Of Turtles and Doves

Lynn Shurr

A Wings ePress, Inc.
Regency Historical Novel

Wings ePress, Inc.

Edited by: Jeanne Smith
Copy Edited by: Heather O'Connor
Executive Editor: Jeanne Smith
Cover Artist: Trisha FitzGerald-Jung
Images: Dreamstime and Pixabay

All rights reserved

Names, characters and incidents depicted in this book are products of the author's imagination or are used fictitiously. Any resemblance to actual events, locales, organizations, or persons, living or dead, is entirely coincidental and beyond the intent of the author or the publisher.

No part of this book may be reproduced or transmitted in any form or by any means, electronic or mechanical, including photocopying, recording, or by any information storage and retrieval system, without permission in writing from the publisher.

Wings ePress Books
www.wingsepress.com

Copyright © 2022 by: Lynn Shurr
ISBN 978-1-61309-344-3

Published In the United States Of America

Wings ePress, Inc.
3000 N. Rock Road
Newton, KS 67114

What They Are Saying About
Of Turtles and Doves

"Shurr is a wonderful storyteller."
—The Romance Studio

"Very easy reads, well written, combined with conflict, believable plots and secondary characters that make the story come alive."
—Jane Lange, *Romances, Reads and Reviews*

"I love the picture the author paints of the time and the way of life, and the characters are strong and interesting."
—Joan Conning Afman
Author of *The Cheetah Princess*

"Lynn Shurr breathes life into the characters and allows each turn of the page to lead up to a pleasurable ending."
—Cherokee
Coffee Time Romance and More

"I love how deep and well-written the characters are."
—Juliette Brandt
Paperbacks and Frosting

"You can count on Lynn Shurr to deliver interesting characters and great romance."
—A.C. Mason
Author of *Deadly Bayou*

Dedication

For Amanda. Welcome to the family.

One

London, March, 1815

 Trouble ahead. Jason Longleigh saw the sign blocking the entrance to the Terrapin Inn as soon as he and his brother rounded the corner in the misty rain. He'd had difficulty enough drawing Joshua out of his warm and comfortable chambers to search out a steaming bowl of turtle soup, a perfect repast for a raw day. Now this.

 Josh held the umbrella high to protect his new brown beaver hat and grumbled, "There, you see. The place is closed. We've walked all this way in filthy weather for naught."

 "Your sunny temperament will not dry up the rain, brother. Let me proceed ahead and determine the problem. I am sure they will serve the younger sons of the Duke of Bellevue."

 "For enough coin, we could have had the soup delivered."

 Ignoring his brother's complaint and any possible damage to his own less costly tall hat, Jason tucked his cane under his arm and trotted up to the door. The dampness had diffused the red painted words spelled out on what appeared to be a full sheet of watercolor paper, the kind his sisters cut to size for their artistic efforts. The weather-beaten carapace of a turtle swinging from a board bearing the inn's name showered the paper with large droplets, making the green blobs in the corners run into the red words to form miserable, muddy brown streaks. Still, he could not mistake the message, "Free the Turtles."

Ah! The green blobs were meant to be sea turtles. Not surprising. What did startle him was the small form of the young woman who held up the sign. Raindrops dripped onto the vermilion cloak she wore. Its hood surrounded a sun-kissed, heart-shaped face framed by wet, light brown ringlets. Her lips had turned blue with the chill, and her small, upturned nose grew pink on the tip, but her eyes—oh, those eyes. Certainly, he had never seen a larger or more beautiful pair of hazel-colored orbs. They shone both green and gray and were speckled with gold, like the sea on a sunny day. He could lose his footing and swim in eyes like those.

Instead, he broke his gaze and said, "Excuse me, Miss. Would you kindly step aside and allow my brother and me to enter?"

She shook her head very solemnly. "Not if you plan to eat turtle," she said in a soft foreign accent.

Of course he planned to eat turtle, the only reason to come to the Terrapin Inn. Joshua caught up and tapped his boot impatiently.

"I pledge to eat no turtle."

"But what of your brother?"

"I have been dragged out in this drizzle to eat turtle soup and so I shall," Joshua proclaimed. "The idea was his."

Ever since his brother had married Kate, he no longer showed any sensitivity toward less sturdy women. In Jason's opinion, Josh's sense of humor had suffered dearly since his brother passed the bar. Why, he'd gotten as stuffy as all the other barristers. Imminent fatherhood contributed to his sibling's general ill temper and wrath as well. Jason overlooked that since it grew out of concern for his sister-in-law. Still, it saddened him to note Joshua saw no levity in their situation and might lay ungentle hands upon the young lady. He must forestall that.

"Do pardon me." Jason reached over the sign and placed his hands around her tiny waist. He lifted the young woman aside and held her easily in place while Josh passed through the doorway.

"I am so sorry I had to do that, but my brother was growing impatient." His hands lingered.

"You are so very b-big and strong. Do swear, no t-turtles," she said, her teeth chattering slightly.

"You have my word as a Longleigh, which is very good indeed."

She smiled, showing small, pearly teeth. He remembered to unhand her and backed his way into the inn, where Joshua held forth just inside the door.

"I say, she must be an escaped lunatic of good family. Where are her keepers, her guardians? And blast, her sign does no good. All the places are taken."

A booming voice spoke up from the nearest table. "We are her guardians, sitting where we can be sure Miranda comes to no harm. My daughter is no bedlamite for certain. But despite her small size, she does have a backbone of steel when it comes to her causes. Sit, gentlemen, sit. We have two spare chairs to make up for your inconvenience."

Joshua immediately accepted the offer. He propped his folded umbrella in a corner of the bow window beneath the quaint, green glass roundels letting in a dim, nautical light and carefully placed his beaver hat on a nearby rack. Bowing slightly to the very portly man bearing magnificent, graying side whiskers and in lieu of a napkin, wearing a soup-stained waistcoat, Josh took a seat across from the slumped and surly young man in the other chair.

"Thank you. Allow me to introduce myself—Joshua Longleigh and my brother, Jason Longleigh. You might be acquainted with our father, the Duke of Bellevue."

"Do you hear, Daniel? We dine with lords. Ain't that something?" The man seized and pumped a hand that had not been offered.

"Americans from the south of your nation, of course," Josh said with some disdain, though the girl's father did not appear to notice.

"Yes, indeedy. We can't hide our accent, wouldn't want to. Eustace Clary at your service, gents. My younger son, Daniel. Now that hostilities are over between our countries, I brought him and my daughter to London to get a little polish. No hard feelings over the Battle of New Orleans, what do you say?"

"Fought after the Treaty of Ghent was signed, I believe," Josh replied frostily.

He could be such a snob. Jason dashed in to save the conversation from going completely downhill.

"My brother is a barrister. He loves to argue. That aside, your daughter is taking a chill. Can you not coax her inside, even though this is not the most respectable place to take a young lady?"

"Looks fine to me—clean, good food. Oh, I see. Only men eat here. Guess we should have asked for a private room, but we been cramped in our lodgings for two weeks. I suppose when I saw the name on this place, I went a little homesick for some good ole terrapin soup. I should have known it would set Miranda off. Mentioned coming here last evening and should have suspected some antics when I saw her wearing her mother's old cloak. She had that sign stashed in the lining. Painted it up in her room last night when I thought she was working on a picture of the Thames to take home. I meant to show her around at some balls, but we ain't having much luck with that."

Daniel Clary drew in his long legs to allow Jason to sit. "What Daddy means is Miranda has destroyed her chances to marry in Georgia because of her peculiar beliefs and um—some unfounded rumors. He hopes to foist her off on some unwitting Englishman who will not appreciate her either," the son, who sported ample, but more subdued curly side whiskers, drawled.

Suddenly, Daniel sat up much straighter. Jason suspected a kick to the shin administered by his father. The younger Clary's heavy, sandy brows lowered over eyes colored much like his sister's, but greener and not nearly as remarkable, in Jason's opinion.

"I was studying maritime law myself until my father demanded my services on this trip to chaperone Miranda. She is far too quick and clever for him to watch, no matter what her failings."

Eustace Clary jumped in with both of his big, booted feet. "My daughter is an heiress and pretty and gentle as a snow-white dove."

"How many pounds does she have to her dowry? Perhaps we could look into arranging some introductions," Joshua said. "There are always unwed younger sons lolling about."

Jason had the greatest desire to administer the same sort of swift kick to his brother. They discussed that sweet waif as if she were no more than meat on a scale. And, he had a feeling Josh might also be referring to him—as if marriage had made his brother the better man.

"Introductions! That's the ticket." Eustace Clary beamed. "Let me buy your lordships some dinner. Waiter!"

A skinny man in an apron deposited his burden of two bowls of steaming soup before his customers and made his way across the crowded room. "What's your pleasure, gents?"

"A refill of my bowl, another basket of bread. Daniel, some more? No. And whatever these gentlemen desire," Eustace Clary ordered.

"I will have the turtle soup. Some mulled wine would go down nicely on a day like this," Joshua Longleigh said. He eyed his brother and waited.

"What have you besides the soup?"

"Oh, a fine roasted breast of turtle served up with herbed potatoes and new green peas."

"Anything, ah—turtle free? A chop. A steak, perhaps." There, let no one say Jason Longleigh went back on his word.

"I can ask the chef, but he will be mightily put out to have his specialties dismissed."

"I believe I can endure his wrath. Bring along a mulled wine for me on your return."

Josh smirked, but Daniel Clary spoke up. "It's those big eyes of hers and that child-like trust in everyone that draws men in, but they cut the line when they find out having Miri means giving up healthy red meat for life. She says she cannot abide the scent on their breath."

"As *I* was saying, my daughter is an heiress—but not in cash money. She comes with her own island, a substantial house, a plantation growing the finest Sea Island cotton in the world and one-hundred-fifty-six head of Negroes to work the fields. Imagine living in paradise." Eustace leaned closer to Jason. "Palm trees swaying in the mild southern breezes, abundant servants to do your bidding—truly a Golden Isle."

"Mosquitoes and hurricanes and brutal heat," added his son. "My sister should not be pawned off like chattel."

"Oh, I must introduce you to my wife and my sister, Pandora. They have very definite views on the rights of women and the abolition of slavery." Josh Longleigh chuckled as a vast shadow fell over the table.

The waiter had returned with the hot spiced wine, the bread basket, and an enormous bald man wearing a soup-spotted apron and holding the bloody cleaver used for beheading turtles.

"Mr. Cobb, here, our chef wants to know why you don't care for his soup."

Jason regarded the large man looming over their table. The cook was easily the weight of both Josh and himself put together. He would hate to skewer the man with a cane sword in his own establishment, but doubted if they could take him at fisticuffs. *Eloquence, try eloquence first.*

"The fame of your turtle receipt distinguishes you and your establishment, Mr. Cobb. My mother, the Duchess of Bellevue, orders it by the gallon during the season to feed to her guests. But you see, I have made a pledge—no, a wager—that I can resist your delectable soup."

That should do it. Men always understood the need to win a bet.

The cook rumbled, "It's that little lady, ain't it? I told her earlier not to block my door, but did not have the heart to haul her off to the gaol. The customers stream right by her, so I let her be."

Jason looked outside at Miranda's small, shivering shoulders. "Exactly. She is not costing you business. Now, your finest steak and those delicious new peas. Their season is so short. What do you say?"

The chef shrugged his vast shoulders and lumbered back to the kitchen to dispatch some more turtles. As he'd said, customers pushed right by Miranda. A burly man intent on hot soup approached the entry and pushed her aside with one heavy arm. She lost her footing on the rain-slick paving and fell, bashing the back of her head against the thick glass of the window.

"Daniel, go fetch your sister and get rid of that damned sign," the elder Clary ordered.

"I am closest. Allow me." Jason rose and went out into the wet to gather the unconscious Miranda to his chest. Her hood fell back across his arm and released a myriad of long, loose curls. He kicked the sign into the street, carried his precious burden inside and deposited her on his chair. When she began to slide out of the seat, he had no recourse but to take her on his lap and hold her tight, now did he?

Their waiter arrived with two bowls of soup in hand and a platter balanced on his arm containing an immense, rare beefsteak surrounded by roasted potatoes and small mounds of green peas. Plunking his burden down, he drew out a bottle of smelling salts and held them to Miranda's little nose. She sneezed adorably and came awake looking up into Jason Longleigh's eyes.

"*'O brave new world that has such people in't.'* Your eyes are as black as the night sky with only two stars shining." She sighed.

"Yours are like the gray-green sea lit by sunshine," Jason answered. She brought out all the poetry in him, and he had quite a lot of it.

"Her first time abroad?" Joshua commented to Miranda's brother.

"Exactly. And she *is* only seventeen."

Josh further ruined the moment by accosting the waiter. "Could you bring us a bit of raw steak or some ice to put on that knot she has on the back of her head."

"Oh, not steak! Not dead cow!" Miranda protested.

"Ice if you have any, then," Jason said, nodding at the waiter to come close. He whispered, "I'd like my food to take away. I keep a large dog at home."

Knowing there was no dog, Joshua rolled his eyes at his brother. The waiter whisked away the succulent meat and the lovely green peas. Jason's stomach rumbled.

"Here, Miranda, if I may call you so. Take a sip of my wine. It will warm and restore you. Now, a bite of bread. I'll wager you have not eaten today you are so light in my arms."

Suddenly, his burden bolted upright and hit her head on his chin. For a moment, he saw stars, but still clung to her. When his vision returned, Miri was rubbing her forehead. With a troubled glance at his face, she asked, "Have we been introduced, kind sir?"

"Indirectly. I have been dining with your father and brother. Jason Longleigh, poet and aspiring barrister, here to serve you."

"*Lord* Jason Longleigh. His mother is the Duchess of Bellevue and his daddy, the duke. Now, wouldn't you like to meet a real duchess, Miranda?" her father wheedled.

"I'd rather go see the turtles."

"And so you shall." Jason accepted a chunk of ice wrapped in a clean rag from the waiter and held it to the swelling at the back of her head. He eased her tiny body from his lap and set her upright, shielding himself beneath the table. He marveled that little Miranda had the same effect on him as Bouncing Bet, the barmaid he'd favored while at Oxford, who often wriggled on his privates in the tavern prior to an assignation.

The brother spoke up. "I will take Miranda to see the turtles in the courtyard."

"Finish your dinner, son. Allow Lord Longleigh here, to escort your sister."

"I am fin—."

"Mind your daddy, son. Here, have some more bread." Eustace shoved the basket at Daniel and waved the couple off through the maze of chairs and tables and out into the courtyard.

Jason kept a steadying hand on Miranda's elbow lest she fall or faint again. Relieved the rain had stopped, he guided her to the first of several large tanks. A keeper, formerly of the king's navy, judging by his ragtag uniform, clumped over to them on his wooden leg. He had the metal hook on one hand required of every storybook pirate and a short, black beard as well.

"How may I serve ye, pretty lady, me fine gentleman? Are ye looking for a fine, fat green turtle from the Indian Ocean? Mind, hawksbills are extra if ye keep the shell for combs and such. We got a huge leatherback from colder waters in that tank right over there. Mighty tasty. So long as they stays in their own sea water, they'll keep for a good three months. Take 'em out, they dwindle and lose their flavor. Fifty fine specimens. Look around. Make yer pick. Amos Gantry is here to help."

Miranda did not peer into the tanks where turtles of all sizes floated. Her horrified eyes had settled on a row of dressed carcasses hanging on hooks just outside the kitchen door. As she watched, Mr. Cobb came outside, snatched a naked turtle corpse from its spike, and nodding politely their way, went back inside to make more soup. Her eyes lowered to two huge, struggling tortoises lying on their backs amongst the cobbles. The small one rocked frantically on its domed back trying to right itself. A bigger, saddle-backed specimen groaned rhythmically in the same endeavor.

"Oh, Lord Longleigh, please make him turn them upright." She dug frantic fingers into his forearm.

"Excellent choice, milady. Come all the way from the Galapagos, they do. I've ate 'em meself when I was at sea. Good as fresh beef roasted. Lucky we had a ship recently come in with a few to spare."

Amos Gantry made good use of his hook by inserting it under the front of the shell and flipping the turtles over. The smaller immediately toiled off toward a small patch of sunlight breaking through the clouds. The other, twice its size, followed.

"Oh dear, it's been on its back so long, its shell has flattened," Miranda exclaimed.

"No, milady. Not at all. Some come flat-topped, others domed like the little bugger, just as God made 'em. Now which will ye have? Dressed out or delivered live to yer cook?"

"Lord Longleigh, dear Jason, they are boon companions. Look how they stay together. I doubt if I have enough shopping money to buy even the smaller and save its life, let alone the larger, and they should not be separated. What is your asking price?"

"That would be five shillings a pound, milady, live weight, shell and all. I'll set him on the scale for ye."

"So much?"

Jason, unable to bear the distress in her voice, spoke up. "I'll take them both."

Gantry inserted his hook under the shell of the smaller domed turtle, dragged it to the scales and encouraged it onto the pan with kicks from his wooden leg. The tortoise retreated into its shell, making the weigh-in an easy matter. The old salt added massive iron weights to the other side of the balance until both sides were in accord.

"An even three hundred pounds. I'll need yer help with the big 'un."

After shoving the first turtle from the pan, Gantry beckoned to Jason. With the keeper pulling with his hook and Jason pushing the hind end, they propelled the giant tortoise toward the scale. It snapped its beak at them all the way and refused to retreat into its carapace once on the pan. Instead, its thick, scaly legs frantically paddled the air as weights dropped into the other pan and raised it into the air.

"Six hundred and six pounds," Gantry called out triumphantly. "Ye can feed a multitude of friends."

"A small fortune," Jason mumbled. "If you would excuse me for just a moment."

He returned to the table where Joshua had finished his repast and blotted his lips on a spotless linen handkerchief. "Josh, may I have a private word with you?"

They stood so close Jason could smell the sherry from the rich soup on his brother's breath. His stomach complained again, but he pushed aside hunger to plead his case.

"As you know, our quarterly allowance will be renewed in a mere two weeks. Since your marriage, Papa has doubled your sum. With Kate in confinement at her parents' estate, you really have no need for the extra funds. Additionally, you've recently collected a fine, fat amount from Lord Latterly for getting him off scot-free on the killing of his wife's lover in her bedchamber rather than on the dueling grounds. Heaven knows, you have boasted about the amount often enough to me. I need a loan of...." He lowered his voice to the tiniest whisper to keep Eustace Clary from hearing.

"Good Lord, man, do you plan to buy your way into the Royal Society with the gift of a turtle! I thought you were more interested in scribbling poetry and pretending to study law than in scientific endeavors."

"No, no, I have no interest in science. Miranda—Miss Clary—is most distressed about the fate of the two gigantic tortoises in the courtyard. I mean to purchase them for her."

"Since she quoted Mr. Shakespeare earlier, I feel compelled to do the same. *'Lord, what fools these mortals be!'* Once purchased, whatever will you do with them if they are not to go into the pot?"

"They will be Miss Clary's tortoises, not mine."

"Why not buy her some jewelry, little brother? You will get off the cheaper."

Jason could tell his brother was enjoying himself immensely at his expense by the smirk on his lips and the rise of his eyebrows. If they were still boys, they would have been pummeling each other.

"Will you or won't you make the loan?"

"Oh, I will if only for the amusement value when you tell Papa how you emptied your account and got into debt. He will suspect gambling debts or soiled doves, but never turtles."

Growing heated, Jason answered, "I can assure you Miss Clary is no soiled dove. I have never met a sweeter, more innocent young lady."

Joshua took a step back and raised his brows even higher. "I said nothing about Miss Clary."

Daniel Clary shoved back his chair so violently it tipped over and crashed to the floor. He bore the red face of the mortally offended. "Who insults my sister?"

Joshua Longleigh held up his hands. "No one, I assure you. Make your arrangements, Jason. I have clients to meet." Calmly, he sat again. "More mulled wine, Clary?"

Jason jogged back to the courtyard only to find Miranda so deep into a conversation with the unsavory tar he hardly seemed to be missed.

"Aye, 'tis true. Slit their gullet pouch. They store water therein like the camels of the desert. No need to give 'em food nor drink on a long voyage, but here Mr. Cobb throws 'em turnips and cabbages to keep their weight up. They graze on greenery like any cow, but coming from an arid clime can do without."

"What amazing creatures. Jason, do come see the immense leatherback in the tub over here. I've never seen bigger even on my beach at home. The pink spot on his head is shaped like a half moon, and my favorite on Ariel Island has a star upon hers. I call her Stella."

Miranda flitted across the courtyard to gaze into another tank.

"Careful there, milady. That 'un bites. Now, milord, are ye ready to deal? The one or the both now that ye know their weights?"

"If you will accept my note and hold it until tomorrow afternoon, I shall take both. The Longleighs are good for it."

"Aye, the duchess is a regular customer. Would you rather I charged her account?"

"Oh, no! The gift is mine to pay."

"Yer bride is a lucky woman, milord."

"Not my bride. Miss Clary is merely a new acquaintance."

The sailor winked an eye. "I get yer meaning. She's a fresh and lively one. I took ye for a new wed man, but husbands are never as generous as this. Where and how do ye want 'em brought?"

"Live and taken to—Miss Clary, might I have your direction for the delivery?"

"We have lodgings at Mrs. Parsons' house the next street over."

"I know the place, milord. Soon as yer note clears, I'll deliver them meself."

The bulk of Eustace Clary filled the doorway to the courtyard. "Come, Miranda, we must leave before the weather turns again. Maybe Lord Longleigh would like to walk along with us."

"I would, sir."

"I took care of the tab. If you could pry my daughter away from the turtles..."

"Of course." Jason offered his arm to Miranda, whose hand lighted upon it as delicately as a small bird roosting. They progressed through the dining room to the front door where Daniel Clary, Joshua, and a large, seeping package waited.

"Your dinner," his brother pointed out.

"For my hound," Jason contradicted. "Carry it safely back to your chambers for me. I will meet you there after seeing Miss Clary home."

"Pleased to do so. Good day, gentlemen, Miss Clary. Yes, a very good day. I cannot tell when I have ever enjoyed sharing a meal with my brother more. The additional company perhaps."

Joshua retrieved his hat and umbrella. Holding the wrapped beefsteak well away from his expensive coat and trousers, he stepped out into the weak sunlight and made his way down the block and around the corner.

Hoping the Clarys would not notice the sound of Josh's laughter echoing in the streets, Jason guided Miranda around the puddles and piles of horse manure. He was supremely glad his brother had gone too far away to hear Eustace Clary say, "When do we meet the duke and duchess, my fine lad?"

Two

Jason Longleigh waited two days for the spell to wear off. Women often seemed enchanting on first meeting, but their charms usually dissipated like the rain clouds over London on second acquaintance. He had to see Miranda Clary again simply to get her out of his mind. He told his brother that very firmly.

Josh burst into inappropriate laughter, pounding his desk and gasping, "Beefsteak for your dog! Turtles, in debt to me for turtles!" And so, he had gone to call alone.

Now, he stood outside Mrs. Parsons' lodging house. The neighborhood was respectable enough that an unholy uproar coming from the rear of the place drew people to their windows to peer out and wonder why. As soon as he heard Miranda's cries, he ceased hesitating on the doorstep and let himself in by jumping a low gate giving egress to the back of the place. The scene unfolded before him.

Miranda, clothed in white sprigged muslin, lay draped like a virgin sacrifice over the domed shell of the smaller tortoise. The larger beast stood nearby hissing and snapping its beak. An irate, buxom woman of middle age waved a cleaver every bit as sharp as the one Mr. Cobb used at his establishment in the direction of Amos Gantry and the male Clarys.

"I said no pets, no filthy animals at all! If they aren't for your dinner, they must go. As for you, Amos Gantry, I told you never to darken my door again. You—and that disgusting parrot flinging fruit about and drawing vermin, not to mention the droppings. I regret I ever allowed you to room below my stairs."

"Now Annabelle, Miss Rosita loved you. She still calls yer name in the night. Annie, pretty Annie," Amos Gantry mimicked.

The woman grew so enraged she forgot all modesty. "That feather duster bit me in the backside, Amos."

"Aye, she was jealous of yer beauty. Didn't I stay ashore for ye? Didn't I get meself a respectable job as turtle keeper for ye? I must do my deliveries as I am bid."

Mrs. Parsons advanced on the sailor. Jason wondered if he could snatch the cleaver from her hand if he attacked from the rear as well. He took the chance, grabbing her by the waist and wresting the weapon from her hand. Miranda stood and clapped her hands in delight at his manly performance. He wanted to bow, but the proprietor of the boarding house jumped on him, attempting to get her cleaver back. He held the cleaver away in one hand while circling Mrs. Parsons' chubby wrists with the other as he tried to inculcate reason into the situation.

"Now, now, the fault is mine. I gifted the tortoises to Miss Clary, and she wishes to keep them as pets. Mr. Gantry simply delivered them. Perhaps I could pay for allowing them to stay in your yard until we can find a better place."

The landlady stilled instantly. "How much?"

"The price of a single room?"

"Done, but you have no more than a week to get rid of them. As for you, Amos Gantry—be gone!"

"Going, me sweetheart, going." He limped away as fast as his peg would carry him to a cart waiting at the rear gate.

Mr. Clary and Daniel relaxed their stance, but Miranda flew across the small space and flung her arms around Jason.

"Oh, thank you. You have saved the turtles again!" She brushed his cheek with her long lashes and perhaps the slightest touch of her lips, a butterfly kiss.

Mrs. Parsons shook a plump finger in Eustace Clary's face. "I see now you are no respectable family at all. Who knows what your daughter did to earn the cost of a turtle that size? And that spook of a servant of yours. I want all of you gone, same as those great beasts, by week's end."

"Where, oh where, shall we go?" Mr. Clary said, pounding a fist against his chest and looking directly at Jason Longleigh. "We are strangers cast up on a hostile shore. I only wanted the best for my daughter—a good marriage to a kind man—and now all hope is vanquished by these turtles."

"Oh, Daddy, don't be silly. There are hundreds of lodging houses in London. First, we must arrange for the tortoises to be shipped back to the Galapagos Islands. Then, we shall remove to another location. Lord Jason will help us, I am sure."

Once more, Longleigh found himself gazing into gray-green eyes as deep as the sea. Her small, pink lips had merely brushed his cheek, and he still felt their imprint warmly.

"I suppose I could inquire about the cost of such a venture."

Daniel Clary snorted. "Don't be an idiot, man. The sailors would take your money and sell or eat the turtles themselves."

"But Danny, they cannot stay here. Mr. Gantry says they come from a much hotter clime and are not used to all this cold and rain." Miranda's smooth brow creased with concern.

"Nor are you, Miss Clary. Please do put on a coat and bonnet. I doubt if your landlady will provide us with refreshments, so allow me to escort you to a very pleasant tearoom nearby for a hot drink and perhaps some cakes. Your father and brother are invited as well. We will use our wits and solve this problem." Jason listened to Daniel Clary snort again and murmur, "Imbecile."

~ * ~

Miranda had eaten only two small iced cakes and sipped tea sweetened with honey and lightened with milk. Eustace Clary worked through the Scottish scones on the first level of the tiered plate up to the dainty watercress sandwiches on the second and finally to the petit fours decorated with candied violets sitting on top. Daniel Clary drank his tea black and sat peering into the brew as if he wanted to know his fortune.

Jason Longleigh took a big, lemon-flavored gulp from his cup and said brightly, "I believe I know a good place to take the tortoises. My mother has a conservatory at Bellevue Hall where she keeps her potted orange and lemon trees during the winter, along with many other exotic plants. It's kept quite warm at all times and has a delightful fountain and small pond."

"Oh, yes!" exclaimed Miranda as if he had given her the moon and the stars beyond.

"Wonderful idea, my boy! We will present the duchess with a magnificent gift of tortoises. She will want to show them off to all her friends. Think of the connections, the possibilities for Miranda to meet the right kind of people." Eustace Clary rubbed his hands together.

Daniel Clary suppressed a smile by popping a cake into his mouth. He watched with amused green eyes as the truth dawned on Jason Longleigh. He'd become his brother's debtor to buy an outrageous gift for his own mother. He could do nothing but stumble forward with his plans.

"The drawback—Joshua and I keep only a pair of riding horses in the city. The carriage will not be available until the duke and duchess arrive for the season. Poor weather has kept them in the north. The journey to Bellevue takes several days, and I don't suppose that a carter would be any more trustworthy than a sailor when it comes to turtles."

"We ain't paupers, son. We'll hire a coach and off we go in the morning. I look forward to meeting your folks."

The cakes consumed, the tea drunken to the dregs, the party set out to find a coach and settled on a stout equipage of some age but good appearance with room enough for six to ride. The interior smelled slightly of sweat and sausages, but Mr. Clary found that no impediment. A debate arose as to whether the tortoises would ride inside or out, be crated or not. Miranda would not have them exposed to the weather. Her father insisted on crates.

Jason left the Americans debating on whether the tortoises needed a bed of warm bricks to rest on for their comfort, which Miranda demanded along with a sack of cabbages for their provender. He suspected she would get her bricks as they would add to everyone's comfort in the drafty coach, but hoped her father would hold out in his opinion that the tortoises would keep for a few days without food and water. Hadn't Mr. Gantry told her so? Personally, he hoped Mr. Clary won out on the latter. He had no idea if turtles suffered from flatulence, but all animals defecated if fed. In a closed coach with an already gamey aroma, the trip would seem very long indeed.

Exhausted by the energy of their plans, Jason straggled back to his brother's quarters. They could send out for their supper, enjoy some port in front of a cozy fire. He would allow Josh to ridicule him about his predicament and get that out of the way. Truth be told, he missed their time together, their spats and their escapades, since his brother had become an old married man leg-shackled to the shrewish Kate. All right, Kate was more practical and clever than shrewish. She had no lofty ideas, no refined principles, no poetry in her soul—while Miranda was all dreams and moonlight, sensitive to the plight of even lowly turtles and willing to fight for them.

Jason let himself in and passed by the chamber where Joshua practiced law and the sitting room where his clients waited. He went directly into the private section of the rented house. He kept his own quarters on the floor above, but if he were being honest, his brother lived in more comfort because Kate saw to that. *My God! The place had been ransacked.*

In the small dining room, the contents of a tipped bottle of wine pooled around a dinner plate with a chop and a hunk of bread upon it. A half-eaten apple butted up against a small wedge of cheddar. The chair sitting before the plate lay overturned. Jason heard clunks and rustling coming from the bedchamber down the hall. Going softly, he approached the room. A shoe hit him in the face before he could duck. He drew his cane sword and prepared to use it on the intruder.

His brother straddled a chair. Josh cursed as he attempted to shove his foot into a tall riding boot. On the bed, an overstuffed saddlebag lay with the sleeve of one shirt dangling out the side. Discarded clothes littered the floor.

Wild-eyed, Joshua said, "The baby is coming. I must go to Kate at once."

"I believe the process takes quite a while. Surely you could finish your meal and go in the morning. I have a great deal to tell you, a very amusing story."

"No time!" Josh said. He gave his boot a final tug, rose, shrugged into a warm riding coat and popped his beaver hat on his head. After tossing the saddlebags over a shoulder, he paused in his frenzy to hand Jason a small sign hung on a fine chain.

"Here, lock up for me and put this on my chamber door. Help yourself to what is left of my dinner. I will send word of the outcome."

Jason looked at the sign. *Closed until further notice.* By the time he raised his eyes, the rear door to the mews had slammed. He wandered back to the dining room and picked a note up off the floor. It came from the country home of Kate's parents, where she had gone for her confinement.

My Dearest Husband – My travail begins. I am in the very best of care. There is no need to hurry or concern yourself. Come at your convenience to meet your child. Yr. Ever Loving Wife, Kate.

Avoiding the spilled wine, Jason took a seat at the table and shaved off a piece of the cheese. He popped it into his mouth as he uprighted the bottle. Ah, still enough of a rather good vintage to fill a glass. For a moment, he almost missed Kate. She would have very level-headed views on how to deal with the Clarys, and she would not ridicule him. No help for that. He was on his own and on his way to Bellevue in the morning to present the duke and duchess with two exotic tortoises and three unusual Americans.

Three

Jason Longleigh packed only a small box he could manage himself, and that was well, since the Clarys had shifted three enormous traveling trunks to the top of the coach, leaving room for little else. Eustace Clary had paid Amos Gantry to crate the tortoises, and Miranda used her wiles to persuade their landlady to fill the coach floor with hot bricks for the comfort of the reptiles, not the human passengers. Tenderly, she tucked blankets in around the crates. The tortoises, heads and feet drawn in, eyes closed, seemed blissful rather than merely torpid. Jason would be blissful, too, if Miri's little hands attended to him that way.

The tortoises, however, left small room for the passengers. Jason lifted Miranda into the space between the crates, and she sat very primly in the center seat. Eustace Clary used one of the crates as a stepping stone and heaved his bulk onto the squabs, leaving his legs outstretched as if the tortoise below served as an ottoman. Jason was about to clamber over a crate and claim the space beside Miranda when a woman's voice, rich and deep, spoke up behind him.

"Pardon, Mastah Lord Jason. I must sit by Missy."

He turned to look into the red-rimmed, dark eyes of a woman matching his six feet in height. Her blue-black skin stretched over broad cheekbones. Though she had the color of a wild African, an aristocratic nose rose above lips as full and dark as ripe plums. A turban of purple and gold-shot silk covered her hair, and hooped golden earrings swung from the long lobes of her ears. Her dress of sturdy indigo-dyed cloth with large horn buttons down the front covered an impressive bosom made modest by a white linen fichu.

"I am sorry. I did not know we expected another passenger. Allow me to assist you."

Jason held her elbow as she doubled nearly in two to get by the crate and settle next to Miranda. He followed, taking the seat directly across from the women, which allowed him some leg room. Daniel Clary sat on the edge of the last seat and swiveled his legs over the crate. Their hired coachman slammed the doors and took his place on top. With a slap of the ribbons and the snap of a whip and no farewell from Mrs. Parsons, they were off to Bellevue Hall.

"I have not had the pleasure of making your acquaintance," Jason said to Miranda's companion.

"Oh, silly me. This is Ida, my mammy. She served as my wet nurse and is now my maid and companion and a mother to me since my own mama died," Miranda twittered.

"A slave?"

"Much more than that. Though she came to us from Haiti, Ida was once an African princess."

"Ain't they all?" drawled Eustace Clary from beneath his cocked hat where he was attempting to sleep.

"She knows cures and spells, too. I once asked her to turn Daniel into a frog when he was being very mean, but Ida uses her magic only for good."

"For the protection of my family," the servant said. She stared pointedly at the place where Jason's boot touched the toe of Miranda's slipper.

"Ah, yes, well." He pulled his foot back against the seat.

~ * ~

The interminable journey progressed day after day in such close quarters that despite the increasingly chill air, the men took turns riding with the driver. Considering the value of their cargo, the coachman slept armed inside the carriage nightly. Jason shared quarters with the Clary men, sometimes sleeping three across in the same bed if the inn was crowded with gentry swarming to the city for the start of the cultural and mating season. Jason could attest that Eustace Clary had a snore like a steam whistle and Daniel talked nonsense in his sleep.

On two occasions, he had gone to the coach and stretched out on the seats across from Jinks, the coachman, who smelled slightly of gin and willingly shared his bottle. A nip or two did no harm on a cold night so long as the driver turned up sober in the morning. However, the aroma in the coach grew steadily riper, being especially noticeable in the mornings when the cages were levered up to receive a new base of hot bricks. All pretended not to notice, and the tortoises did not murmur a sound either.

More than glad when they turned off the London road and cut toward Bellevue, Jason savored the thought of comfortable quarters, warm and well-prepared food, and the freedom from turtle stench that lay ahead. The awe he noticed in the faces of his guests when the Hall came into view behind its iron gates took him aback. A flight of marble steps led up to the portico, raised on four soaring Corinthian columns. Two impressive wings with arched windows on their lower floors stretched away on either side of the central block. Built by his great-grandfather, the place was simply the home where he'd run wild as a child.

Anticipating a surprised and delighted greeting from his parents, he got none. They had gone into Westbrook, his father to attend to some last-minute estate business before leaving for London, his mother and sole unmarried sister to get final fittings on their new gowns for the season. They expected to have dinner with friends and return in time for supper, according to Busby, the butler.

"Well then, Busby, we will need three bedchambers for my guests and a place for their maid and the coachman. Also, send your stoutest footmen around to the outer doors of the conservatory. We have two very heavy crates to unload—gifts for my mother."

"I am sure the duchess will be delighted with any new additions to her collection of rare plants," Busby answered.

He stood there the epitome of a butler, tall and dour, thin-lipped and long-nosed, not a thinning hair out of place. Try as he might, though, he could not suppress a slight flaring of the nostrils. Tactfully, he suggested, "Your guests might wish to bathe, rest, and take a meal in their chambers before the duke returns. Then, they will be fully prepared to meet his lordship in the drawing room before supper, milord."

His superior gray eyes roved over the assemblage of Americans as if he had never seen their like nor smelled it either. They huddled together, resembling unwashed savages peering up at the soaring ceilings and down at the checkerboard marble floor, looking out the arched windows with their sidelights and elegant pilasters, ogling the scalloped niches holding nude Greek statues, and staring open-mouthed at the fine ornaments of the Palladian mansion that was Bellevue Hall.

Jason got the point. Even Miranda, who changed her frilly, high-waisted frocks daily and usually smelled sweetly of orange water, had acquired the gamey scent. Daniel, always the well-turned-out Southern gentleman with his neatly trimmed, curly side whiskers and cropped sandy hair, stank of turtle, too. His boots bore scuff marks from resting atop the rough crates. Mr. Clary, a voracious but not tidy eater, wore some of his breakfast on his clothes. As for himself, he'd spilled gin on his jacket to add to his own aroma.

"Excellent idea, Busby. See them to their chambers. Once I finish unloading our surprise, I will want a bath also. Attend to it."

Jason had Jinks take the coach around to the conservatory doors, where they were met by a phalanx of footmen in blue and silver livery. With levers and boards, many hands and lots of muscle, they deposited the tortoises inside the doors and opened their crates. The creatures declined to move until they were dumped from their cages. Then, cautiously, the largest one rose up on his legs and stretched out his neck. He plodded off toward the trickling fountain and pond with his smaller, lighter companion soon passing him in a slow race to the water.

Forgetting himself, one of the footmen said, "Lud, you ever seen a turtle that big, Willie?"

"No, I ain't. That's soup for a month of days, that is," his fellow footman replied.

Jason grinned. For all their powdered wigs and fine uniforms, they were only overgrown country lads with whom he'd played as a boy.

"Good work, men. We'll leave them to settle in. Now, do not say a word to the duchess. I want to surprise her."

Satisfied he'd pulled off the escapade without Joshua's help and come out smelling like a rose—or more like a drunken tortoise, Jason Longleigh sniffed his jacket and went off to take a bath.

Four

Flora Longleigh, Duchess of Bellevue, removed her bonnet, and with assistance from Busby, her close-fitting coat, and handed them to a maid. One knew one had passed fifty years of age when a long session with the dressmaker, a dreary lunch with poor Elinor, and a longish ride home left one so fatigued. Of course, she'd had to endure Pandora, the most difficult of her ten troublesome children. That alone wore one down to a nub. She watched her black-haired daughter dart up the stairs without so much as a pleasant parting word.

Busby lingered, effectively blocking her own way to the staircase and her bedchamber. He might have towered over her small frame and trim body, but her own commanding gray eyes won out every time, even if she did have to look up at her butler. He wished to say something, and she wanted none of it at the moment.

"I believe I will rest in the conservatory instead of my chambers, Busby. Have a tea tray brought there."

"Yes, Your Grace. However, I must inform you that Lord Jason arrived earlier today along with several guests and—"

She cut him off with a wave of her small, ring-ornamented fingers. "How inconvenient, when my son knows we will be embarking for London in a few days. Well, we shall do our best to entertain them for a short period of time. Then, they must leave."

The duchess turned on her heels and walked swiftly to the conservatory before Busby could burden her with other household matters. Surely, whatever it was could wait until after she'd had her restorative tea. Ah, the warm, moist air inside the glass house attached to the back of Bellevue Hall wafted over her skin as she entered. Certainly, it would plump out the fine lines in her face and relieve the stress of visiting Elinor, her dearest friend.

The woman had every right to be upset, with Napoleon on the loose again and both her sons serving in the army being gathered to defeat the emperor of France. As a younger son, Trent had chosen the military as a career, but what had possessed Tarleton, the eldest and holder of the title, Earl of Edgemont, to enlist? His duties consisted of running his estate, getting an heir, and caring for his frail mother. So far, he had done none of them very well.

Of course, she should not judge. Her own husband, Pearce Longleigh, Duke of Bellevue, had a hale physique and looked good for another twenty blissful years of marriage. Fortunate because their oldest son, James, seemed more interested in unearthing ancient civilizations than in marrying and providing for the Longleigh succession. However, with Joshua's Kate about to give birth, that problem might be solved soon. Justinian, her last boy, quite the scholar and too young to marry, matriculated at Eton. As for Jason, if he really desired a career in the law, he must stop dallying with inappropriate women, fooling with poetry, and apply himself.

Now Pandora was another matter altogether. Shortly, she would begin her third season in London and turn twenty-one in the autumn. Not a suitor in sight. She had good looks enough, and all the accomplishments money could provide, in addition to a fat dowry, but her strident and often-expressed opinions and cool demeanor drove men away. Euphemia, her baby sister, had barely set foot out of the nursery when she was snatched up for marriage, quite literally, but Phemie had the kind of softness men adored. The other four girls had married well despite some mishaps that seemed to go with being a Longleigh. The duchess often wondered if she'd been cursed by the Shawnee witch, Snakeroot, during her stay in the colonies, since she'd had so much trouble with her numerous children.

Lady Flora supposed Pandora would become the daughter to take care of her parents in their old age. Every family had one. What had the girl said today at the fitting? Oh yes, "New frocks will not get me a husband, Mama. Allow me to apply myself to other endeavors." Dear Pearce had warned her about giving their fifth daughter such an ill-omened name, but she had not listened. Sure enough, Pandora had a box of troubles. Nevertheless, her unwed daughter would endure one more season, as would the duchess, no matter how tired. Others depended on her presence and her matchmaking skills to prevent any disastrous marriages from occurring.

The duchess strolled down the gravel path running among her palms and pineapple plants toward the small pool, her favorite place in the conservatory. Before she rounded the bend to where the fountain burbled merrily, she came across the temptation of a cushioned wicker settee. The plump pillows beckoned to her, and no one lurked to see her sit and put up her tired feet. Resting her head against one arm, she cared not one bit if the dampness frizzed her fair curly hair, gradually going white, under its small, lace cap. Plenty of time to repair the damage before supper and deal with these unexpected guests. She dozed off listening to the pleasant tinkling of the fountain.

Footsteps plodding on the gravel woke her, but she did not open her eyes.

"The tea, Your Grace."

"Set it down anywhere. I shall pour it myself."

The tray rattled as it came to rest on a hard surface. The maid crunched down the path, and Flora Longleigh had the place to herself once more. She stretched and sat up. The tea set rested at a tilt on top of a curious table resembling the shell of a huge turtle. How odd. The boys were always accumulating curiosities and dumping them here—small grass snakes and wounded songbirds and stray dogs when they were younger, now gifts from exotic lands fresh off the London docks. She'd take a closer look later and be sure to thank Jason for the oddity, hideous as it was with its dull brown color and grotesque, big-nailed feet.

Flora poured a cup of tea and added sugar and cream. Cook had thoughtfully supplied a small plate of biscuits, a bit of Stilton cheese and some preserved fruits. Though she prided herself on retaining a slim figure after bearing ten children, she did need to build herself up in order to entertain the unexpected guests this evening. She chose a wedge of sugar-glazed pineapple from her very own plants. Excellent. She reached for another piece but fumbled it, and the fruit fell into the gravel. Disgusted with herself over the waste, she sipped her tea instead.

The tea tray rattled ominously. The duchess was aware of earthquakes that could destroy civilizations, thanks to her son, James, but none had ever occurred here in the North Country. Before she could flee to the safety of the main house, the hideous table began to grow taller. Flora screamed as it sprouted a head as gray and wizened as an old man. The wrinkled beak that served as a mouth opened and snatched up the piece of pineapple. The tea service cascaded off its shell. The beast began to rummage among the fallen refreshments for more fruit, but kept a beady eye on her. Flora slung her teacup at it, but the horrible creature merely ducked inside its shell.

Sensing she had time to retreat, the duchess rose slowly and backed away. One should never make sudden movements around animals. The thing looked like a gigantic turtle, but who knew how fast it could run? Thank heaven heavy footsteps came at a run along the path. She knew their owner. The duke, her dear huge husband, charged to her rescue just like he had in the olden days in America. The immense tortoise paid her no mind. It poked out its head and sampled a chocolate biscuit.

Pearce, dressed in his antique finery of greatcoat, knee breeches, silk stockings, and lace-trimmed neckcloth, arrived brandishing a saber like a gentleman privateer of yesteryears. Obviously, he had grabbed the weapon from the wall display when she screamed.

"My God, what is that creature, Flora? Should I behead it for you?"

Right on the duke's heels, Busby said, "Oh, I would not, Your Grace. *That* is the surprise Lord Jason brought home—along with the Americans."

~ * ~

The duchess made a wonderful story of her encounter with the beast. Those gathered around the supper table laughed mightily, all except the young lady who assured her the tortoises were harmless vegetarians. Someone named Mr. Gantry had told her so. The duke jested that should they decide to attack, turtle soup would appear on the menu. Little Miranda had grown teary-eyed. She observed Jason patting the girl's hand to comfort her and jumping in to add reassurance.

"These tortoises are not for eating, Papa. They are rare. Think of how all your friends will be green with envy when they know you possess a pair of unique Galapagos turtles to ornament your conservatory. All of the ton will want one for a pet."

Ah-ha, Jason had formed another ill-advised attachment. She understood the tavern maids he considered worthy of poetry, even the rapacious widows flattered by a young man who wrote odes to their eyes. Boys needed to sow their wild oats somewhere—but not in a very innocent, if somewhat odd girl, who would turn eighteen two days hence. Why the child still wore her curls pulled back and held by a green ribbon as if no one had yet taught her to put her hair up. Still, she was clever. She'd let slip that birthday remark, probably expecting some token from Jason. He should be cautious. Miranda's father watched Jason's every move, and her strapping brother scowled at the merest touch that passed between her son and his sister.

She noted the girl had accepted the French onion soup and a bit of whitebait but waved away the joint of beef, the haunch of venison, the smoked pheasants. The child did partake of every vegetable side dish: the pickled beetroot, the honeyed carrots, the early peas, and so on. No wonder Miranda remained so tiny, with no red meat in her system. The child-woman did find the sweets, the fruits and cheese acceptable, however. Cook had done very well on such short notice.

She had seated Mr. Clary to her right and Mr. Daniel Clary to her left with Pandora on the young man's other side across from Miss Clary, who sat dwarfed between her father and Jason. Daniel Clary presented a fine, masculine figure an inch or so taller than her own son but much fairer in complexion. She found his short-cropped sandy hair and side whiskers attractive and his lowering brows over changeable green-gray eyes a feature any young woman might find alluring. Best of all, his speech flowed slowly like honey dripping from a spoon.

So far, Pandora had not savaged him with her tongue. Earlier, she had asked Daniel if any Red Indians lived on their islands.

"No," he'd replied in that low, slow voice of his. "I am sorry to say they caught the white man's plagues and died off, though some of their blood might have mingled with the Spaniards and Negroes. When I attended the College of William and Mary, I was acquainted with descendants of the Indian princess, Pocahontas, who married a tobacco planter named John Rolfe. Some of the best families of Virginia lay claim to native blood. Their daughters put me in mind of you with their raven hair and sparkling dark eyes, Lady Pandora."

She'd seen her daughter speechless for the first time, but not for long. "My papa is half Shawnee, which explains the resemblance. Generally, I do not find favor with English gentleman because of my darker complexion. Tell me more about the American Indians."

And so, their conversation had continued throughout the meal. Hmmm. Pandora's treatment of men drove off suitors, not her complexion. Her daughter dismissed all of her English beaux as idiots, imbeciles, tulips, or fops. Perhaps someone more hardy, someone from a foreign land far, far away, would have appeal. Imagine Pandora's sharp tongue and ill temper residing across an ocean. How peaceful Bellevue Hall would become. No, no, she must not think it. But what if the young Mr. Clary *were* a good match?

"Tell me, Eustace." He had already begged the duchess to use his first name. "About your islands, your plantations."

"Well, Your Highness, there are three of them covered with fields of the best cotton in all the world."

"Your Grace," she corrected mildly.

"We usually say grace at the beginning of a meal, not the end, but I would be happy to oblige."

"No, I meant I am referred to as Your Grace or simply The Duchess."

"Be easier if I could just call you Flora."

"Yes, it would." But she did not grant him permission. Unlike Daniel, Mr. Clary twanged like a banjo and was not sweet to the ear.

"You see, I come from Georgia hill country, but the sea called to me. I invested in a cargo ship and made several very profitable voyages to Africa before I settled down. I bought those islands one by one. Old indigo plantations, they were, but I put them to cotton. We have the perfect weather, the right soil, the heat and the rain, needed to grow long staple soft as a cloud. See here."

Eustace Clary pinched up his daughter's skirt without thinking and exposed her petticoat, thankfully mostly hidden beneath the dinner table, and encouraged the duchess to roll the fabric, patterned with stylized cotton blossoms on a pale green background, between her fingers. The duchess did, if only to end the ordeal.

"Yes, very soft indeed."

Miranda blushed and Jason, like the good gentleman she'd raised, averted his eyes and spoke to his father about the weather. Daniel Clary turned red in the face, and Pandora gaped. Eustace patted his daughter's skirt back into place as if nothing untoward had happened and continued his story.

"They showed as Clary's Islands on the maps until I married. My dear departed wife was fanciful and loved that Mr. Shakespeare. She renamed them Caliban, Prospero, and Ariel. Hell, she even called our daughter Miranda from that play, *The Tempest*. I named my boys Roger and Daniel, good strong names. Roger will inherit Caliban where I built my biggest home out of good, red Georgia brick atop the only hill. Daniel will come into Prospero, and my daughter's dowry is Ariel with its own house, servants, and field hands."

Eustace paused to gulp some wine. Pandora attacked.

"Tell me, Mr. Clary, how many enslaved human beings do you have on your islands?"

Oblivious to her tone, he replied affably, "Why, upwards of four hundred, maybe more as they reproduce all the time. The climate agrees with them, being similar to Africa. Roger, my oldest boy, keeps the count. Daniel, here, takes little interest in our property, though he ought."

Pandora shifted her chair several inches further from Daniel as if he carried one of those plagues he'd spoken of earlier. His face burned again. She had plenty of room to move with no one on her right at the socially unbalanced table. She turned on the younger Clary.

"And you, sir, are a slaveholder. You traffic in human flesh!"

"My father owns the property, not I. I have only a manservant who has been with me since childhood, not unlike the servants who work at Bellevue."

Still without understanding, Eustace Clary continued. "But don't you worry, Miss Pandora. Daniel stands to inherit over a hundred head like Miranda. He is a good catch for any gal."

Ignoring the man, Pandora spit out, "Can your man quit if he wishes, come and go as he pleases? Did you leave him behind lest he seek his freedom in France?"

"Horace has a comfortable life waiting upon me as do your servants, but should you turn one out without a reference, what becomes of him? If you enclose your lands, what happens to your cottagers?"

Before Pandora could slap Daniel's face, the duchess rose and announced, "Ladies, to the withdrawing room."

Miranda stood up trembling, but Pandora continued to stare into Daniel Clary's unflinching green eyes.

"Pandora, you will come at once. While you know where our sympathies lie, this is not proper dinner conversation. Leave it to the men."

Her daughter arose and sticking her nose into the air as if she smelled a great stink, turned her back on Daniel Clary and marched from the room.

~ * ~

Tea and conversation awaited the ladies in the drawing room while the men pored over port and politics. The duchess attempted to soothe the nervous Miranda, parted from her menfolk for the first time, but Pandora sought out a chair in a dark corner. She still steamed like the teapot. That's the way it always was: women taken off to discuss household matters, babies, and adorable pets while the men got down to the real stuff of life. She wanted to scream, but if she dared, Mama would send her to her room. She sulked silently instead while that insipid girl rattled on about turtles.

The men were soon with them again. Her mother glided over to her dark corner and said quietly, "You will now make your apology to Mr. Daniel Clary for your insulting behavior. How he makes his living is of no concern to you."

"It should be of concern to all the world."

"Of course, you are right, but I will not have anyone say my daughter is ill-bred. Go."

Pandora kept her seat. "I do not care for the man. He talks like he has a mouth full of treacle and is too lazy to speak crisply. And his eyes—they change color, now green in dimness, then gray in the light. He is fickle like all men."

"Mr. Clary can hardly be faulted for the color of his eyes or his accent. I thought it refreshing that a man stood up to you instead of backing down or running away." The duchess paused thoughtfully. "Are you still burning over your rejection by Tarleton Heaton?"

"Hardly! I despise that soft slug and his slimy friends. I cannot believe you betrothed me to him in childhood." Pandora folded her arms under her ample bosom, the only soft part of her. She often felt the rest of her body was all jagged edges hidden under deceptively rounded limbs. Why couldn't she be like Phemie or that lunatic turtle lover, all fluttering lashes and dainty hands? No, her nature would not allow it, and she rejoiced in that.

"I have told you before, the betrothal was simply a fond wish between close families, not a contract. He might have settled on Phemie, if she hadn't been swept away by Ian McLaughlin, or even one of the twins, though he wasn't ready to settle down when they came out. Elinor and I hoped one of you would become the next Lady Edgemont, but it was not to be."

"I will never be a countess or a duchess or a viscountess or a..."

The duchess had had enough of her behavior. Pandora could tell because the lines by her mother's mouth grew deeper and her gray eyes darkened. She had pushed too far.

"No, but you will be polite in your current state as Lady Pandora Longleigh. If you will not apologize, you will stay here while the rest of us depart for London."

"As if I cared for another season of being dragged about the ballrooms!"

"Oh, it won't be the balls you miss, only those meetings of the Abolition Society. Will you tender your apology to Mr. Clary now?"

Sometimes she could not decide if her mother was a witch or merely ruthless. She stood and strode across the drawing room, no gliding or mincing steps for her, to where Daniel Clary conversed with her father and his. Jason had rushed to Miranda's side on the settee the moment the men entered the room and sat gazing into those big, mooncalf eyes of hers. Might as well get this over with and then feign a headache and return to her bedchamber.

"Mr. Clary, might I have a word with you?"

The young man hesitated. He was afraid of her, like all men. His boorish father encouraged him.

"Go on, son. See what Miss Pandora has to say."

"Very well."

He accompanied her to another dark corner of the room. She knew all eyes but those of Jason and Miranda watched. She would do this her way or no way. Pandora smiled up at him, trying to emulate his foolish sister. Evidently, she showed too many teeth because he did not smile back.

"If you are a true gentleman, you will nod and pretend to accept an apology from me for speaking my mind."

Daniel nodded. "Is that all?"

"No. I know what you and your slave-holding family are up to. You think to pawn that ninny of a sister off on Jason and marry her into wealth and nobility. Let me tell you, my brother is merely a third son. He gets an allowance from Papa but must make his own way in the world. His title is honorary. Chances are he will never come close to inheriting Bellevue. So, why do you not take her back where she came from and leave us alone?"

"I would be pleased to do that. The thought of leaving her behind in this cold and hostile land appalls me. But you misapprehend my sister. She is no ninny. She uses her innocence as a shield to protect the things she cares about most deeply."

"She cares more for stupid reptiles than for enslaved human beings."

"I can assure you, all who dwell on Ariel Island are well-clothed, fed, and decently housed. Mammy Ida and Miranda care for them if illness strikes. We cannot keep an overseer there because my sister will override every punishment, so we use head men of their own race. As for marriage, Miranda has had offers since the age of thirteen, but they fell aside for one reason or another. The brothers of her schoolmates were put off when she expressed her peculiar beliefs about eating animals, especially turtles. Daddy would have forced her to wed a time or two, but the men never made it to the altar. You do not know everything, Lady Pandora."

There, he did it again, drawing out her name so long and slow he seemed to be covering her in a warm, light blanket. She grew hot and had to throw it off.

She heard Miranda coo, "Oh Jason, we should visit the turtles and see how they do. I am sure your papa frightened them badly with his ferocity this afternoon."

"Excellent idea," Pandora said with her voice harsh and sarcastic. "Let us all go see these marvelous beasts. I missed their attack on Mama earlier today."

Miranda, like a beautiful white wraith, drifted across the room in the candlelight and touched her arm. "Do not be afraid, Lady Pandora. The tortoises are the gentlest of creatures."

"I am *not* scared. I will lead."

She made for the door and snatched up one of the candlesticks meant for the guests to light their way to their bedchambers. She lit a candle off the one left burning and moved toward the dark conservatory. The others did the same. Her father paused to take up the saber he had used during his last venture into the hothouse. They entered a steamy world, a jungle of vines trained up pillars and tall palms grazing the glass roof. Rivulets of moisture ran down the wide panes. Waxy orchids gleamed in the rays of a cold March moon penetrating the gloom. The only sounds came from their own footsteps on the gravel and the splashing of the fountain.

"I think I know where they might be," Miranda said as she flew past Pandora. "Yes, look, here they are enjoying the pond."

Half-submerged in the shallow pool now sullied with mud the turtles had dragged in, the tortoises turned their bulbous heads toward the guests in mild curiosity. The statue of a naked nymph pouring water from her jug into the pond seemed quite dismayed about the use of her bathing area.

A shriek loud enough to rattle the panes shook the air. Everyone jumped. The tortoises retreated into their shells. The duke charged back along the path to where his duchess, her gray eyes wide with horror, stood. Pandora half-expected to see Busby's body covered by turtle bites and lying in the foliage.

"My pineapples! Those beasts have crushed them down and eaten all the fruit. What shall I give to my friends in the city now? They have come to expect a Bellevue pineapple at the start of every season. And all these droppings!" The duchess turned her face into her husband's broad chest and wept.

"Now, now, my dear. Shall I dispatch those monsters?"

"Please, no!" Tiny Miranda tried to pry the saber from his grip. "It's not their fault. We neglected to feed them. Mr. Gantry says they will eat any greens, even thorny cactus."

"I have no cactus—and now no pineapples," the duchess wailed. "Look at the mess they've made."

"Come now, Mama. You used to let your lapdog do his business in here when snow was on the ground. What are those droppings but more manure to feed your plants?" Jason said. "I think the turtles are full for the moment, but tomorrow we will throw them some cabbages and turnips. When the grass grows tall again, they can eat the clippings. In fact, I'll wager they could graze outside in the summer along with the sheep, eh?"

Flora blotted her eyes with a delicate hankie Pandora had shoved her way. "I suppose you are right. Let it never be said the Duchess of Bellevue is unfair to anyone or cruel to animals. However, my nerves are shattered for the evening. Come, dearest, take me to my chamber."

The duke handed his saber to Jason. "In case they turn on you. I must console my duchess and take her mind off those pineapples."

Jason and Pandora exchanged glances. Their parents were at it again. How could anyone mistake the wicked gleam in their father's black eyes? Honestly, he did not need to scoop Mama up and carry her to the bedchamber as if she weren't capable of walking on her own. Pandora would never understand them.

Five

"So glad you could come on short notice, Elinor. The Appletons should arrive shortly. We shall view the exotic creatures Jason brought home and then have a late supper. It is my great pleasure to be able to return your hospitality so soon."

The duchess guided her frail friend into the drawing room where Elinor could sit at ease and wait for the rest of the company. The poor dear lady had aged terribly since Tarleton had taken the notion to join the army, a thoughtless deed for the Edgemont heir. The tortoises might afford her a little gentle amusement since Elinor's heart beat too weakly in her thin chest to survive the arduous trip to London and the amusements of the season.

Flora chattered on. "I thought daylight to be a better time. As we learned last evening, the gigantic turtles appear quite hideous at night. Oh my, I'd forgotten young Lady Appleton is *enceinte*. Married in October and Sir Guy's heir well on the way. Do you suppose seeing such beasts will affect the baby? What if it comes into the world resembling a tortoise? But then, all of them do resemble wizened, old tortoises when first born."

That comment made Elinor laugh. Her friend of nearly the same age had gone from fair to white-headed in the last few months. She had only the two boys, as Dr. Gudikunst had advised her to have no more because of an irregular heartbeat. Her boys gave no comfort in her old age. Flora thanked God she had daughters, now scattered all over Great Britain with their husbands, to be sure, but still a solace—all except for Pandora, of course.

"Oh Flora, you do know how to amuse." Elinor's ever-cold hand patted hers. "Even if the Appleton child does look like a tortoise, its parents will adore the baby regardless."

"Bella Appleton is quite pretty and cheerful, and Sir Guy has a pleasant face and is easily pleased, so I suspect you are right. I have warned Pandora to mind her manners as she tends to be rude to anyone who is perpetually happy, and I won't have little Bella upset."

Elinor commiserated. "We all know Pandora and her notions."

"My daughter has taken a special dislike to one of our American guests, Mr. Daniel Clary. I thought I detected some attraction at first, but then Panny discovered he is a slaveholder."

"Oh my! Well, some women are meant to have causes rather than husbands," Elinor replied.

"And me, known as a matchmaker, unable to find a husband for my last single daughter. I must endure the embarrassment as best I can. Ah, I hear the Appletons have arrived. Remain seated, dear. I will have Busby bring everyone to you."

The Appletons, possibly the two most sunny-natured people on earth, soon appeared to pay their respects to Lady Edgemont. Both of them slightly plump and rosy-cheeked, they glorified the brisk but cloudless day and the wonderful diversion of being invited to see the curiosities. Bella Appleton had passed beyond the misery of the first months of pregnancy and now fairly glowed, her big blue eyes sparkling, her blond curls bobbing as she spoke. The rounding of her belly showed plainly beneath her charming high-waisted pink morning dress flecked with a rosebud print. Her breasts, enlarged in anticipation of the child, nearly popped from her low neckline, but a lacy tucker kept them in place.

The duchess introduced her guests to the Americans, who had been drawn from their various rooms and amusements. Obviously, meeting people from Georgia held as much interest as the giant tortoises, but she did not want to delay the meal. She'd heard Lady Appleton's stomach gurgle. Women with child tended to be voracious once the sickness had passed, as she well knew. Flora herded her company toward the conservatory.

Her dearest husband had offered his sturdy arm to Elinor, which left her to accept similar support from Eustace Clary. She simply did not care for the crass and overstuffed man. The Appletons, still in the throes of early love, paired off. Jason immediately companioned Miranda, and Pandora—ah, Pandora—refused the arm of Daniel Clary and went on her own.

"We have had to make some accommodations for the creatures. Duncan, my gardener, built them a compound of field stones in a corner. They can rest beneath the shade of several palms, but we will have to provide them with their own pool. The tortoises broke out yesterday and made directly for my lovely pond again."

The group entered the glasshouse. Elinor noticed first. "Oh Flora, what has become of your pineapples?"

"Sacrificed to the appetites of my new pets, I'm afraid. Duncan trimmed the plants as well as he could. We hope to have a new crop later in the year. Meanwhile, I shall make the best of the situation. I am having the turtle droppings raked up twice a day and will give sacks of the manure to my friends instead of pineapples. I am sure exotic *merde* will do wonders for their plants."

No one dared to disagree. They approached the fountain where the statue of the naked nymph poured water into the previously sullied pool, now pellucid once more, and turned toward the turtle compound. At once, all noticed a rather vigorous liveliness uncommon to this sort of creature.

The large tortoise bellowed and rammed the other. It circled its smaller domed companion, nipping at its feet and pecking on its carapace. The little one kept moving forward until it came up against the low wall and could go no further. Then, it retreated into its shell.

The attacking tortoise pulled back and heaved its bulk on top of the other, jacking up its companion's carapace by engaging two knobs on the bottom of its own shell. Its fleshy tail swung forward between its legs and forced itself into a vulnerable opening. The big tortoise's long neck snaked out, its bulbous head bobbing and looking for all the world like a male organ. It began to groan.

The experienced matrons stared at one another. Bella Appleton giggled behind a dimpled hand. The gentlemen began to chortle, all but Jason.

Miranda cried out, "Jason, please make them stop! They are not close friends, it seems. The big one is hurting the little one."

"Oh, I do believe they *are* close friends," Daniel drawled.

Jason took Miranda's hands in both of his and gazed into her eyes. "I would wrestle the Nemean lion for you, but believe me, he is not hurting her. They are—they are—making baby turtles."

"Oh! I understand now. Among the sea turtles I've studied, only the females come ashore to lay their eggs. No one knows where or how they—make baby turtles in the deep of the sea, though I believe the correct term is copulation."

"A mystery of nature. Who knows what passions flare in the depths of the oceans where the turtles dwell?" Jason replied, after his surprise that Miranda knew the word 'copulation.'

"Oh, spare me," Pandora grumbled to herself.

Daniel standing nearby, his color rising, said between his teeth, "I should call your brother out for simply looking at Miranda that way."

"She started all this with her sympathy for turtles. Harm one hair on Jason's head, and I will come after you myself with a loaded gun," Pandora answered, her voice growing louder.

"I would like to see your savage blood come to a boil—Lady Pandora." He drew out the last syllables one by one.

Pandora fisted her hands on her hips and rose up on her toes to get as close to Daniel's face as possible. "And I would like to see you at the bottom of the ocean."

The audience turned from the tortoises to the quarreling couple. The giant turtle groaned louder as if to reclaim their attention. He had a regular rhythm going.

The duchess clapped her hands. "We have all seen the creatures. Let us go into dine and allow them some privacy to finish their—uh—sport."

~ * ~

Pandora Longleigh usurped Lady Edgemont's seat by her father's right elbow despite his scowl. The poor woman drifted away and took a chair by her best friend, the duchess. Though Pandora pitied Elinor for her wastrel elder son, and the danger the younger would encounter on the battlefield, she was not about to sit next to Daniel Clary again. However, Sir Guy had been displaced and moved down one, still holding his fluffy wife's hand and slipping their affectionate clasp beneath the table top. Daniel, with no lady on his arm, arrived last and ended up by the duke's left hand directly across from her. Her haste and rudeness had done no good. She must look into his changeable green eyes for the entire meal.

Her mother had planned an informal dinner served *á la française* with dishes already on the table to be passed from person to person. A good thing, since the clatter of dishes and requests for various bowls, platters, and condiments covered the lack of conversation. Now and then, a gentleman would chuckle, recalling the tortoises, and Bella Appleton would burst into a fit of giggles when she was not eating for two. Miranda accepted no meat and dined on an excellent salad of lettuces fresh from the cold frames, bread, and the side dishes. Pandora made a point of taking a large slice of beef and tearing into it like a starving tigress. Across the table, Daniel Clary appeared to be enjoying the ham.

Her papa cleared his throat and made an attempt to enliven the meal. "Did you know, sir, our Pandora is an accomplished musician? She plays piano and harp and Spanish guitar. She is also uncommonly skilled at mathematics for a woman and can figure in her head, which makes her formidable at cards."

"I believe you mentioned the first last evening after supper. Not the cards." The younger Mr. Clary continued to concentrate on his food.

So that was the game, trying to marry their unacceptable daughter to this foreigner and send her off to America where they would never have to hear her opinions again. She noticed Papa had not mentioned her loathing of needlework or her inability to draw. Men did not need to tout their talents in the marriage market, but perhaps they should.

She focused on Daniel's eyes. "Tell me, Mr. Clary, what are *your* accomplishments?"

He hesitated only a moment before answering. "Why, I am glad you asked, Lady Pandora. I study the law like your brothers. I enjoy a brisk ride daily, am a crack shot with pistol and rifle, but not quite as handy with a sword. I prefer to take my exercise swimming in the sea when I am home. The waters are warm and caressing for a good part of the year in South Georgia. You should try them sometime."

Damn the man. Having four brothers, she was well aware that men often swam nude, a freedom not accorded to women. Now she envisioned those broad shoulders cutting through the breakers, his bare bum rising as he dove beneath the waves, his long muscular legs following. She swallowed.

"Panny, your brother has asked for the mustard pot three times. It is right there in front of you. Do pass it on," her father prompted.

She thrust the mustard at Jason. "I cannot swim, as Mama would not allow me to learn and so would have no interest in coming to South Georgia."

"There are other amusements, I do assure you."

At the other end of the table, her mother, getting her hopes up again, beamed at them. Pandora clamped her lips into a thin line and continued eating in silence. At last, the cheese, nuts and fruit were placed on the table, but no sweets. Pathetic little Miranda would have to do without sugar today.

The duchess tapped her glass for attention. "I have an announcement to make. Our dear guest, Miss Miranda Clary, turns eighteen today. Cook has prepared a special dessert for her."

The servants paraded in with a three-tiered cake and many small dishes of sweets, the cleverest of which were plates of marzipan turtles. Pandora recognized the receipt for the cake. She'd had the same for her birthday—layers stuffed with chopped nuts and raisins and frosted all over with butter cream. She seized a marzipan turtle and bit its head off.

As plates of cake were passed around the table, her brother slipped out and returned with a bouquet of daffodils twined around with one of her own blue hair ribbons. The stems still dripped from the vase. He presented them to Miranda along with a box of bonbons.

"How lovely. How very nice. I do like flowers and sweets—but I'd rather have another turtle," she said.

Everyone laughed as if the simpleton had said something witty.

Daniel Clary spoke up. "You have a great many of those flowers in bloom around your garden, haven't you, Duchess?" He picked up a chocolate identical to the ones in Jason's box from a dish and popped it into his mouth, to make the point that her brother had spent nothing on his gift.

"But we do have another present for Miranda. Busby, please bring it in," the duchess countered.

The butler brought a hatbox from the milliner in Westbrook and placed it in front of Miranda. She raised the lid and took out a bonnet of pale gray in the latest cabriolet style. White ribbons circled the base of the high crown along with a stuffed dove nestled in a clump of pink silk cherry blossoms. Miranda dropped the bonnet back into the box.

"Now then, I sent to our milliner and asked her to deliver a hat for a young lady turning eighteen. You should wear your hair high up on your head to accommodate it. My maid will arrange it for you. Also, you must begin to protect your complexion. One can never start too soon," the duchess continued with motherly concern.

Daniel scowled at the implied criticism of his sister. Pandora rejoiced. How nice that she wasn't the one being criticized for a change. *Pandora, do not wear your hair so severely. Allow a few curls. A bit of bosom might show, just a bit.* She anticipated the party atmosphere her mother wanted to achieve was about to change quickly.

"I am so sorry, but I cannot accept your gift, Duchess. You see, there is a dead bird sitting on it."

Jason did his best to save the moment. "I am sure this is merely a replica of a dove covered in feathers."

"Taken from other dead birds," Pandora could not stop herself from adding.

Mr. Clary, sitting next to his daughter, looked closely into the box. "No, I can see where the eyes have been taken out and glass beads glued in."

"Oh!" squeaked Miranda.

"Well, it does not please you. We shall go into town tomorrow and find one more to your liking," the duchess said.

"I like it very well, Mama. May I keep it?" Pandora asked, merely to show her disdain of the foolish Miranda as she ordinarily had no care for new bonnets.

"It does not suit your coloring, Panny."

"Remind me again of how brown I am. This is all Papa's fault!"

Daniel Clary seemed to measure her distress and said, "No, I agree with your mother. That pale hat does not suit you, Lady Pandora. You should be clothed in vermilion and cloth of gold, in fabrics the color of jewels as rare as yourself."

Again, Pandora found herself speechless. That simple Lady Appleton sighed.

Unfortunately, Mr. Clary spoke out. "When we spoke last evening, how big a dowry did you say comes with Miss Pandora?"

Her father had the grace to redden under his bronze skin. "Now, now, Panny. Do not be upset. I would never force you to marry. You may remain an old maid as long as you wish."

Ignoring the duke, Pandora turned on Daniel. "So, will I bring as much as one of your slaves at a sale, Mr. Clary? Am I worth twenty-thousand pounds like my five sisters, or more because I am a nuisance to be rid of? Do you know how you should dress—like the privateer and fortune hunter you are!"

"Pandora Jane Longleigh, you are excused from the table. Go directly to your chamber and stay there."

Her mother's orders, not her father's, naturally. Pandora pushed back her chair before a footman could assist her and sailed out the door. Her parents would be some time making apologies for her. She might as well retrieve reading material from the library to while away the afternoon. The Dukes of Bellevue had been accumulating books for ages. They filled the room on shelves from floor to ceiling, leaving space for only a few equally tall windows. She found the section she wanted and blew the dust from several volumes on America, among them St. Jean de Crèvecœur's *Letters from an American Farmer*, and his later *Voyage dans la haute Pennsylvanie et dans l'etat de New York*. Nothing on Georgia—which did not matter as she had no intention of going there. Pandora tucked the books under her arm and started for her chamber.

She would like to go to the former colonies, however. Her parents spoke often of their sojourn among the Shawnee with her mother emphasizing Indian women of that tribe could be civil leaders and divorce their husbands by merely putting the man's belongings outside the door, the last said to tease her father. So unlike England where women, especially married women, had almost no rights at all. To her mind, women's suffrage and the abolition of slavery went hand in hand. Perhaps she could convince her father to release a portion of her dowry for travel abroad with a suitable companion, one of her brothers, maybe. Justinian, the youngest, was easily led.

The heavy sound of men's voices and the lighter patter of ladies' traveled down the hallway. She knew she had been out of line earlier and had no desire to invoke further punishment or to appear to be disobeying her parents' orders and so slipped behind one of the ballroom doors to wait until the company passed. They had gotten between her and the staircase and stopped by the conservatory doors. She put her ear to a crack. The groan of the male tortoise continued to vibrate the glass panes. Quickly, the women decided to risk the chill in the air and take a postprandial walk in the formal gardens instead. The men lingered behind, trapping Pandora for a moment longer as they made a few bawdy comments amongst themselves.

She heard her father's deep voice say, "Still at it, by George. Who would have thought it of a turtle?"

The elder Mr. Clary answered. "More stamina than my best stud."

The younger men laughed heartily, Daniel Clary's voice booming out above the rest. Their group moved to follow the women. Pandora came out of hiding a moment too soon. While most of the guests had followed the duke onto the terrace, Daniel lingered by the doors. Startled, she dropped a book, stooped to retrieve it, and fled his mocking smile. The man was nothing but smoldering looks and sly compliments, all given to get her dowry. His broad shoulders and narrow hips—the devil could take them and that toothy grin, too. She would go to her chamber and read about American farmers until she banished all thoughts of copulating—copulating turtles, that is.

Six

"Mama, may I take Miranda to the Indian lodge?" Jason asked.

The company had walked past the magnificent fountain of Triton, shut down until all cold weather passed, and now stood on one of the side paths leading into the wooded, less formal part of the garden. Lady Appleton exclaimed over a patch of purple crocus and early daffodils. His mother promised to have Duncan dig some of the bulbs for her once the blooms had passed and the foliage died down. She answered her son absently, "Certainly, but we will be right behind you."

He grasped Miranda's hand and urged her along until they were running down the path. He needed time, time alone with Miri. The wigwam built of bent saplings and covered with bark sat in a clearing just off the meandering way. In a few weeks, his mother would have the gardeners put in a plot of Indian maize, pumpkins and beans to give the place more color and charm, but for now the glade sat barren, covered in last autumn's fallen leaves. Jason pushed aside a tanned deer hide that served as a door and held it to allow Miranda to duck inside.

"It's very dark in here without any windows," Miri said.

Some late afternoon sunlight penetrated the smoke hole and shimmered on the ashes of a cold fire. As their eyes adjusted, the forms of sleeping platforms overflowing with bear furs and buffalo robes became visible. A baby's cradleboard hung on the wall.

"Yes, it is, but very cozy in winter I'm told. Papa and my mother once stayed in such a lodge and sometimes they come out here to—uh—camp."

In no way could he explain to innocent Miranda about his eccentric and randy parents. Nor did he want to. His deepest desire remained to steal a kiss from her pink bowed lips, a long lingering kiss, while he pressed every inch of her small body against his. He moved toward the object of his desire, and she turned aside.

"Jason, we must get back to London."

"Certainly. We will travel along with my parents next week and take you to balls and the opera. My quarterly allowance is due soon. I shall take you to see the sights and eat ices."

"I do not care for any of those things. If I wish, I can dance on the beach in the moonlight by myself. But Mr. Gantry told me the big leatherback's days are numbered. If he is not sold soon, Mr. Cobb will chop him up for the pot. We cannot allow such a magnificent creature to die. We must purchase it and return the turtle to the sea."

"As I recall, that magnificent creature tried to take a bite out of me when I passed its tub."

"You would be irritable, too, if your home was the ocean, and you had to live in a tank."

"Miranda, I am short on funds just now."

"I will give you all I have and ask Daniel for more, but we must be away tomorrow at dawn before any of the others are up and can stop us."

The romance of it caught him by the throat—and perhaps his genitals. He could envision them fleeing to London on a noble quest, no one to stop them from doing anything they yearned to do.

"I will make the arrangements."

"Jason, are you in there?" His mother's voice sounded.

His father pulled up the deerskin flap, and the group swarmed in. The Americans were clearly unimpressed, but Lady Appleton clapped her hands in delight at being in a real Indian lodge. However, after fingering the bear pelts and showing off the buffalo robes, the moccasins made by the duchess's own hands, the wampum belt, and the scalp of an enemy which elicited a cry of horror from Bella Appleton, there remained little to see and they started back to the Hall. Jason could only be grateful his parents had not gone on to tell the tale of how the scalp was taken and by whom, or broken into the Green Corn Dance. To think they considered Miranda an oddity!

On the way back, Jason fell behind and accosted his father with a request. "Papa, I am a trifle short on funds at the moment. Might I have a note for an advance on my allowance?"

"What have you gotten yourself into—gambling debts?"

"Never! You see, the turtles cost a bundle, and I bought them selflessly to please Miranda."

"And dismay your mother. So, it's woman trouble, then. I remember those days. I'll pen a note to my banker in London to release your allowance early when we get back to the house, but this time, spend it wisely."

"Thank you for your understanding."

"A man is only young and very foolish once, but I would take care around Miss Clary. These Americans might be setting the parson's mousetrap for you."

"I believe I would gladly step into it."

"Bide your time for a while. Look around at other offerings."

"As you did with Mama?"

"A different circumstance altogether. Let us move along. Our guests are preparing to leave."

~ * ~

A maid carried Pandora's supper tray to her bedchamber, and so peace reigned at the dining table. Civil conversation ensued. Jason could barely eat, waiting for the meal and the evening to end. The note to the London banker weighed in his pocket as if it were actually solid gold coins. Miranda's lovely hazel eyes lit every time she glanced his way. As for Daniel Clary, he looked supremely bored, but who cared about him?

Over tea and coffee, Miranda asked to see the turtles again. She whispered to Jason that she wanted to say goodbye and make sure they were doing well in their new home. The duchess agreed to another candlelit foray into the conservatory if "the beasts are behaving." His mother sent a footman to make sure the groaning had stopped. The servant reported back. Indeed, the groans had ceased, but now a strange scuffing sound emanated from the enclosure. He had been reluctant to venture too far into the greenery.

"For heaven's sake, man, they are only turtles. Where did I leave that sword?" The duke led the way, candle and saber in hand again.

They found the male tortoise resting, completely tuckered, his tongue lolling out one side of his beak. The female, however, industriously dug a hole with her hind legs in the soft loam covering the conservatory floor.

Duncan McLaughlin, the gray-haired head gardener, leaned on the stone wall and observed, "She's been at it for several hours now. I canna seem to tear myself away from these two."

Miranda squeezed Jason's arm. "She's nesting. Daniel, quickly, run to my chamber and get my notebook from Ida. It's in my trunk. Could someone get me a measuring stick?"

Duncan went for a measure. Daniel departed at a run for the upper floor.

Eustace Clary rested his wide backside on the top of the wall. "Might as well be seated. We'll be here for some time." He sighed as if all his dreams were crumbling like the sides of the turtle nest.

"Jason, you must lift me over the wall," Miranda declared.

"You're going in there? No, I cannot risk you."

But Miranda simply lifted her skirts and began to clamber over the barrier without assistance. Relenting in an attempt to protect her modesty, Jason swung her over the obstacle and jumped into the enclosure right behind her. He would protect her if he must. His father offered the saber, but otherwise seemed more fascinated with Miranda's lack of decorum than shocked. Jason refused to look at his mother.

Duncan returned with the measuring stick and handed it to Miranda. "I will need your lantern as well," she said. She gave the lamp to Jason and asked him to hold it close.

Daniel returned with Pandora on his heels. In the commotion, no one thought to send her back to her bedchamber.

"What is all the uproar?" she asked.

"The female turtle is nesting. Miranda needs her notebook to record the process."

Daniel settled a candlestick on the wall, withdrew a black lead pencil from the spine of the notebook and flipped it open to the page where Miranda had drawn very accurate pen and ink sketches of the tortoises and recorded their weights and habits as related by Mr. Gantry. She'd also described in detail their earlier mating ritual, probably scribbled down while the others dressed for the evening meal, Pandora noticed, as Daniel rested the notebook on the rough surface and prepared to write.

Kneeling in the dirt and heedless of soiling her gown, Miranda called out, "Daniel, record the depth of the nest as eleven and one-half inches. I believe she is nearly finished. How long has she been digging, Mr. Duncan?"

"Och, she wandered around a wee bit after the male got off her, then chose that spot. I'd say a good four hours, lassie."

"Daniel, did you get that?"

"Yes, Miranda."

The female tortoise ceased her laborious digging and poised herself on the edge of the nest. Her audience waited in complete silence. She strained and a white sphere stretched the skin under her tail. It popped out and dropped into the pit. Another egg followed, wet and glistening. Then, another and another. Miranda counted them as they came, caught one in her hands, described its size and shape to her brother, wiped the slime on her skirt, and replaced the egg carefully in the nest. She stopped counting at twelve.

The mother tortoise rested for a moment, but not for long. She began to hide her eggs by kicking the dirt back into the hole. Miranda helped, pushing the mounds of loam gently over the shells. Satisfied with the covering, the female backed over the nest and urinated copiously on the top. Some splashed on Miranda, who continued to observe without flinching.

"Daniel, record she laid twelve eggs and sealed her nest with dirt and urine."

"I have, Miranda."

No longer concerned with either her eggs or her audience, the tortoise plodded across the enclosure and came to rest next to the male. Miranda arose and brushed off her skirts with dirty hands. She beamed at the duchess.

"Now you will have something better than exotic manure to share with your friends—baby tortoises."

Looking doubtful, the duchess asked, "When might they be expected to hatch?"

"I cannot say. The sea turtles on Ariel Island dig their way out of the nest at approximately sixty days, but these eggs are larger and might take longer. Mr. Duncan, would you note the time and date of their hatching and how many survive? Please send me the details. I will give you my direction."

Jason cast a doting glance at Miranda and added, "Oh yes, this reminds me. Kate's time arrived, and Joshua bolted to her side the second the message came. That would be the day before we left London. Sorry, it slipped my mind. You should have word soon."

"Slipped your mind! The arrival of my grandchild slipped your mind. I won't rest a minute tonight after all this and now for worrying about Kate," the duchess said.

Her husband put his large hands on her delicate shoulders and rubbed his thumbs along the back of her neck. "There, there, I will help you to relax. We have a bevy of grandchildren already and nothing has gone wrong to date."

Another inappropriate display of affection, Longleigh style. Pandora sighed and inserted herself between her parents and Daniel Clary to block the view.

"I apologize, sincerely this time."

"No need." He seemed more amused than offended.

"I meant your sister is not a ninny. She is a naturalist."

"Exactly. I blame myself. My brother Roger and I spirited her down to the beach one night to see the turtles come ashore and make their nests. She was only ten at the time. We let her count the eggs as they were laid. Then Roger snatched one up and squeezed the yolk into his mouth. Miranda flew at him, all tiny fists and sharp teeth. She'd noticed that the turtle cried as it labored and could not bear the thought of anyone eating the babies. She set Ponce, Ida's boy, to guarding the nest and when the turtles hatched, the both of them drove away the gulls and raccoons that would eat the nestlings as they escaped to the sea. She's kept records on the Ariel Island turtles ever since—their variety, number of eggs, when they come ashore."

"Impressive. I suppose neither the Royal Society nor any all-male scientific contingent in your country would consider publishing a paper written by a young woman."

"Miranda had her observations on the painted bunting published under the pseudonym of M. Clary, Esq. when she was only sixteen. The Ornithological Society considered it brilliant."

Perhaps she had misjudged Daniel Clary. He adored his sister and aided in her pursuits. How many men would take time from their own self-involved interests to assist a woman? Would a man who did marry only for money?

She cocked her head and asked, "The painted bunting is a bird?"

"A finch common to our islands." He flipped to the front of the notebook and showed her a bright watercolor of a small but remarkably colorful specimen.

"Let me read to you, Lady Pandora. *During the mating season, the male painted bunting puts on a gaudy display, flitting through the thickets, showing off its violet-blue head, green wings, and red breast and rump. It is my belief that buntings pair off for life, but at this time, I have no way of proving it."*

Daniel's eyes appeared as black as hers in the dim light surrounding them but that green glow still lit them from within. "Lovely," she said.

"We also call the painted bunting a Nonpareil, the same word you Brits use to describe a beautiful and totally unique woman." He looked at no one but her.

Pandora felt all her jagged edges begin changing into smooth and rounded forms like beach pebbles molded by the sea. The silence around them grew intense. Even Miranda, with a daub of mud on her small pointed chin, ceased smiling up at Jason and turned their way.

"Looks like we ain't done yet," Eustace Clary had to say.

Seeing his daughter's back go up quick as a black cat and her swift turn away from Daniel, the duke intervened, booming out his words in an attempt to drown out anything more the elder Mr. Clary might add.

"All this excitement has done me in. The duchess and I shall retire for the night. Come along everyone. Busby will see to your needs."

Jason stretched and covered a faux yawn with his hand. "Yes, I believe I will turn in as well. We have another exciting day ahead."

"Do we?" questioned the duchess.

"Who knows what the turtles will attempt next? Come, Miranda. Up and over the wall."

He took advantage of the gloom to hold her close, filthy and reeking of tortoise urine as she was, for a moment. She always smelled of orange blossoms and fresh ocean air beneath the odor of turtle. He sniffed her loose curls. There it was—that sweet and heady scent. If only he had not looked up to see her father's heavy-lipped smirk.

Seven

The Duke and Duchess of Bellevue passed an arduous night. They decided mutually to sleep late and have their breakfast sent up on trays, consuming it side by side in their nightclothes, uncaring what the servants thought.

"Did you enjoy my imitation of the male Galapagos tortoise, darling?" Pearce said as he stirred sugar into his second cup of coffee.

"I did find the little nips and bites stimulating, but did not care for being curled up in a lump with my rump raised in the air for all that time. Although after a while, I did forget about my discomfort and began to enjoy the experience. Mayhap the female tortoise feels the same. The constant groaning, however, I could do without."

"But my stamina was impressive, was it not?"

"Always, dearest." Flora patted his arm and pecked his cheek. "Finish up now and be gone. I must call my maid and dress. Our guests have most likely finished their meals and are wandering around at loose ends."

"A final word. If you do not fancy Miss Clary as a daughter-in-law, you must get her back to London and show her around at the balls. Jason is so smitten, he emptied his bank account to purchase those turtles."

"Miranda is sweet, but so very eccentric. Poor thing has no mother to guide her and needs a strong man to protect her from the world. Jason really should consider finding someone like Kate to steady him, since he is so fuzzy-headed with romance himself. Miranda and Jason together—they would believe they could live off of nectar and dewdrops as they counted turtle eggs and wrote poetry."

"My opinion, if it matters: one more eccentric would do the Longleigh family no harm if he is set on her. We have a passel of them already. Kate believes in ghosts, sensible as she normally is, and Phemie's husband builds steam engines in a dungeon during his spare time. I could go on and on."

Reluctantly, the duke slid from the bed and took his coffee to his own chamber through the connecting door hidden in the paneling. The duchess arose and finished her toilette with the help of her maid. She chose an opaque, high-necked inset to cover a few "turtle bites" that the low bodice of her morning gown would not conceal and was satisfied with her appearance. Morning! Ha! The clock sounded twelve.

Busby waited for her as she descended the stairs. He held out a silver tray containing the morning mail. She sorted through various invitations and inquiries as to why the Longleighs had not come down to London as yet. Then, she found what she most desired, a letter from her son, Joshua. She tore it open and read it right there in the hallway. Joshua did go on about his agony over waiting hours for Kate's travail to end as if men truly knew the severity of birth pangs. Finally, he got to the crux.

Smiling at her butler, the duchess said, "Kate and Joshua have a son. All is well with mother and child."

Busby quirked up his thin lips. "Wonderful news, Your Grace."

"Where is everyone? I must share our happiness."

"His lordship is in the library reading the newspapers with Mr. Eustace Clary. Lady Pandora took breakfast in her room and has not yet come downstairs. Mr. Daniel Clary broke his fast, then requested a mount and went for a morning ride. Lord Jason and Miss Clary and her companion left for London at dawn as planned. His note is here under the rest of the mail. I believe he said you would be joining them in a day or two, and he would see to opening the townhouse."

The duchess crushed her letter when her hands flew together. "Summon the duke! We must go after them at once. This is but a ploy. I know in my heart they are eloping to Gretna Green."

With not so much as lifted eyebrow, Busby set the mail aside and stalked to the library to request the presence of the duke. Eustace Clary, unrequested, followed the duke's large form to the foyer where Flora wrung her hands.

"Good news and bad, dearest. Kate and Joshua have a son and all is well."

"That's my lad," the duke replied, bursting with pride.

"I'd say the compliments go to Kate, but we have a more serious matter on our hands. Jason and the Clary girl have run off together. He says to London, but I believe that is only a tale to throw us off. I know the hearts of young men and women, and I say they have eloped to Gretna Green."

"Now Flora, let me see the letter. No, it says they are going to deal with an important matter in London and will meet us there shortly."

"What matter is more important than marriage?"

~ * ~

Pandora Longleigh descended the stairs just in time to see Daniel Clary, windblown and ruddy-faced from a morning ride, enter the house and join the noisy group in the foyer. She felt gritty-eyed from lack of sleep, all her thoughts of the mating rituals of tortoises and painted buntings disturbing her rest. That, and the eerie groans emanating from her parents' chamber. Daniel would notice the dark smudges under her eyes and her total exhaustion, not any sort of dusky beauty, if he bothered to look her way. He took no notice of her at all but was drawn into the maelstrom of shouting voices at once. His voice rose above the others.

"What? My sister has run off with that penniless fool!"

"Penniless, you say?" his father said.

"As are all younger sons in a noble family, Daddy. His title is merely honorary as well. Why do you suppose so many of them came to America? You should spend more time studying British society and less eating their food."

"Daniel, get back on that horse and fetch your sister immediately."

Her mother shrilled at them. "My son has an adequate allowance when he isn't wasting it on turtles, and he will be a respected barrister with a good income one day. Any young lady would be proud to wed him, even one as odd as your daughter."

"Nothing but a lousy, lying lawyer. I might have known," Eustace answered. "Sneaky and underhanded, all of them."

"No, here in England that would be a solicitor," the duke corrected.

"No matter what he is called, he is a scoundrel, after my daughter's inheritance."

"Be quiet before I strike you down. Now Busby, exactly what did Jason say and do?" the duke demanded.

Busby repeated what he had told the duchess, adding, "I had Cook make up a hamper for them to take on the way, nice fresh scones and sandwiches, some of the preserved fruit, a good bottle of wine. I handed it to them myself."

"They won't starve for their love," Daniel remarked dryly. "At least not until they try to live on his allowance."

"Scotland is closer than London. I tell you they mean to throw us off with that note," the duchess said.

Pandora turned on her heels and retreated to her room. She felt sure Daniel Clary's glaring eyes followed her as she went. She called for her maid to help her into her riding habit and sent another scurrying down the servants' stairs with a message to have her mare brought round. The rumpus in the foyer had not abated by the time she returned. She stepped into the middle of it and parted the Longleighs from the Clarys with her arms.

"Mama, we waste time. If you feel they made for Gretna Green, I will show young Mr. Clary the way to the most likely road. If they are headed to London, they must mean to marry by special license and that will take a week. I suggest you continue our arrangements to remove to the city, which were half ready before these Americans arrived. If no sign of the couple is found on the Scotland road, we will all pursue them in the other direction."

"No one can say you lack sense, Pandora. It's a good plan. Go, go immediately," the duchess replied, fanning her flushed face with a hand.

"Are you with me, sir?" she said to Daniel.

"I am."

They met the horses at the door and walked them the distance to the gates of the estate.

"Simply give me directions. You will slow me down," Daniel made the mistake of saying to Pandora.

"I hunt foxes riding on a sidesaddle. I hardly think I will be a burden. Follow me."

"You mean to go all the way to Scotland?"

"They are in an old and heavy coach. Papa's thoroughbreds will overtake them long before the Scottish border, I assure you. Certainly, you do not think I would trust you to bring them back unwed. I've seen through your plot to weasel your way into the British nobility by preying on a young man as unworldly and full of poetry as my brother and by tossing shallow compliments my way. You say your sister is an heiress, but we have no way of knowing that."

"We hired a confoundedly expensive coach to bring those wretched turtles to Bellevue, and you believe we are paupers?"

She watched his face turn red before replying. "Many a gentleman lives on credit and buys what he can never repay. I go along, or I will not divulge the directions. You will waste time asking the way."

"I would do anything right now to prevent a Clary from marrying a Longleigh. Lead on!"

They rode all afternoon, stopping to make inquiries at inns along the way. None had seen the hired coach pass. No one answering Miranda's or Jason's description had stopped to buy refreshments or ask for fresh horses. All said they would remember a tall Negro woman, never having encountered one before. They checked side roads and byways. Pandora and Daniel returned to Bellevue Hall in exhausted silence.

"Where have you been, Pandora Jane Longleigh?" her mother said before they could shake the dust from their boots. With raised eyebrows, the duchess accused, "You could have gotten to Gretna Green and been back by now. What am I to think of the two of you?"

"Don't get your hopes up, Mama. You aren't rid of me yet. We had no sign of them. Prepare to leave for London in the morning."

Eight

Their romantic flight down the length of England had not turned out exactly as Jason Longleigh hoped. When he took a seat in the coach next to Miranda, figuring she would bump against him with every rut in the road or even fall into sleep on his shoulder, Ida inserted the picnic hamper between them and watched his every move from the facing seat. The black woman certainly had a stare saying she *could* turn men into frogs if she wished.

Stopping for the evening, Miranda's companion arranged at once for a single room for the women, leaving Jason to decide if he would get his own or sleep in the carriage. For the sake of saving money, he shared the coach seats and gin with Jinks, the driver. During the daylight hours, they ate and slept some more as they traveled and handed Miranda's notebook back and forth so many times, he felt he'd grown up on Ariel Island and knew all its denizens.

Arriving stiff and unkempt in London, he suggested they go immediately to Bellevue House and take advantage of the small staff preparing for the arrival of the duke and duchess, but Miranda insisted they repair at once to the Terrapin Inn and make certain of the leatherback. The creature still lay, unhappy as ever, in its tub of

North Sea water and snapped at all who passed. Despite his warning, Miranda ran her small hands down its rubbery, black-hided back and along the ridges that did look like stitched leather running its six-foot length. She stroked the white margins of its flippers and murmured reassurances it would soon be free. The turtle calmed and did not attempt to nip. How envious of the beast Jason felt, wishing those soothing strokes might be his and not wasted on a cold-blooded reptile.

~ * ~

Sailor Gantry, scenting another easy mark, appeared at Jason's elbow, the one nearest his purse. "What can I help ye with today, lad?"

Jason sucked in a large amount of air and let it out slowly. "How much for this leatherback?"

"We must get him on the scales." Gantry summoned enough men to lift the tub like pallbearers heaving a coffin and, letting the beast bite at his hook as a distraction, set it on the scales. The weights piled up, the needle waivered, and settled on 1,050 pounds. The sailor deducted the fifty pounds to adjust for the tub and water. Still and all, the thing weighed as much as a beef cow.

Seeing Miranda's beseeching hazel eyes on him, Jason responded. "I will have the money in the morning. I suppose we will need a cart to shift him to the river."

"Oh no, not the river. I've seen the Thames. It is very muddy and dirty. He won't survive the journey to the sea. We must release him directly into the ocean. Where is the nearest beach?"

Miri's little hand stroked his arm just as it had the turtle's hide, exactly as he had wished a moment ago. He swore enchantment dwelt in her touch because he heard himself say, "I do not know, but there is a good, direct road to Brighton since the Prince Regent is building his Pavilion there. We would need the cart and dray horse for several days."

"I'll ask Mr. Cobb to throw in the transport since ye paid such a royal price for the beast. In fact, I'll drive it meself. I could use a good sniff of sea air," Gantry proposed.

"We'll all go! It will be a grand adventure. Jason, see your banker. Ida and I will take a room above stairs for the night and watch over the turtle," Miranda said with a voice full of enthusiasm.

"While the Terrapin Inn is a perfectly respectable place, I would not think of leaving you here alone. Let me deal with business, and I will be back as soon as I can. Meanwhile, Mr. Gantry, I charge you to look after Miranda and her woman."

"I wouldn't hurt a hair on her head, I swear," Gantry replied, looking not at Jason but at the towering black woman a head taller than himself.

Hard as it was, Jason parted from Miranda and took advantage of having the coach to make the rounds of the bank, his own chambers, and his father's townhouse. The banker, knowing the ways of young men, thoroughly disapproved of dispensing an entire quarterly allowance all at once in currency and showed it in his mouth pulled tight as purse strings. As for the visit to his own digs, the place sat as deserted as the day Joshua left. He replenished his trunk with clean linens and extra clothes suitable for a trip to the beach and took himself off to Bellevue House for a good wash and shave. No need to concern himself about his family. They would most likely be returned from Brighton before the duke arrived with his entourage.

Back at the inn and very grateful Mr. Clary had rented the coach for a fortnight paid in advance, supposing they would all return to London shortly, Jason bid farewell to Jinks, who held out a hand looking for his vails to replenish his gin. Jason doled out the coins and went to find Miranda, who had established herself in a comfortable chamber accessed from an outer staircase without having to pass through the dining area or bar.

He paid for his own space and arranged for their supper in a private room. Ordering up a fish dish, all the vegetable selections available, cheese and bread, and a crisp, white wine, he contemplated gazing into Miranda's eyes in the candlelight as they ate, taking her hand and receiving a kiss for a sweet dessert. Unfortunately, Ida took the trays as they arrived and elected to serve them herself. She hung over the meal like a deep shadow. In the end, he had no choice but to see Miranda to her door and return to his own chamber nearby without so much as touching her fingertips.

~ * ~

"Mammy Ida," Miranda whispered just before she blew out her bedside candle. "You said the spell you cast upon me when I turned thirteen would disappear when I met my true love, the one I wished to marry for life."

"Yes, child." The slave woman unrolled a pallet next to the door. She found the knife she carried hidden in her garments and placed it under the mattress. They slept in a strange inn on this cold and foreign isle. No doubt, the young man would rush to their rescue if Miranda cried out, but women must be prepared to defend themselves in any way open to them. She'd learned that young when torn from her mother's arms and placed aboard the slaver that took her away to Haiti. A cold draft crept under the door and chilled her bones. She stuffed the pallet into the crack and settled herself for the night. Once she got her charge home safely, she planned never to leave the warmth of the Sea Islands again.

In the darkness, Miranda spoke. "I think I feel the spell dissipating every time Jason is near."

"No need to be hasty. Take your time in choosing and then I will see you have the man you desire."

"I am fairly sure I am falling in love with Jason Longleigh. I know he has used all his money to indulge me and will never be titled or rich like the duke, but I do not need a wealthy man, now do I?"

"No, *bébé*, you are an heiress, but choose carefully."

"He seems to understand my need to study the creatures of the earth and protect them. He ordered the sort of dinner I like, while I know he would have preferred a roasted fowl. He has poetry in his soul, Mammy Ida, but his family regards him lightly."

"A person cannot dine on fish *or* fowl and pay for it with poetry, child. His family knows that."

"His brother, Joshua, and the Lady Pandora are frighteningly practical, and I suspect the duchess could be fierce if she took a dislike to a person. I find the duke very sweet. He loves his wife so and is not afraid to show it. Jason, I suspect, takes after him. We could live on my island and dance in the moonlight and wait for the turtles to come ashore."

"A pretty thought. I will see you have more time to test Jason Longleigh. Sleep now, child, sleep."

~ * ~

The Bellevue entourage of carriages and carts finally arrived in the city, a trip tedious in the extreme over at last. The duke had brought along several riding horses to allow the gentlemen some exercise along the way. Eustace Clary declined a turn, preferring to sit in the carriage with the duchess and pick at the victuals packed for the trip. Pandora immersed herself in Abolitionist tracts, holding them directly in front of her face, but she had been otherwise forbidden to bring up the subject. When she lowered her papers, all she saw was Mr. Eustace Clary's piggy eyes and heavy jowls. However had he sired such an attractive son? A conniving and very ruthless son, but attractive nonetheless.

Daniel preferred to stay on horseback for the duration. After stopping for the afternoon meal, the duke generally joined his wife in the carriage and both he and old Mr. Clary snored away the time until the supper break. Pandora had her sidesaddle placed on her mare and took her exercise then, carefully staying on the opposite side of the road from the man who drew her like metal to a magnet. Occasionally, passing coaches forced her closer. At these times, he spoke to her politely, commenting on the differences of the British Isles to his own.

"Our roads are no better. I have a sloop I run up the coast to Savannah, where I hope to have my law practice one day. I use a smaller vessel between our islands when I am home."

"I've had no opportunity to travel abroad with the recent hostilities between our countries and Napoleon running rampant all over Europe...only a short trip on a coastal vessel to Scotland," she replied, despite herself.

"I believe the open sea would suit you."

"How so?"

"Because both of you are so very strong and magnificent, dark and tumultuous."

Pandora felt his allure again. She was sinking into the depths of his eyes, light green and sparkling like waves in sunlight today, but still drawing her down. Quickly, she set her heels to her mount and cantered out ahead to the safety of the other side of the road.

She and Daniel were still astride when they entered London and stopped before Bellevue House. Her mother began directing everyone at once.

"Pearce, darling, take Daniel's horse and go at once to see if Jason has applied for a special license. Busby, ask the staff if they have seen Lord Jason and supervise the unpacking. Pandora and I shall take the carriage and visit amongst our friends to see if any knows what has become of our runaways."

"What shall we do?" Daniel Clary asked eagerly as he stood beside his corpulent father.

"Wait. You do not know London or its society."

Busby returned. "Lord Jason stopped in briefly for a wash yesterday and went off again without saying where. He did not come back to sleep, Your Grace."

"He is up to no good if he has hidden Miranda away. If he so much as touches a hair on her head, I'll have Daniel shoot him dead," red-faced Eustace Clary declared.

"It would be my pleasure," Daniel answered.

Pandora glared at him. "If Miranda were not such a mooncalf, she would not have run off with a man she hardly knows. Not that Jason would do anything dishonorable."

"Let us not underestimate your brother, Panny. He is a love-struck man. I assure you if Jason has taken advantage of Miss Clary in any way, he will do what is right by her," the duke said.

"And gain a plantation while my daughter gets a penniless, titleless third son who writes poetry and reads law. I call that an unfair exchange," the elder Clary blustered.

"We will rectify the matter if it comes to that. Now, we waste time again. I am off to see about the matter of the license." The duke mounted Daniel's horse and left the melee to his duchess, who was more than up to the task of ordering them all.

His dust had barely been swept away by the breeze when another horseman approached from the opposite direction and came to a stop before Bellevue House. About to re-enter her carriage, the duchess hesitated, then turned and opened her arms to the dismounting rider.

"Joshua, dear boy, how is Kate and your new son?"

"Thriving, Mama, but Kate told me I had neglected my practice long enough and must return to the city. She will come along as soon as she is mended from her travail. Where is Papa? Since James is a laggard about marrying, we plan to christen the boy Pearce William George Longleigh the Second." Joshua frowned at the company.

"What are the men with the turtle-mad girl doing here?"

"Jason gifted me with a pair of huge tortoises at Bellevue Hall and then eloped with Miss Clary. Have you seen him anywhere?"

"I've been by our house. He isn't there. He left the cheese out to mold and mice. Kate would have his hide. But his horse is still in the mews, so he can't have gone far."

"Oh, he had the advantage of a hired coach. They could be anywhere by now. I was just about to make the rounds of our friends to see if any had knowledge of your brother."

"Younger brothers, what are we to do with them? I should have known he'd get into some scrape he could not manage alone."

"I beg your pardon, but I am a younger brother, and I assure you I would never do anything as stupid as run away with a young woman I hardly knew," Daniel Clary added with ire.

"I see. Mama, you are fatigued from your journey. Why don't you rest, and I will inquire among our friends. Pandora can entertain the guests."

"Why am I to be stuck with the Americans when I could be out searching as well?" Pandora objected.

"Because it is your duty," the duchess snapped. "Go along then, Joshua. See what you might find out."

~ * ~

In the end, no one wanted to be entertained. They went to their assigned chambers as soon as those rooms became available and gathered to confer over a light and hastily put together supper.

"No sign they have applied for a license," the duke reported as he helped himself unhappily to yet another cold dish.

"Our acquaintances have seen nothing of them. Of course, I did not mention Miss Clary's name in the same breath with his. I merely asked if Jason had sought their company while I was out of town and spread the glad tidings of our new son. We are still safe from embarrassment," Joshua said.

"Why? Because your brother wants to marry an American?" Daniel challenged.

"I was circumspect for her sake as well as ours. This may still turn out happily for everyone."

"Forgive me if I doubt that." Daniel went back to dissecting a piece of pudding he never raised to his mouth.

The duchess rose. "Gentlemen, enjoy your port. Pandora, come play some soothing music for me. I have a headache."

Once away from the men, the duchess ordered a tisane for her malady, closed her eyes and rested her head against a cushion. Pandora did as she was asked and picked the gentlest of tunes, even adding a lullaby that made her mother smile. What possessed her to switch to crashing chords and fancy finger work when the men entered the room, she did not know—the devil perhaps. She arrived at the bottom of the page so swiftly she tore a corner off the music in turning it. Her mother woke abruptly and upset her herbal tea. The duchess held her hands to her ears.

"Please, Pandora, something quiet. Young man, go turn the pages for her before she rips the songbook to shreds."

Daniel obliged. "You do play very well, Lady Pandora, but I suspect my sister sings more sweetly."

"Like the painted bunting, no doubt."

"I don't believe the female buntings sing very much. They nest low in the bushes and have a green color for disguise. Stillness becomes them. We do have a blackbird with red wings that sings brilliantly, though."

"Another male, I am sure. The female of the species is always relegated to sit quietly on the nest."

"I believe you are right. More's the pity. They should have a chance to sing as well."

He was doing it again, luring her with words she wanted to hear and believe. "I am tired of playing," she told him.

"Then let me sing you a song I learned from the sailors who come to our islands. It tells the tale of a white man in love with an Indian maiden, but he must leave her for a time. It's called 'Shenandoah.'"

Daniel folded his hands in front of his broad chest, closed his eyes and sang the lyrics in an extremely pleasing baritone. Pandora found that even with his eyes shut, she could not take hers away from his face.

Oh, Shenandoah, I long to hear you.
Away, you rolling river!
Oh, Shenandoah, I long to hear you,
Away, I'm bound away,
'Cross the wide Missouri.

The white man loved an Indian maiden,
 Away, you rolling river!
With notions his canoe was laden
Away, I'm bound away,
'Cross the wide Missouri.

Oh, Shenandoah, I love your daughter,
 Away, you rolling river!
For her I've crossed the stormy water,
Away, I'm bound away,
'Cross the wide Missouri.

Farewell, my dear, I'm bound to leave you.
Away, you rolling river!
Oh, Shenandoah, I'll not deceive you,
Away, I'm bound away!
'Cross the wide Missouri.

He opened his eyes, and she was caught again in their green depths. She had to turn aside and seek help from her parents to break another Clary spell. They sat side by side on the settee. The duke's arm had strayed around the duchess's shoulders. Her mother mopped tears from her eyes.

"Yes, very moving. Daniel has a passable voice, but we are no nearer to finding my daughter," Eustace Clary, ever the spoiler, remarked.

"While I sang, it came to me where they might be. Miranda wanted another turtle for her birthday. We should try the Terrapin Inn."

"Then fetch her, Daniel, fetch her at once, and take care not to startle Ida. You know how she protects Miranda."

"That is why I am sure we will find my sister untouched unless they have married."

All of the men except Eustace went on the hunt to the Terrapin Inn. He stayed behind partaking of a bedtime snack. The duchess steadied her hands with needlework.

She spoke softly to Pandora. "If your father had sung to me like that instead of bellowing all the time, we might have married even sooner."

"Oh please, Mama. Papa could not love you more. Besides, he cannot carry a tune in a bucket."

"I know you think I want to be rid of you, but truthfully, I wish you could have a love like ours for your very own, Panny."

"Unlikely to happen."

The men came back too soon.

"They were at the inn in separate rooms but decamped for Brighton early this morning, drat it!" the duke declared.

"Brighton, oh dear!" The duchess dropped her needlework and pressed her hands to her face.

"What is the matter with Brighton?" Eustace asked, brushing cracker crumbs from his waistcoat. "A town on the sea, am I right? Miranda loves the beach. It does figure."

"You see, Brighton has a rather racy reputation. The prince cavorts there with his cronies and the town abounds with Hussars and Cyprians. Not during the London season, of course. The town will be deserted except for the sick taking the waters. I am sure Jason will protect Miranda from any unwanted attention."

"So, your son has taken my little Miranda to a love nest by the sea. Daniel, you must go after them at dawn, if not immediately."

"They are riding in a dray bearing a thousand-pound turtle. Mr. Cobb said, lunatics that they are, they plan to release it into the sea. We should have no trouble catching them if we leave early tomorrow."

"I insist upon going along. Miranda might want the comfort of another woman," Pandora said. "I will ride my mare. She is a thoroughbred herself."

"Yes, a magnificent creature," Daniel Clary agreed, though he seemed not to be talking of horseflesh as his green eyes dwelt on Pandora.

"We shall all go and straighten this out at once. Busby, did you hear? We will want the carriage ready to go at dawn. We are all bound for Brighton," the duke boomed.

Nine

The first day out had gone wonderfully. With all of them riding the dray along with the one-ton turtle, they progressed slowly, making only half of the forty-seven miles to Brighton. Miranda, determined to make an adventure of the trip, dressed as a country lass in a plain blue gown wrapped around with one of Ida's white aprons. A simple straw hat with its broad brim pulled down by the black ribbon tied under her chin shaded her face and her eyes of dreamy gray-green.

Jason had gotten into the spirit of the venture and donned brown trousers stuffed into his boot tops, a coat and vest of the same dull color worn over an unadorned white shirt open at the neck. He topped his head with a low-crowned, broad-brimmed hat rather than his usual silk. Ida and Mr. Gantry came as they were, with the addition of the sailor's parrot, Miss Rosita, ornamenting his shoulder.

"She needs an airing and loves an outing," Gantry claimed as he handled the reins rather deftly with hand and hook.

The parrot clacked its sharp yellow beak at Ida, who sat beside the seaman, and cocked its bright red head to glare at her with one beady black eye. Ida stared right back. After a moment or two, the bird ruffled its green body feathers and beat a claw-over-claw retreat across Gantry's back to the seaman's far shoulder, where it beat its wings and complained until finally settling down. The bird talked more along the way than Ida, who chanted softly to herself and threw small objects she fashioned with her hands into the roadway.

She'd settled Miranda quite comfortably in the dray, padding its rough boards with pillows and handing her a sunshade. Jason was left to get splinters in his backside. For some reason, an imbalance in the cart perhaps, the water from the turtle's tank always splashed on his feet when the wheels jolted in and out of the many potholes along the way, but never on Miranda's dainty slippers. Even the turtle had more shade as they'd covered it with a tarp to disguise the value of their cargo. He pulled his hat down low and made the best of the situation.

When the sun stood high in a blue sky, they stopped beneath a tree and ate the provisions Miranda had wheedled out of Mr. Cobb: a mellow cheese and fresh bread, a crock of pickled vegetables, last autumn's apples, a few slices of brandy-sluiced fruitcake, a jug of aged cider gone a little scratchy, and a bottle of decent wine. The latter made for a merry company when they got underway again.

Jason felt moved to sing "The Gypsy Rover," one of his sister Phemie's favorite songs, in his fine tenor voice, making sure to use the version where the gypsy who runs off with the great lady turns out to be a wealthy lord. Miranda, her sweet light soprano soaring, answered him with the same song, different ending in which the lady elects to stay with her poor gypsy no matter how many jewels or comforts her abandoned husband offers. They sang the chorus together, their voices blending perfectly, his dark eyes never moving from her wide hazel gaze.

Mr. Gantry entertained them with some sea chanties, stumbling over the lyrics as he tried to expurgate any words offensive to the female sex, but the parrot insisted on filling in those blanks and got them all laughing. Ida sobered them up with a mournful song, sung in the cotton fields, Miranda said. Her companion had a rich contralto fit for an opera house. Jason suggested they should free the turtle and seek employment on the stage in Brighton, they were that good. The idea appealed to Miranda and even Mr. Gantry, who claimed he could add in a hornpipe dance, wooden leg or no. Ida quelled them all with a dark look and common sense.

"We need to stop soon for the night."

Mr. Gantry turned the workhorse up a farm lane. They begged their supper from the gaunt housewife reigning over a thatched cottage with a sagging roof. She took their pence but eyed them shrewdly and offered up her only bed for a few more coins. She and her old man could sleep in the loft. As Jason reached for his purse, Ida politely declined for all of them. They would make a camp and sleep with the wagon for a smaller fee.

"Suit yerself then. I'll cobble up a stew."

"Meatless, please," Miranda asked.

"Meatless is easy to come by in this house," the housewife answered, as she pushed a few greasy strands of gray hair under a cap in need of washing and went back to her cooking.

"I thought only of Miranda's comfort," Jason rushed to explain.

"And I think only of lice and bedbugs, Mastah Lord Jason," Ida answered.

"Good point."

The stew proved to be decent fare with potatoes and onions, lumps of a bony fish and fresh herbs swimming in a milk and butter broth. Mr. Gantry got the use of a kettle in exchange for half the packet of tea he drew from his coat pocket and entertained them with his jig as the beverage brewed. Miranda insisted on doing her version of a gypsy dance and raised her arms high above her head as she twirled, her unbound golden-brown curls lashing around her shoulders. Her narrow skirts belled out slightly, permitting Jason a secret peek at her stockinged ankles. When Miranda began swaying her upper torso, dipping low enough to give Jason a fair look at her small, flushed breasts, Ida called an end to the performance.

"Sit, child, before you become overheated and catch a chill. Do as Mammy says."

"I will if you do an African dance for us." Pouting slightly, Miranda took a seat on a blanket and cooled herself by waving a hand across her chest.

Jason found he could barely remove his eyes from that hand to Ida's quick stepping feet. Their dark companion held her skirts up slightly to show off her footwork, but Mr. Gantry focused on the sway of her big hips exclusively. With slightly scandalized expressions, the farm wife and her wizened husband in from the fields watched from their doorway until the bizarre entertainment ended with a few merry songs from the sailor and a plaintive duet sung by Jason and Miranda. After arranging for a breakfast of fried eggs and potatoes in the morning, Ida settled them all for bed with a spiritual song sounding almost like a prayer.

She made a nest of quilts and pillows for Miranda and lay down next to her charge in the dray. Gantry pulled a bundle of cords from a worn sea bag and strung his hammock between two close-growing trees. He rolled into it along with an old blanket while Miss Rosita climbed up one of the ropes to perch on a branch. Soon all were asleep except Jason, who hadn't thought to bring along any bedding. He grabbed a spare tarp like the one covering the turtle and crawled under the wagon, thinking the boards above would keep off the dew. The leatherback sloshed in his tank as if he mimicked swimming to the mating grounds, and water dribbled down on Jason no matter where he moved. Both Gantry and Ida snored. The night turned into a sleepless misery.

He had more hours to reflect on his actions than at any time since meeting the Clarys. What was the third son of the Duke of Bellevue doing sleeping beneath a leaky wagon on the hard ground? Who was he and what did he want out of life? His father had once asked the same question, hoping his son would choose the way of the warrior. Pearce Longleigh had killed men with both rifle and his bare hands long ago and respected the military life. But though Jason had been taught by the best to ride and shoot, fence and box, he lacked any desire to fight, kill, or maim. His skills were good enough, as he'd proven himself against Josh over and over again. He'd disappointed his father in his choice of careers, but not his mother, who feared for all her children. She'd urged him toward the church, but he had no feeling for religion either.

Sandwiched as the two brothers were between six sisters in birth order, they shared a natural rivalry. With his fine education and superior debating skills, Joshua chose the law, and he had blindly followed his brother, declaring he would make an even better barrister. Unlikely. He hated arguing. He loved poetry. Was this dalliance with Miranda merely a way to delay eating his terms away with the elderly barristers and being called to the bar at last?

Still, he'd never met an original like Miranda Clary, so lovely and pure, yet so passionate and intelligent. He'd done his stint at Almack's, where the debutantes raised their noses at a younger son with two brothers before him. They cooed and flitted about at balls and in the shops as much alike as a flock of pigeons waiting for a hunter to bring one of them down. So long as the hunter had money or a title or both, they were content. He scrubbed his weary face with his hands. He'd impoverished himself to buy turtles. What did his parents think of him now?

More water slopped through the boards, and he rolled over again toward the front of the dray. He believed he lay directly under Miranda's warm nook, and his mind began to travel in other directions that made him no more comfortable. He imagined he heard her soft voice calling to him through a crack in the boards.

"Jason, are you awake?"

"Yes, Miranda."

"I want you to know titles and wealth mean nothing to me, no more than they did to the lady who ran away with the gypsy rover."

He thought he might have dreamt this, but his physical discomfort was strong enough to keep him very awake. She worked her little finger through the crack, and he raised his to link with hers. He felt a bond so strong, he cared not that he would wake sore, rumpled, unshaven, in debt, and an object of mockery to his entire family. He loved Miranda Clary and believed she loved him, too.

Ten

The ducal carriage hitched to six speedy horses bowled out of London just past daybreak, when the shadows still lay long across the road. Riding light with only one footman, the vehicle carried the duchess, Eustace Clary, and provisions for the day trip. Certainly, they would overtake the eloping couple with ease and bring them home for a judgment.

Regardless, Jason would be forced to marry Miranda Clary, who was far more cunning than she seemed, Pandora thought. Her father, always very aware of his honor, would insist. These Americans! They all wanted to insinuate themselves into noble families now after tossing away old King George, who still occupied the throne and the madhouse.

She insisted upon riding with the men and, though Joshua disapproved saying she would slow them down, her father granted permission. He knew full well she'd spent her early years trying to keep up with the two brothers born just before her and could ride either of them into the ground. Bless his big heart. He was hard on his sons but soft on his daughters.

All four of the outriders rode ahead and never saw what spooked the carriage horses or caused the coachman to pull up so sharply he put the conveyance in a ditch. They did hear the animals scream and the unmistakable sound of a crash and turned round as one to dash back.

The duke arrived first at the toppled coach. His complete concern would be for Mama, Pandora knew.

"Dear Lord, Flora might be crushed beneath Mr. Clary!" He ripped open the door to find it the other way around. The duchess sat on Eustace Clary's huge paunch and appeared very ready to get off. With strong arms, he lifted her from the carriage.

"Dearest, are you hurt?"

"No, no, I had a soft landing." The duchess righted her hat and straightened her garments.

"Here now, a hand up needed," Mr. Clary called out, stuck as he was between the benches with his feet in the air. The duke's massive shoulders strained, and he heaved the man out.

Mr. Clary turned round to rummage in the coach. "See here, the hampers are intact. Not a single wine bottle broken. All is well."

"The horses?" the duke asked of his coachman, who was running his hands over equine legs.

"Bruised and shaken but nothing serious. They can pull 'er from the ditch, but I'm afeared the left front wheel is shattered. We'll have to send for another."

"Whatever happened, man? The way was clear except for a few carts bringing produce to the city."

"I whipped up the team good because you ordered me to make haste, but the lead horses shied. I could of swore I saw a tree fallen in the road and pulled up sharp to avoid it. There ain't no tree, I can see now. My fault, Your Grace."

Joshua got down and knelt in the grooves where the coach had left the road. "No tree at all, only a strange twig wrapped round with colored strings."

He held the object up. It bore a knob on one end and was forked at the other as if it had legs. Wrapped around with different colored threads, the center was distended by a huge gall resembling a big belly. Daniel Clary sucked in his breath. Pandora looked at him sharply. He knew something.

Daniel spoke up quickly. "No fault of yours, Mr. Coachman, but a simple mistake caused by the long shadows across the road. I suggest Lord Joshua ride back to town for help. Lady Pandora should stay with the coach and comfort her mother. The duke will want to guard his carriage, I'm sure. Let me go on alone and bring the runaways back to you."

"Yes, Joshua, do go back to the city and make the arrangements for repair. The day is young, and we aren't far along. I am sure Mr. Clary would not mind staying with the coachman and footman to guard the horses and carriage since we are well provisioned for the day, eh?" the duke replied. "However, I feel duty bound to straighten out my son in person and must ride on."

"But Papa, you know how mule-headed Jason can be. You might need my help to subdue him," Josh protested as he remounted and tossed the sinister stick aside.

"I am sure you would enjoy that, but no. You are a married man, a father now, and have greater responsibilities than getting your brother out of scrapes. Do as I bid you."

"I am certain Mr. Clary could watch over Mama as well. She doesn't seem in need of comforting at all. I must ride on with you. Remember, a woman's touch might be needed," Pandora said before anyone tried to dispose of her again.

"True, I am fine. No need to delay for me," her mother agreed. "Let Panny ride along with young Mr. Clary and yourself.

"As you wish, dearest." The duke lifted his wife up, hardly an effort for him, and kissed her forehead on the way. "Don't worry, darling, all will be well."

"Take care, my love. Watch out for sticks in the road."

The duke roared with laughter that rolled off the surrounding hedges and up into the sky. "I will not be stopped by sticks. Let us ride on."

The remaining three continued their pursuit and made good progress, though Pandora's temper shortened more every time she sought to ride with the men and Daniel Clary blocked her way. They approached a farm lane, where a haggard woman sat on an upturned bucket and shelled peas into a basin. A little before reaching her, the duke pointed out a puddle in the road.

"By damn, not a cloud in the sky. I'll wager that water came from the turtle tank. I'll ask the goodwife if she's seen our quarry."

Pandora's father raced ahead and she tried to follow, but Daniel held her back again by grabbing at her reins. She flailed at him with her riding crop.

"Be cautious, sir," Daniel shouted after the duke.

"As if my father is ever cautious," she snapped, then opened her own mouth wide to shout a warning, too.

The small puddle shimmered in the sunshine and grew larger, slicker, deeper. The rear hooves of the duke's huge, black mount sank into the morass and slid beneath its belly. The horse reared up and tossed Bellevue back over its haunches. He landed hard on his backside and then fell back, hitting his head on the packed dirt of the road.

"Papa!" Pandora shook free of Daniel and went to her father's side. By the time she arrived, the puddle had shrunken, dried, disappeared. Right behind her, Daniel dismounted and poked his toe at some small object in the road. He stooped, picked it up, and pocketed whatever it might be.

"Are you injured? Can you stand? Here, let me see your head first."

"Do not fuss, Panny. My thick skull can take a minor blow like this, but I think I might have broken my tailbone. Daniel, lad, give me a hand up. I'm too much for Pandora to handle."

She watched her father's normally full lips flatten with pain as he rose. The country woman approached leading the duke's charger, its hocks still caked with mud. The hag nodded sagely. "And so it came to pass."

"What exactly do you mean by that?" Pandora asked.

"Last evening, come a strange troop of folks looking for a place to camp. First, I thought they was buskers on their way to Brighton. They sung and danced around the fire, but their speech was too fine for that, all but the sailor, so I knew them for quality having a lark playing at being gypsies. Had a parrot, the seaman did, rode right on his shoulder. Then, there were the black woman looked like she come right out of Africa, but she knew the King's English, too."

"We are on the right trail then. When did they leave?" the duke asked, even as he gritted his teeth against the pain in his back.

"At dawn. That Negress, she give me some coins to sit here wasting the day at the foot of my lane waiting for fine gentlemen to come racing by. Well, they come all the time heading for the Prince's Pavilion down there by the sea. If any were hurt near my place, I was to take them in and would profit mightily for my help, she swore. They'd be nobles who would pay me well. I guess she were a witch who could foretell the future because here ye be."

The farm wife eyed the men, searching for fat purses, Pandora guessed. "Come, Papa. Let me help you down the lane to a soft bed, where you can rest until the carriage arrives. I will pay this woman to continue watching."

"No, no. I'd rather wait here. Hitch my horse in the shade and bring me a chair and cushion from the cottage. Then, the two of you ride on and retrieve Jason and Miranda. We will most probably meet you coming back."

Their hostess looked down the long lane and sighed. "My hip is ailing me today."

"I will fetch the chair and pillow. I am good at fetching." Daniel Clary started down the cart path to the farm. Pandora raised her skirts slightly and followed after him.

"What did you find in the road?"

"Nothing of concern. You should stay behind with your father."

"And let you to stand up for Jason and Miranda's marriage in some non-conformist chapel? My impractical brother might yet escape your sister's clutches if we find them in time and keep the story quiet."

"I am no happier than you, Lady Pandora, at the idea of leaving my sister behind in this cold land and tied for life to a feckless younger son. The climate would kill her, let alone if your brother should prove unfaithful, as all these English lords are."

"The Longleighs are noted for their fidelity. Aha! You are trying to distract me from the object in your pocket. Believe me, if you won't show it, I am not too shy to search you."

"Oh, I never thought that. While it might be a pleasure, your father watches us from the road, so be careful where you put your hands or I might be forced to marry *you*. Then, I'd be stuck with a wild bride in need of many nights of taming."

Pandora's cheeks turned a dusky rose, but she jumped nimbly over a pile of horse apples left behind by the dray horse and continued to harry Daniel. "You would be fortunate to have me. No, I will not be deflected by outrageous talk. The object, please."

"Here, then. Don't throw it down again, I warn you."

He extracted a tiny turtle shell from his pocket. Although coated with dried mud, a few strips of bedraggled fabric hung from the openings at either end of the carapace. Pandora pulled on the material and a few small bones from the inside of the shell came out in her hands. They were wrapped round with silk in the blue and silver colors of the Bellevue livery.

"Is it a charm of some kind?" she asked.

"Yes, Ida is adept at making them. While she would never cause a death, she will do whatever possible to protect Miranda and see my sister gets what she wants. My father brought Ida as a young woman to our islands from Haiti, where she'd been apprenticed to an herbal healer. He said she'd serve as midwife and doctor to our slaves, but she already had his child growing under her apron. Herbs and midwifery weren't all she learned, but curses and love potions, too."

Pandora felt the urge to drop the charm but heeded Daniel and curled her fist around it. "This one was fashioned to stop the Longleighs?"

"I believe so, just like the stick in the road was meant to upset the carriage. We should burn this one. There may be others along the way to Brighton. For Miranda's sake, Ida would never harm me, but I am concerned for your safety."

They reached the cottage door. Scattering chickens dusting themselves on the stoop, Daniel bent to enter the low doorway. Pandora hastened to the fireplace and threw the evil object into the flames. She dusted her hands of it. The shell hissed, popped and exploded against the bottom of an iron pot bubbling with that day's dinner, a stew of ancient mutton, by the smell of it.

"I am not afraid to go on, but I will ride behind you if you wish."

"I wish," he said, giving her a rather melancholy smile. "You are the most fearless woman I have ever known."

"Oh, I have my fears. I've often dreamed of drowning. I believe I will die that way and all alone without a family." She felt herself drowning now as the firelight brought out the gold and sea green of his eyes and a deep, deep longing for a man who understood her.

"I could teach you to swim like a mermaid if we had the time, but with your family, you are never alone."

She pushed her way to the surface and said smartly, "Well, we shall be alone soon. Take that chair. It appears sturdy enough for Papa."

Pandora pointed to one of a set placed at a crude table. She went to a bed in a corner behind a screen and picked up a pillow stuffed fat with chicken feathers. The soiled covering displeased her. She rooted in a chest for a clean slip and found one under some moth-eaten blankets. The linen had yellowed long ago, but someone had attempted to embroider a daisy chain along the hem. A sad remnant from an old hope chest, she thought. She had such a box filled with dainty items completed mostly by her mother and sisters because she did not care for sewing and rarely finished a piece. Would those linens turn yellow before she wed, if she wed?

"Take the chair. I will be right along," she told Daniel.

As soon as he cleared the door, she raised her skirt and found the pocket stuffed with coins and banknotes she had concealed under her clothes. She withdrew a guinea and went to lay it on the table, only to find Daniel had done the same. She left the coin regardless. Let this be someone's lucky day.

Pandora followed Daniel down the lane and settled her father on the chair and cushion. "We left payment for his dinner and anything else he might need. Do take good care of him, madam, and you will be rewarded further."

"Nothing as grand as a madam, just plain Mrs. Bert Waisley. Imagine me, taking care of a real duke. Won't my children be tickled. It's magical, truly magical." Mrs. Waisley grinned and, judging by the gaps in her teeth, she had given birth to many and lost a tooth for each one of them.

"Oh, go on and catch your brother, Panny. Do not coddle me. This is the most embarrassing injury I have ever sustained, but I will survive. And you, Clary, take care of my girl and keep your hands off her." The duke folded his arms over his broad chest and resigned himself to the wait.

"I shall, if at all possible, sir."

Daniel cupped his hands to toss Pandora back onto her sidesaddle and remounted his borrowed horse. They rode out together, but he soon requested she keep her promise and fall behind. He strained his eyes for small obstacles and went wide around anything looking out of place. They stopped briefly for a quick meal in a village boasting an inn and a stable where their horses could rest for a while. The sun sat lower in the sky when they continued on and both agreed they must go at a less cautious pace. Not a mile further on, Pandora cried out "No" and cursed the way no woman should. Daniel turned back.

"My horse was going along fine and now she's pulled up lame."

Daniel dismounted and dug his boot toe into the dust of the road. He unearthed a flat, brown pouch and spilled the contents into his hands—a bent rusty nail and some curled, horny material, hoof parings most likely. He checked Pandora's steed.

"She's thrown a shoe. No real harm done. We must lead her back to the inn and see to it, I suppose."

"Another trap, drat it!" Pandora said, sounding terribly like her father. "We won't let them win. Put me up behind you. If the spells weren't cast for you, I should be fine. We'll leave the mare at the stable and collect her on the way back."

"You should stay at the inn. After all, I promised the duke not to put my hands on you."

"And added 'if at all possible,' I noted. Besides, I will be putting my hands on you, not the other way around. Believe me, Brighton has seen worse spectacles than a woman riding behind a man. Papa rented a cottage for us once when the town became so fashionable. We took the sea waters in the bathing machines and had tickets to the Assembly Rooms, but as soon as he learned the disreputable nature of the company, he herded all of his daughters home like a sheep dog watching over his flock. I have always wanted to visit again."

"No time for sea bathing now. We must push on if we want to get there before night and find our runaways."

"Lift me up, and I will put my arms around you."

"If that is your desire, my Lady Pandora."

Eleven

"Why won't he move to the sea and be free?" Miranda sobbed. "The nesting females make the journey above the tide line and back in one night."

She laved the immense leatherback turtle with a bucket of sea water to cool his hide. Mr. Gantry had gone to the docks and found two hefty men and a portable winch to lower the turtle down the seawall to the shingle of the beach. Now, she beseeched the old tar to answer her question.

Gantry scratched his scalp and shrugged. "We don't feed the sea turtles at the Terrapin Inn. Mr. Cobb won't put out for fish, and they'd befoul their water and not keep as well if he did. Might be he's too weak to move."

"Then go at once and find a pail of fresh fish that are still lively." She pressed coins from her reticule into his palm. "Go quickly. Oh, one other thing." Miranda went with the sailor out of Jason's hearing and whispered in his ear.

"Not likely to find that kind of ship out of Brighton, Miss," he answered for all to hear.

"You will."

Jason frowned. Why was Miranda keeping a secret from him? Did she not feel his adoration, know he wanted them to be together always? The sailor continued on his errand, his peg leg slipping now and then on the flat stones as he made for the steps rising off the beach to where their dray waited. The parrot on his shoulder flapped wildly and swore at every misstep. Miranda darted back to Jason and handed him the pail.

"More water, please. I do believe it makes the leatherback more comfortable."

He took the bucket to the sea's edge and filled it. Here he was hauling water like a stable boy for his love, and all her concern went to a turtle. Somehow, Miranda still looked as fresh as when they had started out. This morning, she'd gone into the cottage with Ida and washed and changed into a yellow gown strewn with a pattern of daisies as sunny and delightful as herself. She wore the same straw bonnet with her hair hanging down her back, undressed as usual. The ocean breeze tossed her curls into charming disarray. She pulled the light wool shawl hanging over her small shoulders closer.

Yet, each time she glanced at Ida, he felt he'd been left out of some sort of conspiracy. Unshaven and disheveled without even a plain stock wound round his neck, he must look the rogue to her ingénue, but they were the ones plotting. Hadn't he shown himself to be constant and true? Why did they leave him out of their plans?

Jason upended the bucket and soaked the turtle—and the hem of Miranda's gown. "Sorry," he said, surly as any underling. "Shall I get more?"

Miranda laid a tender hand on his cheek and looked into his eyes. He saw sunlight on the waves, a tall ship pushing through the surf, cleaving the waters, pounding against the warm, liquid body of the sea. His pulse quickened. Ida took the hand away.

"Ida, I do believe we have worked Jason too hard and not fed him either. Let's go find a meal for him while Mr. Gantry completes his mission. Please do keep the turtle wet while we are gone, Jason."

They went off hand in hand, the huge black woman and the petite girl, toward the promenade. He sank down next to the leatherback but far enough away not to be bitten. The reptile hadn't tried to take a chunk out of him since they began this journey, but better safe than sorry. The turtle looked at him dolefully.

"Yes, yes, I know. So close yet so far away. Do not worry. She is going to feed us both soon."

He regarded the deserted beach. The air of late March and coldness of the water kept the invalids off the shingle, though a few well-bundled individuals were being pushed along the promenade in wheeled chairs by their nurses. The bathing machines, little houses on wheels drawn into the water to protect the modesty of the ladies, sat idle above the high tide line. With the prince in London, the town lay dull and lifeless as a dying man. He gazed out at the sea and saw the ship reflected in Miranda's eyes making for the docks. Not his imagination then. The crew scurried to reef the sails and slow its progress as they came into port.

With the constant wars raging in Europe and America, he and Joshua had been denied their Grand Tours. James, the cherished heir ten years his elder, had gotten his chance to go abroad and rarely came home, obsessed as he was with ancient civilizations in foreign lands. Too late now at the age of twenty-three to buy a commission in the navy or run off to sea, Jason supposed. Professional sailors started their careers as cabin boys or midshipmen. He had school chums who had advanced to lieutenant already and prepared to command their own ships. And here he sat at sea's edge hauling water for a turtle. He got up, trudged to the surf and brought another bucketful.

Miranda and Ida returned, already having purchased food from the vendors' carts lining the promenade. He saw they'd brought greasy cones of newspaper stuffed with fresh fried fish and bread rolls. A lidded pail of beverage turned out to be hot coffee from the food mongers. Miranda sank down next to him as Ida poured coffee into tin cups and handed them around. The ship they watched lowered its anchors and sat still in the water. Gulls circled its masts, hopefully seeking a meal of scraps thrown overboard.

Suddenly, he felt full of hope, too, just sitting on the beach with Miranda, gazing out to sea, a cantankerous leatherback by their side.

Limping along on his peg, Amos Gantry returned sometime later with another pail sloshing water over its sides. He set his burden aside, dug into the still warm fried fish, and accepted a cup of coffee. The sea turtle raised its head a bit when a small fish leapt up and fell back into the bucket.

"Aye, the sea air builds an appetite. Oh, for a tot of rum to go with this coffee and I'd be a happy man." Gantry wiped the grease off his fingers with the roll and swallowed the chunk of bread. He offered another hunk to Miss Rosita, who took it in a claw and nibbled daintily.

"Do you know anything of the ship that just came into port?" Miranda asked.

"She's an American vessel full of fancy English goods to tempt the planters of yer country out of their next cotton crop now that hostilities have ended. Captain Fulton plans to sail her to Charleston and Savannah and on down the coast."

"To our Sea Islands. I know that vessel, Mr. Gantry. She's the *Sea Nymph*. We've often traded with Captain Fulton and had him to dine with us."

"Stranger things have happened than a ship bound for America arriving exactly when desired, I suppose," Gantry remarked.

The sailor caught Jason's puzzled look. He directed a furtive glance at Ida, who had sung and chanted away the morning in an odd and foreign tongue unbeknownst to them. "The crew had a strange tale to tell. They left the mouth of the Thames and made their turn to the west, a strong wind blowing, not a cloud on high, when along comes a squall that almost o'er turned them. Bashed the *Sea Nymph* up bad, so they put into the first port to check her over. She'll sail on the morning tide for the high seas if they can get all the repairs done. Uncanny, very uncanny."

"No lives were lost, Mr. Gantry?" Ida inquired.

"Not a one."

Miranda smiled gently. "I am so glad. But we must attend to the matter at hand. Half Moon must eat."

She caught up a fish by its tail from the bucket and dangled it before the leatherback.

"No, Miranda! He'll snap your fingers off."

Jason jumped up and tried to pull her away, but the turtle opened its mouth and accepted the offering as calmly as a parson took tea. She laid out a trail of silvery, flopping bait to lure the turtle to the water. The beast made a massive effort, digging its front flippers into the shingle to reach the next fish, but only progressed a foot. A gull snatched a sardine, and Miranda chased it away, waving the white apron she still wore to protect her gown. More birds descended to feast. She scooped up as many fish as she could save with Jason doing the same and dumped them close to the turtle. The reptile ate while they held off the flock but did not move an inch.

"I feel as if I've done battle and come up with a draw," Jason declared when both fish and gulls were gone.

A few birds had perched on the turtle's hide and pecked, but the creature showed some of its old life and snapped and hissed, turning its neck as far back as possible. The gulls took heed and went off to wait on a nearby railing where scavengers of another sort had started to gather.

Miranda put her hands on her hips and looked out to sea. "Yes, we haven't moved him very far, but at least he shows more life. The tide is beginning to come in and will do some of our work for us, but we must bring him deeper into the water. If we could get him into a bathing machine...?"

"Why not chop 'im up and sell the pieces? We'll help and share in the profits," a navvy suggested from the top of the seawall. Jason recognized the man as one of the winch operators done with his day's work and come back to heckle with some companions.

Seeing the alarm on Miranda's face, Jason reassured her. "They shan't have him. I may not be as brawny as those villains, but I am quick on my feet and good with my fists."

"Aye, and a hook has its uses and serves better than a hand in some cases," Amos Gantry agreed. Miss Rosita fanned her wings and threatened a few straggling seabirds.

"Be about our business and do not regard them," Ida said as she picked up a gray and white gull feather and began drawing it through her thick, black fingers. She mumbled under her breath. More birds congregated on the railing.

Jason and Gantry pulled one of the bathing houses around to the head of the leatherback, since it seemed clear the beast would not back into the vehicle. They put down the ramp crossed over with thin slats to help the bathers with their footing as they descended into the sea. The turtle showed no interest in ascending. Jason scanned the tide line and jogged off to retrieve a warped board washed ashore. He and the old salt levered the creature up onto the foot of the ramp and raised its rear again. The turtle dug in with its front flippers and, using the cross pieces for traction, made its way up to the mouth of the little cabin.

Obviously, the bathing machines had been constructed for upright humans, not wide leatherbacks. Turning Half Moon sideways to enter was not an option they could consider.

Jason took off his hat to mop his brow with a swipe of his sleeve. Gantry fanned himself with his ancient and battered tricorne. Seeing their predicament, the audience jeered, but the sun was setting and the sea boiling closer.

"We needn't get him in the bathhouse. If we all pull, we might drag him into the surf as is," Jason offered.

"I'm willing," Miranda said at once.

She lined up behind Jason and put her hands to the wooden poles usually drawn by horses to take the bathing machines into the water. Amos Gantry took the other side, set his hook in the timber and his peg into the shingle. Ida pushed behind him with as much strength as either of the men. Miss Rosita fluttered to the top of the cabin and encouraged them by chanting, "Heave ho, lads, heave ho."

Laboriously, they drew the little cabin forward. The end of the ramp scored the flat stones of the shingle as it passed. The leading edge of the tide foamed about their feet, then rose over their ankles and up to their knees. Their cart rolled easier in the salt water.

The men on the promenade stopped laughing. "Come, lads. They mean to let our profits swim off," the navvy said. He took a knife from his coat, clutched it between his teeth, and prepared to swing over the railing and drop down to the shingle.

"A moment," Ida requested from her team.

She drew out the gull feather she had tucked behind her ear and began stroking it again. Her voice, the words indistinguishable, blended with the wind from the sea. A flock of seabirds spiraled into the air, making a column thick as a waterspout. Pecking at heads and plucking at clothing, the gulls bore down upon the men on the promenade. Sheltering their eyes with one hand and trying to fend off the birds with the other, the thugs ran, pursued by vicious yellow beaks and strong, flapping wings.

Ida picked up the pole again. "Proceed," she said.

When they reached waist-deep, the turtle began to struggle. He used his powerful flippers to turn sideways on the ramp and push into the surf. Half Moon coursed toward the setting sun, the last rays glinting off the seams of his leathery back. Then without a glance at his saviors, he submerged and blended into the darkness of the sea. Careful of his hook, Amos gave Ida's shoulders a squeeze, and he roared a loud, "Huzzah!" Miranda and Jason applauded and cheered.

As usual, Ida brought them back to reality. "We must return the little house to its proper place or our luck will turn."

They latched the ramp and drew the bathing machine back up the beach. The vehicle seemed as if it had no weight at all minus the thousand-pound turtle. Resting against its side, Jason asked, "And now?"

"Now we celebrate. We dance by the light of the moon," Miranda answered, pointing to the silver orb already high in the sky and becoming more noticeable as the light faded.

Jason regarded her sodden skirt plastered between her legs and clinging to her lithe thighs. The wind rippled over her bodice, the pale yellow made transparent by splashes of salt water. Her nipples puckered beneath the cloth. He forced his eyes skyward.

"Aren't you cold? Shouldn't you change?"

"Dancing will warm me. Do you know the waltz?"

"I've heard it is very *au courant*, but I have been studying law, not frequenting ballrooms."

"It's so easy. See, you put your hand on my back and let it remain there." She placed it so.

"I like this new dance already."

"Then, we clasp our other hands thusly, and I put my free hand on your shoulder. The rhythm is simple, one-two-three, one-two-three. Here we go."

They spun off across the shingle, the moon lighting their path. Jason found he could pull Miranda closer by drawing in his arm ever so slowly. However, when they passed Ida, she used her fist to straighten his elbow again.

Catching the drift, Amos Gantry whisked off his hat and bowed before the woman a head taller than he. "Might I have this dance, me ebony goddess?"

Ida showed her strong white teeth in a wide grin. "Mind that hook now."

She grasped his arm at the stump and allowed his good hand to touch her back. They were off, with his peg proving very useful on the turns. Miss Rosita, full of jealousy, ducked her head and paced the roof of the bathing machine. The exercise did ward off the chill of wet clothes and soggy shoes, but at last, all breathless, the dance came to an end.

Miranda, her cheeks pink, her eyes a golden-green in the moonlight, all the gray obscured, cradled Jason's face with her small hands.

"And now, I must leave you, Lord Longleigh, and return to Ariel Island. I sail with Captain Fulton on the morning tide. Mr. Gantry has arranged it for me and delivered my trunk when he went out to seek the fish. Although my people have been taught to let the nesting turtles alone, spawning begins in April. I am not sure they can resist the lure of the fresh eggs and easy meat. Certainly, my brother Roger will not deter them, and he is in charge while we are gone. He may give them fewer provisions if they get their own and so save his money. You do understand."

"Impossible! You cannot make a sea voyage alone on a ship full of men."

"Ida will be with me, and Captain Fulton has known me since childhood. You need not worry."

"I must worry—if not about that, then about ever seeing you again. No, I must go along to protect you and to—to....don't you know I would follow you to the ends of the earth, Miranda?"

"Do you hear, Ida? He would follow me to the ends of the earth." Her gamine face glowed as she said the words.

"I hear, child. If that is so, we best be going."

"Did you summon Daniel?"

"He is on his way, *bébé*."

"Then we shall all sail together. Won't that be wonderful!"

Twelve

The beating of wings woke Pandora Longleigh from a light doze. Her arms were still locked firmly around Daniel's waist, but her head had nestled between his shoulder blades. She pulled herself erect immediately, but kept her grip. A good thing, too, because a storm of birds caused the horse to rear, nearly throwing her off. Daniel controlled the animal with great mastery and brought them safely to a stop by the side of the road at the mouth of Brighton. They watched with amazement as the swarm of gulls savaged a group of bloodied and ragged men in their midst and drove them from the town out into the countryside.

"More magic?" she asked Daniel.

"Definitely Ida's work. We are getting very close."

They entered the town and passed the Prince's Pavilion with its many turrets and an onion dome, a fantastical oriental palace where excesses of eating and drinking and almost everything else took place, though some parts were still abuilding. Deserted for the nonce, the rising moon set off its filigree work like fine lace in a fan.

Pandora might wish to imagine she had been kidnapped by an Indian mogul who carried her to his harem on his prancing steed.

But ever a sensible girl not given to fancy, she quashed that dream and said, "Do hurry, Daniel. They must be on the beach."

The two of them made their way around knots of chattering people who stood in the twilight and discussed the weird passing of the birds. None took note of a gentleman with a fine lady mounted on his horse. They seemed invisible to the bystanders, but Pandora did catch snatches of their conversation. Guns had been fired and torches waved to drive off the flock but to no avail. She shivered against Daniel's warm, broad back. The sun vanished and a fat moon full of womanly power rose to light their way.

They found the promenade and began to search along its length. Wavelets rolled across the shingle and hissed back to the sea again. Devoid of birds, deserted at night, the beach offered up only a path of disturbed shingle being smoothed by the tide.

"They were here, I know it. I can almost taste their presence in the air," Pandora whispered.

"Gone now." Daniel turned the horse. "I will find you a respectable place to stay, then search the docks. I have a feeling Miranda means to escape our father entirely and be home when the turtles come to nest. They might have put up at a sailor's inn to await a ship."

"My brother would never take Miranda to such a disreputable place."

"I'm not so sure. He buys tortoises he cannot afford and hares off the length of England on a whim to free another turtle. The man has no sense at all."

"Very well then, go straight to the docks. I have a knife if we should face any trouble."

"I have a bigger knife, I am sure, and would rather go alone."

"I have brothers who taught me to use my fists." Pandora balled her hand and punched Daniel in the back. "Go directly to the docks."

"Certainly, milady. As you wish, Lady Pandora. At your service anytime day or night."

She punched him again, and he kicked the horse into a faster gait, forcing her to cling to him. They came up rapidly on the shipping area of the small seaside town. There sat the dray and the people they had searched for all day. Hidden by the now empty but still tarp-covered tank from the eyes of Ida and Amos Gantry, who directed the loading of the luggage into a rowboat, Miranda pressed close to Jason and rose up on her toes. He wrapped his arms around her and lowered his lips to hers.

"Unhand my sister. If you have debauched her, I will slit your throat." A very impressive knife, large enough to skin a deer, appeared in Daniel's hand.

Pandora shoved her skirts out of the way and drew her own stiletto. "I will stab you in the heart if you have caused my brother to do anything dishonorable with your clever wiles and magical spells, Miranda."

Ida came between the couples and flashed her own knife of intermediate size. "No one will hurt these children. They are in my care. Mastah Daniel, put away your weapon and get down. Come morning, we sail for Ariel Island, where no one will hurt my *bébé*. We sleep aboard the *Sea Nymph* tonight."

"Yes, Daniel. I am so glad you arrived in time. Captain Fulton will credit your passage against the next cotton crop. Did you bring a change of clothes?" Miranda chirped, ignoring any threat to her safety.

Bemused, Daniel replied as he dismounted, "Yes, in my saddlebags. For some odd reason I felt compelled to do so."

Without waiting for Daniel's aid, Pandora slid off the horse and landed in a fighter's crouch.

"Oh, come now, Panny. I only sought to warm Miranda. We got very wet returning the leatherback to the sea. I am going with them to see the wider world and watch over Miri. Imagine, I might write a narrative poem about my adventures as fine as *Childe Harold's Pilgrimage*," Jason explained, so obviously smitten with the girl and the idea of traveling to American that Pandora ground her teeth together.

Next to Pandora, Daniel pushed aside her smaller blade with his large one. "You see, mine *is* bigger."

He turned on Jason. "So warming is what they call that sort of embrace. You think yourself another Lord Byron, do you? I am here to see to my sister. You may go back to London. She is no longer your concern."

"But Daniel, he has already paid for his passage and is my invited guest. There are but two cabins available. I will stay in one with Ida. You will sleep with Daniel and become fast friends on the voyage, I am sure." Miranda smiled winningly at her brother.

"He has not done anything untoward?"

"No, you must realize Ida would not allow it."

"True. I suppose I can suffer his presence for a few weeks. I cannot wait to be free of this chilly land."

"Wait! Do you think I will let my brother be drawn into this scheme and not be there to defend him? He has no guile. You draw him into your net to ally yourself with the great Duke of Bellevue and expand your business interests. If Jason goes, I must go," Pandora insisted.

Ida's big chest heaved. She put away her knife. "Her I did not see coming. When I no longer heard two sets of hoof beats, I thought she had stayed behind like the rest of them. I did not consider that she rode with you, Mastah Daniel. She must have some magic all her own."

"More like an iron will. Lady Pandora, you have nothing but the clothes on your back and no way to pay your fare. Be reasonable. I shall see you safely settled at an inn. Your family will be here tomorrow to take you home." Daniel sheathed his knife in a leather pouch cunningly sewed into his jacket where it settled without showing so much as a bulge.

"So that's where you kept it."

Pandora turned her back on all of them and raised her skirt. She put her stiletto into the sheath strapped to her calf, withdrew a pocket tied round her waist, and straightened her riding habit before facing the group again. She held out the pocket bulging with banknotes.

"My mother once managed with no more than a deerskin to clothe her, and I believe this to be sufficient for my fare. I will stay with the other ladies. If I go with you, I can be sure you will not force Jason into an unwanted marriage presided over by the captain, or put pressure upon him once you get to the island. I will look out for the Bellevue interests."

"That is untrue, you know. The captain may only register marriages, births, and deaths aboard his ship, not perform legal ceremonies. I've studied maritime law, you see." Daniel puffed up a little in displaying his knowledge.

Pandora pricked his pride. "Good, one less matter to worry about—if you know what you are talking about."

"But I want to..." Jason began.

"Silence. You have made a muck of things again, big brother. You have no sense, no sense at all. I must go along and look out for you."

"Ahem, the boat awaits to take ye to the ship. The oarsmen wonder at the delay," Amos Gantry said.

"Then, let us go."

Grandly, Pandora led the way and allowed herself to be handed down into the waiting vessel. Miranda and Ida followed.

Daniel shrugged and said loudly enough for Pandora to hear, "She'll be complaining of seasickness and lack of clothing before we reach rough water." Saddlebags slung over his shoulder, he lowered himself into the boat.

Jason bid farewell to Amos Gantry and pressed a few more coins on the man. "Please keep a lookout for the Bellevue coach and explain the situation to her father and my family. They will take Daniel's mount back to London. You are a good man to go adventuring with, sir."

"Tell my father my mare is stabled at the last inn before Brighton. He must collect her, too," Pandora shouted in a most unladylike way to be sure the sailor heard.

"That I will do, milady. I think the same of ye, milord. I never thought living on land would be as interesting as my life at sea.

Bon voyage, as the Frogs say." Gantry whipped out a snappy salute and watched Jason board. Miss Rosita echoed, "*Bon voyage, bon voyage.*"

Miranda waved goodbye as the oars dug into the water and pushed them toward the *Sea Nymph*. She looked ridiculously happy, Pandora thought. As for herself, she had never done anything this foolish in her entire life—except perhaps dressing as a man to aid in her sister's elopement. The thought made her stomach clench. She put on her blank Indian face as her father had taught her, and pretended she had not a fear in the world.

Thirteen

The Duke and Duchess of Bellevue, Eustace Clary, Joshua Longleigh, and Amos Gantry stood on the dock at Brighton and watched the early morning sun glint off the distant sails of the *Sea Nymph*. Soon the ship bound for America slipped over the horizon line and vanished from sight.

"How could we have missed the boat so terribly?" the duchess said.

Her pragmatic husband answered. "By the time our carriage got its new wheel and you found me by the side of the road unable to ride, we barely reached the inn where Pandora left her mare before night fell. We all agreed Daniel and Pandora would find our runaways, and we need not risk our necks driving pell-mell to Brighton by the light of the moon. Simple as that. We had no way of knowing they would escape by ship."

"That is not what I meant at all. It appears Pandora and Daniel have eloped along with Miranda and Jason. How could I have missed the signs when I pride myself on matchmaking and have failed to find anyone else for Panny?"

"You frequently miss..."

"I do not!"

"Oh, I saw the spark between them. Yes, indeedy," Mr. Clary claimed. "We are to be in-laws twice over, it seems. No help for it, Duchess Flora."

He squeezed her delicate shoulders against his bulk, and she wanted to stamp on his toe, but dignity prevented her. Eustace seemed to be adding Pandora's dowry to his bank account already and no longer cared that Jason had neither a title nor great wealth.

"Their spark was more like steel striking flint than the raging fires of passionate love," she said, pulling away from the unwanted new relative and seeking safety near her husband.

"They cannot all be as lucky as you and I are, dearest," the duke said, giving her almost the same embrace. "They must reach their own accord."

"I'd say ye needn't worry, Your Grace. Them two were arguing all the way to the dinghy about keeping Lord Jason and the little missy apart. Lady Pandora even pulled a knife," Amos Gantry clarified.

"I wish you had never given her that stiletto, Pearce. I have told her time and again that soft words win husbands, not weaponry and strong opinions." The duchess stared out over the water as if she could will the ship to return.

"Depends upon the man, I should think. Some men find strong-willed women very attractive." He smiled fondly at his wife. "Besides, I wanted my daughters to be able to defend themselves from the wrong type who would take advantage, not that it did me any good to arm them, considering Phemie's abduction, and now this."

"Nothing to do but go back to London and wait," Eustace Clary said.

"What? You are not going after them?" the duchess inquired.

"I paid a fortune for a London season. One of us should enjoy its pleasures."

And our food and drink and free lodging, Flora thought. They could do nothing more for the moment than hitch the spare horses to the back of the carriage and return to the city. She reckoned without her husband. The moment she noticed the gleam in Pearce

Longleigh's eyes, she knew. It took no fortuneteller to see their immediate future.

"My dear, what would you say to another trip to America? You shall miss the London season, of course, but without Pandora to foist off on some unwitting swain, what would be the point?"

"We have responsibilities to society and the estate, not to mention our other children."

"Our children are grown, Flora, except Justinian, and Thalia will see to him. Let's chuck it all overboard and go adventuring just as we did last year in Scotland. If we should die together, hand in hand, during a gale, James will simply have to stop his wandering and take over. Even if our eldest never marries, Joshua has assured the Longleigh lineage. Won't you go with me to those savage shores again?"

"Savage? My plantations are certainly not savage places. We live in utmost elegance, I assure you." Eustace Clary expanded like a toad in full croak.

"Excellent! Then you shall be *our* host for a change. My love?"

"But your injured back, Pearce?"

"I can think of no better way to mend than on a long sea voyage. What say you, dearest?"

"Well, I will need some time to put things in order and pack, but yes. I find the thought of another adventure with Pearce Longleigh very enthralling."

~ * ~

Pandora woke to the sounds of a ship setting sail: the officers shouting orders, the gulls arising with irritated cries, the canvas snapping then straining in the fresh breeze, the timbers creaking as the *Sea Nymph* turned her face to the waves and began bounding over the sea. She'd slept well, exhausted by the long ride and lulled by the lapping of water against the hull, even though the box bed built into the wall was small and not very comfortable. Of course, Ida had padded Miranda's nest across the narrow way with extra pillows, but she hadn't begged the woman for any special favors for herself. Still, when the buxom Negress lay down on a pallet stretched between them and placed her feet against the door and her knife under her pillow, Pandora felt safe enough to sleep soundly.

She pretended to doze when Miranda arose, used the slop bucket, dressed for the day with Ida's help and went out, presumably to seek breakfast. She'd slept in her undergarments and merely loosened the tight braid so practical for riding that formed a smart chignon at her nape. Eager for her own turn at the chamber pot, she rolled from the bunk and swayed a moment, getting used to the rhythm of the ship before squatting. That precarious duty over, she had no choice but to put on her dusty riding habit and boots and pin her thick braid into a knot again.

Out in the corridor, the sway of the ship pushed her from one side to the other. She tripped over the extra length of her gown, so necessary for covering the limbs when riding sidesaddle, so in the way when trying to walk down a moving hall. Pandora followed her nose toward the scent of food and stumbled across and into the captain's mess. Miranda and Daniel looked up, twins in coloring, culprits who could have been hatched from the same shell if half a dozen years hadn't separated them in birth. They sat enjoying their coffee, eggs and bacon, exactly as if they sat in the dining room at Bellevue. She made her wobbly way to the table bolted to the floor and gesturing to the men not to rise, took a seat, a nice steady seat.

"Good morning. I trust everyone slept well," she said pleasantly, just as if she hadn't forced her company on them last night by offering an extra fee to Captain Fulton, who kept repeating he had no room for her. Miranda had allowed him to accept the money by offering to share her cabin exactly as Pandora wanted.

Admiring a cunning well cut into the table to hold the jam pot and other condiments, she slathered strawberry preserves on a slice of bread, took a bite, swallowed and inquired, "Has Jason finished with his breakfast?"

"Sorry to say your brother was not pleasant company this morning. As soon as the ship weighed anchor, *mal de mer* overcame him. The sickness should pass in a few days once he gets his sealegs.

I see you are unaffected, Lady Pandora." Daniel threw his sister a look that made it seem he boasted about her.

"I must say, I feel very well—the sea air, I suppose." She accepted a plate of bacon and eggs and tucked into the food.

"I knew you would take to the sea naturally, if given a chance." Again, that tone of pride in Daniel's voice.

Captain Fulton excused himself. "Enjoy your meal. I keep a few hens on board so we might have the luxury of eggs. I suggest you see if your brother can keep down some water and sea biscuit, Miss Longleigh. He'll be the better for it. Now, I must make my rounds and take our bearings, since we'll be going further south than I planned."

"After breakfast, would you care to take a stroll on the deck?" Daniel offered.

"Not until I hem this gown. I'm likely to trip and fall overboard." A small shiver went down her spine at the notion. "I should see to my brother, of course."

"I will be up on deck in the fresh air if you should change your mind. I warn you my cabin has the stench of the sickroom." Daniel took his leave.

That left only Miranda for conversation. "I will help you with the hemming and perhaps Ida could alter some of my frocks for you."

"I hardly think…" Pandora stopped herself. She had a bosom thrice the size of Miranda's small breasts. Although not tall like her brothers, she was of middling height, standing several inches above her own mother and other sylph-like women. Still, what was she going to do—wear a riding costume every day for weeks at sea?

"Thank you for your generosity," she answered. "I will repay you."

"No need. I've always wanted to have a sister," Miranda said shyly.

"We do not always get what we want." She watched the girl's expression fall under her sharpness. "And sometimes, we do," she amended. "Let us go see if Jason can be persuaded to eat and drink."

His cabin was not hard to find. They could hear his retching through the door. The women, bearing water and ship's biscuit, knocked.

"Come in. No, go away. I don't want to be seen like this."

"Don't be ridiculous, Jason. We've come to minister to you."

"That you, Panny? You've seen me in bad shape before, but send Miri away. I don't want to disgrace myself in front of her."

"Why don't you take that stroll with Daniel or choose some gowns you won't mind sacrificing for me, Miranda? I will get him up and around."

"Oh, my poor gypsy rover." Miranda's big eyes filled with tears, but she turned and left.

Pandora entered her brother's cabin. It did stink of illness. Jason lay on his bunk. He had his full six feet of length curled into a ball around his stomach. As dark complected as she, Pandora had never seen her brother with that strange tinge of green lying beneath the surface of his skin. Several days' growth of black whiskers covered his chin. His head hung over the end of the bunk above a half-full slop bucket. He peered at her, his usually lively black eyes dull with misery.

"Why is it that Lord Byron never mentioned vomiting up his insides on *his* travels, Panny?"

"Probably couldn't find an elegant rhyme for it, Jason. Now buck up, brother. Try to keep some water down or at least rinse out your mouth."

"I am a disgrace to the Longleighs and an embarrassment to Miranda. Her damned brother sails his own sloop. Look at you, no sign of seasickness."

"None. I cannot explain it. We had a wonderful breakfast of bacon and eggs this morning. Perhaps a coddled egg would stay down?"

Jason dry-heaved over the bucket. "No, it's all out now. I don't want to put anymore in. This is worse than a big head and a sick stomach from drink."

"Come now. Captain Fulton believes you will do better with something to eat, and you absolutely must take some water. It's still fairly fresh this early in the voyage."

Jason accepted a thin slab of hardtack. He placed it in his mouth, bit down and spit it out. "It's hard as a brick. No wonder Gantry has so few teeth. He said he'd suffered from scurvy, but eating this would take its toll."

"Let me soak it in some water. You can suck on it once it's softened. Fresh air might help, too. Would you like me to help you dress?"

"Stay away from my drawers, Panny. I'll try to keep this stuff down and then make a brave show for Miranda. She must think me a complete weakling. I don't know how I will ever deserve her love after this poor showing."

"I doubt she will cast away a man willing to put up with her passion for turtles, her strange diet, and her improper whims."

"You're a hard woman, Panny, and hardness has never won a heart."

"I want slaves to have freedom and women to have equity. I do not need a heart."

"That says it all. Go, go away."

~ * ~

Pandora made inquiries about borrowing a sewing kit and was surprised to be offered several by the seamen. "No women about, ye know. Sails to mend and socks to darn," they told her.

Their needles were coarse and their thread of common cotton, but good enough to tack up her hem. She sat cross-legged, sailor-style, on the floor under the oil lamp swinging from its gimbal in the ceiling of the cabin. She could hardly afford herself of the better natural light on deck, not when she had to strip down to her petticoats and shift to do the job.

Indians also sat this way, she mused. Her mother had told her that and then forbidden her to do it, so of course she had in her own chamber and when she played with her brothers in the wigwam. She'd even caught her mother at it once. The duchess claimed she was preparing for the birth of yet another child by stretching certain parts of her anatomy—no details given as this must have been Justinian, the baby of the family, and Pandora herself only five or six years old.

Well, Pandora Longleigh had no need to prepare for childbearing. She envisioned the life she thought she'd have: passing into spinsterhood this autumn after another failed season, taking up her causes in earnest once she attained twenty-one years, using her dowry to finance her endeavors. She'd be dear, odd Aunt Panny to the offspring of the ever-growing Longleigh family. Even her closest sister, Euphemia, a year younger, had a child, a red-haired boy arriving six weeks early but strong enough to live, his physician father promised. Phemie, caught up in all the romance of Scotland, including her husband, a laird, had given the tiny lad the fanciful name of Ivor Ian Somerled McLaughlin. But no, Pandora had planned her future more sensibly and swore not to be tempted from a straight path to her future as a maiden lady.

Now, she sat cross-legged on a ship bound for America—and not the civilized portion like Boston or Philadelphia but the islands off Georgia, once proposed as a penal colony for the English and where pirates had lurked not that long ago. This explained Daniel Clary's brigand's eyes, green and gray and flecked with gold. "Your life or your honor, lovely lady," she could imagine him saying in that strong baritone voice of his. She pricked her finger and sucked up the blood before it stained the cloth. Her life seemed to be shifting like the lantern above her head and as far out of control as the sea beneath the hull. No, no, merely a detour she'd made for Jason's sake, she assured herself.

Sewing was not her forte. Pandora pulled the thread too tightly and bunched the cloth, then snapped the strand trying to straighten it. The cabin door burst open, letting in Miranda and Ida. Miri's cheeks had been pinked by the sea breeze and her golden-brown hair, tangled by the wind, still hung loose down her back.

"How is Jason?" she asked. "Won't he see me?"

"He has vowed to try to keep down some food, and dress to visit you on deck as soon as his stomach settles, but he wants no visitors."

"Oh." Disappointment filled her sweet, heart-shaped face. "Well then, Ida and I have selected some gowns to adjust for you."

She edged past Pandora in the narrow cabin to the trunk that sat at its back and made no remarks about Panny's unladylike sewing position.

"We thought this deep rose gown would become you, and the white. Both have fuller skirts we can let out and lots of gauze on top to preserve your modesty if we can't alter the bodice enough. I believe the length will do if we let down the hems all the way. What do you think?" Miranda spread the dresses across the top of the box.

"I think you are far too generous to a person who has not been kind to you. Is the white gown very sensible for aboard a ship?"

"Oh, a white gown can be hung in the sun to bleach, and you will be glad of the light fabric once we get near the islands. April is very balmy in South Georgia. You see, it is lawn covered in white work, very pretty. You can change the color of the sashes under the bodice to suit yourself."

"White does not become me, and it is far too pretty to give away."

"I believe with your striking coloring, so like Jason's, you would be very lovely in it. My brother is right, though, you should wear bright colors. The rose is the deepest shade I have. We will remove the flounce at the bottom, let down the hem and put it back again. The silk rose nestled in the gauze on the bodice will look wonderful against your skin. Don't you think so, Ida?"

"Yes, child. Choose one and pick out the hems while I brush your hair. I could braid and coil it at your neck in Lady Pandora's style."

"I hate the weight of it and the pins gouging into my scalp. I don't know how you stand such severity, Lady Pandora," Miranda replied a little pettishly.

"You would do better to pile your hair high and thread it with ribbons. My sister, Phemie, has curls like yours, and we snipped some of them short into a fringe. Very becoming to a face like yours."

"Would Jason like it?"

"Certainly." Jason would adore Miranda if the seagulls plucked her bald, Panny knew.

"We will try that. You should pin it up, *bébé*, if you are to be a wife." Ida gathered the light brown curls and brushed them upwards.

Alarmed by the last words, Pandora stuck herself with the needle again. This time she let the blood well up. "My brother has asked for your hand in marriage?"

"Not exactly." Miranda's rosy cheeks grew redder. She lowered her eyes as she plucked threads from the hem of the rose-colored gown.

"Has he—has he done anything he ought not with you?"

"Oh, no. We've danced and sung and saved turtles together."

"He does not touch her in any bad way. I see to that," Ida said ominously.

"But he did say he would go to the ends of the earth with me. That is practically a proposal, is it not?" Miranda raised a hopeful face to Pandora.

She sighed. Must she always crush this infant?

"My mother counseled that men will say nearly anything to get beneath a woman's skirts. You must not believe them. However, I would like to think Jason meant those words—in a poetical way of course—with no thought of marriage or any other ulterior motive. He is the most impractical of my brothers."

"I believe I feel unwell, Mammy Ida." Miranda dropped her sewing. "I will lie down until dinner."

Back turned to her companions, she curled into the box bed. Her small shoulders trembled and she hiccupped as she sobbed.

"I did not mean to distress you, truly. But until a man actually asks for your hand, you are not engaged. Please, stop crying."

Pandora reached the end of her hemming and bit off the thread with her teeth, a bad habit her mother forbade, but right now she felt like sinking her teeth into something. She shook out the skirt and noticed that like most of her sewing projects, she'd botched it. The hem hung crooked and bunched at the seams. She put it on anyway and buttoned up her riding jacket. She had to escape the cabin and those heartbreaking sounds.

Before Pandora could edge out the door, Ida leaned close. "If it would not hurt your brother and Mastah Daniel, I would hex you right into the sea."

Pandora escaped from the confines under the deck to the clean air above. She noticed Daniel making friendly conversation with the sailors as he sat relaxed on a coil of rope. The wind freshened his color and the sunlight glinting off the water gilded his green eyes. He looked strong and capable enough to help the seamen at their work.

A bleak figure hunched over the railing. When Jason heard her footsteps, he forced himself to stand tall. Coming closer, Pandora saw he was still green round the gills and dark circles underscored his black eyes, but he put on his Indian face and pushed suffering aside.

"Is Miranda with you?"

"No, she is in our cabin and not feeling well."

"I thought she loved the sea and did not suffer from *mal de mer*."

"Her distress is emotional in nature. I merely passed along some advice Mama gave me before my first London season. She took it badly."

"Mama's advice! She can be very blunt and shocking."

"In this case, she spoke an eternal truth. Men will say anything to get beneath a woman's skirts. A young lady is not engaged until she has received a proper proposal. All the rest is nonsense. I found simply laughing at indecent suggestions served very well. I used the stiletto only twice and wished I had been quicker in Phemie's defense when Leo kidnapped her. Now she is so engrossed in her husband and child she barely writes me anymore." Pandora stared out over the water and thought about lost opportunities.

"We all know how proper Papa's proposal was. How could you say such crude words to my sweet Miranda, whom I love and adore? How could you imply my intentions are less than honorable?" The ship lunged into a trough and surged up the other side. Jason took several deep breaths.

"You, I gave the benefit of a doubt, considering your impractical nature, but I'd wager you have never proposed or thought to make a proper offer for Miranda to her father. To think, she ruined her reputation running all over the countryside with you and has nothing to show for it. No wonder she is in tears."

"Surely she knows how I feel, has felt my sincerity."

"Is that what men call it?" Pandora replied, looking pointedly at her brother's pants. "Then, I have known more sincere men than I thought."

"I must go to her and make my intentions clear." Swaying from side to side, Jason struggled across the deck toward the hatch leading to the cabins.

"No, no! She understands this was simply a lark for you. No need to commit yourself now, Jason. Are you listening?"

Daniel appeared at her side. "What have you done?"

"Inadvertently pushed my brother toward the altar. We must stop him."

She tripped over a portion of her new hem, already coming undone. Daniel caught her elbow, steadied her, but Jason had disappeared down the steps to the cabins and careened along the narrow hall by the time they clambered after him. They found him proclaiming his feelings on his knees beside Miranda's bed. Ida watched from her seat on the trunk. Pandora and Daniel crowded into the doorway, but the stream of words once released could not be dammed.

"Miri, I love and adore you. You do know that. If I have been negligent in not saying so more often, I will make up for it now. I have braved the sea for you and will follow you anywhere."

Miranda, her heart-shaped face puffy from crying, her hair falling from the arrangement Ida had attempted, nodded. She offered her small hand, and Jason seized it like a fish takes the bait.

"Hook, line and sinker," Daniel murmured into Pandora's ear.

Her light eyes big as an owlet's in the dim cabin, Miranda answered, "I love you with all my heart, Jason. I would stand beside you for all of my life. Do you have anything else you want to say to me?"

The ship plunged again and rose. Jason pressed the fingers of his other hand to his lips.

"So sorry. This cabin is very stuffy. Stuffy, that's how Joshua has become since he married Kate. Always worrying if he can provide for her as well as her other beau, Harold Brumley, might have. Terrified she might die in childbirth."

Jason's eyes traveled along Miranda's small body. His grip on her hand loosened. He stood and bumped his head on the cabin's low ceiling.

"I apologize. I cannot—I am unwell."

Jason blundered from the room. They heard the door to his cabin slam, but mercifully were spared the other noises he might be making. Miranda wailed as if he had gone overboard and not just down the hall. Ida shooed Pandora and Daniel from the door and shut it in their faces.

"My, my," Daniel drawled. "My sister has been spared from marrying your brother by a case of seasickness and uncertainty."

Fourteen

Two weeks into the voyage and halfway across the ocean, Pandora Longleigh thought she would go mad. Oh, not from fear of the sea, but from sharing a room with a silly girl intent on dying because of a love lost and roaming the deck with a brother who moped and declaimed his latest attempts at poetry, all dealing with crushing the fairest rose that ever bloomed.

Jason had gotten his sea-legs on the fourth day and begun to appear at meals and elsewhere on the ship. Cautious, he ate lightly. Unsure of his shaking hands, he eschewed shaving. His face became sharp-angled and black-bearded, but tanned ever darker by the sun. The wind claimed his hat and tossed it into the waves, so he let his black hair, growing longer each day, stream free. When Daniel Clary stripped off his jacket and waistcoat to help with the setting of sails and do other chores on board the ship, Jason did the same—mostly getting in the way. Otherwise, he folded himself at Pandora's feet, where she sat out of the way reading, and recited from his notebook.

"O my love, my precious love, whom I have failed to love enough…"

"Ridiculous, Jason. You simply did not feel strongly enough about Miri to marry her. She is very young and not stable enough to make a good wife. When we get to Savannah, we shall seek out another ship and go directly home. The family will never speak of this escapade again, and being so far away, Miranda's reputation will remain intact. She will be wiser for the experience."

"Not so! I have wounded her unto death. Yet, I am the one who is weak. This was to be my grand adventure. How I thought I could support Miranda if Papa cut me off or make her endure the dangers of having a family when she is so fragile, I will never know. I could tutor or give poetry readings or learn American law, I suppose, but the other…"

"That young woman was spritely enough with her wall-climbing and egg-counting before you disappointed her and, supposedly, she has a fortune of her own. Women are not nearly as weak as men presume."

"Oh, they are heaving or hoing again. I should offer to help."

"Yes, do. Captain Fulton said he would set a more southerly course today. We are halfway to our destination."

"Only half? Promise never to bury me at sea," her brother said as he went to offer his clumsy assistance.

Pandora buried her face in the copy of *Gulliver's Travels* she had borrowed from the captain's scant library. Her father favored the book, which was written more to the tastes of the last century and very vulgar in parts. Mama had taken it from her hands a few years ago as being unfit for young ladies, but now she had her chance. The sharp satire did make her laugh and if she blushed a time or two, no one noticed. Here she was, having an adventure almost as picaresque, but without giants, tiny people, or talking horses, of course.

She peered over the cover to watch Daniel, his shirt pressed against his broad chest by the breeze, take a place at the ropes. He turned his back to her and set his stance, his buttocks tightening beneath his trousers. With hands steady and sure, he shaved each day and kept his curly side whiskers trimmed and his hair, crisp and growing more golden in the sun, a practical length. She paused in her reading to admire the sight of him, strong and trim like the ship itself.

Jason tripped over some coils on the deck and blundered into Daniel. Daniel, patiently enough, pointed out where he could help while the sailors snickered.

Pandora thought Miranda would adore Jason more than ever if she could see this lovelorn, bumbling poet brought low, but the girl would not leave her cabin. A good thing perhaps, to keep them separate, but how to endure the sight of Miri in her bunk with all the sunlight and sea shine gone from her face? She had gotten so pale, her large eyes turning a dark gray, all the green and gold gone. She accepted watered wine and thin oat gruel, a bit of bread, a bite of the precious eggs the captain supplied, but all in all, she withered away.

Here Pandora sat in the rose-colored gown given to her out of utmost kindness, and altered with Miri's fine stitchery before the girl had taken to her bed permanently. She put it on often because it suited her as she sat on the deck in whatever patch of shade she could find so as not to darken her complexion further. The scrap of lace she wore as a head covering came from Miranda's trunk—even the rags she had used for her monthlies this week. She owed the young woman a huge favor. How could she let Miranda die?

A solid form sat down next to her. Not wanting to hear any more mournful poetry, she pretended to be thoroughly engrossed in her reading. But the man beside her smelled of sea salt and manly sweat, not wine and sorrow as Jason did these days. She thanked heaven the captain doled out spirits to his passengers as strictly as he did the rum ration for the seamen or her brother might have pitched overboard a week ago.

She glanced at Daniel Clary sitting at her feet in Jason's place. Closing her book, she patted the tight knot of black hair at her nape, making sure the wind had not undone it. She'd pulled it straight back and unbraided today; no charming fringes for her, because she was a no-nonsense person, even if wearing a silk rose between her breasts belied that.

Daniel spoke. "I do not know what to do. I visited my sister this morning to beg her to eat a little more, to get some fresh air. She told me she wanted to be buried at sea so her flesh could nourish the sea turtles. I cannot lift her melancholy. Were we wrong to want them parted? They are miserable. Before they were alight with love; now both are crushed." Daniel laid his arms on his knees and lowered his head.

"Not you, too! I do not want to hear the word 'crushed' again on this voyage. I thought you and Ida could bring her around, convince her Jason was unworthy. He certainly feels he is. Someone must administer a stronger remedy and that would be me." Pandora slammed down her book and marched to the hatch to leave Daniel staring after her.

In the narrow corridor, she bumped into Ida, taking out the slops to fling overboard. "You with your spells and potions, why can't you repair your charge, get her to eat, make her dance again?"

Ida regarded her solemnly, then spoke in that rich, coffee-flavored voice of hers. "If the will is strong, magic cannot overcome it. One must believe in the curse or the cure, Lady Pandora, and want to do what is suggested. I have tried. She defies me. Soon, I will lose my *bébé*."

"You will not." Pandora strode to the cabin she shared with Miranda, flung the door open and pronounced, "People do not die of love. They do die of starvation, however. You will come to supper with me and clean your plate."

"You have never been in love, I can tell," Miranda replied in such a small voice it almost lost itself in the covers of her bed.

"Nor will I ever be if a person can catch it like the plague and die of it. Have you no pride to let a mere man bring you so low? If you pass away, who will save the turtles and paint the buntings?"

There, she'd raised a wan smile on Miranda's lips, but the girl replied, "I am not as strong as you."

"Of course you are. I have never defied my papa in a way that might make him want to put me in an asylum—a locked room perhaps, not a madhouse—but you have, and gotten away with it unblemished."

"I was foolish and fortunate in my companion. Jason never pressed me to—oh, oh, I cannot go on anymore."

"Not a tear, not one. The best remedy for your ills would be to put your hair up and your most becoming gown on and strut before Jason as if he does not exist. Show him your island and all he has lost. Live for that."

The slop bucket soused clean with sea water in her hands, Ida stood in the doorway. "That is true, Miranda. We have turned for the Sea Islands, our place of power, where Stella will soon come to nest, and my son relies on your kindness. What will happen to my boy if you are gone? Your father will sell him away. Lord Jason had paradise in his hands and tossed it to the winds. Make him suffer."

"I don't want to see Jason hurt, but you are right. I must think of something other than myself, prove that I am other than a burdensome child. I am responsible for all the creatures on my island and must go care for them. Here, help me up."

Miranda's knees buckled, but the two women were able to steady her easily. Ida brought water, and they bathed the smell of staleness from her body and dabbed her favorite orange water behind her ears. Her companions carefully selected a frock to cover her sharp collarbones and thin arms. Its pink shade reflected some color back into her face and its bodice flounces enhanced her shrunken bosom. Ida piled Miranda's hair high and adorned it with ribbons. They pinched her cheeks to bring up some color and walked her between them to the captain's mess for the evening meal, arriving early enough to seat her before the men entered.

"Eat lightly at first, lest it come up on you," Ida prompted before leaving.

"I am at your side, Miranda, if you should feel faint," Pandora assured her.

"I will get through the meal, never fear."

The male contingent soon entered the room. All three, the captain, Daniel, and Jason, seemed astounded but pleased to see the invalid at the table.

"Might I say you look lovely this evening, Miranda," Captain Fulton said in an avuncular way. "Fully recovered from your malady, I hope."

"So glad to have your company again, dear sister." Daniel spoke as if a miracle had occurred. He looked gratefully at Pandora, who waved her hand as if this feat were nothing, nothing at all.

"Miri," Jason choked out. His dark poet's eyes filled.

"Lord Longleigh, good evening. Please sit and do not delay the meal. I am ravenous tonight. My, this fish chowder is delicious, reminiscent of the one we enjoyed on the way to Brighton. No, no, far better than that. Fond memories, but in the past." Miranda sipped her soup again.

Under the table, Pandora patted her knee. A single tear coursed down Jason's cheek and ran into his black beard. He blotted it quickly and tried again to get Miranda's attention.

"Miri, I—"

"Please, Lord Longleigh, address me as Miss Clary since we do not have an understanding. I believe your sister is correct that I allowed you the familiarity of using my first name too easily and that led me to false expectations. If we maintain some distance and resume our acquaintance on a more formal basis, I believe we will all have a more pleasant voyage." Miranda broke off some bread and made a show of eating it.

Jason bowed his head over his soup and said, "As you wish."

He remained silent for the rest of the meal as Miranda speculated about the fall's cotton prices with the captain and told Pandora more about loggerhead turtles than she wanted to know. She ate a bit of every dish presented and ended with tea but soon excused herself from the table. Asking Pandora if she would like to take a short walk, Miranda linked arms with her cabin mate, and the ladies left, allowing the gentlemen to have a pipe or some port if they wanted.

"I nearly succumbed. I wanted so badly to wipe that tear from your brother's cheek," Miranda confessed.

"Never fear. I will be by your side for the rest of the voyage. I will lend you strength. You will never be alone with Jason again."

"That makes me very melancholy. I really do need to lie down now, but I pledge to be up and about tomorrow."

Ida tucked the young lady in for the evening, and Pandora returned to the men to see if any of them were up for a game of chess or draughts.

Fifteen

The next morning, Miranda ate a boiled egg. Pandora and Ida exclaimed so much about this, she might have laid it herself. Still, the girl needed encouragement, no matter how ludicrous, Pandora assumed. They got her up on deck for some air, though she sat in a well-padded chair, her lap covered by a blanket, her face shielded by a deep bonnet. When Jason appeared to languish by the bulwark, they hauled her back to the cabin.

Like a newborn filly, Miranda wobbled at first but seemed to gain strength by the minute. With her self-imposed dietary restrictions, feeding her remained a problem, especially as the fresh foods ran out and the meals tended to center around stews of salt beef or pork filled out with potatoes. Jason was the first to offer up his breakfast egg, then Daniel. Pandora felt compelled to do the same. Miranda accepted their sacrifice, equally gracious to all.

Miri's brother cast a small net overboard to scoop up any fish in the vicinity, quickly sorting through the trash in the catch, freeing any small turtles, and delivering what was edible to the ship's cook. Daniel Clary would be a very handy man to have about if one were trapped on a desert island, Pandora could not help but notice. He proposed something now to her brother further down the deck.

Light footsteps sounded behind her. Miranda made her way to a seat by Pandora with Ida looming behind. Two weeks had passed, and the girl seemed recovered physically at least. She settled herself and opened her notebook.

"I will not hide in my cabin anymore. Also, I feel as if I might begin to cluck, I've eaten so many eggs. Oat gruel and molasses will do for me very well. It is very fortifying."

Molasses, same as the treacle Pandora had once claimed Daniel's voice reminded her of. How that drawl of his had grown on her. She watched the two handsome men confer as she said,

"Ah, so you are recovering. You've re-grown a spine."

"A major biological feat, I promise you. I got Jason into this predicament, this awfully awkward situation, and I need to show him he has done me no harm." Miranda took up her pencil.

Pandora looked at this prim young lady, her hair up and wearing a proper bonnet. Her small feet were tucked beneath a pale blue and white striped underskirt, while the rest of the lace-edged gown draped gracefully. In her wrinkled white lawn dress with a broad red ribbon tied under her bosom, her straight black locks constantly being tugged from her chignon by the wind despite a pair of borrowed combs, her skin browning terribly regardless of the shared sunshade, Pandora felt herself to be the hoyden, not this young miss. She was comforted by thinking she resembled the Indian maidens her mother talked about, with their flashing dark eyes and bronze skin. When she returned to England, she would have to stay inside for weeks to bleach herself back to an acceptable British paleness.

The two men had gone below deck, making the view of the endless ocean and the seamen at work considerably less interesting. She glanced at Miranda's sketch. Not a seabird or a sailor, but a drawing of Jason, gaunt and suffering.

"You should not do that," she prompted the girl.

"This is simply a remembrance of a youthful adventure—part of the wildlife I encountered in your country, nothing more."

How cool she had become, but Ida saw through her. "You still want this man, Missy. I can give him to you."

"No, no, none of that. We are getting close to Ariel Island now, where we will part ways forever. Lord Longleigh and Lady Pandora will continue on to Savannah and return home. I do not plan to set foot in England ever again."

Ida did not argue with her mistress. Instead, she seemed to change the subject as she watched the waves cleaved by the ship.

"You know the Englishmen, the Americans, and those Greeks of old...they think the ocean is ruled by a white man with a big beard, King Neptune by name. But no, the mother of the waters is a goddess, Mami Wata, her hair long and black, her arms dark and powerful. Her tides are linked to the moon like the cycles of a woman. She is bountiful to the fisherman, but she can be cruel to the sailors when she is in a temper. If I call on her, she will help us."

"What exactly do you mean by that?" Pandora asked, alarmed.

"When Miranda was thirteen, I cast a spell upon her to protect her from bad men. The magic would lift when she found the man she loved. Lord Jason broke the enchantment. Now Missy is unprotected. He should have made her his bride."

"Miri, you are a talented naturalist. Certainly, you do not believe this superstitious nonsense," Pandora said.

"*'There are more things in heaven and earth, Horatio, than are dreamt of in your philosophy'* as my mother's favorite, Mr. Shakespeare, would say. I believe you experienced some difficulties following us to this ship, so you have felt Ida's power. If you hadn't ridden with Daniel, you would not be aboard now. If you had not forced Jason to speak before he was ready, we might still be destined to marry. However, I will not connive to have him. Do you understand, Ida?"

"Yes, Missy. I understand."

Pandora noticed the new command in Miranda's voice and the acquiescence of the servant that did not quite ring true. They both blamed her for Jason's defection. The sea, so vast and powerful, spread out before them, no land in sight. She shivered and pulled her borrowed shawl closer.

Her brother and Daniel returned to the deck hauling a long case. Obviously preparing for a match, they shed their jackets and took sabers from the box. They made a great show of trying the swords for balance and getting the feel of them by slashing through the air while their bodies stretched and assumed elegant poses. A few sailors and the captain watched. The women pretended not to see, burying their noses in reading, drawing and needlework.

"Look at them, Miranda. They are like male painted buntings putting on a show to attract a mate," Pandora whispered, holding her book to cover her lips but not her eyes.

Miranda giggled and glanced rapidly back and forth from the combative men to her drawing. Even Ida smiled as she worked to repair the hem of Pandora's dark riding skirt yet again.

Keeping their distance from the ladies, the opponents assumed a fencing stance and proceeded to get some exercise. From the start, Jason Longleigh's superior training showed. His style, quickness, and grace excelled. Except for their mother, the duke loved nothing better than the clash of swords and the firing of guns and had taught his boys well. If Jason were not weakened by his lack of appetite and moping over Miranda, he should overcome Daniel with ease, Pandora figured.

However, Daniel Clary, more powerful with his workmanlike strokes and used to the roll of the ship and the obstacles on deck, made a worthy opponent. They did not dance upon a fencing strip but on the sea itself. The sea loved Daniel Clary like a passionate mistress. The ship lurched suddenly. Trying to keep his balance, Jason dropped his guard. Obviously, Daniel meant only to touch his saber to his opponent's chest, but the ship rolled back again and pushed the sword through cloth to flesh. Red welled through the fabric of Jason's shirt.

Miranda gave a small cry and started to rise, but Pandora held her back. "I've seen worse damage when he takes on Joshua. They always get carried away when they go at it, but Daniel has admirable restraint. See there, they are examining the wound. It's nothing to cry over. Quickly, go back to your drawing. Jason looks this way and must not see your concern. You have no obligation. He is no longer yours."

"Yes, I understand."

Miranda picked up her pencil and put the finishing touches to a drawing of the fencing match where Jason appeared to be winning. She shut the notebook when the men paraded past, smelling of sweat and blood and jesting about the mishap.

"Nothing serious. No need to worry," Jason called out to them.

"We are not worried," Miranda piped up as coldly as she could, but the response came out lukewarm and half-hearted. She had to turn her face away from the injury.

"Do wash before supper, brother," Pandora added.

Ida muttered to herself. Suddenly, a seagull swooped from the sky and dove, attracted perhaps by the shining combs of abalone Miranda had loaned Pandora to keep her hair in place—or so everyone would say later. The bird ripped a small patch of black hair from Panny's scalp and left her bleeding, too. Red droplets marred her diaphanous white gown. The men dropped their case and drove the gull away. Miranda, showing some of her old quickness, raced to a barrel of sea water and wet a handkerchief to press on the head wound. Pandora gasped as the salt stung the cut. Daniel grasped her hand.

"The salt is good for the injury. Really, it's no more than a peck, but scalp wounds tend to bleed. Here, I have some cheerful news. If the birds are back, we are nearing land. Your journey is nearly over."

"Thank you for telling me that." Pandora should have been joyous, but her head throbbed and her heart had a letdown feeling she could not explain.

"Do fix yourself up before dinner, Panny. Your hair resembles a bird's nest," her brother taunted, getting back some of his own.

Jason idly flipped through Miranda's notebook and came to his picture. "Ah, I see I still merit some attention."

Miranda's cheeks flamed. "Give me that! I drew you for lack of any more interesting creatures."

"Time to wash up for supper, children," Ida said.

~ * ~

Pandora came out on deck to watch the sunset at sea. The captain thought they would reach the islands by tomorrow afternoon. A good thing, because the coffee was long gone. Fulton had not expected so many passengers, and burnt hardtack boiled with water made a poor substitute. She had such a hunger for greens, she thought she could graze in a field once on dry land again. Still, the sea did offer some compensation.

The sun blazed red and trailed streamers of orange and pink behind it as it descended below the horizon. In the rose-colored frock she had exchanged for the bloody white gown, Pandora felt dressed for the fiery display. She half expected the sun to set the sea to boiling, it seemed so huge and bright. Not a single lamp competed with its glory, not a tree or building impeded the view. She sighed.

"Yes, a sunset at sea is a beautiful sight to behold." Daniel had come up behind her. "A red sky at night means good weather tomorrow, and we have been blessed by fair winds and freedom from storms this entire voyage. With Miranda and Ida aboard, I should have expected nothing else."

"You think Ida is able to control the entire sea with sticks and turtle shells? She talked earlier about casting a spell over your sister to protect her from bad men. She can whip up a mud puddle and break a carriage wheel, I'll grant you, but stir the ocean or keep a girl safe from men who would harm her, I doubt it."

"I don't know about the entire sea, but all of Miranda's previous suitors have perished."

"Your sister is barely eighteen. How many suitors has she had?"

"The first when she turned thirteen. My father's cousin came from the hills for a visit, a forty-year-old man who dined at our table and never took his eyes off Miranda. Our mother lay two years in her grave after dying from a lung inflammation, but I understand my sister resembled her at the same age. The man made an offer for her right then and there. I was home from the university for a visit and thought my father would laugh the proposal away. I should have known better. He saw an opportunity to save money and make a profit at the same time. No boarding school for Miri to continue her education—and he demanded a bride price. He always said he had paid one for my mother, purchased from a dirt-poor farmer when he made a trip inland. The story embarrassed Mama, but he told it often. My mother was no older than Miranda at the time. Maybe this offer seemed normal to Daddy."

"The thought makes me ill." Pandora stared into the black sea and waited for the moon to rise and the story to continue.

"Another cause for you, Lady Pandora: child brides. A great deal of money changed hands that evening. I was ordered to take them to the mainland in the morning to be married by a preacher. Then, Daddy's cousin and Miranda would continue on to his home by horseback with her belongings to follow afterwards. I thought I might take a pistol and drive the man away, bear the chance of my father's wrath for my sister's sake, but I had no need. Ida served at dinner that night. Servants have ears, even if they pretend not to hear."

"What do you think she did?" Pandora asked skeptically.

"The sail was a short one, a mere four leagues to the nearest town with a preacher who required no banns to be read. My father gave me a signed paper endorsing the union and accompanied it with cash. He charged me to stand witness. I swear we would never have entered the chapel doors, but my proposed heroism proved entirely unnecessary. A whirlwind came from nowhere and tipped our boat. Miranda and I swim like porpoises and know to hold on to the hull if possible. The inlander did not. We were rescued hours later. They found my father's cousin washed ashore and eaten by the crabs."

"A freakish accident," Pandora proposed.

"Daddy had no other use for his daughter after that and sent her off to a ladies' academy in Savannah. Miranda can sing like a bird and plays the piano wonderfully. Her knowledge of the natural world from her own observations excelled. My mother, who was wholly ignorant before Daddy found her and had her tutored to be his wife, loved learning and passed that on to Miri. Still, my sister had only the children of our servants and two rough brothers for company and did not know how to get along in society. The other girls poked at her like a wild creature in a cage. She ran away and came back to Ariel Island when she was fifteen."

"I escaped my boarding school at the age of fourteen," Pandora said with some pride. "But Papa said I had a duty to return and protect my sister, Phemie. He made me practice what he called his Indian face, completely stoic except for the fierce, murderous dark eyes. When Phemie and I were taunted for the color of our skin, the blackness of our hair and eyes, I would put on the face and stare the girls down. Of course, putting toads and small snakes in their beds helped, too. I think my French instructor was terrified of me as well. Perhaps Miranda and I have more in common than I thought."

"Yes, she has more spirit than you give her credit for, while yours is obvious. We had a mainland neighbor, Raleigh Poundstone, a man up in years who had buried three wives and numerous slaves. People far and near feared his temper, yet Daddy listened to his offer for my sister and agreed to accept some parcels of land in exchange for her hand, since she had defied him by running away from her school. I stood with Ponce, Ida's son, when Poundstone came to the island to collect her. Ponce is very large, but simple-minded and utterly devoted to Miranda. Still, he understood he could not hit a white man. That was to be my job. Ponce simply stood in his way blocking the door, while I made ready to defend my sister. Poundstone carried a horse whip wherever he went. He raised it against Ponce and laid down one stripe. He readied the whip again and dropped down dead when he lifted his arm a second time."

"An elderly man with a choleric temper. He died from a heart seizure or apoplexy surely." With the moon unrisen and only the few ship's lanterns sending their glimmers out on the sea, Pandora spoke in the darkness.

Daniel's smooth baritone voice continued. "Daddy sent Miri back to the school. I half think her strange diet developed there as a means of starving herself to death. The headmistress summoned my father and a man of the cloth to minister to her about her peculiar beliefs. The preacher had permission to examine my sister in the most intimate way. He concluded she had a devil inside her because she fought him off so strongly. The best way to drive the devil out involved his marrying Miranda and using all the means at his disposal to subdue her. My father assented, thinking only to keep his hands on Ariel Island, promised to Miranda, and be rid of a troublesome daughter. Leaving the ladies' academy that evening, the preacher was thrown from his horse and broke his neck. Witnesses said something large and dark spooked the animal—a black panther, they thought."

"That could be true. A simple accident caused by a wild beast."

"I've lived in Georgia all my life and have never seen such a creature, certainly not near long-civilized Savannah."

The moon made an appearance. Knowing it showed her face strained with concern, Pandora needed to ask, "Does Jason have to fear for his life?"

"I think not. Although she is putting on an amazing show of not caring, Miranda still loves your brother. If Ida believes hope remains for them, she will not harm him. You should save your worry for yourself. You stand in their way by encouraging my sister to resist any reconciliation."

"You pursued them as well to stop their marriage."

"I pursued them to make sure your brother did not take advantage of my sister without paying the price."

"Marriage?"

"Or his life. I would have given him the choice, naturally. Unfortunately, I have become too well acquainted with him. He truly loves Miranda. My head aches from listening to his verse at night, but I believe killing a poet, no matter how bad, brings ill luck."

Pandora used an accusation to suppress her smile. "Then you admit you would have assisted in their elopement once ashore."

"Strangely, I no longer believe they meant to elope. Miranda went running back to the islands, and Jason followed her. He didn't seem to think beyond what a great adventure epic he could create."

"That does sound like my brother, all impulse and no common sense."

"None, I agree. He became involved in my father's latest scheme to be rid of Miranda totally by mischance when he stopped for turtle soup. Between the deaths of her suitors and the poisonous gossip the other young ladies at the academy spread about my sister, she had no prospects in Georgia. Daddy has become desperate enough to offer the island for her hand, providing he gains some influence in Britain, a source of ready cash, and maybe a title for his family. I came along as much to protect Miri as to pursue her on his orders."

The moon soared high, edging the dark waves with its light, igniting Daniel's shadowed eyes with green and gold, and probably streaking even her black hair with its rays. In its magical aura, anyone would appear beautiful.

"I should be grateful my papa would never force me to marry, no matter how much trouble I had given him."

"Yes, I recall you may remain an old maid for as long as you wish. Have you turned down many offers?" Daniel inquired with a smile.

"I've had none. Mama says my opinions and my tongue are too strong."

"Strong, yes. So unlike the simpering belles of Savannah who tormented my sister." He raised a hand to her hair. Though she had carefully covered her injury, he found the spot unerringly.

"Still hurting?" he asked.

"Not so very much."

He replaced his hand with his full, firm lips and let them to travel to her bared ear and down the side of her face to her own mouth. He cupped the back of her head to hold her as he pressed, coaxing her lips to open and accept a deeper kiss.

In the back of her mind, she heard her papa say, "Your stiletto, Panny!" but for once, she ignored sound advice. Her fingers rose and sunk themselves into the crisp curls of his hair, preventing him from ending their contact. The throbbing of her injury vanished and reappeared in her heart. From there it spread, settling low in her body. She must be glowing like the moon, she thought, until a sailor whistled and another made a low comment to his mate.

Pushing Daniel away, she said coolly, "Still after my twenty-thousand pounds?"

He raised her chin with one finger, forcing her to look directly into those sea change eyes. "Never, never mistake me for my father, Lady Pandora."

He offered his arm. They strolled across the deck as casually as if they were walking in Hyde Park on a pleasant afternoon. He saw her to her door, bowed, and went to the cabin he shared with the lovelorn poet.

Pandora entered her room where Miranda slept soundly, though Ida still crooned to her as if she were a babe in need of comfort. She allowed the servant to help her out of the rose-colored gown and too short petticoat to her undergarments for sleeping. The white dress, its bloodstains worked out of the fabric with sea water and soap by the slave woman, hung drying on a peg like a ghostly bride.

Bride. Pandora closed her eyes and breathed evenly and deeply to induce rest, but she still felt the imprint of Daniel's lips on hers. Ida continued to hum, and gradually her body relaxed. She was not quite asleep when the tune ended and the servant stretched out on her pallet between the box beds. Drifting, drifting, she thought she heard Ida say not a prayer, but a promise.

"If you want Mastah Lord Jason, you shall have him, my *bébé*."

Sixteen

The wind seemed eager to blow Miranda home. By late afternoon, Daniel pointed out a smudge of blue on the horizon to the women.

"The islands. The captain will bring the ship around the tip of Ariel to the leeward side and drop anchor. We'll spend the night on the ship and take the dinghy to the dock in the morning."

That evening at supper, they toasted the successful voyage with the last of Captain Fulton's wine and then went above to watch the ship draw nearer and nearer to land until they could make out the low mound of Ariel and the higher elevations of Caliban and Prospero. The captain called for a new setting of the sails to slow and turn the ship lest they run up on a sand bar at their current speed. With some regret, Pandora watched Daniel help at this task for the last time.

Miranda, her cheeks rosy, her eyes big and bright again, hung by the railing taking in the view of her home and snatching a few sidelong glances at Jason, who helped with the sails to the best of his ability. He had improved, Pandora thought, as she stood by the hatch leading to the cabins. The pure white dress flapped around her ankles like the wheeling gulls and the breeze seemed intent on plucking the pins from her hair.

Ida came up the steps and went straight to her young lady. She trailed a strange scent of orange water and fragrant herbs behind her. Twined in her strong dark fingers, she carried the purple and gold-shot silk scarf she often wore as a turban. Along with an immaculate white apron and headpiece, the slave woman wore a red dress Pandora had never seen. Until a moment ago, the servant had been singing in her native tongue and thumping the boards below as if she did some exotic dance. Only Pandora stood close enough to hear her.

"Have you been singing to your goddess, thanking her for our safe arrival, Mammy? I see you wear her favorite colors tonight," Miranda remarked.

Ida did not answer her question. "Come, Missy. You must go below now and get your rest for tomorrow."

"But I want to stay up until the stars come out and they set the anchor."

"Think, there may be turtles come ashore tomorrow. You will be up half the night counting their eggs."

Pandora watched the slave woman release the scarf into the wind and flick her fingers behind her back.

Miranda exclaimed, "Oh, Ida. You have lost your best tignon to the sea. I must buy you another."

At the same moment, Jason tripped over his own feet as the ship changed course, and coshed his head against one of the masts. The broken skin oozed blood and a knot swelled on his forehead.

While Miranda did not run to him, she did place her hands on her hips and say in mock exasperation, "I suppose we should take *him* with us and clean him up. Staggering as he is, he might go overboard."

"Yes, we will take care of him. Come, Mastah Lord Jason, I have remedies below for a sore head."

As they passed, Pandora caught that sweet herbal scent again. Just a whiff lingering around the hatch made her feel a trifle dizzy. She went to Daniel, now free from his chore, but not yet back in his jacket. The last rays of the sun turned the foam running up on the distant sandy beach a brilliant gold. He, too, seemed eager to be home.

"You should stay a few days and see the islands."

"I don't think that would be wise. Jason is easily seduced by the idea of foreign climes and might not wish to leave. Then, we would have to sunder him from Miranda again. My brother and I had best stay aboard and say our goodbyes here."

"I suppose you are right. I had some idea I might show you we do not mistreat our people."

"Your slaves, you mean." Pandora leaned her back against the railing.

"As I've said before, I have only one given to me when I left for boarding school. My father owns the rest. If allowing Horace his manumission papers would convince you to stay, I would free him tomorrow. Of course, he has been with me all his life and has nowhere else to go, but I would gladly pay him a salary to serve as my valet if that would give you a better opinion of me." He leaned against the railing, too, leaving only a small space between them.

"You have my good opinion," Pandora assured him. "I have seen that you are strong and able to defend yourself, that you extend your protection to those who are weaker. Why, you even sought to save me from Ida's spells on our mad dash to Brighton when I had not been kind to you. Unlike Jason, I believe you have no fear of marriage and family and would make an admirable husband. But I could never align myself with a man who stands to inherit a hundred or more enslaved human beings."

"Lady Pandora, I have no desire to be a planter. I plan to sell out my interest to my brother and practice law in Savannah. Besides, love and passion are not about alignments." With his fingertips, Daniel caught a strand of her straight black hair freed by the wind and stroked down its length. He tucked it behind her ear again.

She struggled to explain while his proximity and light touch distracted her mind.

"Among the gentry in England, marriage is very much about alignments among families. Love and passion are sought elsewhere.

I do not want to become some man's property because I am a duke's daughter worth twenty-thousand pounds who was born of a woman with the incredible capacity to produce ten living children. I want to be able to pursue my causes without being locked away if my husband does not agree. Why should I spend all my life being ordered about by a man?"

The wind stiffened, shifted. Instantly alert, Daniel looked past her to the south. A mass of black clouds writhing like sea serpents in a watery sky raced toward the ship. The chop of the waves began to slam broadside against the *Sea Nymph*. Seamen raced to lower the sails and put up a storm sheet.

"Go below. Go below at once before they close the hatches." Daniel gave Pandora a slight push in the right direction.

"Now that is just what I mean. I am simply to obey without question your better judgment. Do you believe I haven't enough sense to get out of the rain without some man telling me to do so?"

Pandora held her place. She would go when the drops began to splatter and not before.

On the beach of the island, the tide had changed its mind and flowed back into the ocean, so far back that fish caught unawares flopped on the sand. Snags and sandbars lay exposed. Daniel grasped her shoulder.

"Daniel, do you see…"

As tall as the highest mast, the great wave rose from the ocean. A glassy mountain of black water rimmed with white, it washed over the ship, turning the vessel nearly on its side. When the pressure passed, the *Sea Nymph* sprang upright again. Manhandled by the crosswind, she turned off course and sped to the north. In the riggings, sailors cried out to God or their mothers and wives and cursed the fickle sea.

~ * ~

Below deck, Miranda Clary, soothed by Ida's singing and the herbal haze rising from a now extinguished concoction in a clay dish, slept, oblivious to the storm. Across from her in Pandora's bunk, Jason Longleigh, who had taken the tisane Ida offered him for his headache, lay unconscious. Oh yes, he was handsome as an enchanted prince, the slave woman noted, with his long length and black hair unruly over the wound on his forehead. When the storm hit, neither of her charges awoke or even tipped from their beds because she cared for them. Ida continued her chant to Mami Wata to bring the wind and the waves, but soon she would stop, since all impediments to uniting these young people in marriage had gone.

Seventeen

The wave engulfed Pandora Longleigh, took her overboard and pressed her toward the bottom of the sea. She would die as she had dreamt so often—drowned and unmourned by a husband or children. Her parents would grieve, but secretly might they be glad to be rid of such a troublesome child? Soon her breath would fail, and she'd take in sea water with her next gasp. Unable to swim, her doom awaited. But being a Longleigh, she could not stop fighting. She pushed upward with her arms. Some creature grabbed at her gown—the legendary giant squid, a bloody-minded shark or some other horror of the deep? She did battle with it all the way to the surface though its claws grasped the hair the sea had unbound.

"Stop it, Pandora! Don't struggle. I will put my arm around you, and the waves will carry us to the island. Be still, please be still."

If she lay in the arms of Daniel Clary, then she must be drowned, dead and gone to a paradise where being a duke's daughter attracted to a common slaveholder no longer mattered. The sons of Allah believed a hundred virgins awaited them in heaven. The stout Vikings populated their hereafter with blond Valkyries ready to serve them. Why couldn't a woman have one desirable man for all eternity?

She sighed out and breathed in a bitter mouthful of brine. She spat and began to struggle again, not dead yet.

"Do not fight me. We are nearly there." Daniel's voice shouted above the raging storm.

The wave tossed them carelessly over a sandbar and into shallow waters where broken shells tore at their clothes and flesh as they skidded onto shore. They came to rest on a low mound with a lone palm tree growing on its top...two Noahs, no ark. The surge continued up the beach and smashed against the wall of the island.

"The tree, hold on to the tree!"

But why? Her mind slowed, seemed to almost stop. Her legs turned to rubber. Daniel's strong arms gathered her and pressed her against the palm. He held on for both of them.

~ * ~

Curling back on itself, the wave returned, trying to pry its victims loose and suck them into the ocean. Steadfast, Daniel gripped the tree and denied the sea its prey. The great wave vanished, but the sky remained black with clouds. Large swells still broke on shore. In the distance, the *Sea Nymph*, one white sail spread, ran north before the storm.

Daniel watched the ship go as he slowly released his death grip on the trunk of the palm with Pandora Longleigh crumpled at his feet. Had he crushed the life out of her while trying to save her? He knelt by her side. She breathed. Her chest rose up and down. The sea had claimed the gauze inset that modestly covered her bosom and pulled down the scanty bodice of the borrowed white gown to reveal ample, brown-tipped breasts. The fragile, tattered lawn of the skirt exposed her limbs. He wanted to praise God for the pale dress that had allowed him to find her in the sea and pull her upward. He wanted to thank the Devil for this glimpse of her body, tinted by her Indian heritage, and her hair, all her black hair glossy and wet from the water. No time to stare and give way to prurient thoughts.

Daniel arranged her rags for modesty and began to tug the soaked bodice up across her bosom. Perhaps he brushed her nipples slightly or took too much time or pleasure about the business because suddenly, her dark eyes opened.

"What are you doing?"

"You fainted. Your clothes are—um—in disarray. I was arranging them prior to carrying you to a safer place." Aware he still held the wet cloth raised, he let it sink back against her chest where it molded itself to every curve and pucker and barely covered those enticing brown nipples.

"I never faint. Fainting is a tool women use when they cannot control a man in any other way. I was merely overcome by the sea." Pandora felt along her limbs and realized the extent of her nakedness. "I have lost my stiletto and my borrowed stockings and slippers."

"Yes, the ocean has disarmed and disrobed you. King Neptune felt playful." Daniel grinned at her.

"King Neptune had nothing to do with this. Ida and her sea goddess tried to kill me." She struggled upright and tugged at her bodice, trying to keep at least her nipples covered.

"Then you would be dead, and I would not be here to protect you. I think she meant to put us ashore on a deserted beach in order to have time for Jason to reach some resolve with my sister. Come, we can't stay here with the weather uncertain. We must find shelter. This mound leads upward. Let me carry you. Your feet are bare."

"Among other things. Surely, I can walk."

Daniel offered Pandora a hand up. She took it and her legs turned to jelly again, either uncertain from her ordeal or his touch. Before she could crumple again, Daniel had her. Sure of his footing, he carried her from the mound of clam and oyster shells, sloshed through a dip where the ocean still poured and mounted a path to the high ridge of the island gouged out by the sea. He set Pandora down, carefully keeping a supporting arm around her and surveyed their surroundings.

"Do you have any idea where we are?"

"Oh, we're on Ariel all right. Ida set us down on Horseshoe Bay. Lucky for us. The natives once camped on that shell mound and my brother and I played here as children. The sea claims more of it each year. We need to find shelter. Mild as this climate is, our wet clothes will chill us until the sun returns."

"Why not simply walk to Miranda's house?"

"It's on the other side of the island facing the mainland, a distance of several miles. No one will be out in this weather to assist us. They won't know to look for us until the *Sea Nymph* makes its way back. But I have an idea."

Without consulting her this time, Daniel scooped Pandora into his arms again and began to trek inland. He hadn't gone far when he set her down again and showed her a hut much like the wigwam at Bellevue. Rather than being covered with bark, palmetto leaves shingled its rounded sides. A woven mat of grass covered the doorway. He raised the mat and helped her inside. Someone had made a camp fire ready to light ringed round by white stones. On its far side, a plump mattress of striped ticking lay with an old woven brown cotton blanket neatly folded over it. An assortment of bottles and bags hung from leather straps on the walls.

Daniel deposited her on the springy pallet and searched among the clutter. He found a small pouch and crouched by the arrangement of sticks and curls of dried Spanish moss. He shook out a flint and steel and after several strikes and much blowing on the moss, got the fire started. Pandora leaned forward to warm herself, one hand holding up her bodice which had a great determination to slip. Her long black hair twined around her, getting in her way. She tossed the heavy, wet strands behind her shoulders.

Daniel rummaged some more among the supplies. He opened two leather-covered bottles, sniffed and drank. "Water, fairly fresh."

He handed one to Pandora, who was more than glad to wash the bitter, salty taste of the sea from her mouth. "How did you know this shelter would be here untouched by the storm?"

"Because Ponce, Ida's son, builds them every spring when the turtles come to nest. He watches the beaches for Miranda. If the weather turns bad, he takes shelter in them. Unfortunately, Ponce is far too fond of fire, but I've taught him to use the flint and steel and be careful. Here, dried meat, raisins, and dessert—sesame candy, *praline au benne,* Ida calls them."

Pandora went directly to the food she craved. "Oh, brown sugar and the taste of butter. It melts upon the tongue."

She followed the praline with a handful of raisins, then went to work on the tough, dried meat, tearing at it with her teeth. "I am told in America anyone can hunt, not just lords and gamekeepers," she said, as if compelled to make polite dinner conversation while eating with her hands.

"True," Daniel replied. He sat on the other side of the fire, eating his share of the provender. He raised the water bottle to his lips. A few drops dribbled down his chin and into the curly light brown hair on his chest. Pandora followed it with her dark eyes.

He debated in his mind what she observed. The sea goddess had toyed with him as well, tearing open the top of his shirt and raking her nails down the stouter fabric of his linen shirt to make a few openings. He was tanned to the waist and beyond from swimming in the surf, not like the pasty English gentlemen who haunted the ballrooms seeking to court an heiress. The ocean temptress had molded his trousers to his private parts, but she had not unbuttoned his pants, leaving that for some other female to do.

"Lady Pandora, are you well? You've stopped eating very suddenly."

"I've had my fill. I believe since you have saved my life, you should address me as Pandora."

"Kind of you, but I believe I prefer calling you Lady Pandora—as if I've abducted a noblewoman and taken her to my lair." He licked a bit of brown sugar off his lips and smiled.

"We should rest until morning," she said suddenly.

"I think you'll find that moss mattress comfortable. Pull up the blanket if you are still chilled. I'll keep the fire going until we are both warm through and through."

He took a piece of dry driftwood from a small stack and added it to the fire. Flames of green and blue magically rose from the salt saturated log as if enchanted.

She lay down on the pallet, pulled the cotton blanket over her and swept her long hair over her shoulder to dry nearer the fire. "Daniel."

"Yes, milady."

"You must be very tired from your fight with the sea. It is silly and impractical for you to sit up all night when there is room enough on this tick for both of us."

Those low, heavy brows of his rose slightly. "An invitation?"

"Yes, to lie down on the other side of the blanket. No one will know. No harm done."

Thoughtfully, he put more wood on the fire and came to stretch out on the far side of her, first on his back, then on his side. His arm enclosed her. He went to sleep, exhausted by his ordeal and entirely certain he'd missed a great opportunity.

~ * ~

The wind continued to blow, shaking the palmetto leaves that kept it outside and whisking away the smoke from the fire through the hole left in the ceiling. Pandora lay awake, wondering if her parents had experienced this same strange intimacy in that wigwam in the Ohio country. They had formed a special, unshakable bond so long ago. Their mutual adoration continued to be an embarrassment to their children, raised in a society where married couples rarely showed such affection.

Pandora shut her eyes, but still felt his manhood pressed against her through the blanket and what was left of her dress. Other men had pulled her close and exposed their arousal. While not distended, Daniel's was indeed lengthy. For the first time she felt no need to laugh with scorn.

She knew she could sleep all night and Daniel Clary would not lift the blanket unless she asked him to do so. The thought was tempting, very tempting. But then, her mother had returned from the New World with the first of her ten children.

Use your good sense, Pandora, she chided. Go to sleep.

~ * ~

Bright light rimmed the mat hanging over the door of their shelter. Pandora awoke bereft of Daniel's warmth, the strength of his arm, the safety of his presence. Where had he gone? She wrapped the blanket around her, went to the opening of the hut, and raised the covering. She found his salt-encrusted boots turned upside down and drying on two stakes pushed into the sandy soil by the entry. His stockings lay drying on top of the palmettos. Had he walked off barefooted to find help?

The wigwam sat on the edge of a grove of low-growing live oaks hung with long, silvery moss and twisted by the ocean winds. She could not see beyond them, so dense was their shade. Birds flittered and called—buntings? No, larger and blue-gray. Walking forward, Pandora came to the edge of the embankment overlooking the sea. The tide ran out, the sun loomed far higher in the sky than she'd thought at first in the darkness under the oaks. The sea, a deep blue, met a cerulean sky at the horizon, no sails in sight.

Below, Daniel waded along the low, rough reef that had probably taken a toll on her gown when they were washed ashore. With his trousers pushed above his knees, he was shirtless and unashamed as he waved to her. He held up a sack made from his garment.

"Breakfast," he called out to her.

She made her way carefully down the shell mound, wincing when her tender feet trod on a sharp-edged shell now and then. By the time she reached the beach, Daniel had made his way in from the water.

"Barefooted and wrapped in a blanket, your hair all loose in the breeze, you could have been the ghost of Pocahontas standing up there on the bluff."

That pleased her more than he knew. "What have you got there?"

"Oysters fresh from the sea. Ponce kindly left his shucking knife in the shelter, and I've pried loose a feast."

Daniel held up a broad-handled, short knife with a strong but not very sharp blade and, dropping his bundle, selected one of the rough, narrow shells he had collected and slit through the muscle holding the oyster shut. He threw away the top shell and offered her the meat served up in its own cup with a broth of brine. She opened her mouth and accepted his offering.

"The best I have ever eaten."

"Yes, small but tasty. Spread the blanket; we'll have some more."

Peeping to make sure she had adequate coverage, Pandora spread the cover out on the pale gray sand. Daniel shucked until they'd both had enough.

"We can save the rest for roasting in the fire later."

"Shouldn't we be trying to find the house?"

"Ah, Lady Pandora, they will come searching for us soon enough and that will be the end of our freedom. Why not spend this day worshipping the gods of sun and sea? I could teach you to swim."

"I am not sure the ocean *goddess* would like that—or me."

"Come, it will be an adventure. We are castaways like Robinson Crusoe. Do you know his story?"

"I read it on the ship after I finished *Gulliver*. Captain Fulton seemed fond of fantastic travels. I must say, you are beginning to sound a bit like Jason."

"Do I sense a little of Miranda in you?"

"Absolutely not!"

"Well, you look nothing like the Lady Pandora I met at Bellevue. You need a new name, an Indian name. I shall call you Raven."

"They aren't very attractive birds. I've seen them at the Tower. Very big beaks and coal black." Pouting, was she pouting? Pandora Longleigh did not pout. She argued her opinions clearly. One bird should be as good as any other.

"For the color of your hair and eyes. Besides, the raven is a magical bird full of supernatural powers, I've heard." He drew a strand of her hair through his fingers, following its length as he had done on the ship.

"Indeed, then not so bad. I rarely tell anyone this, but one of my middle names is Black Wing after a Shawnee woman my mother knew."

"Very fitting."

"What shall I call you—hmmm—Wooly Goat like the satyrs of ancient Greece."

She dared to poke one finger into the deep curls on his chest. She'd seen enough bare-chested men with all her brothers running about but had never actually touched one. He was much hairier than the Longleigh men with their Indian ancestry, and she found that strangely attractive. Could she be flirting for the first time in her life?

"Yes, Wooly Goat," she asserted.

"I take umbrage."

"Then you should keep your shirt on. Wooly Goat, Wooly Goat!"

"You must answer for that."

Before she could resist, Daniel plucked her from the blanket, carried her into the surf and dumped her in the water. She sputtered and panicked for a moment before she found her feet.

"See, you need to learn to swim. Come out with me a little further. Lie back across my arms and let the water hold you."

She did as he asked, but only because she rested on his arms, not on the deceitful sea. Then his arms were gone. She floated a moment, then thrashed.

"No, let the water bear you. Rest on the swell with arms spread, your limbs relaxed."

She did, because Pandora Longleigh was not a coward. To her amazement, she did not sink. Daniel's arms returned, rolling her over on her belly. She was well aware that her shredded skirts sank and bared her.

"Kick. Not so hard. Stretch out your arms and pull the water back." He moved along with her, supporting her efforts until she moved freely through the water.

"I'm swimming—good as any man."

"Yes, you are. Now, let's ride the waves in."

He took her hand, and they rode the surf to the shore. Just before emerging from the water, Pandora squatted down and adjusted the remains of her gown again. How long had she been bare-chested? Daniel hadn't said a word, that Wooly Goat, already drying on their blanket. She went to lie beside him. He found her hand and raised it to his lips.

"You were brave, my Raven, very brave."

"Yes, I was. My mother has an Indian name that she will not reveal to anyone. My father sometimes calls her his Little Yellow Flower, but I don't think that is it."

"Oddly, I don't want to be reminded of your parents, the Duke and Duchess of Bellevue, at this very moment."

He rolled over, covering her with his big, half-naked body. She knew she should lock her knees together, but somehow, they wanted to spread apart. He settled between them but raised his body up on his elbows. All that he touched were her lips with his. The kiss might have gone on much longer if Pandora had not opened her eyes and seen the sun shut out by a cloud—not a cloud, a bank of fog extending across the sea in their direction.

"Daniel, stop."

He rolled aside, his hand across his eyes. "I understand. You do not trust me. I am a common slaveholder not good enough for Lady Pandora Longleigh."

"No! The fog is coming in."

He bolted upright and raised her with one heave of his arm. "This isn't natural. Another of Ida's tricks, I'm sure. Bring the blanket."

Daniel rushed her along, pausing only to grab his shirt full of oysters resting in a small pool by the mound. They barely reached the hut when the heavy mist engulfed them, cocooning them so tightly they could see neither right nor left nor forward.

Slipping inside the hut, Pandora turned to Daniel and asked, "What are we to do?"

"Roast oysters and wait."

Eighteen

The *Sea Nymph* made her way carefully down the leeward side of the islands, keeping to the deepest waters off the mainland. Captain Fulton called the roll. After the terrifying night, he expected to find more missing than two of his guests, but all the crew, somewhat bruised and battered, answered. Several sailors attested they'd seen Daniel Clary and Lady Pandora washed away by the freak wave. As captain, he had to tell sweet Miss Clary and the English gentleman the fate of their relatives, but according to the servant woman, both still slept soundly.

Fulton wished he had been able to do the same during the storm that had driven his ship far north of Prospero and Caliban. For a while, he thought the *Nymph* would race all the way to the Carolinas, but at last the wind died down. He'd taken the bearings and brought her about, finally regaining Clary's islands in the morning and finding the channel to take them to the gentler side of the sea. Now, Ariel Island lay just off port.

His remaining passengers wobbled from the hatch like newborn ducklings. Miranda looked once again like the disheveled girl who loved to roam the beaches, rather than the proper young lady she'd become under Lady Pandora's management. Her hair cascaded down her back and her gown, the same worn yesterday, hung in wrinkles. As for Lord Longleigh, he'd turned green again under that dark, unshaven complexion of his. Perhaps he hadn't slept through the entire storm. At least the purple bump on his forehead had diminished in size. Both gulped fresh air and shielded their eyes from the sun high above the mast.

Miranda recovered as soon as she saw the island. "I am home, home at last!" she shouted with joy.

Lord Longleigh put on a long and doleful face. For all his poetry, good looks, and desire for adventure, here he must part from Miranda, the woman he professed to love. Young folks, so tangled in their emotions. Captain Fulton thanked the good Lord he had a loyal wife and six healthy children awaiting him in Charleston and was through with such nonsense. Well, he could indulge in drifting thoughts or do his duty. He approached the two as they stood by the rail gazing at Ariel's dock and the double row of tall palms that led to a white house in the distance.

"All is well with the sailors and the *Sea Nymph*, Captain?" Miss Miranda asked. "I understand we had a storm last evening."

"Aye, we did. The crew is accounted for, and they are checking her over now for damages. Could we go to my cabin for a moment, Miss Clary, Lord Longleigh?"

"So formal, Captain Fulton, when you have known me for years. Can't we talk here? The air is so stuffy below it's given me a slight headache. Before you leave, I do want to give you a sack of coffee beans. As unexpected passengers, I know we strained your larder. In fact, if you could remain a day or two, most probably my sister-in-law would like to look over your goods. I could ask Daniel to bring her to Ariel," Miranda chattered on innocently.

"About your brother." This was the worst of his duties, informing families of deaths at sea. "A great wave engulfed the ship last evening. Daniel stood near the rail and some of my men saw him washed into the ocean. We stood off Ariel at the time. He might have gotten to shore. And Lord Longleigh, your sister went overboard with him."

"My brother is a strong swimmer. Why, he might be waiting for us at the house as we speak. Yes, certainly that must be the case." Miranda's hazel eyes opened wide and hopeful and strained to see her brother's figure coming from the distant building.

"Pandora cannot swim." Jason's undertone went from green to gray. He squeezed his dark eyes shut for a moment and gathered himself behind closed hands before looking up again.

"Miranda—Miss Clary, I know you want to be rid of me and I have no right to set foot on your island, but I beg of you, let me search the beaches for her corpse and give my sister a decent burial, if possible. My escapade brought her to her death, and I can do no less. I believe you were friends with Panny at the last, so for her sake, could you endure me?"

Miranda opened her slender arms. "My poor boy. Of course, you must stay and search for her. Daniel is very resourceful. He might have saved her. Right now, they could be having tea on the verandah and worrying over us."

Lord Longleigh bowed his great height over her tiny shoulder and wept. Captain Fulton turned his eyes away. The sea seldom gave back its dead, but that was not for him to say. If anyone were on the verandah, they would have hailed the ship by now. As it were, only one huge man, dark as a walnut husk in autumn, shambled down the long lane. Other slaves worked the vegetable garden on either side of the road, but looked up only briefly.

"Let me take you ashore, then," the captain offered without hope.

"Their trunks are packed, and I put what little Mastah Daniel and Lady Pandora brought with them into the boxes."

Fulton had no idea how long the tall, ebony woman had stood there waiting to say her piece. A fixture on Ariel Island for as long as he'd stopped here, she never failed to chill him. He hadn't been pleased to have her aboard, but he'd done his best to show no doubts. Sailors were superstitious enough without giving them more to fear. He'd heard the mutters that Ida had called the storm, but he would be rid of her shortly.

"Look, Ida, Ponce has come to greet us. He might have word." Miranda cupped her hands around her mouth and tried to shout over the expanse of water, "Is Daniel home?"

The big man shook his head and pointed to his ear.

"Could we go right now, Captain? You must come and dine with us. We will send fresh stores to your men who brought us safely here. After we are refreshed, we will begin our search," Miranda suggested.

"I'd as soon forgo the meal and start looking for them at once," Jason countered, raising his woeful countenance from Miri's sodden shoulder.

"And faint along the way? Do be practical. You haven't eaten since early last evening and might still be dizzy from your wound. I will send some of my people to the nearest beaches to search while we eat."

"Yes, Miss Clary."

Obviously, their brief truce had ended. The lad seemed dazed by her authority. Captain Fulton suppressed a smile. He might be in command aboard his ship, but when it came to the household, his wife ruled. This young man should learn that lesson before he attempted another proposal to any female.

He called for the ship's boat to be lowered, the trunks brought, and guests helped to board the smaller vessel. At the dock, the huge slave helped the women ashore and startled everyone by first throwing Miranda into the air and catching her, then whirling Ida around in a circle.

"Mammy and Missy come home!" he shouted, giving them a huge, face-splitting grin. "Missy, two big head turtles come, but not Stella yet. See, I count the eggs for you like you show me and mark the nests."

The big fellow drew out a scrap of bark from the pouch of his homespun shirt and eagerly showed his mistress his crosshatches for every five eggs, one column per turtle.

"Very nice, Ponce. I shall add these figures to my records. But remember, the big-headed turtles are called loggerheads. Thank you for watching the beaches in my absence. Now tell me, is Mr. Daniel home?" Miranda looked up at him so hopefully.

"No, Missy, not at home."

Her shoulders hunched, and Jason reached out to console her as she had him, but Miranda drew herself up again.

"Very well, we will get people searching for him and Lady Pandora as soon as we reach the house. Shall I send Ponce for a vehicle or do you care to walk? It's but a mile."

"At this point, I would like to stretch my legs on dry land," Jason admitted. He took a few steps forward and swayed from side to side as if he'd never left the ship.

Captain Fulton slapped him on the back. "Never fear, your land legs will come back soon enough. Me, I'm not so fond of walking. I'll remain behind and come up to the house with the baggage."

~ * ~

Miranda and Jason continued toward the house with Ponce gamboling in front of them like a playful Great Dane puppy, and Ida a few paces behind. They entered the alley of tall palms rustling their fronds in a light breeze. To the right and left, dark-skinned men and women advanced in age and half-grown children tended a vast garden with new crops of maize and beans, melons and sweet potatoes, already green and growing. Huge cabbages and the root vegetables—beets, carrots and turnips—were just finishing up. Beyond a windbreak of trees, Jason could see other black figures tending the young cotton. The men doffed their hats as they passed and the women and children called out their welcome homes.

They came to a semi-circle of small houses made of a peculiar whitish material and roofed with shakes. More grannies watched little brown children at play in the dirt.

Trying to take his mind off Pandora, Jason remarked, "Interesting building material."

"That's tabby," Miranda answered flatly, her mind elsewhere. "It's a mixture of crushed shells, lime, sand, and salt water poured into forms and left to harden, very durable in this climate and certainly less expensive than wood, as we have all the ingredients in abundance. We learned the trick of it from the Africans. Our barn and the lower story of the big house are made of it also. The headmen have the larger dwellings. We don't use overseers on Ariel."

"I see," said Jason, although he didn't, not having the least idea how plantations were organized.

Ponce interrupted their desultory conversation. "Missy, Missy, Missy," he said while walking backwards to face them.

"Should you allow this fellow to be so familiar?" Jason asked.

"Ponce is Ida's son. He was so big at birth a physician had to be called to draw him from her body with forceps. He came into the world simple-minded and knows no other way to be. Besides, he is my brother."

Jason winced at the all too candid description of the black man's birth. Miranda was truly unusual among women, much like his own mother. "Yes, I know Ida served as wet nurse to you both."

"No, I mean he is my half-brother, sired by my father."

While Jason continued walking in stunned silence, the huge, melon-headed Ponce sang out again, "Missy, Missy, Missy, Mastah Daniel not at home."

"Yes, Ponce, I understand. We must go look on the beaches for him."

"Ponce know where he at. I seen him before the fog come in on Horseshoe Bay. He playing man-woman games with an Injun girl—or maybe she Mami Wata come out of the sea. Very beautiful with her long, black hair. Now he must always be true to her. Right, Mammy?" he asked his mother.

"They are alive! Oh Jason, alive!" Miranda hugged him tight, then turned to dance in circles with Ponce's big hands in hers.

How he had missed Miranda's quick, impulsive embraces, her use of his first name. How glad he would be to have his sister restored to him—with some of her high and mightiness washed away.

"Did you say man-woman games, Ponce? What exactly would those be?" Jason asked.

"You know," Ponce giggled, a massive hand over his ear-to-ear grin. "Naked games in the water, then like them horseshoe crabs, one on top of another."

"My son, I have told you never to spy on people, especially when they are playing those sorts of games," Ida corrected sharply before he could do any more damage.

"I go to see if any turtles come in the night and put a stick by their nests. Instead, I see Mastah Daniel with Mami Wata. Then, Mami Wata sends the fog so I cannot watch anymore. I run fast, fast before the mist catches me, and I come home."

"Yes, yes, one must be careful what one asks of Mami Wata. She can be a trickster. So, we know both are safe. We need only go collect them," Ida said in a soothing voice.

"Safe! Daniel has dishonored my sister. To think I felt I deserved that scratch he gave me on the ship when all along he lusted after Pandora." Miranda's hand touched Jason's arm, and he felt that longing again for what he had thrown away.

"Jason, Ponce is not the most reliable of witnesses. We must go rescue them at once and hear their story. I'll call for a cart, and we will take along food and water and some medicines for any wounds they might have suffered in the surf."

By then, they had passed the massive tabby barn and approached the big house, the entire structure white-washed and glittering in the April sun. The massive lower story had only narrow gunports for windows, but the upper portion of frame accessed by an outside staircase sat light and airy like frosting atop a heavy cake. Shady verandahs provided views of the sound where the *Sea Nymph* rested, and if a curious fog hadn't enveloped the other half of the island, its seaward side as well.

A round, brown woman hurried from a two-story cookhouse connected top and bottom to the main dwelling by lattice-covered walkways. She wiped her hands on her apron as she came.

"Missy, Ida, so good to have you home safe." The cook inclined her head almost reverentially more in Ida's direction than toward where Miranda stood.

"Matilda, prepare us a cold meal quickly and a basket of provisions. Ponce, ask our driver to hitch some mules to a wagon and bring them round. We'll need another to fetch our trunks and Captain Fulton from the dock. Two wagons, Ponce," Miranda said, making herself clear to him by holding up two fingers. "Come, Jason, I will show you my home while we wait."

Jason, she'd said his name again, forgetting all formality. He followed Miranda up the outside stairs just as he'd said he'd follow her anywhere. Below them, Ida and the cook conferred with their heads close together.

Miranda showed him into a small parlor expensively decorated with blue-and-white china from the orient and scented with a potpourri of roses, cinnamon, and orange peel sitting in a bowl on a round, gilded table. She offered him a seat on a white and gold-framed settee covered in pale green brocade. Over a fireplace with a mantel of blue-veined white marble hung a portrait of a young woman who could have been Miri if she hadn't been wearing the clothes and hairstyle of the previous century. A dark-haired boy of about six stood in the crook of her arm while a younger lad with a head of light curls and dressed in a blue velvet suit played with a spotted puppy at their feet. Heavy draperies of the same green brocade edged in golden fringe covered the long windows and doors, floor to ceiling. Miranda drew the cloth behind gilded tiebacks and threw open the doors on both sides of the room.

"There, now we have some air and light. During the summers, we must keep the rooms in shade during the day or roast." She moved around the room, admitting the sunshine and breeze and pushing out the dark and stuffiness as she opened the curtains.

"If you will excuse me, I will take a moment to set myself to rights. Please, take an armchair if you would be more comfortable. I will only be a minute." She uttered the words of a perfect hostess.

Miranda slipped into a side room. Jason caught a brief glimpse of a high bed draped with mosquito netting and canopied and curtained by white fabric printed with colorful flowers and fanciful butterflies. The door clicked shut behind her. He had no desire to rest and a great one to follow her into her airy boudoir. Instead, he paced to the far side of the parlor and opened that door.

A long table of polished rosewood filled the dining room, along with twelve graceful chairs and a matching sideboard ornamented above by a seascape that could have been painted by Turner. A small crystal chandelier tinkled in the wind from the open parlor door. He moved to the far side of the room, where more brocaded curtains blocked the view, and drew them aside to disclose another door to the upper gallery and a bank of windows looking out over cotton fields that spread to the far end of the island. This isle, this lovely home, could have been his if he'd had the courage to propose to the lady he still loved.

Miranda must have read his thoughts because she said from behind him, "I suppose Ariel Island seems paltry compared to Bellevue Hall. The house is very small. The entire bottom floor houses the stores for the plantation, and of course, it can be easily defended if we are attacked by pirates or Spaniards or the English, whoever wants to take the islands from the United States at the moment. They lurk just south of here in Florida."

"No, I find the island to be beautiful and mystical, much like its mistress." She did not smile at his delicate compliment.

"Are you truly troubled by pirates?" He imagined himself defending Miranda from a crew of ruffians, shooting down half and dueling to the death with some bearded captain.

"No, the Navy has taken care of most of them. Besides, I suspect my father has always been on good terms with the corsairs. He dealt heavily in contraband goods during the embargo. Anything that turns a profit, you know. I thought we would dine outside, since the day is pleasant."

She had brushed her long hair and tied it with a ribbon again. Her pale fresh dress hung in diaphanous folds from her shoulders and tied under her bodice with a pink ribbon threaded through eyelet lace. She was his Miri again, not that cold, stiff, formal woman Pandora had turned her into on the ship. Now that he knew Panny was safe, he felt some resentment toward his sister.

They retreated through the parlor where Jason pointed to a portrait. "Your mother and brothers, I presume? You resemble her, a lovely woman."

"She was a strong mountain girl and, as you can see, had no trouble producing children. My father took her north on a trip to New York City, where she contracted the lung disease that killed her. Cities, cold and damp, all pernicious."

Was she casting aspersions on London, on his beloved England? He no longer understood her.

They went out onto the verandah again. A linen cloth had been thrown over a table aged gray by the salt air. Four simple rush-seated chairs sat around it. A young black woman dressed in indigo blue and a frosty white apron and cap set full plates on the table. The food covered the willow pattern of the china with its abundance. Steam rose from a basket covered by a napkin. The servant poured two stemmed glasses full of lemonade. Jason held Miranda's chair for her to settle, then he sat himself.

"Matilda say the food was ready when you come and hot is better," the maid announced with a final curtsy before she went to the stairs.

"Tell Matilda I am happy to be eating her cooking again," Miranda said as she picked up her fork and dug it into a mound of rice and beans.

Next to that sat a pile of greens cooked with small cubes of turnips. Miranda offered the basket to Jason. He removed a piece of cornbread baked into the shape of a cob and placed it next to the thick slab of ham Miranda's dinner lacked.

"In England, we feed maize and turnips to the cattle," he said and immediately regretted his words as he watched Miri's face wash with red.

"I know you are used to finer fare. Matilda was preparing food for the hands, but we often eat the same. I will ask her to prepare something else for you."

"No, no, I didn't mean to criticize. I was making conversation. I mean, I am having an adventure and would love to try the indigenous foods." He stuffed his mouth with greens, swallowed and tried his corn stick.

"Good, very good." He cut off a bite of ham and used it to get the taste of the greens out of his mouth, then followed that up with a gulp of lemonade. "These beans, delicious."

"Black-eyed peas, we call them. We have orange and lemon groves and never lack for citrus."

"How wonderful," he said, wondering how they could be exchanging such stilted, formal words when they had danced on the beach at Brighton and eaten fried fish out of newspaper cones together. When the clomp of boots sounded on the steps, he was almost grateful.

Captain Fulton took a seat at the table. The maid followed with his plate.

"Greens, how I crave them after a month at sea. Ah, food that reminds me of home. What a peculiar fog bank lies on the edge of the island. No matter, this breeze should move it away."

"We've had good news, Captain. Ponce has seen Daniel and Lady Pandora stranded on Horseshoe Beach. We will go to fetch them shortly."

"Take care you don't fall off the edge of Ariel in that fog." Fulton laughed to show he jested. "My men are filling the barrels from your cisterns and Ida has sent the coffee beans along. Are you sure I can't tempt you to look at my wares, some of the first from England since the war ended?"

"Not at this time of crisis for us. Do stop at Caliban and show them to Roger's wife. She loves her luxuries. Here comes the wagon. Lord Longleigh, are you finished with your meal?"

He'd made a good show of trying everything on his plate, but still he'd become Lord Longleigh again. "Yes, let's go rescue our siblings. Captain, if you will excuse us."

"Go, please. Miranda, could you send up more greens?"

"Certainly. No one makes better than Matilda."

Ponce and Ida rode in the back of a wagon well-stocked with provisions and blankets. A driver held the reins of two red mules. Scant room remained on the front seat for Miranda and Jason.

"Here, let me drive. Your man must have other chores to do," Jason offered.

"Are you familiar with the southern mule, Lord Longleigh?" Miranda asked.

"Certainly not much different from horses. I am quite adept at driving."

"Then by all means."

He held out a hand to help Miranda mount to the seat, then climbed aboard and claimed the ribbons. He slapped reins against the back of the sturdy red mules. Both turned their heads to glare at this stranger who presumed to rule them. Their regular driver took off his battered straw hat and swatted the nearest rump. "Git on now."

The mules set off at a leisurely pace as if they were going on a picnic instead of a rescue mission. Jason called to them to go faster. They ignored him. He considered using the whip mounted on the box but knew he would sink in Miranda's estimate if he did. Slowly, they advanced along the palm alley that continued on the other side of the house and ran toward the bank of fog. Eventually, they did arrive, but the red mules would go no further. They balked as soon as their noses touched the mist. One simply sat down in the traces. Both rolled their eyes and tossed their heads.

"Very well then. We must walk the rest of the way. What lies ahead, Miss Clary?"

"A grove of oaks, then the road that runs around the island and a drop off to the beach."

"Seems straightforward enough. Allow me to go ahead."

Jason got down and strode into the fog. One step in and all behind him vanished. He took two steps ahead and collided with the stout trunk of a tree. The low branches raked his hair. Several side steps and he bashed into another trunk. Finally, he cupped his hands and shouted, "Panny, Daniel, where are you?"

Birds with a cry like a rusty pump handle called back, but he heard nothing else. From behind, Miranda cried out, "Jason, please come back!"

He twirled, not knowing which way to go.

"Here, here, to me!"

Two small hands reached into the fog for him. He clung to them like a lifeline and emerged back into the sunshine of a perfectly normal day. Miri's distress showed plainly on her face. He kissed her palms. "My savior."

"Oh, you have injured yourself again." She produced a hankie and dabbed at a scratch on his hairline. "You disappeared completely."

Ida stood next to her. "Mami Wata is not ready to release them. Ponce took fresh supplies to the hut recently. He planned to watch there for turtles coming ashore tonight. He said someone had started a fire and slept on his bedding, and then he saw the people on the beach and the fog descending. They will be well enough until the fog lifts."

"More turtles come tonight, Missy. Do we camp on South Beach?" Ponce asked eagerly.

"I believe so, since we can do nothing else here. I would like you to see the turtles nest, Lord Longleigh, before you leave me forever. Then, you might understand me better."

Forever. How could he be without her forever?

Nineteen

Pandora stood at the entrance to the wigwam and listened to the rusty cries of the jay birds and the incessant drip of moisture from the oak leaves. Rivulets coursed down the palmetto leaves covering the hut and beaded on the grass mat she held aside. The thick fog enveloped them like biological specimens packed in cotton wool. She strained to hear the call again. Nothing. She could have sworn someone summoned her a moment ago.

"Come back inside. Have some more roasted oysters," Daniel said, in that enticing voice of his.

He'd placed the rough shells at the edge of the fire until the oysters popped open, ready to eat. What's more, someone had come to the hut while they were on the beach and left fresh water and a sack of small, sweet oranges. She went to sit beside him on the pallet.

"I thought I heard someone calling us. We should make an attempt to find our way to the house. We have responsibilities to attend to, people to look after—if they survived the storm."

"As I am sure they did with Ida aboard. Lie down. Rest. We'll have a long walk when the fog lifts."

"Can we not try to find our way with a stick as the blind do?"

"The road may have washed out in the storm. There are bogs on the island as well. Sections of the bluff collapse after heavy rains. We had best stay where we are."

"It worries me that someone might have seen us on the beach."

"Only Ponce, I assure you, restocking the place for a turtle watch. He will have told someone where we can be found and that we are well."

Pandora licked her lips and tasted the salt of the oysters, the sticky juice of the oranges. Daniel lowered his mouth to hers and added the taste of himself.

"Lie down, my Raven. Do not fly away. Let me ease you."

"We cannot do that. I must collect Jason and take him home. My family will be relying on my good sense in the matter."

"Not what I meant. Lie down and roll over. I will rub your back."

What could it hurt? An intimate service to be sure, but just between the two of them locked in this enchanted place. He began to stroke her back, using his broad, strong thumbs against her shoulders. He had magic in his hands. Magic. She fell asleep as heavily as any bewitched princess.

~ * ~

The pavilion set up on the south beach had been outfitted as lavishly as any pasha's tent. Ida had the servants unroll oriental carpets on the sand and heap pillows of brightly colored silk and light cotton throws in the corners, should anyone want to rest until the turtles came. Candles ensconced in hurricane glasses burned at either end of a long table and lanterns hung from the frame above a feast. Miranda pointed out various delicacies to her guest.

The table held beakers of wine, sparkling glass pitchers of lemon and orangeade, two golden goblets, a porcelain bowl of strawberries fresh from the garden and another of oranges that had been stored away at their peak. A cold roasted fowl sat beneath a heavy cover, and a napkin sheltered a plate of the thick, white baked rounds the locals called biscuits. A pot of honey stood nearby along with butter and a preserve of figs. Small containers held the indigenous nuts: pecans, salty and roasted or glazed with sugar. A fat Dutch cheese ensconced in red wax squatted ready to be served on a cutting board.

They had wrung, plucked and roasted the chicken for him, of course. The rest of the refreshments were designed for Miranda's tastes. All seemed destined to be eaten with the fingers, as no utensils other than the butter and cheese knives and a jam spoon had been provided. Jason selected a large cushion and sat upon it cross-legged. He supposed chairs would sink in the sand.

Outside the tent, Miranda conferred with Ida. Jason heard her soft voice rise. While Pandora had goaded Miri to adopt a new authority, he'd never known her to speak harshly to Ida before tonight. He leaned closer to the draped wall, but could not make out their words. No matter of his. For the moment, he felt rather like a sheik waiting for his chosen concubine to arrive.

She came to him barefooted and simply dressed in plain white cotton tied with a red sash, a matching ribbon tying back her hair, her notebook and pencil in one hand, her slippers in another. She placed the shoes beneath the table.

"They only get wet and filled with sand," Miranda said. "Please eat if you want. The turtles prefer to nest at night, maybe to avoid the heat of the sun, perhaps to hide from predators. We could have a very long wait, and there is no guarantee any will arrive."

"Waiting in such luxury will not be a hardship. Waiting in *your* company will be a pleasure." Jason rose, picked a strawberry up by its stem and offered it to her.

"Thank you, but you need not pay me hollow compliments." Still, she accepted the bright red berry, rolled it in her hands and finally ate.

Jason did not want to attack the fowl in her presence, but his appetite waxed. He hadn't done justice to their earlier dinner, strange as it was. He cracked the seal of wax on the Dutch cheese and cut a wedge, put strawberries on his plate and helped himself to one of the biscuits, which was not sweet at all. It tasted far better slathered with butter and syrupy preserved figs. The wine he poured ran like liquid rubies into the golden goblet with a single red stone set in the side. Some pirate's loot traded for Eustace Clary's supplies?

"Would you care for some?" He raised the equally ornate beaker.

"I'd rather have the orangeade in the pitcher, please."

He poured her choice into the other goblet set with a blue stone, surely not a sapphire, but why not? Everything about Ariel Island seemed exotic and enchanting, including his hostess, who fidgeted with nervous energy and barely touched the food. She sat away from him to nibble a buttered biscuit oozing honey down its sides.

They had finished their meal in a silence suddenly broken by Ponce shouting out, "Two turtles coming, Missy! Two!"

Miranda came to life, grabbing a lantern and her notebook and rushing from the tent. Jason followed after taking another lantern to find his way. Two low, bulky forms struggled up the slight incline of the beach and through the debris line left by the tide. They pushed onward to the loose dry sand near the low bluff with its scattered trees and vines and began to dig.

"Loggerheads ten and twenty-two. See, I've painted the numbers on their shells," Miranda whispered. "Let's not disturb them with our lamps until they begin to lay. Ponce, go watch the other beach for more to arrive."

Quietly, they waited in the moonlight. A breeze sprang up from the south and rippled the cloth sides of the pavilion with its warm breath, lifted Miranda's hair and played with her curls. The turtles dug their nests and began to produce their eggs. Kneeling in the sand next to the reddish-brown carapaces, Miranda counted one nest and Jason the other—one hundred sixteen here, one hundred twenty there. The females covered their nests and began the laborious trek back to the sea. Miranda placed markers near the disturbed sand.

"Did you see their tears, Jason? Did you see?"

"I did. I don't believe I will ever crave turtle soup again. But I could use another cup of that wine. Counting eggs is thirsty work."

"Stay a moment. I'm not ready to go back to the tent. The eggs will hatch in about sixty-five days. I wish you could see that. The babies are so adorable, and we must scare off the raccoons and the seabirds that would eat them on their way to the sea. Ponce and I race around the beach waving our arms. It's great fun. But you will not be here." She paused.

Again, a pregnant pause, again that choking feeling—not because he feared the responsibilities of marriage or the jeopardy a wife faced in childbirth, but because he could not bear the thought of life without Miranda. She must despise him for his cowardice in not making an offer for her, for his total lack of honor. He must try again to say the words that would make her his forever, even if she laughed in his face and told him to leave her island. Wine, he needed more wine. Now.

"Let's go back to the pavilion, have some drink, talk."

"I suppose that is what we must do then."

She picked up her lantern and led the way, a slim white figure holding a fairy light as if she would lead him to a magical kingdom under a hill. Instead, they entered the enchanting pavilion. Ida had been at work while they watched the turtles. Small dishes of chocolates, sesame sweets, and a butterscotch-colored candy enrobing more pecans sat before the two goblets filled to the brim with the fine red wine. Plump pallets covered in white linens awaited their rest.

Jason reached for the goblet bearing the red stone. Miranda covered it with her hand. He shrugged and tried to lift the other.

"Not that one either. Don't drink from these cups. Have the orangeade, if you thirst."

"What? Is it drugged like the tisane I drank on the ship, the potion that rendered me unable to help in the storm, to possibly save my sister?"

Miranda looked at him helplessly mute for a moment before Ponce again cried out, "Stella come, Missy! Next beach over."

"Stella is back. She did not arrive last spring and I feared she had ended her life in some soup pot. She often vanishes for several years, then returns to nest on our beaches, sometimes half a dozen times. She's a leatherback like Half Moon. Perhaps they met and mated in the calm Sargasso Sea while we crossed the ocean."

"Yes, perhaps. You've mentioned her before. A leatherback, not my favorite breed."

She laughed, a sound like small bells chiming. This was his Miri, alight with joy in her turtles, not some sorceress intent on seducing him with aphrodisiac-laced drinks. He took her offered hand, and they raced from the tent across the long beach, past the new nests to the pile of rocks forming a breakwater where Ponce stood shouting. Jason helped her scale the slippery stones and lifted her down the other side. Far down the next stretch of sand, the moonlight revealed an antediluvian form humping its way from the surf and entirely intent on acting upon ancient urges. Stella.

~ * ~

Pandora awoke with Daniel molded to her back, one of his large hands resting possessively on her breast. He slept heavily, but something had disturbed her rest. She removed the hand and slipped from the pallet. Lifting the mat at the door, she saw the fog being ripped to shreds by a wind from the south. It sang through the gaps in the palmetto leaves sheltering them. The oak grove stood revealed but ominously dark. The pale ribbon of the road running around the island glimmered in the light of the moon. She heard a shout, followed by laughter borne on the breeze.

Going to Daniel, she shook him. "Wake up, wake up, you old Wooly Goat. I hear voices again."

Groggy, he said, "Just the wind in the oaks most likely, but it might blow the fog away."

"It has. Come see."

He arose, stretched and went to look. "So, the fog is gone, but night has come. We should wait until morning and not go stumbling in the dark."

"Do you love this place so much? Hurry, people are searching for us."

"It's not the place I love. Very well, let me get my boots on, and you must wear my stockings to protect your feet. I'd suggest you wrap in a blanket again in case we do come across someone."

He looked meaningfully at her tattered gown as he pulled on his stiff, salt-encrusted boots. She rolled his stockings up her calves and turned them over several times at the top to make them fit her slimmer thighs. Daniel watched, not gentleman enough to turn his back. Oh, what did the proprieties matter now? He'd seen more of her than her limbs and had not pressed himself on her. Well, he had, but not in *that* way. Could it be she was not attractive enough with her wild black hair and tinted skin? Ravens were not pretty birds.

She stood wrapped in the blanket. They started out along the path to the south with the moon showing the way. If she tripped over a vine growing across the road, Daniel, always there to prevent a fall, caught her elbow. The bluff they walked sloped downward toward another beach. A side path led to the water and also to a curious structure tucked into the space where the lane merged with the sand. The white pavilion glowed with inner lantern light and the breeze lifted the entry flap enticingly.

"What is that?"

"No one is searching for us. This is the tent Miranda uses when she is watching for turtles. Ida stocks it with refreshments and a pallet for her to rest upon. Ponce keeps guard and calls out if he sights any of the beasts. You probably heard his voice."

"Marvelous. We have only to wait there to be discovered. Do you suppose Miranda has anything to drink? All those oysters have left me thirsty."

Pandora darted down the lesser path with Daniel following more slowly. She entered the tent, spied the full goblets, raised one to her lips and drained it before her companion joined her.

"Somewhat fancier than usual," Daniel remarked. He raised the goblet studded with the blue stone and took a sip. "My father's best Burgundy. He will not be pleased when he gets home and counts his bottles. I've never known Miranda to drink anything but fruit juices when she is doing her science. She rarely touches wine."

"Burgundy, real Burgundy. How did you manage to get your hands on that?"

"We are not at war with France—while the English are after Napoleon again."

"Well, we simply can't let Nappy run amok, now can we?" Pandora lifted the lid of the covered tray. "A chicken. Aha! She must have Jason with her." She ripped off a leg and began to eat.

"Could be intended for Ponce, but he usually eats the same as Miranda. And all these sweets. Ida usually limits what Ponce can have, as he will make himself sick, just like a child."

"They are very tempting." Pandora selected a chocolate, soft and melting in the warm night, its center a sweet white cream, and popped it into her mouth. She licked the residue from her thumb and forefinger and returned to eating the chicken leg.

"I cannot say you are a dainty eater, Lady Pandora," Daniel remarked, watching her over the rim of his cup.

"Because I am suddenly ravenous. The Raven is ravenous. But I love the way you say my name, the way you draw it out." She withdrew the wooden spool used to serve the honey from its pot and dribbled some on her tongue. "Now I am honey-tongued, too. Want to taste?"

She cast her blanket aside and stumbled toward Daniel, put her lips to his and worked her tongue inside his mouth. There, women could do this, too. No need to wait for the man to begin. The chicken leg dropped from her fingers. She needed them free to run through his side whiskers and hold his face close to hers.

When he paused for breath, Daniel said, "I think someone drank their Burgundy a little too quickly."

"Yet, I still thirst. I need some more." Pandora refilled her cup and topped off Daniel's, though his was still half full. He quaffed nearly half again, and she drank deeply, though not so fast. She began to feel very warm and as swollen as a bud in May down there between her legs. She waved a hand before her face.

"I am sweltering, Daniel. We should go bathe in the sea again."

"Not a good idea at night, Pandora. You've only had one swimming lesson and..."

~ * ~

She flitted from the tent. He sat on a cushion to struggle with his stiff boots again and the other annoying stiffness in his pants that the kiss had caused. She would drown if he didn't follow immediately. He dashed after her and caught the remains of her gown full in his face as she released the scraps to the wind. He tossed it aside in time to see her disappear in the surf, her nicely rounded buttocks accented with two dimples in the small of her back illuminated by the light of the moon.

Daniel followed the markers made by his discarded stockings and other bits of torn undergarments until his feet were washed by the foam. Where was she? Had a riptide seized her because he had not come to claim her fast enough?

"Pandora," he cried out.

"Here I am!" She popped up from where she waited crouched down in the water, her dark hair across her face like a mask. She threw her glistening black locks over her shoulders and raised her arms to the moon. "Come get me, Wooly Goat."

She stood only knee deep in the sea. The shallow water roiled around her. The moon shone on her full breasts, the brown tips shiny with sea water, a droplet caught on the end of each one. Oh, how he wanted to lick them off. He felt warm himself, no, hot, burning, totally without restraint for the first time since he'd met Pandora Longleigh. He stripped off the remains of his shirt and tossed it away.

"Let's see how hairy you really are, Wooly Goat," she taunted.

What a superb idea. He unbuttoned his trousers and pulled them down with his drawers, stepped out, and raised his own arms to the moon. He knew the mat of curls on his chest continued down in a thick V to his crotch where a heavy bush housed his penis. The curls continued lightly down his legs and across his backside, but his back was bare of hair—for which he'd always been grateful. Right now, those curls between his legs hid nothing. He had an erection large enough to be the envy of any satyr. He waited for the sensible and virginal Lady Pandora Longleigh to cringe at the sight of him— or laugh.

Instead, she splashed water his way and opened her arms for him. "Come to me, my Wooly Goat."

His mind felt wooly, too, all his thoughts gathered in the bulging head of his shaft. Was she a nymph made of dark sea water, a raven that would transform and take flight when he reached her, an Indian princess who bathed in the sea without shame, or that goddess Ida revered, the Mami Wata who seduced men by the water's edge? Pandora Longleigh might be any or all of those creatures tonight. He plunged into the ocean and drew her out further when she tried to jump into his arms and lock her legs around his waist as if she intended to impale herself upon him without any further delay.

The water gave her buoyancy, and she leaned back on his supporting arms and tried again, not succeeding. "Please," she begged.

"Rest on the water, my Raven, my Indian maiden, my goddess." He supported her with one hand and used the broad thumb of the other to rub the small, throbbing peak hidden in the folds clothed in silky black between her legs.

She writhed and cried, "Too much, too much," but he did not relent until she mouthed another kind of cry, the one he wanted to hear, his cue to bury himself to the hilt inside of her. Her legs floated free, but he held her up and continued his drive to fruition like any other monster of the deep. She might have called out again, but the sound was overcome by his bellow, not a goat but a bull from the sea.

For a while afterwards, he held her against his chest where she burrowed content and let the waves wash them. Then, he carried her up the beach to the glowing pavilion where they could dry themselves, lie on fresh linens and repeat the act again.

~ * ~

Age was catching up with her. Ida came out of her doze. She had intended to stay awake all night to make sure everything went well this time: that Ponce did not interfere, that Jason Longleigh did not do any real harm to Miranda once the potion took effect. After he'd taken Miri's maidenhead, she planned to burst into the tent and shame him into marrying her *bébé*, who wanted this man so badly the protective spell had shattered. Instead, she'd made herself too comfortable in the back of the wagon parked deep among the live oaks rimming the island and slept. Now she heard the cries others might mistake for seabirds calling or a bull on the loose. No, these sounds came from a woman in rapture and a man who had spent his seed.

Her legs had stiffened, but Ida got down and used a stick to make her way to the road, then to the side path leading to the pavilion. She tried to go quietly, but soon realized the lovers inside the tent would not have noticed the bluff caving in on them, they were making so much noise.

"Again, my Wooly Goat, my bull, my god of the sea!"

"I adore you, my Raven, my princess, my goddess!"

Raven? No one would look at the fair Miranda and call her that. From what Ida had seen of Jason Longleigh, he was dark and sleek, not wooly at all. She hesitated to raise the flap of the tent. What had Mami Wata done now in return for a purple silk scarf, a bottle of perfume, and some fragrant herbs?

Twenty

The female leatherback named Stella burped and sighed. Laying eggs amounted to very hard work. She had not taken to Jason, but allowed Miranda to stroke her back and give comfort in her travail. Jason instead sat at her hind end and counted the eggs as they plopped into the hole.

"Ninety-five." The turtle belched again. "She hasn't very good manners," he joked.

Miranda took offense. "Nor would you if giving birth."

"I know. I spoke too lightly of a serious matter. Speaking of which..."

"Yes, the wine was drugged. I confess." By the light of the lantern, Miranda's cheeks shone as pink as the star-shaped mark on the turtle's head.

"Ninety-six," was all Jason could think to say as another egg emerged and dropped.

"Mammy Ida asked if I still wanted you. I said, 'Yes, with all my heart.' She said she would put a potion in the wine and fill the cups. I was to drink lightly but allow you to finish yours. She claimed I would feel warm and yielding, and you would be filled with great ardor—enough to consummate our love. In the morning, your Longleigh honor would compel you to marry me."

"Ninety-seven. Why did you relent?'

"Oh, Jason. If I cannot bear to see turtles kept in a tub, how could I trap and cage a man I would love forever? I know you think I am too eccentric and weak to fulfill the role of a wife. I've been to Bellevue, seen where you were raised, the fine foods you eat. My island must seem insignificant to you, not a tempting dowry at all."

"Not so! I will never come into Bellevue. This is a small and perfect paradise, especially because you dwell here. I could even learn to love greens."

There, she smiled through her tears. Another egg fell into the nest.

"Don't lose count."

"Ninety-eight. The fault is all mine. I feared responsibility and the hazard of losing you in childbirth, but living without you would be far worse. I never stopped loving you. Since I am already on my knees in the sand—though at the rear end of a turtle—Miranda Clary, will you marry me? Ninety-nine."

A strange cry rent the air. A bellow followed.

"Drat it, the bull has gotten out again and is bothering the cows in the salt meadow. They've all calved recently and have no use for him."

"Miranda, please, have you any use for me?"

"Of course, I do—as my husband."

She leaned over the turtle's broad back and placed a kiss sweet as honey on his lips. Jason half expected Ida to emerge from the shadows, pull them apart and hustle them off to the nearest preacher, but Stella took the woman's place by hissing before she emitted another egg.

"One hundred!" they said in unison.

~ * ~

Ida saw them strolling hand in hand across the beach. They paused now and then to share a chaste kiss, their lanterns held aside. Once, they stopped to pick up a piece of white cloth and laughed when they held it up, a woman's tattered undergarment. Obviously, neither Miranda nor Jason had partaken of the potion. When the young couple noticed her, they, so full of youth and love, broke into a run.

Unable to contain herself, Miranda shouted, "Stella laid one hundred eggs, and I am to be a bride. Mammy Ida, he said the words and I have accepted!"

"Hush, hush." Ida put a dark finger to her broad lips.

"But why? I want to sing and dance and celebrate."

Miranda and Jason joined both hands and whirled in a circle, their lanterns flashing by time and again, the pouch containing the notebook bouncing on her hip. A deep groan emerged from the tent followed by a woman's gusty sigh. They stopped in mid-romp.

"Who is in there? Not Ponce?" Miranda's concern showed in her voice.

"No, I told him he had done well, to go to the wagon and rest. I left some sweets for him there."

"Some of our people out in the night? I know they do roam after dark sometimes. I've heard their drums since I was a child."

"No, not them. We should not enter. Let's hitch the mules and return to the house. We have moonlight enough to find our way. Mastah Lord Jason may sleep in your mother's room."

"But who?" Jason asked.

"More, more, more, my beloved Daniel," a female voice urged inside the tent.

"Pandora, my sister Pandora?"

For once Ida was not quick enough to stop him. Jason charged the entry and skidded to a stop just inside the pavilion.

"Don't come in here, Miranda." But she was already by his side. She covered her eyes, then peeked out. Ida, shaking her turbaned head, joined them. Six wide eyes beheld the scene.

Stretched out in splendor, breasts exposed, Pandora Longleigh lounged on the long, white pallet. Daniel Clary, resting on an elbow, dangled a strawberry over her lips. She sucked it from his fingers. Both of their faces were smeared with bits of red fruit and dark chocolate, especially around the mouth. Pandora's tanned breasts appeared to be coated in something golden and sticky that also matted the hair on Daniel's chest. Primly, he drew up the blanket covering them to the neck and fell back, arms behind his head.

"Oh look, Panny, we have guests. So sorry, the wine is all gone."

"All gone," his lover echoed.

Jason moved to loom above them. He made a motion to pull Daniel from the covers but thought better of it. Instead, he struck his fiancée's brother across the face.

"You have debauched Pandora. You will marry my sister or die!"

Daniel rubbed his jaw. "No need to get angry. I want to marry my Lady Pandora. We shall live in a wigwam by the sea and survive on oysters and oranges."

Agreeing, Pandora nodded. "And chocolate and strawberries, honey, and the finest of Burgundies." She giggled and snuggled into his hairy chest.

"And who do you think will pay for all that? How do you propose to support my sister in her accustomed style? She cannot abide slavery."

"I have agreed to free the only slave I own. Now nothing stands in our way. We will bathe in the sea and exist on love. Isn't that right, my goddess?"

"You are always right, Daniel. But please, help yourselves to the feast. No sense in having the chicken and those odd biscuits go to waste."

Pandora gestured to the table like the best of hostesses. The blanket slipped. Daniel pulled it up again as if he were hiding secret treasures.

"If I had a weapon, I would kill him right now." Jason clenched his fist, but Miranda opened it and kissed his palm.

"Think, Jason, we could all live here and swim in the sea and enjoy the bounty of the island."

"Life is not as simple as that. We all have serious responsibilities to fulfill. They might have conceived a child. Dear God, how will I explain that to the duke and duchess?"

"Mastah Lord Jason," Ida intervened, "I have said before my potions and spells cannot make anyone do what they do not wish to do. This would have happened eventually—maybe not in this way—but Lady Pandora and Mastah Daniel have always been drawn to each other, I sense. Come, let's coax them to the wagon and back to the house."

Jason was able to raise Daniel high enough for Ida to wrap the sheet from the other pallet around him while Miranda shoved the boots onto his feet. With Daniel's arm slung across his shoulders, he tried to walk the man from the tent, but Daniel turned back.

"Look at me, Panny. I am Antony and you are Cleopatra. *A horse! a horse! my kingdom for a horse!*"

"Wrong play, brother," Miranda told him. "Now shoo while we make Lady Pandora decent."

"I don't want to be decent. I want to be with Daniel," Pandora proclaimed.

"Then let's knot this blanket over your chest. Yes, you may take the strawberries. Up we go. Lean on Ida now."

The astonishing procession made their way up the path and over to the wagon with Pandora strewing strawberries along the way. Both of the drugged parties crawled into the back of the vehicle willingly and curled together as if they'd done it before with one of Daniel's big hands on Pandora's breast. Her brother removed it, but the hand crept back.

The mules refused to obey Lord Longleigh, so Ponce and Ida led them by the bridle. Ponce asked his mother, "Man-woman games?"

"Yes, son."

"Knew it. I was right. Knew it," Ponce answered in a sing-song voice.

Miranda looked back from her seat at the entwined couple. "They look so very happy. Do you think—?"

"We shall be even happier—and very soon," Jason promised her.

Twenty-one

Pandora winced as Ida drew the comb through her straight, raven hair and worked out another snag. With the lightest of touches, Miranda rubbed salve on the cuts and abrasions and bruises she'd acquired in the storm—and some that had come after, but Miri did not need to know. It soothed a burning red mark on her neck and another high on her breast. She could see them clearly in the gilt-framed oval of the mirror hung over Miranda's dressing table.

Miranda offered her the small pot. "Perhaps you have other areas that need attention and would rather tend to them yourself."

Of course, she did. Both of the women would have noticed when they bathed her like a nurse does an infant in a tub of warm water, dried her, lowered a loose night shift over her head and put her to bed next to Miranda, the mosquito netting tucked in all around them last evening. She raised the shift discreetly and rubbed the salve on the worst areas between her thighs. After wiping her fingers on a piece of linen embroidered with the butterflies that seemed to be the motif of the room, she raised the tin cup of black coffee to her dry mouth again. Her shaking hands could not be trusted with fine china for the moment, and oh, the headache that beat against her brow every time Ida teased out another knot.

"You sure you don't want a tisane for your pains, Lady Pandora?" Ida asked again.

"No! No potions, no drugs. You must realize neither Daniel nor I were in our right minds last night. He should not be held to any promises he made. After all, no one knows what happened on this island but us. We should proceed as before. I will take Jason home to grow up. Perhaps this adventure will settle him with no lasting harm done to you, Miranda."

Miri smiled, her face all aglow. "But, Panny, last night Jason asked for my hand in marriage as we counted Stella's eggs. He's already spoken to Captain Fulton about taking us over to Caliban in the morning. We are to have a double wedding. You will be my sister twice over since Daniel said he is willing. We still have your rose-colored gown which is so becoming. The early roses have opened, and my mother cultivated one the exact shade of the silk flower on the bodice. We could twine some in your hair. I will wear white and braid a chaplet of mock orange and tiny white rosebuds for mine. Roger and his wife shall welcome you to our family and have a preacher, a feast, and a frolic waiting. Word was sent ahead while you slept."

"Miranda, stop!" Pandora looked around the room, where all the light draperies had been drawn out of deference to the sensitivity of her eyes. "How long have I slept?"

"Why, all day, and Jason has taken charge in the most exciting ways. If you feel well enough, we will have supper on the verandah shortly."

"Jason in charge? Miri, you must go at once and tell him I release Daniel from his promise. An intoxicated man cannot be held accountable. They both study the law and know this must be true."

"But why?"

"Just go now before things get any more out of hand."

~ * ~

Jason rapped sharply on the door of Mrs. Clary's former chamber and entered before Daniel could answer. He caught the man standing in a shallow tin tub behind a screen made to protect the modesty of a small woman. Daniel's head and shoulders rose above it. His hair, side whiskers, and three days' beard foamed with soapy bubbles as did the hair on his chest from which he scrubbed the residue of honey. No doubt where Panny had gotten those burns on her throat and chest. His insides cringed when he thought of it. His own beard had grown in thin and silky during their voyage. Miranda claimed it tickled, but he should consider shaving it off before their wedding night out of consideration for her delicate skin.

"Longleigh," Daniel said. "Pull up a chair while I make myself presentable."

He did, sitting on a spindly thing with bowed mahogany legs and no arms and thus meant for a lady with full skirts. Daniel raised a pitcher from a stand and poured the water over his head, shaking himself afterwards like a wet hound. He began to towel dry, turning his back to Jason. The deep scratches high on his back and a bite mark on his shoulder became clearly visible. Familiar enough with the marks of lust, Jason entertained no notion that Pandora had been trying to fight off the man.

Wearing his drawers and a loose, open shirt, Daniel emerged from behind the screen. As he whipped up more soap in a cup with a shaving brush, he asked, "Afraid I will run off now that I'm conscious?"

"No, I believe you do have a sense of honor and want to do right by Pandora. You were concerned enough about your own sister."

"Thank you for that." Daniel soaped his chin, then drew a razor from the case on the shaving stand. Deftly, he sliced off foam and beard, cleanly delineating his side whiskers. Wiping his face dry, he trimmed those whiskers with a tiny pair of scissors taken from a sewing basket on top of the dresser. Throwing open an armoire, he sorted through a stack of clothes until he found a pair of buff trousers and a waistcoat to his liking. He selected a plain neckcloth from a drawer and hung it around his neck as he buttoned up shirt and pants.

"Haven't you a valet?" Jason asked, putting off the announcement he was reluctant to make.

"I have a body servant who remained behind with Roger. My daddy was sure he'd run off to Europe. I plan to free him as a gift to Pandora. Fortunately, I always leave some clothing here for when I visit Miranda and can dress myself, unlike you English lords."

That stung. "I did well enough on the ship and maintain my own quarters in London."

"I think Pandora and I took care of you on the ship because you were too sunk in misery to do it yourself." Daniel sat to pull on his boots, polished but still in sad condition from their soaking. He shrugged into a loose brown coat that reached his hips and removed a straw planter's hat with a wide black band from a rack.

"There now, do I look like a bridegroom?"

"Pandora has released you from any obligation to her. But I intend to marry Miranda regardless. I have asked for her hand, and she has accepted. In the absence of your father, I ask for your blessing."

"Did Ida poison you, too, to get your courage up?"

"No, I realized I love your sister more than I love adventure, more than I want to write great poetry, more than..."

"Enough! You have my blessing. Pandora and I figured out we should not have come between you after we were shipwrecked. But why doesn't your sister want me? Last night, she held nothing back. We were joined like the sun and the sea at the horizon."

"I do not want to hear the details—though that is a pretty simile."

"I know I am a commoner, a lawyer, a man who will eventually inherit an island and a parcel of slaves—all manner of things Pandora might hate. But I know she trusts me after our days together. I thought we had come to understand each other." Daniel threw his hat on the bed and paced the room.

"She says you were not in your right mind nor was she. I might point out love and trust are hardly the same emotions."

"I believe I have loved your sister since I first laid eyes on her, but I had the sense to move along slowly, consider her pride and her opinions—instead of running off with her to happy turtle land."

"Ha! Panny would never have eloped with you. She would have skewered you first. Now that she has come to her senses, I will take her home along with my bride. The duke and duchess will understand the circumstances of being marooned momentarily unhinged my sister. The rest need not be mentioned. The Longleighs shall see she is taken care of along with any other unfortunate results."

Despite the implied insult that he could not care for Pandora and that any offspring of his would be considered unfortunate, Daniel stopped pacing. He went to the top dresser drawer, removed a slim wooden box and placed it into the deep pocket of his coat.

"Let me speak to her in private before any decision is reached."

"I have known Pandora all my life and can tell you she is the most hardheaded of my sisters. She never relents. But, be my guest. And Daniel, if she should agree to marry you, you have my blessing."

~ * ~

"I would rather have a tray brought here. I am not up to dining on the verandah," Pandora said, even though Miranda and Ida had persuaded her into clean undergarments and new silk stockings tied up with rose ribbons.

Now they worked on braiding her hair and piling it high on her head. The rose-colored dress, smoothed by an iron, lay waiting on the bed along with a flower Miranda had darted downstairs to pluck from a bush by the kitchen door.

"Daniel wants to see you directly, and he can hardly do that if you remain in your undergarments."

No sense in reminding Miranda that Daniel had seen her in considerably less clothing. Her cheeks warmed to a shade of dusty rose. "Didn't Jason speak to him?"

"Certainly, he did, but Daniel insists. Of course, if you lack the courage to face him after last night, I do understand. The Longleigh honor and bravery belong only to the men. A woman could not be expected to possess those qualities," Miranda insinuated.

Pandora straightened and raised her arms for the lowering of the gown. She suspected Miranda and Ida exchanged winks while she was blinded by the fabric. They fluffed the gauzy netting of the tucker to cover most of her brush burns and bruises and tucked the deep pink rose into her hair.

"Do you need help in walking?" Miranda asked solicitously.

"I am perfectly fine. Tell Daniel I will receive him in the parlor." She stood and made her way into that room, choosing to light in one corner of the settee and leaving space for another to sit. Her legs wobbled a little on the way, but that was understandable after her ordeal. The mirror at the dressing table had revealed her color as high under her dusky skin and her black eyes large and bright with nerves. He must never know that. She folded her shaking hands and waited only a moment before Daniel entered from the other bedroom.

He filled the dainty room with his size, his masculinity. He dressed now as a planter, not in English finery, but she remembered what the clothes covered and saw him still as he stood on the edge of the surf, naked and erect. She had beckoned to him, lured him, that much she recalled. Her eyes drifted shut for a moment. She supposed he would begin with an apology and take away that feeling of feminine power she had experienced. Then, he would say he felt obligated to do his duty by her, thus ruining every moment they had spent together. Head up and refusing to be ashamed, she opened her eyes and looked directly at him.

"Pandora, I have something to offer you."

She expected a ring, an heirloom inherited from his mother or some bauble Miranda had supplied, but the gift came in a narrow wooden box. She opened it and drew from a leather sheath a stiletto, its blade of good steel, its hilt made of an open weave of metal. She hefted it in her hand—nice balance.

"Not as fine as the one claimed by the sea goddess, no jewels at all, but still of good quality. It seems that in exchange, she has given me to you. Now, I know I am a lowly commoner to the Longleighs, but I stand here before you the well-educated son of a wealthy planter. If you would consent to get down off your high horse and listen to me..."

"I can see you did not spend enough time at Bellevue. The Longleighs are so terribly eccentric none of their daughters has married without a scandal of some kind and all are rapturously happy, another oddity. I never thought to be one of them." She held the steel dagger upright, allowing the candlelight to illuminate its blade.

"I did notice your parents care a great deal for one another, unlike mine."

"You do not know the half of it. Our—romantic interlude—would hardly shock them."

"Very well. Moving on. I noticed the scorn your father has for lawyers, and I do plan to practice with a specialty in maritime law. I was very close to hanging up my shingle in Savannah when my father summoned me to go with Miranda. I will never be a planter nor own slaves again once I free Horace."

"Daniel, two of my brothers read the law. Papa was jesting as usual. But you will inherit more slaves." All her nerves had settled. She enjoyed countering his every sentence while holding the stiletto in her hands, all her power returned.

"Long before last night, I considered how I might lift that burden. I believe I could sell my inheritance to my brother before the fact. That would give me the wherewithal to support a family until my law practice grows large enough."

"Have you forgotten we could live quite comfortably on my dowry?"

"Actually, I did. Pandora, I would fight for your causes, emancipation and equity for women. I will take up English law if that will convince you to have me."

She nearly cut herself on the blade as the stiletto fell from her hand. "But you would give up your birthright for me?"

"I don't believe Americans are as entrenched about birthrights as the British. Most of my relatives still make a living selling untaxed liquor up in the hills and these plantations were purchased from the profits of selling slaves—not a very proud heritage. But if ever I betray or harm you in any way, please feel free to drive that dagger into my heart—my Raven, my Indian Princess, my goddess of the sea."

"You do remember and are not revolted by what I did?"

"Hardly. I recall the sight of you standing in the ocean and beckoning to me. After that, yes, the evening blurs. Here, may I tie on the stiletto? I would never want you to be unarmed."

Coyly, she raised her skirts, and he knelt and tied the thongs of the sheath around her calf. "I remember one other moment as the potion wore off. I am certain I heard you say, 'Daniel, you are always right.'"

"Just more proof that you were out of your mind last night. Why, you could not even quote Mr. Shakespeare correctly."

"So you remember also." He looked up at her, his eyes going deep sea green.

"A warning—never expect to hear those words again for the rest of our lives together. Oh, come up here, my Wooly Goat." She ran her fingers through his side whiskers and drew him beside her.

"For the rest of our lives together?"

"Yes, Daniel Clary. Who else would keep me as warm at night in frigid Britain?"

"I suppose I must share a bed again with Jason tonight."

"And I with Miranda, but not for long. I understand Jason has taken charge, and we must marry posthaste."

"Then let him be in charge a little while longer."

He stroked the one unruly lock of her hair that had escaped its pinned captivity and brought his lips to hers.

~ * ~

The palms susurrant in the breeze, the sea thrumming in the distance, Jason Longleigh enjoyed the blue hour just after sunset from the upper gallery. Smoke rose from the chimneys of the small cabins as the hands heated their evening meal. Good scents arose from the kitchen. He leaned his chair back and put his feet on the railing. A bird colored so brightly it caught his attention even in the dim light flitted by. A painted bunting, had to be. He would tell Miranda when she ceased primping in the bedroom. All he desired to make the evening simply perfect was her presence, and perhaps—"

"A cup of Burgundy, Mastah Lord Jason," Ida said.

His feet hit the floor. For a big woman she moved so silently. "Ah, no, I don't believe I will."

"No potions tonight. Do not fear."

She offered the cup again. He accepted. She set the rest of the bottle on a table bedecked for a celebration with fine gold-rimmed china bearing pictures of different birds and crystal, also gold-edged. Lighting the single candles in gilt holders, she lowered the glass covers over them before the breeze could snuff them out.

"The mosquitoes will not bother you tonight." With her face lit from below, Ida resembled an old crone about to tell a ghost story. "You know," she said. "Some folks say I poisoned Eliza Clary, Miranda's mother."

Jason choked on his wine and grabbed a snowy napkin to blot his lips.

"Not so. We were as sisters. In the country of my birth, men of high status often took several wives, had many concubines. I bowed to Eliza as head wife, though she was only a year or so older than myself. She gave the master two strong sons. After, he lost interest in her. When he saw me in Haiti, he wanted me, so different from his wife. He paid a large sum for my skills as a midwife and herbal healer, he said. I was eighteen years at the time, but had apprenticed with an old woman since I came from Africa."

"Yes, there is no denying you know your herbs." Jason set his cup on the table.

"I carried Ponce in my belly by the time we arrived here." Ida made a curved sign over her stomach. "When I got too big to entertain the mastah, he returned to Eliza and got her with another child, our Miranda. The night Ponce came, the mastah ranted he would lose his investment if I died and called for a doctor to cut my baby into pieces to bring him out. Instead, this man used a device that gripped the head and yanked my son from the womb. A ten-pound boy, how

Mastah bragged. Miranda arrived, small and sweet, with no trouble at all, but she was only a girl. Ponce grew and grew, but his mind stayed small as a child's. Miranda, how bright and lively she was. Eustace Clary ignored them both and sought out other women."

"Swinish behavior," Jason remarked.

"Yes, exactly. And so, I used my herbs to quell this desire to roam, this interest in other ladies. His appetites turned to food and drink. He grew fat as a hog and unable to pursue the female sex. Still, he liked to show us off when he traveled, his white wife, his black concubine. Eliza took a chill in New York City that worsened as the ship sailed home. Despite all that I tried, she died shortly after we reached the island. She entrusted me to raise and care for her daughter and asked Daniel to watch over Miranda as a father might, since Mastah Clary regarded the girl as simply one more thing he could sell for profit. So, you understand now why we are protective. We want you to make Miranda very, very happy for all of her life and most especially on her wedding night. Do you understand, Mastah Lord Jason?"

Jason eyed the wine again. "Um, yes. I am not without experience. Older women tend to be very outspoken in what they desire, and ah—well, you do get my drift."

"That is good. Widows make fine teachers." She nodded a head swathed in a red silk tignon.

"I don't suppose you intend to have this same conversation with Daniel regarding my sister."

Ida chuckled with that deep, throaty voice of hers. "No need for that. Lady Pandora is a very strong woman. She is favored by Mami Wata, the water goddess. Daniel will always be true to her."

"If she agrees to marry him."

"Even if she does not."

"Well, so far, I haven't heard any screaming or accusations coming from the parlor. Panny hasn't scratched his eyes out or threatened him with any of the dire consequences she wished on her brothers. In fact, it is far too quiet in there. I should knock and see how it goes."

"Maybe you should."

"And Ida, perhaps we could use just a soupçon of that potion on our wedding night."

Showing her very strong teeth in a big white grin, Ida nodded. Miranda came softly from her chamber and took Jason's hand. He kissed her fingertips.

"Where have you been for so long, my beloved?"

"You see, the inside door to the parlor was open a mere crack. I couldn't come to you until I knew. We *are* going to have a double wedding tomorrow. But they will soon realize both bed chambers are empty. We should go inside and congratulate them at once before they choose one and lock the door."

Twenty-two

Despite the numerous toasts honoring the engagements made by Captain Fulton and the other gentlemen the night before, the *Sea Nymph* sailed on the morning tide and the southern breezes toward Caliban Island. The couples stayed above deck, watching as the ship passed the north end of Ariel and the channel between it and Prospero, a long, narrow island devoted wholly to the cultivation of Sea Island cotton. The ship could not move swiftly enough for Pandora, who squeezed Daniel's hand as they passed by his inheritance. She swore her pulse beat in time with his. This man, this man willingly had given up so much for her.

Bulky Caliban hove into view with its foursquare red brick mansion squatting on the hill. Rows of windows with shutters of dark green stared out at sound and sea, and the two white pillars of the small portico appeared to be garbed in greenery and flowers for the festivities. From a widow's walk, someone watched for their arrival and dashed from the railed platform to relay the news.

By the time the ship dropped anchor and the passengers settled into the dinghy for the trip to the dock, a welcoming group had gathered on the shore. As soon as the women were helped from the boat, Miranda took the lead in embracing a young matron, handsome, blue-eyed and dark-haired, and a man who had the look of a Eustace Clary in his prime, not the bloated figure that man had become. She doled out introductions.

Regina Clary, Roger's wife, produced a deep bow and curtsy. "Lord Longleigh, Lady Pandora, welcome to Caliban Island. To think little Miranda and dear Daniel are both to marry British nobility on the very same day in my home. My own family is descended from the younger sons of some of the best English families who settled in Virginia as early as 1670. They made their fortunes in tobacco. I met Roger when he studied at William and Mary, one of our finest academies of learning."

She patted her husband's arm. Two small boys gamboled like puppies around the outside of the group. "Our sons, Jefferson and Rolfe."

"Uncle Daniel, Uncle Daniel, what did you bring us from England?" the boys screamed.

"A new aunt."

Their small noses wrinkled and their mouths turned down in disappointment. "No, a real good present."

"I am afraid I left England in haste and had no time for shopping, but Captain Fulton brings a ship full of treasures. We will try to find something to please a boy."

Her eyes still on the Longleighs, Regina apologized. "Such manners. Their mammy does spoil them. I have done my best on such short notice to provide a suitable celebration for this double marriage. Two pigs are roasting in a pit. My cook and her helpers have been up since dawn baking and making side dishes. Of course, my father-in-law keeps an extensive wine cellar. Beverages will be no problem. We shall give the hands the day off after the feast, but I am afraid other guests will be in short supply. Those who can attend will be brought at noon from the mainland along with the preacher. We've had to settle for a Methodist since the Episcopal priest refused to preside without the banns being read, but I understood we had no time to waste when we received Lord Longleigh's communication.

Regina's eyes drifted to the stomachs of the two women. She jerked her gaze back to Jason's handsome and now clean-shaven face.

"We did not wish to delay our joy. That is all. Please, you must call me by my given name," Jason told her.

Pandora swore the woman shivered like a hound stroked by its master. She summoned up her best imitation of her mother being gracious. "Yes, yes, do address me as Pandora. I am sure all your preparations will be more than satisfactory."

If she were being honest, she could not wait for the nuptials to be over so she might rest in Daniel's arms again. Once her passions had been released, there seemed to be no way to shove them back into the box. Her attempt to go to Daniel last night had been thwarted by Ida, who slept on the day bed at the foot of Miranda's mattress and woke instantly when her feet hit the floor. She'd been offered the chamber pot and a nostrum to help her sleep. Miranda, the oblivious bride, rested like a child exhausted from counting turtle eggs, exactly what she was. Ida still dogged their steps on the boat and now to Caliban Island. The slave woman wore her own idea of finery, the red silk turban and gold hoop earrings along with a purple gown and a pleased smile on her wide lips.

While Roger offered hearty congratulations to the men, Regina surveyed Pandora's rosy dress, which had been smoothed again that morning.

"I am closer to your size than Miranda. Perhaps you would like a fresh gown to wear for the ceremony? I understand you arrived without your baggage."

Pandora's lips bowed. "Thank you, but I am fond of this frock. In the morning, we might try something else. However, I believe Miranda wants to raid your flower garden."

"Oh, yes! We must go to the house immediately and dress our hair with posies and make up lovely bouquets," Miranda exclaimed.

"Whatever Lady Pandora wishes," Regina replied, dropping another low curtsy as if the Prince Regent stood before her. "Come, the carriages wait to take you up the hill."

Of Turtles and Doves

~ * ~

Was there any task more tedious than twining flowers into chaplets, Pandora wondered? Where was the preacher? Surely noon had come and gone by now. Regina Clary, so enraptured by the idea of nobility about to become members of the family, rattled on and on until Pandora wanted to stuff two of the small, white rosebuds into her own ears to drown out the sound.

"Not only nobility, but the son and daughter of Pearce Longleigh and Lady Flora. Their story was so romantical, it gave me the courage to leave my native Virginia and become Mrs. Roger Clary, the mistress of Caliban Island." Regina sighed, making the bosom of her becoming and lacy pale blue gown swell and the long brown curls gathered over her ears tremble. She closed her wide blue eyes for a moment.

"You speak as if you know the Duke and Duchess of Bellevue," Pandora said.

"I know *of* them. Of course, their adventure took place before I was born, but I found the account in my father's library when I was but fifteen and read it over a dozen times. Your tale is nearly as good—two noble Britons eloping on a ship in order to marry American commoners. A pity you will not be disowned and forced to live on the islands, forever exiled from your native land. That would be a more sympathetic ending, but Pearce Longleigh would never do such a thing to his children, I am sure."

"No, that would surprise me. Papa can be very unorthodox himself." Though he had tried to tempt Daniel into marrying her by dangling her dowry, Pandora thought.

"Because he carries the blood of a noble Indian chief in his veins," Regina whispered, as if not wanting Ida to overhear.

"Papa is half Shawnee on his mother's side and quite proud of that, but his father was the previous Duke of Bellevue," Pandora corrected as she stuffed yet another rosebud in among the mock orange withes.

As soon as she bound the whole in white ribbons with streamers down the back, her chore would be completed. Miranda danced about, poking so many deep pink roses into her black hair, Pandora feared she would attract bees as she walked down the aisle.

"No, I am certain the chapbook said an Indian chief fathered Pearce Longleigh on a duke's captive daughter who carried her baby home to England to become the heir to a great fortune and a title."

"That is not exactly how English succession works," Pandora answered.

"Let me go get the book. I begged it from my father before my removal to the island."

Regina stood and fluffed her skirt to remove several clinging white petals. She handed Ida the bouquet created of shining magnolia leaves and pure white blossoms bound with satin ribbons and left the room. She returned shortly, holding a slim brown paper volume flaking on the edges.

Pandora perused the title—*The True and Exciting Adventures of Pearce Longleigh and the Rescue of Lady Flora as told to this correspondent, Elias Meriwether, Esq.* The frontispiece showed a huge man dressed in a buckskin hunting jacket and leggings, a coonskin cap atop this head, carrying a dainty, bare-chested woman whose curls just managed to cover her nipples and breasts. Panny set her project aside in order to read, and Ida took up the chaplet to put on the finishing touches.

The duke had taken part in many outrageous escapades during his life and told the story many times of killing a bear with his bare hands when he was thirteen during his manhood rights, but Pandora had no idea he had also wrestled a bear to death as a naked tot of three. An illustration showed this event. She'd heard the story of her parents' marriage often enough. Their annual recreation of the pagan wedding dance was a family embarrassment. The duke and duchess never mentioned that Flora was about to be burned as a virgin sacrifice to heathen gods when Pearce stepped in to marry and thus save her. While Pearce Longleigh preferred the life of a savage, he had nobly given that up to follow the ransomed Lady Flora home to England and assume his title of Viscount Laughlin, later Duke of Bellevue.

Pandora knew her brows shot up several times as she read. While she suspected the last statement might be true, much of the rest of the story had to be patently false. She gave the booklet back to Regina.

"This is not exactly the way my parents have told their tale over the years."

"Oh, are they not totally devoted to each other eternally?" Regina showed her distress.

"Devoted? That and more," Pandora assured her.

She grew restless again, yearning for Daniel. Ever since her coming out, she'd been sure she had escaped the unruly passions of the Longleigh family, quelled those urges with common sense. Now, she burned in a raging inferno twice the size of anything her sister, Euphemia, had experienced, certainly.

Ida set the completed chaplet on Miranda's head. She straightened the ribbons down the back and placed a single red bud in the bow at the top. A similar flower adorned each of the magnolia bouquets.

"No, no, no, Ida," Regina said, plucking the red flowers out. "They do not match. Oh, the darkies do so love bright colors. White for purity—and deep pink to better match Lady Pandora's complexion."

"The red is for luck, Missus," Ida claimed.

Pandora suspected red represented passion or served as an offering to Mami Wata, but she said nothing because the plantation bell rang out in greeting. The boats had arrived at last, bearing the preacher and the last-minute guests.

"I must go tell those children the bell is to be rung only after the ceremony. Now brides, remain here. I will see the guests are seated and the men in place. We have a very fine fiddler amongst our people, and he will play a processional tune. When you hear the music, come down the stairs and into the parlor. Take your place beside your grooms and stand before the preacher to be united in holy wedlock." Regina hurried out to organize all to her liking.

Miranda and Pandora exchanged glances and burst out laughing.

"How do you stand her, Miri?"

"She's not as bad as the girls at the ladies' academy I attended in Savannah. Mostly, I suspect she is lonely here on Caliban and relieves herself with tales of romance and parties to draw company from across the water. I know she yearns for a daughter and tried to take me from Ida's care when she first married Roger, but Daddy would not allow it. He said I was best left alone on Ariel as I brought bad luck to people. He did not want Roger's family tainted."

"You are not bad luck, *bébé*," Ida answered as she tucked the red buds back into the bouquets. "Your father brings bad luck on himself. Look how well we have done without him. The music sounds. Now go to the men you love and be happy."

Miranda hugged and kissed the woman who had raised her. Pandora hesitated, then said, "Ida, I owe my present happiness to you, however accidental. Believe me when I say I will work tirelessly to free your race with Daniel by my side."

Ida gave her that white-toothed, almost feral smile. "You would have done that with or without Daniel. You are a strong woman favored by Mami Wata. She has given you Mastah Daniel. Stay true to each other, and prosperity and good luck will follow you all the days of your lives."

No more remained to be said. The music called the brides to descend the stairs. Regina Clary stood by the door, plucked out those red flowers once more, and followed the women to the front of the parlor to stand before a black marble fireplace filled with magnolia boughs and in front of a reedy Methodist preacher. Ida took a place among the household servants standing along the walls. The grooms fell in next to their intendeds.

For Pandora, no one else in that room existed but Daniel, his appearance primped and polished by his body servant, Horace, who was to become a free man today. In minutes, she would be his lawful wife. In hours, they could escape to a bedchamber and forget about storms and shipwrecks, magic and potions—if only Regina would shut her mouth and let the parson proceed.

Regina stood by her husband, who served as best man and witness for both couples. As the minister opened his Bible, she whispered to Roger. "Who are the four men in the last row?"

"I have no idea. Perhaps they were visiting in town and came along."

"I do hope no riffraff looking for a free meal got aboard the boats."

The black-clad preacher gave Regina a pointed look, cleared his throat loudly for silence, and began the solemn ceremony. He quickly came to the phrase, "If any know why these couples should not be wed, speak now or forever hold your peace." Glancing up briefly at the small gathering, he stopped, his mouth hanging open for a second. "Is there an objection?"

The men in the back row moved forward, led by the youngest among them. All were big and dark-visaged with eyes deep brown, narrow and cold, four of a kind. Two wore beards and long hair past their collars and appeared to be identical twins. The second fellow, largest of them all, hadn't shaved in several days and shambled along loosely behind the leader. All but the first one wore loose clothes, country-style. Only the young man had groomed himself for this happy occasion and dressed in close-fitting city attire. He'd slicked his dark brown hair back and shaved so closely he'd nicked himself in several places. He positioned himself to address Daniel and Roger.

"Let me introduce myself. I am Ransom Clary, your daddy's second cousin. We don't know each other because Eustace Clary thought himself too good for the people he come from and visited but briefly up in the hills. Once, he rode in with all his money and his fine clothes, and he left with Eliza Puckett, the prettiest gal in the mountains, some say. My pa was waiting on that child to ripen, but Eustace paid for her, young as she was, and took her away. Gave the Pucketts enough cash money to move into the valley and buy a good farm. Pa, he had to settle for second best. I heard that all my life. Then Ma died, and Pa heard Eliza had passed on, too, but she left a daughter her exact image. He came to this island and made a good offer for the girl, paid out a high price."

"Excuse me, young man, but white women cannot be bought and sold," the minister said.

"Preacher man, anything can be bought and sold. Ask Eustace Clary. Next day, my pa drowned on his way to the chapel. Never got his bride nor his money back. So, I come to collect one or the other."

Roger Clary spoke up. "My father is currently visiting in England. I am sure he will make some sort of reparation upon his return. Please take your seats and allow the ceremony to continue."

"See here, I been waiting in town for Eustace Clary a month now. Nothing much to do but sit by Pa's grave and consider the matter. I come of age a few months back, and I'm of a mind to take a bride. Town folk say Miranda Clary is pretty as a wild rose but peculiar. Close up, she looks fine to me."

Ransom reached out and fingered Miri's curls. She shrank back, and Jason slapped his hand away.

"I heard about you, too, a proper English lord like the kind we threw out of this country some time back. Those fancy handwritten invitations going around yesterday said so. This would be your sister, Lady Pandora. Funny how she looks like a half-breed."

Pandora drew herself up and stared directly into Ransom Clary's eyes. "I am one-quarter Shawnee and proud of it."

The unshaven man spoke. "I know some Shawnee. They live up with the Cherokee."

"Hush, Custis. This ain't a social call."

"I like her. I want a bride, too, Ranse."

Ransom Clary cocked his head. "You might be owed one as well, deprived of a father as you were. This man with the size of the Clarys and the look of the Pucketts is responsible for Pa's death. He sailed that boat. Seems he owes us a blood price. Don't you, Cousin Daniel? Your life or your wife. What do you say?"

Daniel's face reddened. "Don't be absurd. A whirlwind overturned our boat. Miranda and I clung to the hull for hours waiting for rescue. Your father's death was an act of God."

"I don't miss Pa very much and don't want your life. Can I have the woman instead?" the shambling man said.

"Shut your mouth, Cuss. Pa beat my big brother around the head one time too many, but that don't mean he ain't owed."

Regina Clary, unable to contain herself any longer, burst out, "You were not invited here. Go at once. I will assign a man to row you back to the mainland."

"Well, Missus, meet the rest of the family—Cousin Robbie and Cousin Ray Clary. Twins, they be. I brought them along in case we didn't see eye to eye on this matter."

The silent, bearded men threw back their coats and revealed their weapons, a pistol and a large knife, each soon in their hands. Custis fumbled with his jacket but managed to produce the same armaments. The twins turned to face the stunned guests. Apparently, none of the company expected to need arms at a wedding as no one made a move or voiced a protest. Custis covered the wedding party and the preacher.

Pandora fumed. At a gathering of Longleighs, someone would have brought a sword cane or a small pistol. These men thought they were going to rob her of her wedding night. At least *she* had worn her stiletto strapped to her calf, mostly to allow Daniel to take it off in the privacy of the nuptial bed. Clearly, Jason had come to the altar unarmed as he shook his head slightly when she looked his way for support. Poets...never prepared!

"All right now. Cousin Miranda, come stand beside me. Everyone stay seated while the preacher says the words over us." Ransom Clary beckoned to Miranda with a crooked finger.

Pandora expected Miranda to faint or burst into tears, but the girl merely shook her head, setting her long, loose curls bouncing under the floral chaplet.

"I am sorry for the loss of your father, Cousin Ransom, but I can marry only my one true love. Terrible things befall those who have tried to force me. For your own good, put down your weapons and await my father's return for a settlement."

"Now ain't that a crock of shit. You mistake me for some superstitious hick from the hills. Come here, I say."

Ranse pulled Miranda to stand beside him. Jason drew her back.

"Custis, if you please, put a bullet through milord's head."

"No, no! I'm coming." Miranda took a place next to her long-lost cousin.

"Preacher man, say the words over us."

The Methodist minister swallowed so hard his Adam's apple bobbed visibly in his skinny neck. His hands grasped his Bible tightly and his eyes closed as if he were about to come to glory.

"To marry an unwilling woman is against the law of God and man. I will not do it."

"Kill him, Custis."

"We can't, brother. Kill a preacher, and we go straight to hell. The Bible says so, don't it?" Custis looked to the Methodist for an opinion.

"Yes, yes, it does," the man of the cloth said, opening his eyes.

"Damn, looks like no one dies today. There are plenty of gospelers roaming the hills. We'll use one of them. Cuss, collect your woman. Boys, cover us as we leave."

Someone had to do something, take action. Pandora dropped her bouquet of magnolias and swooned back into Daniel's arms. Rose petals fluttered down like dying butterflies. He lowered her to the floor and stayed the hand she moved towards her stiletto.

In such a low voice he only appeared to be comforting her, Daniel said, "Don't, Panny. Keep your secret. We will be right behind."

More loudly, he spoke up, "Go with them quietly and take care of Miri. He is right. No one should die today."

"See there, sweeting. You deserve a better man than that. He won't even take a bullet to save you. Custis might not have much in the way of brains, but I know he is entirely satisfactory in other ways. Come along now. Get her up, Cuss. And you, Missus." Ranse Clary pointed to Regina, who trembled in her husband's arms.

"Why me?"

"To tell the servants to keep out of our way and do as they are told. See that clock on the mantel? Anyone leaves this house in the next hour and you will find Missus Clary here dead on the dock with her throat slit. Understand?"

Roger nodded. Miranda stood on her tiptoes and kissed Jason on the lips. Pandora, already wrapped in Custis Clary's bristly embrace, wished she had done the same with Daniel.

"Oh, my love, I've lost you again!" Jason cried.

"Never fear, my dearest. We will be together once more even if it be in heaven," Miranda answered tremulously.

"For crying out loud, this is a kidnapping, not a fairy tale. Come on, gal. Let's head for the hills." Ransom Clary took the knife from his cousin Ray and prodded Miranda and Regina down the aisle before him.

Pandora followed with her idiot escort holding her close, the dark twins backing behind them, pistols drawn. Her eyes darted toward Ida, whose lips already moved with some sort of prayer or incantation. She made her own vow as they passed from the parlor and she scooped up one of the red blossoms left on a side table. She hadn't been able to save her sister, Phemie, from a kidnapping, but by God and maybe by Mami Wata, she would save Miranda.

Twenty-three

Daniel went to the parlor window and carefully peered out from behind a corner of the draperies. Jason stood directly behind, crowded by Roger.

"What are they doing?" Roger Clary asked.

"Cutting the traces on the second carriage. Now I assume Regina is telling your coachman to take them all down the hill to the boats," Daniel answered.

"Mastah Daniel," a soft, low voice said from behind the wall of tall men.

"Yes, Horace."

"The boatman, Peter, he say those men come wit' rifles and leaves 'em under the seats."

"That's good to know, but as of today, you are free. You need not address me as Master anymore."

"But Mistah Daniel, you not married yet."

"Regardless, Roger will see to the paperwork if anything should happen to me. Roger, your word."

"As you wish. What goes on now?"

"They are nearing the boats. One has jumped down and is removing those rifles. He's using the butt to stove holes in the other boats."

Captain Fulton's voice boomed out. "Never fear, I can summon the ship's boat at any time. We have two small cannons aboard and..."

"Not with the women as hostages. They are getting on the last of the boats and pushing off. Your oarsmen are moving at a good clip, Roger."

"As would you with a gun to your back. If we pursue them immediately, Regina will die."

"We can't merely stand here watching. What arms can you offer? Let's prepare to go as soon as the hour is up," Jason interjected, his voice impatient.

"Might I suggest we all pray," the high voice of the preacher said.

"Fine, lead our guests in prayer while we dress for the pursuit." Daniel dropped the curtain, his last view the boat bearing Pandora and his sister away across the sound.

Daniel, Jason, Roger, Fulton, and several other men wanting to help left the room as the rest of the company raised their voices to God to ask for the salvation of the women. They passed Ida standing by the side table. She rolled the red flowers in her dark hands. Jason turned aside to address her.

"Miranda says you can summon storms. Can't you cast some spell to save them?"

Ida lifted woeful, red-rimmed eyes to his. "The spell protecting Miranda from bad men lifted when she fell in love with you. Should I send a whirlwind now, all might be drowned. My *bébé* hasn't even the red bud I tucked into her hair for luck on her wedding night. But I will pray to my goddess while the preacher prays to the white man's god. Who knows what they might do together?" A tear coursed from the corner of a dark eye, followed the groove beside her mouth and dropped onto the bodice of her purple gown.

"We will save them if everyone does their part." Jason followed the rest of the men.

~ * ~

By the time the clock in the parlor struck the hour, Jason and the others stood dressed for a rough pursuit with pistols pocketed, swords by their side, knives in handy places, and rifles slung over their shoulders. Fulton signaled his ship and summoned the boat. Horses stood ready to get the men down the hill as rapidly as possible. Inside the parlor, the preacher whipped his temporary congregation into a frenzy of prayers. A sweet odor barely covering the stench of burning cloth filled the halls of the red-brick mansion. Her hair wild and wiry without her red silk head scarf, Ida appeared to see them off.

"Care for the guests in the absence of the mistress," Roger ordered. "They will need food and drink after all that praying. Allow the hands to have their feast as well. No sense in food going to waste. I do not know when we will return, but see the carpenter mends the boats and everyone gets home."

"Yes, Mastah Roger." She bowed her uncovered graying head.

Jason paused. "I know you will do all within your power."

"Mami Wata has accepted my best red scarf in return for Miranda's safety. She will aid you if you do not anger her."

A chill went up Jason's back, but he nodded and went to answer Daniel's call. They were off with a clatter of swords and the sound of hoofbeats to the waiting boat. Captain Fulton tested the direction of the breeze with a wet thumb as they approached the dock.

"Strange. I could have sworn the winds were out of the south. They seem to have shifted and blow from the east now. We can put up the sail and cross the sound in half the time as the oarsmen."

"Must be all that prayer," Daniel said, giving the eye to Jason, who nodded.

With winds so fair and a crew so experienced, their boat soon bore down on the public docks where Regina stood waiting and weeping and telling her story to anyone who would listen.

She ran to her husband.

"Oh, Roger, I am unharmed, but those ruffians said if they were pursued too closely, they would take Miranda and Lady Pandora into the Okefenokee Swamp. What shall we do?"

Daniel replied, "Roger, you have a wife and sons to care for. If we must go all the way to the hills, our lives will be forfeit most likely. Stay home. Captain, our thanks for getting us to this point so quickly, but you have a ship waiting with goods to sell. As for the rest of you gentlemen, we appreciate your willingness to help, but Lord Longleigh and I can go faster and more quietly by ourselves. Now, if we could have the use of some swift horses..."

"Take the racehorses. I keep them stabled in town for the meets. Don't spare them if it means getting Miranda back." Roger clapped his brother on the back.

"But it will be four against one," Regina pointed out as she rung her hands.

"I believe we shall manage. You do not know her well as yet, but Pandora can be very fierce when roused," Jason answered her.

"In all ways," Daniel commented. "And do not discount Miranda. She is wiser than anyone assumes."

Twenty-four

The roads across the lowlands were few, running as they did between marshy areas. The flatness of the land yielded few hiding places. Whenever a crossroad appeared, Ransom Clary paused to consider turning right or left, now toward the hills, then toward the swamp to make pursuit more difficult.

At every juncture, Pandora Longleigh shook her head, leaving a trail of wilting rose petals behind as they went along the chosen path. Ranse might have noticed, but he rode in front with Miranda forced to cling to him or be trampled by the other horses if she tried to jump. Custis had placed Pandora in front of him and took such great joy in pressing his loins against her backside, he seemed oblivious to all else. As for the twins riding in the rear, their iron-shod horses ground the petals into the dirt of the byways. Jason, she trusted, would remember their childhood Indian games.

The sun lowered in the sky. Ranse pushed through some thick brush to a grove of live oaks overshadowing a creek running with water the color of brewed tea. The men began to set up camp, throwing down bedrolls and gathering branches twisted off the trees by previous storms. The twins hobbled the horses in a grassy patch near the stream to fend for themselves.

Miranda looked down at her toes and pleaded to Ranse. "Please, I need to answer the call of nature."

She glanced at Pandora, who immediately said, "I must also."

"Custis, tie a rope around each of their ankles. Make it nice and tight now. You ladies, don't even think of untying yourselves and running off. The woods are full of scary creatures at night—snakes and wolves and panthers so black you never see them pounce."

The other men laughed heartily as they watched Miranda's eyes widen with fear. "We won't go too far, will we, Pandora?"

"Daniel says there are no such things as black panthers in Georgia," she answered, disgusted by Miri's meekness.

"Shows what he knows. Off you go now. Don't be long, or you won't get fed tonight."

Ranse played out Miranda's rope while Custis kept a loose grip on Pandora's binding. She figured she could make a dash and pull it from the man's hands, but on unfamiliar ground and chased by four men, her chances of escape remained small. Rather, she must save her strength until Daniel arrived. Pushing through a row of bushes, she popped out into another small clearing. A large dead limb from one of the oaks lay on the far side of the space. Miranda headed directly there.

"If you really do need to go, do it now," she directed Pandora without the least quaver in her voice.

"I believe I shall." Pandora squatted down in the deep shadow of one tree. "You had better take care of matters, too. I doubt if they will allow us another trip."

Coming close, Miranda whispered, "Take off your petticoat. We might have a need for it."

Puzzled, Pandora did as she was asked. She fumbled with the tapes that held the garment up, as Miranda searched beneath the trees and finally flourished a stout, forked stick.

"We can't hit them, Miri. They will simply overpower us."

"Help me roll this log over."

She did, putting all her strength into it. The rotten limb crashed back into the brush.

"What are y'all doing back there?" Ranse shouted. "Make it fast now, or I'm coming in."

"We needed a log to sit on," Miranda answered.

"Women," he said, annoyed. "Just squat down somewheres."

"Say, Custis, me and Ray were thinking you might need some help breaking in that bride of yours. We could take turns and get her all trained for you. We know Ransom won't share his, because he's a tight bastard, but you are one generous man, Cuss."

Pandora shivered. She would need to use her knife sooner than expected and make a run for it if necessary.

"Ignore them. Tear your petticoat down the seams and make a sack of half of it," Miranda ordered.

She used the stick to prod the rotten leaves exposed when they rolled the log. The detritus began to writhe. Fat, arrowed-headed snakes emerged with tongues flickering frantically. The smell of cucumbers emitted by the reptiles filled the glade. Even in the fading light, Pandora could see they were crosshatched with ominous hourglass markings of dull orange. Miranda raised one on the end of her stick. Quickly, Pandora ripped the petticoat and formed a bag. Miranda dropped the snake inside and went back to fork up another.

"What are you up to now?" Ranse jerked the rope tied to Miranda's leg. The second snake tumbled back to the ground. She worked the stick again before it slithered away.

"Woman problems," Pandora answered, hoping to give Miranda time. "We need rags."

"Which one of you?"

"Both. The shock of our abduction has brought on our monthlies."

A collective groan went up from the men on the other side of the bushes. "Shit, aw hell," Robbie or Ray said.

"Do what you got to do, take care of it, and get on out here." Ranse jerked the rope again, but the second snake fell safely into the sack.

"All right now. Hold the top shut and give the sack to me," Miranda whispered.

"Will they do the trick—whatever that might be?" Pandora watched the sack bulge as the vipers coiled within.

"They are good-sized copperheads, but probably won't kill anyone. However, the bites are extremely painful and sure to slow a person down. We have some on the island that most likely came in with a load of wood. Mammy Ida sent these to help us, I am certain. Rattlers would have been better, but they do make a racket." She tied a loose knot in the top of the bag.

"I'm not so sure. But wait, our monthlies."

Pandora drew her knife from its scabbard and, gritting her teeth, cut a long shallow line along her inner thigh above her stocking top. She tore strips from the second half of the petticoat and soaked two of them with her blood.

"You have your knife?' Miranda marveled. "You wore it on your wedding day?"

"A good thing, too. A gift from Daniel, actually. I lost my other in the sea. Here, stuff this in your undergarments." Pandora did the same. "It might not keep them off of us, but we must try."

"Bridey, oh Bridey," Custis called as he jiggled the rope. "I miss you. Come out."

"Go first and shield me as you are taller," Miranda said.

She hefted the snake-filled bag. Pandora peeked out through the verge of the bushes. The men had started a small fire and fried bacon over the flames in a pan Ray had hauled along with a small coffee pot and a little brown jug. They passed the jug, each one taking a swig, wiping off the mouth on a sleeve and passing it on. The bedrolls lay unfurled in an outer circle, ready for use.

Pandora emerged and walked slowly, stepping daintily over the nearest blankets with her skirt held out. In one hand, she clutched her half of the petticoat like the white flag of surrender. She resisted the urge to bolt when she heard the small thump of Miranda's release of the snakes into the bedroll. As they neared the fire, all Miri carried was her half of the petticoat smelling faintly of cucumbers, an odor soon overpowered by the scent of sizzling bacon and camp coffee boiling in the pot. Submissively, they folded their legs and sat in the space between Custis and Ransom across the blaze from Ray and Robbie and the infested bedding.

Pandora began ripping strips from the petticoat. Miranda did the same until the pan was removed from the fire and slices of bacon were laid out on top of cold pones of cornmeal. After the grounds settled, Robbie poured the coffee into four tin cups. Custis, almost chivalrous, offered his portion to Pandora first.

"Here, Bridey. This will make you feel better. Woman problems can make a lady mighty sick, Ma said. If you dip the pone in the pan drippings, it won't be so dry."

"Thank you, Custis, but my name is Pandora and that is what I prefer to be called." She rolled up the strips in a tight bundle and neatly tied it off. "Perhaps you will put these in your saddlebag for our use tomorrow."

She waited to see which bed roll he would approach, but he merely reached behind and pulled his saddlebag closer to stuff the rags inside. Not him, then. The simple one would not suffer.

"Pandora, that's a strange name," Custis said.

"Pandora was the first woman ever created, according to the ancient Greeks. She brought troubles into the world by opening a forbidden box, but saved hope for all mankind."

"We don't believe that, do we, Ranse?" Custis asked his brother, as if unsure.

"No, Cuss, we believe in Adam and Eve and what the Bible tells us, not a bunch of Greeks. Eve caused enough problems without any help. Sop up those drippings before they get cold."

"But, we must all hold on to hope," Miranda said. She offered her slice of meat to Ransom and explained that she did not enjoy eating the flesh of animals.

"They said you was peculiar, but that leaves more for me. Explains why you're so puny, too, I'd guess."

Miranda cast her eyes down. "I've always been very small and weak."

Ranse called to Ray to pass the jug again before they settled for the night. The twins shook the crumbs from their beards and sucked on the whiskey before passing it on.

"Tomorrow, only cold pone and water. We got to make time and get back to our territory before they catch up with us. You ladies, take care of your needs before we go because I ain't stopping until the sun is overhead." Ranse beckoned Miranda into his covers and pulled her close.

The twins stayed up drinking from the jug and arguing in a friendly way about who should keep watch, but Custis imitated his brother. He held his captive bride tight under the blanket. Pandora felt a hand grope her thigh. She thanked the Lord and whoever else might be watching out for them that Cuss had started his explorations above the knee and missed the thongs that held her knife in place. He soon encountered the cut still sticky with blood in the warm, humid night. His hand retreated. He wiped it on their covering. The twins laughed.

"I ain't so squeamish, Custis. Send her over here." Ray, a mite drunk, fell back chuckling into his blankets.

Nearby, Pandora heard Miranda saying, "Please, please don't," to Ransom Clary. Had the snakes slithered back into the bushes, leaving them to face the untender mercies of the Clary boys? How quickly could she kill Custis and move to rescue Miri?

Having lost the guard debate, Robbie settled cross-legged on his blankets and shook the coffee pot to see if any of the brew remained. Whatever happened, he clearly intended to watch or help out.

"You go on, Ranse. Why wait for the wedding night, huh?"

Ray screamed high-pitched like a panther in the night. He stood up, flailing, with one copperhead attached to his neck and the other to a hand. Plucking off the snake entangled with his beard, he threw it into the bushes. The other viper retracted its fangs, dropped to the ground, and wound away in the dark.

Miranda broke Ranse's grip and rose, shrieking, "Snakes, snakes, we have lain down in a nest of vipers!" She gestured slightly to Pandora, who put her all into screaming, too, as she jumped from the covers. Between Ray and the two of them, anyone for miles around would hear their cries.

"Lord, Lord, feels like my head is on fire! My lips are going numb. Robbie, help me."

"I can tie off your arm and cut across the bite to drain out the venom, brother, but I can't do nothing about that neck wound without killing you. Stay still. You're making it worse."

Screaming hoarsely now, Ray fell to his knees. No words made their way out of his ballooning lips. His arm swelled, stretching the cloth of his coat. Deep red blood blisters appeared on his hand.

"Quiet, you two. I got to see to my cousin. Don't make a move in any direction. Custis, make sure there aren't any more of those varmints around." Ranse moved to kneel by Ray, now cradled by his twin. "What's he trying to say?"

"Kill me," Robbie answered. He lowered his brother to the ground.

Pandora held Miranda close, as the girl rested her head against her shoulder. Miri's lips moved quietly close to her ear. "He'll die. Bit in the carotid artery. Nothing can be done."

"Did Ransom molest you?"

"Above the waist. He squeezed my bosoms. Panny, you must stab Custis tomorrow and shove him from the horse. Race back along our trail. I doubt they will follow as they came for me alone."

"I will not abandon you."

"Save yourself."

Custis came stomping behind them. He prodded the oak duff with the long barrel of a rifle and tossed their blankets.

"You can set down now. I scared those snakes off."

The women sank to the blankets but still clung to each other, the better to make plans. On the other side of the dying fire, Cousin Ray Clary convulsed and died. A new stench filled the glade as the dead man's bowels released. His brother laid him on the bedroll and straightened his limbs. He crossed Ray's bloated, purplish hand over the other.

"We need to bury and pray over him."

"Pray all you want, but we have no time to bury him. Don't even have a shovel," Ransom said.

"I won't leave my brother for the wild beasts. We can scrape out a holler with a branch and pile rocks atop him," Robbie insisted. He squeezed his eyes tight but two tears escaped into his beard.

"I'm not looking for rocks at night in a place teeming with copperheads. We'll tie him in his blankets and take him with us. First settlement we come to, we leave some cash for his burial and a cross. Best I can do for him."

Robbie nodded. He folded the blankets over his brother's nearly unrecognizable face and along his body. After cutting two lengths of rope, he bound the legs of the corpse together and tied the arms across the chest. For lack of knowing any other prayers, he mumbled the one dedicated to the Lord and recited the Twenty-Third Psalm, forgetting a few lines, Pandora noted.

Keeping Miranda with her, she stretched out on the blankets and folded the girl into her sheltering arms. "Pretend we've gone to sleep, Miri."

"Just bad luck," Custis said, attempting to console.

From under her half-closed lids, Pandora watched Robbie stare their way. "The little gal said she brought bad luck to her suitors."

"Ray had too much to drink and didn't check his blankets for snakes, is all," Ranse insisted.

"He did look before he chose his spot. My brother was no idiot." Robbie flicked his eyes towards Custis.

"Neither is mine. Cuss will take the watch. Get some rest."

"No, I'll sit up with Ray."

"Suit yourself. The women are down. No sense in stirring them up again. They've been enough trouble tonight. Here, Custis. Take one of my blankets."

Ranse handed his brother one of the covers. They settled down side by side not far from Pandora's face. She could feel the heat of their bodies, adding to the discomfort of the humid night. At least she and Miri were safe until morning.

~ * ~

"A scream! More than one." Jason Longleigh bolted up from his resting place against the trunk of one of the low-growing oaks that dotted the land.

"Could be a panther. They cry like a woman in the night," Daniel told him.

"We should investigate. We did not ride swiftly enough. Who knows what might befall our ladies?" He picked up his saddle and started for the sweat-streaked horses.

"Darkness overcame us. Do we want to go bumbling around in the night, making enough noise for the Clarys to set up an ambush? A poor idea. Here, finish off the provisions and get some rest."

Daniel handed over half a ham sandwich as large as a brick and a packet of dried fruit the sympathetic wife of the stable keeper had packed for them. He drank from a canteen of fresh water, warm and tasting of the wooden container.

"We have gained on them. Our horses are swifter, and we are not burdened by extra passengers. With Panny leaving signs for us, we've barely had to stop to track them. So obvious, the two horses carrying heavier loads, the rose petals trampled into the soil. We must overtake them tomorrow." Jason paused to take a bite out of his sandwich.

"Clever girl, your sister," Daniel remarked. "I admit I never thought a lordling poet like you would have any tracking abilities."

"Penniless third sons do have their uses, though some might not think so."

"Nothing against you, Longleigh, but I did not want my sister to be sold off far from all she loves for some fancy title and the sake of my father gaining influence for his trade."

"With me you get neither, but some unusual skills. Our father felt all of his sons should know how to track, swim, fish, and hunt as if we might be required to leave for the American wilderness at a moment's notice and move in with our red brothers. Actually, we had immense fun. Few great lords take such an interest in their sons, especially the second and third. My eldest brother had gone off to school. Four sisters were born before me and Joshua. We had the duke all to ourselves. Well, of course Panny wished to tag along, so Papa allowed her and Phemie to be the quarry. When we were small, the girls dropped hair ribbons and posies along the way."

"Rose petals?" Daniel allowed himself a smile at the thought of a very young Pandora strewing roses along a woodland path.

"Often. Our sisters grew quite cunning as we got older. By the time Joshua and I left for boarding school, we had to rely on broken twigs and disturbed moss on a stone to find them. They had footsteps so light a wind would blow their tracks away, and they often erased their path with branches or stepped from stone to stone or crossed water to throw us off. Panny delighted in thwarting us."

"I believe she would enjoy outwitting her brothers or any other man."

"Exactly. Once, the girls did too good a job, and we failed to find them before dark. My mother grew frantic, but Papa said his daughters had Shawnee spirit and would survive unharmed. We found them the next day curled up like bear cubs in the base of a hollow tree with leaves and boughs covering them for warmth—one of the duke's favorite tales, but not one of my mother's."

"Are the Bellevue holdings so vast, then?" Again, Daniel considered how little he had to offer Pandora in comparison. His voice must have given his thoughts away.

"Oh, yes. But none of it will come to me, so stop thinking yourself too low for my sister. I have no island and am deeply in debt for turtles. The duke holds acres of forest, heath, and farmland, but no dogs or beaters for us when we hunted. Papa expected us to follow the deer in silence, find where they grazed, and lie in wait for them."

"Were you forced to use bows and arrows?"

"No, the duke said even the Shawnee had taken to rifles." Jason went silent for a moment. "Those screams. I cannot banish them from my mind."

"We will find our ladies tomorrow." Knowing he'd given little comfort, Daniel added more wood to the small fire they'd built to keep away the mosquitoes and wildlife.

Jason repacked what was left of the food, stretched out on a blanket and used his saddle for a pillow. He pulled up a second blanket, not for warmth, but to deflect the annoying buzzing insects determined to suck his blood. Daniel did the same. Nearby, the tethered horses cropped the grass.

"I am sorry, but I have to ask."

"What now, Longleigh? We should get some sleep."

"If those fellows have despoiled Pandora, will you still marry her?"

"Since I was her first despoiler, yes. It wasn't that way, really. Your sister and I—we only sought an excuse to do as we wanted. Ida's drink simply helped us along."

"If there should be a child?"

"Much as I hate to think it, that child would still be a Clary, no matter who the father is. I believe I am man enough to say I would raise any child Pandora gave me." Daniel slapped at a mosquito dining on his cheek. His hand took away a splotch of blood big enough to take an oath on.

"Now I must ask—will your feelings toward Miranda be changed if they ruin her?"

"Some English lords would cry off worried about their succession. As a third son, that is not a great concern of mine. Miranda could never be spoiled for me."

"A solemn pledge then, since my palm is already bloodied. We will find our women and marry them." Daniel stretched out his arm and clasped Jason's hand. "Tomorrow."

Twenty-five

The Clary boys broke camp while the women took care of their bodily functions with Custis holding both of the ropes bound around their ankles. Pandora coyly asked him for the roll of rags before going behind the bushes and raised a great blush on the simple man's cheeks.

"Be quick about your business," she told Miri as she tied a strip of cloth to a bush to let Jason know they had come this way. "Leave the rags in your undergarments. I have no desire to bloody myself twice."

She began plucking rose stems from her hair. Most of the petals had flown away, but she saved what she could along with the sepals and the swollen ovaries of the flowers. These she hid in her bosom to drop along the way. They lay on top of the red bud she'd taken from the wedding. She touched that one for luck.

"A plump bosom must be a handy thing to have, so good for secreting items. I am afraid anything I put in there would fall right through to the ground," Miranda remarked as she rose from her squat.

"A way with serpents might be more useful. Very well done last evening."

"Truly, I didn't mean to kill Ray, only incapacitate him."

"He got what he deserved, or would have deserved if he'd touched me. We can only put them off for so long and must even the odds in any way we can. My true monthlies aren't due for two weeks. Yours?"

"I never know when the Curse will arrive. Sometimes not for months, then two or three times in a row."

"A lack of red meat," Pandora said, sounding regrettably like her mother.

"Let's not argue. We have another long day ahead."

"Here, let me run my fingers through your hair."

"Whatever for? I do not care how I look for anyone but Jason."

"For this." Pandora held up loose hairs she'd combed out from the curls. She nestled them with the remains of the roses between her breasts. "More to guide Jason to us."

Custis jiggled the ropes. "Time to leave, ladies."

The horses stood saddled and ready, one bearing the odiferous bundle of Ray on its haunches. Robbie passed around cold pone and cups of water. His eyes looked puffy and bloodshot as if he'd cried in his sleep.

"Either of you females ride?" Ransom asked.

"Not very well," Miranda confessed.

"I am an excellent horsewoman," Pandora replied.

"Then, you get the honor of riding with Ray this fine morning. Tie her hands, Cuss, so she don't try to ride off and set her up there sideways. So sorry, milady, we don't have a sidesaddle for your convenience. You just hang on any way you can. Lead her horse, Custis. We're going to walk the horses upstream this morning. Yesterday, we had to make time. Today, we got to make sure we lose whoever is coming after us. No chatter, understand? Come on little gal, you're with me."

Ransom lifted Miranda to his saddle, mounted and led the way down the bank to the sandy bed of the creek. The dour Robbie brought up the rear. They headed upstream in the shallow water. Pandora watched the slight current erase the hoofprints of Ranse's horse as they passed. She hoped for mossy rocks to be overturned, but this seemed to be a land without stones. Turtles out for an early sunning abandoned half-submerged logs as the riders' shadows washed over them. Minnows scattered away from heavy hooves. Neither would give Jason any clues to the way they'd gone.

They came to a rookery of white, hunch-shouldered birds. One shout would startle them, but perhaps too obvious. Ranse might gag her for that infraction. She'd done her best to direct her brother before Custis placed her in the saddle and would try again when they left the streambed, unless a more subtle sign could be managed beforehand. Up ahead, a huge blue heron plucked a crayfish from its hiding place.

"Look!" she exclaimed as if delighted by the sight.

With the crayfish still struggling in its beak, the big bird took wing, flying back along the course of the water. Ranse turned in his saddle and said, "You make another sound, and we'll stop and bind your mouth, too."

She nodded submissively. "Such a magnificent bird. I was overcome."

"Common as dirt in these parts. You'll see plenty more, so hush."

Not much further on, their party came across a dip in the bank where deer came to drink or cross to the other side. Their cloven hooves had cut the sandy soil into a cuneiform design. Ranse nodded and steered his mount toward the side of the natural ford. As the horses climbed upward, Pandora removed her foot from the stirrup and slid down the side of her horse as if falling. She landed on her knees, digging in her toes and rocking back on her heels until Custis came to return her to the saddle.

"Stomp out those marks," Ranse told his brother. "Take her with you if she can't stay on."

Happily, Custis untied her hands and hoisted her in front of him again, leaving the defunct Ray alone on the other horse. Pandora was not sure which companion she preferred as both were silent and odiferous in the increasing heat of the day. At least Custis did not draw flies, but his bristled chin rubbed against her cheek far too often. She used that as an excuse to flinch away from him, shielding her bosom with her hands long enough to extract a few rose hips to drop along the way. The hips would not fly off with the breeze, and Jason needed a direction to follow.

After traveling uphill for a short while, their group burst out onto a level plain. A ridge rose up in the distance. Ranse headed in that direction, following the game trail. Suddenly, two shots of a pistol sounded from the direction of the creek. A cloud of small, white egrets, startled from their roost, wheeled toward the distant swamp.

"They're close! Let's ride," Robbie shouted.

As the horse sprinted forward, Pandora dropped one, two, three rose hips and prayed none of the wildlife would find them tasty.

~ * ~

Jason Longleigh looked up as the huge blue heron flew overhead and continued down the course of the stream. A bit of offal fell from the bird's beak and hit him squarely in the face. He showed the object to Daniel. Unaware that its tail remained in the gullet of a bird, the crayfish continued to snap its small pincers as it died.

"Be glad you weren't hit by a deposit from the other end," Daniel remarked.

"Something disturbed that bird recently. It had no time to devour its catch. We might be only a mile or two behind. If we make haste..."

"We will give them notice or miss their trail. Be cautious."

Ignoring his companion, Jason urged his horse to move faster on the shifting sand of the creek bed. The thoroughbred objected, sidling and tossing its head. The animal reared up and came down on the end of a thick branch hanging over the water. A dark-scaled, muscular snake rose from the leaves and flashed its white, open mouth and sharp fangs. The horse reared again. Without thinking, Jason drew his pistol and shot its two balls into the reptile. Unused to any abrupt noise other than the starter pistol, his mount shied, bunched, gave a great kick that sent Jason flying, and headed back the way they had come at a good clip. The white birds perched in the tree exploded into the sky.

"Now the beast wants to run. At least neither of us is snake bitten and sand makes for a soft landing." Jason picked himself out of the water.

"Ida always cautioned us to leave the cottonmouths alone, back up slowly, and let the snake go its way. You've probably angered that serpent goddess of hers, not to mention giving away our position. I will fetch your horse, and you may cool your heels." Daniel shot a look at Jason, standing ankle-deep in the stream, before he turned to pursue the skittish animal.

With nothing better to do than keep company with a stinking dead snake under a tree streaked with guano, Jason walked up the streambed, searching for signs. He saw the cut in the bank from a distance—a natural place to leave the water—and cursed himself for being so stupid a moment ago. Patience was a virtue he did not possess. Oh, he knew how to track, but a hot meal always waited at home, whether he stalked and killed his quarry or not. He'd enjoyed the game, but never before cared about the outcome so dearly, discounting only the time his sisters had gotten lost.

Pandora had done all she could, shedding blossoms where her captors had turned off the road to make camp, leaving that white rag in the glade obviously used by the women as a lavatory, setting her feet one in front of the other into the soil of the bank to show which way they had gone. He'd checked the far side of the stream to be sure no horses had passed there, then followed Panny's lead. They had come close, he was certain.

Daniel returned with the blasted racehorse. He remounted and, letting his animal pick its way, headed toward the cut in the bank. There, a clumsy attempt had been made to obscure evidence of the women. But Panny had dug her heels and toes in deep. He could still see the impression of the point and heel of a woman's slipper within the stamp of a boot.

At the head of the cut, he found the rose hip split open by a horse's shoe and a few more scattered along the game trail. The Clary boys were heading straight for that ridge, had probably gotten there by now. He found the exact spot where their horses dug in for a sprint. No need to speculate about the time. That would coincide with the shots from his pistol. Cursing himself, Jason set his heels to his horse, and Daniel followed.

~ * ~

Once on top of the wooded ridge, Pandora studied the great swamp stretching for mile upon mile to their left, a wilderness of towering cypress and tupelos shallowly rooted in a basin of water-covered peat. Staying on the high ground, Ranse picked up the pace even more. Pandora let one rose hip slide down the horse's withers like debris caught in the saddle during their passage through the brush. She dropped the others a few paces along the way. They galloped onward.

Past noon, Ranse sighted a cluster of cabins ahead. "We stop here and trade Ray's horse for a boat and some supplies."

"And give my brother a decent Christian burial," Robbie said, speaking up for the first time all morning.

Ransom did not answer his cousin but simply rode on until they reached the small settlement. Hides on stretchers littered the place: deer, bear, beaver, otter, muskrat. Three dark-hued men sat around a fire cooking their morning catch impaled on the ends of green sticks. Pandora had to admit the scent of cooking fish had never smelt better. Even Miranda in a silent stupor all morning, probably still blaming herself for Ray's death, raised her head and sniffed the air.

"Looks like we got a darkie, a Injun and a greasy dago to deal with," Ranse told his brother. "This should be easy."

He maneuvered his horse close to the fire. "Any of you boys want to earn some money digging a grave for my dead cousin here? After, we'll trade his horse for one of those dugouts you got pulled up on shore and some vittles. What do you say?"

The Spaniard, who seemed to be the leader, rose from his squat. He swept off a floppy felt hat with a hawk feather in the band and bowed to the women. "Don Diego de Saltillo at your service, *señoritas*. My companions, Bear-Who-Walks-Like-A-Man and Toby. As for your request, *señor,* I would rather trade one of *our* horses for one of *your* women."

Giving them a broad grin glittering with a pair of gold teeth, Diego wiped a finger along his mustache. The creases by his eyes and mouth deepened with his mirth. He gestured toward two skinny pinto ponies cropping marsh grass from a manger inside a corral of pine poles.

"However, you are welcome to share our meal before you go on your way."

Miranda said softly without inflection. "*Los hombres son muy malos. Socorro, por favor.*"

Pandora had planned to use her fluency in Spanish to beg for help as well, but Miri had spoken first—for all the good it did them.

"*Lo siento mucho, señorita bonita.* This is not my problem. Get down. Eat. You seem tired."

Ranse dug his hands into Miranda's shoulders and shook her hard. "No more of the foreign lingo, you hear."

"She merely greeted him and asked for his assistance," Pandora quickly interjected.

"You speak his language, too?"

"Yes, I am fluent in French, Spanish, and Italian. I have some German as well."

"Great lot of good that will do you as my brother's wife."

"Cuss can just about speak English," Robbie had to add.

Pandora suppressed a shudder. Mentally impaired though he might be, Custis could certainly overpower her if he grew amorous. She felt the urge to touch the knife strapped to her calf. Not now. Patience. Patience.

Ranse shoved Miranda off his horse. She would have fallen if not for the Spaniard, who caught her elbow. Custis, showing more consideration, dropped Pandora gently to the ground. The men dismounted, all but dead Ray, whose scent began to overpower the smell of the fish.

"Can't eat with a corpse stinkin' right there. I'll dig you a hole, but I can't go down real far befo' I hits water. Best we make a shallow grave and pile the dirt over him," the Negro man said.

Uneasy in the presence of the dead, the black man clenched his bare toes in the sand and waved off the flies with a battered straw hat. Both his arms and legs stuck out from his homespun shirt and trousers as if he'd outgrown his slave clothes after making a run for freedom. He was young, well-muscled, and not much darker than his Spanish and Indian friends.

"Not here," the Indian said. "Away from house. How this man die?"

"Bit by a copperhead snake right in the neck," Ranse answered.

"No copperheads in this swamp. Plenty rattlesnakes and cottonmouths."

"Not here, back yonder. Robbie, go with this boy, Toby, and see it's done to your liking. Custis, go back the way we come and watch our trail while I parley with our friends here."

"But I'm hungry, Ranse."

Ransom Clary pulled up a stick threaded with small fish and thrust it at his brother. "Go on now. No time to waste."

Ranse sat by the fire next to the certainly counterfeit Don Diego, who had the grand gestures, but not the refined accent of any Spanish nobility Pandora had met in London or at Bellevue Hall. Her captor gestured after the burial party.

"Fine buck like that most likely has a bounty out on him."

"Toby came from Florida with me for the trapping. He is a freedman."

"I heard about that—how the Negroes run off south of our borders and offer to fight for Spain against the Americans. You got whole towns full of these so-called freedmen."

"They thrive under Spanish rule."

"Then, they sneak across the border again and poach our furs."

The faux Don Diego declined to answer, but his lip curled into a sneer of disdain worthy of any hidalgo. He took his fish from the fire and prepared to eat.

Ranse appropriated the black man's meal, shoving a couple of the fish off the stick with his knife and onto a palmetto leaf placed near the fire for the purpose. He gave that portion to Miranda and Pandora to share and kept the rest for himself. After waiting a moment for the fish to cool, Miranda split it with her fingers and delicately pulled out the bony spine before raising flakes of steaming, white meat to her lips. Pandora copied her.

All the while, the Indian studied the women as he ate. Pandora began to fear the Spaniard had not been jesting about buying them. Near Jason's age, this man had a handsome, high-cheeked face, a strong nose, full lips and large dark eyes. Except for his deeply bronzed skin, he could have passed for any of her brothers, though he was stockier and shorter than Jason or Joshua. He'd covered his straight, black hair with a turban of scarlet calico ornamented with a display of religious medals and the plume of a snowy egret. He wore his loose, calico shirt bound round his waist with a sash of red. He'd adopted Spanish pantaloons and had the tops laced into a high pair of deerskin moccasins.

"You Injun?" he asked.

"Partially Shawnee," she answered, knowing that thanks to her mother's passion for Pearce Longleigh, she would be answering this question for the rest of her life, even in the American wilderness where all sorts of people dwelled.

"Me part Shawnee. My father Shawnee. My mother Creek. We come back to my mother's people when she a widow. Her people gone south. Now, we Seminole."

"How very interesting," Pandora said. How strange to be making dinner conversation with a savage of her own blood.

The young brave called out in a musical, exotic language. A woman she mistook for Spanish because of her bright red calico skirt and blouse, white apron and black hair pulled back into a bun came from one of the cabins. She carried corn cakes in a split cane basket and had a jug tucked under her arm. Close up, Pandora could see she must be the young man's mother. Her features were the same, her hair threaded with silver. The woman offered the cakes and the container to her guests.

Ranse sniffed the jug. Obviously disappointed, he poured molasses on a corn cake and passed it along. Pandora drizzled a small puddle of treacle onto the palmetto leaf and dipped her cake into it. Treacle, sweet and syrupy, the way she'd accused Daniel of talking. How she wished she could hear his voice now. Was this how her mother had felt, waiting and hoping Papa would rescue her somehow? Had she longed for him in the night? Perhaps her mother was not so ridiculous after all.

"Corn Tassel, my mother," Bear-Who-Walks-Like-a-Man said.

"What clan, you?" the woman asked.

"Bear, or so my papa tells us. I have a sister whose middle name is Corn Tassel. Quite a coincidence, don't you think?"

"Bear clan good. We bear clan. Corn Tassel a good name." The Indian woman nodded her approval.

"Tassie cooks, keeps the camp for us while we are trapping," the Spaniard explained. "She helps with the hides, a very useful woman like all squaws, no? That is the kind of wife you need out here. Not these fine ladies."

All during the meal, Miranda beseeched Don Diego with her wide hazel eyes. Pandora thought the girl had lost the magic that had so enchanted her brother, but perhaps not.

"You offering to trade?" Ransom asked as he licked his fingers clean of the molasses one by one.

The young Indian jumped up, offended, and glared at his trapping partner. Don Diego held up his hands.

"No, no. You misunderstand. These *senoritas* will not last in the swamp. You should leave them behind with the horses. I will watch them for you until you finish what business you have in there."

"Our business is none of yours. It's time to make a deal, dago." Ranse stood up in one smooth motion, drew his knife and held it to Corn Tassel's throat.

"You keep your woman, and we'll keep ours. We need two of those dugouts, supplies, and a guide to bring us somewhere safe. You tell no one where we've gone. You can have the use of our horses, but they better be here when we come back."

"But *Señor*, we planned to leave this place soon and take our furs to market in St. Augustine before the worst of the heat sets in." Don Diego gestured toward a small building up on stilts and securely padlocked.

"Not my concern. Injun, go clean out the smokehouse."

"No got much now," Bear told him.

"Whatever you have, put it in a sack."

Custis tore into camp. "Someone coming. Far off, but raising dust."

"Good work, brother. Go in the cabin and see if these folks got any more cornmeal and molasses. Salt and coffee, too. Pack it up. Robbie, time to travel. Say goodbye to ole Ray and get your ass back here."

Robbie came running, stumbling over roots in his haste as he entered the clearing. "I give the darkie some coins to finish the job and carve a cross." Seeing the situation, he drew his pistol and went to stand behind Don Diego.

The Seminole returned with the meat from the smokehouse. He showed Ranse the contents. "Bear hams, venison, big smoked fish."

"Good. Custis!" Ranse called.

"Coming." He emerged from the cabin with a sack slung over his shoulder, a rough, shambling St. Nicholas grinning over his bounty.

All the while, Pandora thought, "Should I use my knife now?" The answer came back "no." Ranse could cut Corn Tassel's throat in a second and be on her in a thrice. Robbie would shoot the Spaniard with no more thought than he would give to killing a rabbit. Wait, wait.

"Now which of you fine fellows wants to take us into the swamp?" Ranse eyed Diego and Bear.

"I will go. I know a place the women can have some comfort," the Spaniard said. "Can any of you *hombres* pole a dugout?"

"We'll figure it out. Ladies, get up. Don't give any trouble in the boats, or you'll be gator bait. Robbie, bring the saddlebags and rifles."

Ranse motioned them all toward the dugouts. Still gripping Corn Tassel, he ordered the kidnapped women into one of the hollowed cypress logs, gray from age and use. Custis got into the second with the supplies and saddlebags. Robbie attempted to stave in the third boat with the butt of his rifle, but the thick cylinder of wood resisted his blows. Giving up, he took the pole, stepped into the boat with Custis, and shoved off from the bank. Wobbling the dugout and leaning heavily on the push pole, Robbie waited for Ranse's next command.

"You next, dago." Ranse pushed Corn Tassel away hard enough to take her son to the ground when he attempted to break her fall. The woman scrambled up and ran for her cabin.

Getting his pistol out, Ranse backed to the dugout and got between Miranda and Pandora. "Shove off."

Corn Tassel reappeared, hauling an ancient musket. She thrust it at her son, but by the time he had it primed, ready, and aimed at Robbie as the best target, the dugouts had moved among the cypress trees. The shot fell harmlessly, making small circles in the water. Ranse did not bother to fire his pistol, a waste of a ball at this distance.

Mildly, he said to Custis, "Brother, didn't you notice they had a weapon in there when you was getting the supplies?"

"Sure, but we got plenty of guns. Didn't you say to get food?"

"Damned fool idiot nearly got me killed," Robbie complained, but he kept pushing his dugout forward, nearly butting the first boat.

The Spaniard poled his craft through the peat brown water of the Okefenokee. They threaded their way among cypress trees with trunks the size of millstones, their knobby knees thrust above the surface, their branches heavy with gray swathes of Spanish moss. With pointed tops against the sky, they resembled witches bathing with their hats still on, Pandora thought. She was becoming as fanciful as her poetic brother and needed to be far more practical.

Whining mosquitoes, darting in for a meal of blood, hung over their craft along with annoying gnats that sipped their sweat. Pretending to scratch an insect bite on her bosom, Pandora recovered the light hair she'd combed from Miri's curls that morning and balled it in her fist to wait for the right moment of its use.

Small frogs thrummed as they approached, ceased their noise and took it up again once they'd passed. They startled a huge red-headed bird tearing into a dead black gum tree with its stout ivory bill. With a flash of black and white wings, it was gone, all eyes following its flight through the trees. In that moment, Pandora crimped the fan-shaped leaves of a palmetto and left behind a few strands of Miranda's hair.

"Lord God, what was that?" Ranse said.

"Woodpecker," answered the Spaniard.

"We got woodpeckers in the hills, but none that size."

"Many strange creatures live in the swamp."

They moved on. Pandora snagged strands of hair on the rough edges of stumps and the thorns of the greenbriers. With all his attention on keeping the dugout upright, Robbie failed to notice and Custis just kept gazing upward, his mouth half-open, at the green light filtering through the branches of the immense trees. Finally, they glided from the tangle of cypress to more open water festooned with water lilies around the edges.

Pandora pretended to be beguiled by the lovely white flowers raised up on thick stems above the pads. She plucked one, placed it in her bosom and left behind the bedraggled silk rose from the bodice of her gown. Ranse faced away from her, his eyes on Miranda's slight back. If the Spaniard saw, he did not give her away.

Don Diego pushed through a mass of lilies and out into a lake. "We paddle now and go faster. Head to that dead cypress."

He knelt carefully on a strip of deer hide and, pulling up his pole, took a paddle in hand. Ranse reached for a second paddle. Behind them, Robbie struggled through the lilies, cursing and annoying a good-sized alligator that sunk from their sight.

"Custis, you gotta paddle, too. I'm tired of doing all the damned work."

The second dugout tore free of the mat of lily pads and came behind. One by one, Pandora plucked the white petals from the lily and dropped them, hoping they would not drift away on the still water in the stifling air. Custis and Robbie paddled over them unconcerned. They moved toward the dead cypress standing white against a blue sky and rounded the end of an island. Following its shore, they arrived at an open area with a small, sandy beach. A rickety dock thrust out into the water, but the Spaniard simply drove his dugout onto the slope of the island, jumped out with Ranse, and pulled the boat up further. Politely, Diego helped the women out. He gestured to a small log cabin raised up on cypress posts and thatched with palmetto leaves.

"My trapping camp—shelter, a small cistern to collect drinking water, much fish and game. I come back for you in *dos semanas*, two weeks." He held up his brown fingers to indicate the length of time.

Robbie and Custis came ashore. Cuss slung the bag of provisions over his shoulder and headed for the cabin. Robbie walked out on the dock a short way. Pandora and Miranda huddled together on the shore. They needed to talk.

"Is there a necessary, Don Diego?"

"So sorry, no. Only the bushes."

"If you will excuse us, gentlemen." She led Miranda away.

"Watch out for snakes," Ranse called after them, his voice taunting. "And gators, don't forget the gators."

The women encountered Custis on his way for another load. Pandora held out her hand.

"Our rags, if you please."

"I'll get 'em." Face burning red, he found the saddlebag in the dugout and handed over the roll without looking either lady in the eye.

"*Adios*, Don Diego," Miranda called out as if she still hoped the man would come to her rescue.

"*Vaya con Dios, senoritas.* I must go now to be back before dark," the Spaniard said.

"You run along, then. Two weeks, remember." Ranse pushed the dugout off the sandy slope.

The women had gotten halfway to the first clump of bushes when a pistol fired. They turned to see Don Diego plummet from his boat. Robbie still had his gun extended, a wisp of smoke coming from the barrel. A sizeable alligator emerged from under the dock and with two sweeps of its mighty tail, nosed against the capsized boat and sank from sight. No body floated upward. All that remained of the Spaniard was his floppy hat floating on the surface and his overturned dugout. No one made a move to retrieve either.

"Now what did you do that for?" Ranse Clary asked his cousin.

"He warn't coming back for us, and we need two boats to get out of here. We lay low two weeks. Then, we go back, kill off those others and come out of this with a full season of furs to sell. You got the women, but so far all I have to show is my twin brother dead. We was close, real close. You said there was supposed to be a ransom, split by all, but I can see that ain't about to happen. Custis may be dumb as one of those cypress stumps, but I got a brain." Robbie came off the dock and got close enough to his cousin to tickle him with his beard hairs.

Ranse took a step back. "If you are so smart, you go on out there and get that boat. I hope you know the way back, too."

"I will, once the gator goes away. Won't be that hard to get out of here. Turn at the dead cypress, go back through those lilies, and keep going until we hit that ridge line again. I think the Spaniard kept turning this way and that just to confuse us."

"You better be right." Ranse turned on the women. "Go do your business and get back here."

Miri trembled in Pandora's arms. "Don Diego was a nice man. He tried to help us. He would have led Jason here."

Pandora moved her into the privacy of the bushes. "We don't know that. I left signs for Jason. He will find us."

"Before dark?" Miranda asked, her hazel eyes wide with fear.

"I cannot say. We must keep them busy in any way we can. Chin up. The Longleighs always prevail, and you shall soon be one of us. Meanwhile, we must keep up the pretense of having our monthlies. Use the facilities, if you must. I swear I've perspired so much I haven't the need. The Spaniard said the heat is only beginning."

"That is certainly true, but on Ariel Island we catch the sea breezes all summer long."

Pandora slapped at her wrist and wiped the blood from the squashed mosquito off with a rag. She pushed through the thicket to the water's edge and tied the strip of cloth to a willow branch anyone approaching by water would notice. On her return, she came across a shrubby tree with small, red berries half decayed ringing its base. She stooped to examine them.

"Miranda, might you know if these are poisonous?" Pandora asked hopefully as she rolled a few in her palm.

"Mildly, perhaps. I've read in early accounts that the Indians made a tea of native holly berries in order to purify their bodies with purges and vomits."

"Purges and vomits, you say. Gather as many as you can and tie them in a rag. A man who is vomiting will be thinking of little else. Today, we shall offer to do the cooking."

Twenty-six

The sound of the musket blast convinced Jason and Daniel to spur their horses until they were almost upon a clearing by the side of the road. Jason slowed, noted the leavings of a fish dinner beneath a live oak tree, and turned to Daniel.

"Someone watched for us here."

"Obviously. Let's go carefully, then."

They proceeded at a slow pace into the small settlement only to find a musket turned on them from the porch of a cabin. Two Indians, a man and a woman, stared at the new arrivals with hostility.

Jason held his hands up. "We come in peace."

He turned to Daniel and said, "Come now, hands up. Show them we mean no harm."

"I believe you've read too many romantic sagas, Longleigh. We are armed to the teeth. Why should they trust us?"

The Indian woman squinted hard at Jason. "Longleigh? You Longleigh—bear clan?"

"I believe you refer to my father, Pearce Longleigh, once known as Great Bear among the Shawnee."

"I know Great Bear many years ago. He go away, follow Little Yellow Flower. Never return. You his son?"

"Actually, the son you refer to would be my brother, James. But yes, I am a son of Great Bear."

"He have many sons?"

"Four sons and six daughters."

"Ah," the woman said, clearly impressed. "He still live? And your mama?'

"Oh my, yes. He's as virile as ever, I'm afraid, and my mother is quite spry. You might have seen one of my sisters come this way in the company of some very bad fellows. Her name is Pandora. She resembles me but is a bit darker-complexioned. Same sort of hair and eyes, but much more feminine, of course."

The woman signaled with her hand. A black man armed with a long rifle stepped from behind a tree. He held the weapon steady on them.

"He is bear clan. No shoot," she told him.

Though he relaxed his stance, the Negro stayed at the ready. "Bunch of hill folks come this way with two women and a snake-bit corpse, big bearded man all swole up with poison. Seminoles don't like to handle the dead, so I buried the body. They took off with two of our boats and all our supplies into the swamp."

"How long ago?" Daniel asked.

"An hour or so, I guess. They had our friend, Don Diego, to guide 'em."

"The women were our kidnapped brides. Do you know where these men have taken them?" Daniel continued, getting to the crux of the matter far more swiftly than his verbose companion.

"Maybe. Diego has more than one camp in the swamp."

"If you show us the way, you shall be richly rewarded," Jason said expansively.

Daniel frowned. They hadn't brought along much money or provisions in their haste. What did he intend to offer?

The young Seminole stepped forward. "Bear-Who-Walks-Like-A-Man will guide his clan brother. No reward. Toby go with Corn

Tassel and furs to St. Augustine. No wait for bad men to return." He folded his arms across his calico-covered chest.

"Can't argue with him once he's set. Bear, I will take care of your mama like she was my own. I'll leave your horses with enough feed and water to get 'em through a few days. I figure those robbers owe us an animal for all they took, so there will be five including yours in the corral when you get back. Tassie, gather up what you want to take."

The black man led the thoroughbreds to the corral now crowded with milling horses, unsaddled the beasts, and turned them in while Jason and Daniel refilled their canteens from the cistern. He caught two pintos and a sturdy bay the marauders had left behind, tying them to the fence in preparation for loading the hides.

Corn Tassel, flicking off a few ants, offered the men the corn cakes and the leftover fish abandoned by the now ashy fire. A steady stream of insects had invaded the molasses jug, but she indicated they could have that, too.

Jason bowed. "Thank you, madam. You are most hospitable. We have had only crusts and a bit of dried fruit this morning, but I would not take the last of your food."

"Eat. We catch more fish. Get rabbit on our way. How are you called?"

"Jason, Jason Longleigh—or Lord Longleigh, if you wish. But no, we are in America now. Jason will do." He accepted the corn cake and a small fish.

"I am called Corn Tassel. You Jay's Son." She pointed to a largish, crested blue bird who scolded them with its harsh voice from a nearby tree.

"No, nothing to do with birds. I have a Shawnee name as well—Rattler."

Corn Tassel sucked in her breath. "You not speak his name. He dead."

"Yes, very. My father took his..." Jason thought the better of telling that tale. The woman might be a relative of the late Mr. Rattler, for whom he had been named out of guilt. "I've never cared for the name as I abhor snakes. We had a nasty encounter with one not too long ago. Do call me Jason. You see, Jason was a daring adventurer who sailed a large ship in search of a golden fleece and had many strange encounters along the way."

Politely, Corn Tassel sat by his side to give full attention to his story, but the less talkative Daniel had finished his meal while Jason chattered.

"Another time, Longleigh. We must go while we still have some daylight."

Jason stood, bowed again to the Indian woman. "Another time, perhaps. Have a safe journey, Mrs. Tassel."

She rose and nodded. "You tell Great Bear I have a brave younger son, too."

"When next I see him."

"Longleigh, enough!"

Daniel moved toward the last of the dugouts where the Seminole man had stowed their armaments, saddlebags, and a few blankets. He waited patiently, push pole in hand, for the two white men to be seated before giving a mighty shove to send the boat into the water. Bear did not look back at his mother as he moved them into the grove of cypress.

Jason rode in the prow, taking in all about them. After a while, he felt moved to memorialize their adventure with poetry.

"I list' to the murmurings of the cypress/ Towering magnificent o'er my head/As with our Indian guide, good man Dan/And I glide water bourn seeking our brides. /We shall leave the villains no place to hide/ As we traverse this marsh called....What is the name of this place?"

"The Okefenokee," Daniel replied unhappily.

"Five syllables. That won't do. What does it mean?"

Bear steered them toward a tiny island and jumped ashore. Small trees rooted on the hummock of floating peat quivered.

"Trembling earth. See." He jumped up and down again to demonstrate, then returned to the dugout with amazing agility.

"Excellent. As we traverse this marsh called Trembling Earth."

"Would you just keep your eyes out for signs of our ladies and your mouth shut," Daniel said. He wiped the sweat from his forehead with his sleeve and brushed away the gnats swarming round his side whiskers.

"I can watch and compose at the same time, my good man Dan. Even my red brother has a greater appreciation of poetry than you. How can you despise iambic pentameter when you were raised on the Bard of Avon?"

"Because your verse has very little in common with Mr. Shakespeare."

"Miranda adores my verse."

"Then we should put all our efforts into finding your sole admirer."

Bam-bam. Bam-bam. Bam-bam.

"More gunshots!"

"Sounds like hammering to me."

"No," Bear told them. "Big redhead bird nearby. I show you."

He began to steer the dugout in the direction of the sound, but Daniel stopped him.

"We have no time for tours if we are to rescue the women today."

"Over there," Jason cried. "See the broken palmetto."

"Any animal could have done that."

Stoically ignoring their spat, Bear steered for the broken fronds and plucked the strands of light hair from the leaf. "Your woman?"

"Yes, Miranda. I would recognize her beloved curls anywhere."

Daniel nodded. "My sister's hair."

"We go this way." Without waiting for assent, the Seminole set his pole and moved them on. All three looked sharp for more signs and found the hair snagged on rough bark and spiky plants, the last of it just before they left the trees and entered a field of lily pads.

"Two paths broken through. Certainly, the Clary boys," Jason assumed.

"Could be alligator trails," Daniel countered.

"No, see that spot of pink on one of the pads. All the other flowers are white. Bear, my friend, take us there."

He did.

"I believe you might remember this, Daniel."

"The rose from Panny's bodice. My apology for doubting you. If I might have it?"

Jason handed over the silk rose. He'd saved the strands of Miranda's hair. It seemed they both had their talismans now. He searched the large, empty lake before them.

"There, a drift of white petals floating away from us. Follow them."

Bear shook his head. "They go to Diego's island. See us coming. We go around back. Take them by surprise."

"Wonderful strategy, don't you think so, Daniel?"

"Yes, a good plan. Can we get there before dark?"

The Seminole shook his head. "No, we must camp soon. Sun go away. I know a place."

Bear took them along the edge of the lily pads in the opposite direction of the floating petals. Alligators, torpid most of the day, roused themselves from the hummocks and slid into the water for their nightly hunt. A specimen as large as the dugout accompanied the men for a distance until a proud mallard leading a harem of three brown hens crossed its path. The reptile submerged. One sharp tug and the green-headed duck disappeared beneath the surface. His mates took flight, paddling furiously to gain altitude.

"Mighty alligator, swamp lord/ Behemoth of the marsh, armored reptile," Jason murmured.

"Gators not so bad," the Seminole said. "Jump on back, hold mouth shut, they no bite."

"True, all the strength of their jaws is in the snap. I've seen Indians wrestling them in Savannah for a few coins and the entertainment of a crowd. Miranda would say if you leave the alligators alone, they will let you alone," Daniel added.

"Really? What if an alligator had you in its monstrous mouth and dragged you inexorably into the depths of the swamp?"

Bear answered. "Poke eyes, hit nose. He let go."

"How interesting. Are they good to eat?"

"Would you hush up? Last night, you were ready to run off in the dark to save our women. Today, you are all optimism and poetry and curiosity," Daniel snarled.

"Last night, we had four enemies. Today, only three. With brother Bear along, the odds are now even. I suspect Pandora will have softened up her abductors for us by now."

"The man died of snake bite. That would be Miranda at work."

"Surely not. My darling bride loves harmless turtles and small birds."

"She has an affinity for all reptiles and would have cried over that cottonmouth you shot. You have much to learn about my sister."

"You have no idea what you are getting with Pandora."

"Indians quiet. White men crazy. Talk, talk all the time. We make camp here. No more words tonight." Bear steered them ashore.

Twenty-seven

"Supper about ready, ladies?" Ranse called out as he lounged in the cabin doorway.

He passed the whiskey jug to Robbie, who sat on a stump serving as a step. "All gone. Now we're stuck here with nothing to drink but water and that little bit of coffee we ground before we left home."

"Ready for your beverage, gentlemen?" Pandora said brightly.

She'd had no idea how to prepare the coffee, but did know how to serve elegantly. She tipped the black brew into their tin cups without spilling a drop. Her recipe: cistern water, a handful of grounds, and the native holly berries she'd gathered in the woods; the ingredients well boiled together in the pot hung over the campfire on the Spaniard's iron tripod.

Ransom Clary spit out his first mouthful. "Jesus, God! That's vile."

Pandora covered her lips with her fingers to express dismay and hide her smile. "Oh, I am so sorry. You see, I've never prepared coffee before. I saw a sugar loaf amongst the provisions. Let me get that for you. No sense in wasting our beverage."

She stepped around Robbie and over Ranse's legs, entered the cabin and returned with the cone of hardened white sugar. The men knocked off chunks of the sweetening with the handles of their knives and dissolved them in the coffee. Custis used three lumps.

"Lots better, Miss Pandora," he said.

Miranda lugged the small iron pot from the fire and set it in the sand near the men. "Bear stew," she announced proudly. "Panny, do bring the corn cakes."

Their captors gathered round the pot and drew out hunks of bear ham from lumpy white gravy on the tips of their knives. Pandora brought palmetto leaves holding the corn cakes cooked at the edge of the fire. She passed them around, then settled herself next to Miranda, who had arranged pieces of the smoked fish on another of the leaves Custis had cut for them, along with chopping up the bear ham.

"As you might have noticed, Miranda does not eat meat. I shall keep her company by dining on fish and leaving more of the bear stew for the three of you." Pandora passed the tin cup once belonging to the late Ray to Miri, who sipped the cistern water they were sharing.

"Tastes kind of funny," Robbie said as he fished another piece of meat from the stew. White gravy dribbled into his thick beard.

"Try the corn cakes," Pandora urged.

Custis cracked open one of the cakes, ashy and charred outside, the inside still raw dough. He shrugged and dipped it in the gravy, oblivious to the lumps.

Robbie said, "Worst meal I've ever et, Ranse. You done stole women who can't cook. Means they only good for one thing, and I'll be having some of that tonight, I swear."

Miranda placed her hands over her eyes and sobbed. "We tried so hard. Neither of us has ever cooked before."

When she revealed her face again, her lashes fluttered and tears overflowed from her big, hazel eyes and splashed down her cheeks. Pandora hugged her.

"There, there, Miri, we did our best. Both of us have been gently reared and know little about preparing food. But we do have other talents. We can play the pianoforte, and I have mastered the harp and guitar as well. We sing beautifully, of course."

"You got a pianoforte at your place, Ranse?" Robbie mocked.

"We could buy a guitar," Custis offered. "That'd be nice, singing in the evening."

"We can sing for you now. Rise up, Miranda. Do you know the Shenandoah song?"

"Certainly. One of Daniel's favorites."

Standing together, hands clasped before them, the women blended their voices as loudly as possible. If Daniel heard, he would discover them. Miranda knew several more verses and continued on in a sweetly quavering voice as day turned to dusk. The men ate thoughtlessly, sopping up the remains of the gravy from the pot. Pandora poured the last of the coffee into their cups.

"That was awful pretty," Custis told them as he sweetened his brew with a large lump of sugar.

Robbie picked his teeth with the tip of his knife. "What's this here thing?" He rolled one of the berries between two grubby fingers.

The women looked at each other. All innocence, Miranda spoke first.

"Berries we found in the woods. The birds were eating them, so we knew they must be safe. We thought they might add some flavor to the stew."

"All I tasted was flour, salt, bear grease and a kind of bitterness," Ranse said. "They can learn to cook. Tonight, we teach them their other wifely duties."

"Sounds good to me. I'll bet the dark one could take on two of us at once. Be careful you don't kill the puny gal." Robbie slapped his knee and roared when the women hugged each other tight.

"It's such a lovely evening." Pandora swatted a mosquito dining on her neck. "Wouldn't you like to hear more singing?"

"I'd like that, Miss Pandora. Besides, ain't we supposed to take our brides to the preacher first before we do them other things?" Custis said, wrinkling his low brow.

"Cuss, once we bed 'em, they're all ours. Those other men will swear off. But I could stand a little more music. They sure sing better than they cook, and we got all night long."

Ranse stretched out against the stump serving as a step for the hut and motioned for more tunes. He kept time with one hand as if he were leading a church choir.

Pandora and Miranda ran through a repertoire they'd performed in elegant drawing rooms and fine parlors. They strived to remember every piece, every verse they had by heart, and filled in the parts forgotten with newly forged lyrics—anything to avoid their fate.

Finally, Ranse cut the air with his hand. Looking a little bilious, he said, "Enough. I need to make use of the bushes, then we're going to bed. No arguments."

He bent over as a cramp hit his gut. Robbie got no further than a corner of the hut before he vomited up the bear stew full of tiny, red berries. Custis simply ran for the shrubbery without saying a word. His big feet pounded the sand and one hand fumbled to unbutton his trousers. Robbie, doubled over, overtook him in the race for relief.

"Quickly into the cabin. We can bar the door." Pandora scrambled to the top of the stump and helped Miranda into the crude shelter.

There was no bar, only a chock of wood with a long nail driven through it into the unchinked pine logs, just strong enough to keep the door made from a single plank of cypress closed against wind and weather. Pandora turned the block to the horizontal position, knowing the device would not keep out a hurricane or even an angry man.

"What shall we do now? They have their knives with them. The pistols and rifles are stacked in here, but I have no idea how to use them. Do you, Panny?"

"I have no skill with a rifle, but only last year persuaded my father to teach me the use of a pistol. Unfortunately, I shot my brother-in-law quite accidentally and am a bit nervous about using one now, even though he survived. We could try, but if we don't gauge the powder correctly, it might blow up in our faces. Jason says a pistol is good only until its shots are spent, and then it is best used as a club.

I suppose we could attempt to beat them over the head, but I suspect any of them are capable of overpowering us."

"At least we have all of the food." Miranda studied the cabin as if preparing for a siege. "And none of the water. The air will heat as soon as the sun rises."

"An oversight on our part, but we must hold out another night until help arrives."

"Do you believe we can be found here?"

"I must."

Swearing and complaining, the men returned. Through the gaps between the logs, the women watched and listened to their conversation.

"They poisoned us. They for sure poisoned us," Ranse muttered.

"That or the one your pa wanted does bear a curse. I feel like I been cursed below the waist and above." Robbie moaned, not quite over his miseries.

Custis scratched his head. "Maybe the bear meat was off. They're so pretty and sing so sweet. Wouldn't harm a flea on our coonhound, would they, brother?"

"Not Miranda. Anyone can see she's a timid thing without a thought in her head, but the other I don't trust. We got to teach her a lesson."

Miranda huffed at the insult. Pandora felt moved to complain in a low voice. "Why is it I am always blamed? This is no different than home. If I could summon tears the way you can, I'd never be accused."

"An easy trick. Pluck out an eyelash while your hands cover your face."

Ranse leaned against the cabin for a moment, then mounted the stump and began thumping at the door. Pandora and Miranda put their backs against the plank. The pounding stopped suddenly.

"Lord God, I have to go again. I'm weak as a newborn pup, and I done lost all my urges. Listen here, ladies. You can have your way tonight, but we plan to keep this fire burning. Come morning, we'll smoke you out if we must. Meanwhile, have pity and throw out a few blankets. I got the shakes."

"All of you go far away, and we'll give you bedding," Pandora offered. Softly to Miranda, she said, "No sense in making them angrier. We will have to go out in the morning."

"I'm going back to the bushes. Cuss and Robbie are coming with me. See, we're going."

The women watched as their captors backed away and started round the shack. Miranda gathered an armful of blankets and prepared to throw them out when Pandora opened the door. Quickly as she moved to toss the bedding, Robbie came on faster, bolting back around the corner to charge the opening. His foot caught in the tangled blankets and missed the top of the stump. He tumbled backwards and hit his head on the ground. Pandora rammed the door shut and turned the chock.

"Cursed," he said before getting up to join his cousins. "Cursed."

The captives watched the men return and settle by the fire for the night, all but Ranse, who paced wrapped in a blanket and steadily used up the Spaniard's pile of firewood. Unfortunately, Don Diego had left a good supply. The Clarys would have ample fuel to smoke them out in the morning. Gingerly, Pandora picked up a pistol.

"Good, it is already primed and loaded. I shall sleep with it by my side in case they should try to force the door. I do not care if it does blow up in my face. I'd rather that than rape."

Miranda's eyes widened at her words. "Some would say we should shoot ourselves before allowing that to happen."

"What utter nonsense. An accidental death trying to defend myself is one thing, but taking my own life is another quite similar to a meek surrender. I personally will live to kill any man who rapes me first chance I get."

"Me, too," Miranda swore.

Pandora shook her head as if she could not imagine the turtle lover, the adorable little dove, to be capable of any violence. "I will do my best to defend us both. Shooting another human being is a terrible thing, and I would not have you suffer over it. My mother told me that once, and I did not believe her. Try to sleep. We will take turns watching the door."

The women spread their blankets, made brief plans about how to handle their captors in the morning, and took a moment to pray to God that Daniel and Jason would arrive at first light.

~ * ~

Dawn arrived wrapped in hot pink clouds and brought along as her guest another sweltering, humid day in the Okefenokee. She did not bring Daniel and Jason.

Having decided they could not kill all the men with pistols before being overcome and slain themselves, the women emerged from the cabin and offered a tin of tea from the Spaniard's supplies as a peace offering to the men around the fire. All had dark circles under their eyes. Robbie's beard harbored the remains of regurgitated bear stew.

"I will scrub the coffee pot after we've attended to our morning ablutions," Pandora said as if she meant to make amends.

She made sure the Clarys saw she carried that roll of rags with her. Before going to the bushes near the edge of the island, she shared a cup of water at the cistern with Miranda. The stuffiness of the hut had them yearning for a drink already. Having eaten little the night before and sweated in the stuffy cabin, their bodily functions took no time at all. They noticed the shrubs appeared more beaten down than before, but had precious little time to care. The rest of their minutes alone needed to be spent in conniving.

"What can we do to deter them next?" Pandora pondered.

"I know our time is running out. If we are not found soon, Panny, we will meet the fate worse than death." Miranda wrung her small hands.

"Stop saying that! It's not worse than death, but could be terribly unpleasant with these men."

"Psst. *Aqui, señoritas.*" Don Diego dropped down from a live oak that shattered their retreat.

Miranda hugged him like a long-lost uncle. "You are alive! I knew you would try to help us if you were able."

With his floppy hat gone, the Spaniard looked much older. His hair hung long, gray and greasy. Cuts and scratches, some quite deep, marked his wiry brown body.

"Were you watching us?" Pandora asked, not in the least friendly.

"I could see nothing from my perch—except that knife the dark lady has strapped to her leg. Do not be afraid to use it when you must."

"I am not afraid," Pandora asserted. "What were you doing up there if not spying?"

"A she-bear chase me here from the end of the island when I trip over her cubs last night. Being a wise *hombre*, I stay up there long after she goes to her den."

"But how did you escape the alligator? Where is your wound?" To Pandora, Miranda sounded as if she wanted to record the whole incident in her journal.

"I think these bad men no let me go so easy. I see from the corner of my eye, the bearded one about to shoot. So, I fall into the water, go up under the dugout like a turtle into its shell. The alligator, he tried to pull me out, but I hold on and hit his snout again and again. The boat, she gets pushed to the end of the island. I start to walk back, then, the she-bear."

"If you could draw the bear into camp, that would create more havoc," Miranda suggested.

"Easy to do since she got cubs," Diego agreed.

"But she must not be hurt. She has babies to care for."

"Oh, Miri, it may be her or us. You must give up some of your sensibilities for plain common sense." Before Pandora could say more, Ransom Clary began calling.

"Time is up, ladies. If you run off, you will be sorry. Something mighty big was thrashing around in those bushes last night. Could be we got a bear on this island."

"As indeed we do. Don Diego, if you will draw her here again, *gracias*." Pandora tipped her head to him.

"I will do my best, *senoritas*, and run my fastest. You must take shelter in the cabin. *Adios*." The Spaniard slipped through the brush, quiet as an Indian.

Pandora threw a few of the rags on the ground and dumped the coffee grounds and suspicious berries on top. The roll must get smaller each day, or the men would suspect another ruse. Taking a deep breath, she led the way back into camp and went directly to the cistern to wash the pot.

A spot of tea would go down very well right then. The men had started preparing breakfast without them and simmered the black leaves in a pot. The tea would be wretched if they had not allowed the water to come to a boil first. That much she did know about cooking. She dipped the cup into the kettle but had no time to enjoy her beverage. Ranse began ordering people about.

"Cuss, I want you to go down to the dock and see if you can pull in a few catfish. My gut is calling for fresh food. Take Miranda with you. You tie her by the ankle again and keep that rope wound round you. I don't want her running back to the cabin for any reason. No sense in making her any more skittish than she already is."

Robbie, drinking his tea and casting dark looks at Pandora, said, "Don't you hate when you have a woman who just lays there and trembles, Ranse?"

"Well, some women need to be taught a lesson, starting with this bird-watching, flower picking, half-English, half-breed bitch. Don't think I didn't know what you was up to. Won't make no difference. Those proper gents will never find you here."

"Want I should help you get started?" Robbie said, grinning into his disgusting beard.

"I can handle her. Keep yourself busy, then you can have a turn."

Custis stood up from tying the rope around Miranda's slender ankle. "But Miss Pandora is *my* bride."

"She still will be when we get to a preacher. Go on, take Miranda down to the dock. You come with me."

Ranse knocked the tea from Pandora's hand before she could scald him with it. He grabbed an arm and jerked her toward the cabin. She dug her heels in, struggling all the way there. He had to lift her into the hut. She splayed out her arms and legs, refusing to go through the narrow doorway.

"You need some help now? She's like an eight-legged cat being put in a sack for drowning." Robbie had a good chuckle over that one as he pried Pandora's hand and foot off one edge of the door and pushed her inside.

She landed on her face and before she could scramble up and reach a pistol, Ranse got on top of her from behind. He began drawing up her gown before Robbie even shut the door. She clawed forward, escaping his grasp. He let her go, pausing to spin the chock into place.

"I like it better face up so you can watch what I do to you, anyhow."

She was face up, crab-walking backward until her back hit the rear wall of the hut. She began to raise her gown, groping for her knife. Now came the time to use it, but damn the inconvenience of women's clothing all in a tangle about her legs.

"That's right. Put up your skirts. Don't make me tear the only dress you got." He threw his body forward on top of hers. Pandora had just enough time to bunch her legs and kick him back against the other wall, where he landed with a loud thud. She screamed, hoping, simply hoping someone who cared drew near.

"Whoo-eee!" Robbie hollered from outside.

She wondered if he watched through a crack like some backwoods voyeur. Faintly, she heard a cry from Miranda. She had to get to her knife, but another scream or two certainly would do no harm.

~ * ~

"Lookee here. I set some lines last night 'cause I couldn't sleep too good. A fish on every one of 'em."

Custis held up his catch for Miranda to admire, but she kept staring toward the cabin. He slit open the first catfish, took out the guts and the mud vein, and peeled the slick skin from the body. Careful of the spines, he beheaded the creature and piled the gaping mouth and eyes on top of the entrails.

"That gator what ate Don Diego is back. Watch."

He flicked the pile into the air. The alligator caught it handily and lingered with only its head above the water to see if more would come its way.

"You know, Miss Pandora kind of scares me with her fancy words and starchy ways. She looks like a Injun, but don't act like one. I'm not afraid of you. You're all soft-spoken and shy. Maybe Ranse means for me to have you for a bride instead."

Slow of mind but not of hand, Cuss had already skinned another catfish and fed its remains to the gator. A loud thump and several screams desperate enough to be heard on the dock made Miranda cry out and pull against the rope tied round her ankle.

"Best you stay here with me, Miri, 'cause I won't hurt you. Ranse when he's riled will," Custis said, pushing her down on the dock with big, gentle fingers slimy from skinning fish.

Miranda put her hands to her face and plucked out another eyelash. She had to hope tears might work again.

Twenty-eight

The rising sun found a gap in the blanket Daniel had rolled himself into and forced the man to wake. He'd kept the middle watch covered to the chin to keep off the buzzing insects after they decided not to light a fire or create any smoke to alert the Clary boys. After checking above for panthers and snakes, he'd put his back to a tree, his pistol and knife by his side, and spent the deep hours of the night staring into the darkness. Bull alligators roared near the water and other critters rustled in the brush. Nothing more dangerous than a mother raccoon with three youngsters crossed through their camp. Bear had relieved him well before dawn.

Now, Jason sat across from him drinking from the canteen and eating a dry corn cake. Bear and the dugout were gone. Daniel bolted from the covers.

"Where did the Indian go? Are we stranded with no way to save our ladies?"

"Calm yourself, Daniel. Bear has gone ahead to scout. He will return for us when he finds the best way to come up on their camp. We will rescue our fair maidens shortly."

Daniel helped himself to water, a corn cake, and the last of the dried fruit.

"Do you know what the worst part of this pursuit has been? Hearing our brides sing "Shenandoah" last evening and all the songs after. What happened to them when the music stopped? We sat here impotent to prevent it."

"Neither screamed, and I assure you, Pandora never keeps her mouth shut. I do not believe they were molested." Nevertheless, the optimism faded from Jason's face.

"Remember, we have pledged to marry them regardless. No fault of theirs if we do not reach them in time."

"Agreed."

Almost without a sound, Bear-Who-Walks-Like-A-Man entered the camp. Both of the other men surged to their feet.

"We go now. Women in cabin. Men sleep near door. One watches by fire. I know way."

"Jolly good." Jason sat down again and began to draw off his boots.

"We are finally ready to go to the rescue, and you are undressing?" Daniel asked.

"Certainly. The surest way to make noise in the woods is to wear heavy boots. I shall go in my stocking feet and suggest you do the same unless Bear has brought along extra moccasins. Walk lightly on the balls of your feet, stay on a clear path and don't rustle the bushes."

"More of your father's training?"

"Exactly. I never thought to put it to use stalking anything other than Bellevue's deer."

"He right," Bear agreed. "Near camp, watch for big stink place. No slip there and show where we be."

"Walk softly and avoid the big stink. I understand—perhaps."

"I wouldn't take that sword," Jason cautioned. "They tend to rattle and get stuck on things."

"Pistols are unreliable. I will muffle it as well as I can."

"We might be able to take one down with a rifle," Jason suggested.

"It would only warn the others and put the women in danger. Bear is right. We must creep up on them."

Neither argued anymore in their haste to get to the dugout and make the crossing to the next island. Daniel shucked off his boots, gathered them and his weapons, and followed the Seminole to the water. Jason seated himself in the prow. Bear pushed off with the pole and took them across the way. He brought the dugout to rest in a tangle of red bay near a game trail wide enough to be used as an alligator slide. Fortunately, none of the reptiles was using it at the time.

The path soon narrowed and passed through a grove of pond pines, their fallen needles muffling the steps of the men. Daniel held his sword close to his side to stifle any clanking. They came to a brushy verge. Daniel wrinkled his nose. The big stink. Certainly, someone had been very sick in the vicinity. Bear motioned around the various piles and puddles. Staying low, they peered through the bushes.

"Miranda," Jason said softly.

She sat on a dock over the water. One of the Clary boys, the simple one, sought to amuse her by feeding an alligator scraps. The bearded twin had his eye to a chink in the wall at the side of a small cabin.

"I take bear-faced man," the Seminole said, referring to the heavily bearded Robbie.

"I shall rescue Miranda from the clutches of that beast," Jason declared in a whisper.

"But where is Pandora?" Daniel asked.

A loud thump, a cry of whoo-ee from the remaining twin, and Pandora's resounding screams sent them into the fray. Running over the sandy soil almost noiselessly, Bear grabbed the bearded Robbie from behind, ready to cut the man's throat. Jason raced onto the dock. Daniel approached from the other side of the hut, his lover's cries disguising his approach. He mounted the stump and shoved against the door.

"Wait your turn, Robbie," Ransom Clary called.

Daniel put his shoulder into it and moved the chock. He stumbled into the windowless single room. The only light came through the cracks between the logs and the doorway, but he could make out Pandora standing against the far wall, her stiletto drawn. Ranse Clary neared her with his own knife held in a strong stance that indicated he could disarm this woman with ease. He glanced over his shoulder, as Daniel drew both sword and knife, and spun to face his attacker.

Immediately, Pandora was on her tormentor, but he did have superior strength. He backhanded her into the sack of supplies before she could do any more damage than nick his free arm. With his big hunting knife pointed at Daniel, he began to circle. Daniel kept Ranse at bay with the long sword and feinted with the knife in his other hand as the man attempted to get under his guard. Out of the corner of his eye, he saw Pandora preparing to attack from the rear again.

"No!" he shouted, fearing Ranse would turn and kill her.

Ranse jumped aside. "Now ain't that just like a woman to stab a man in the back."

"We must do what we can to protect ourselves," Pandora answered him very coolly. No more shrieking now.

"We had your women, both of 'em, lots of times. They ain't worth fighting over. Nothing but two soiled doves now," Ranse spit out. He began circling again.

"He lies!" Pandora hissed.

"No matter. We have pledged to marry them regardless."

"Well, how good of you, Daniel Clary. You can be with any number of women, but Miranda and I are nothing if our honor has been taken through no fault of our own."

"Pandora, this is no time to discuss women's equity."

Daniel placed himself in front of her, but his cousin shifted, forcing him to move again. Ranse came in low, trying to gut him. Daniel parried with his knife and shoved him back. Pandora edged behind her captor again and threw her knife. Sadly, she underestimated the amount of thrust needed to skewer a man.

The stiletto arced low and pierced Ransom Clary at the top of his buttocks.

"What the hell!" Unable to stop himself from glancing at his backside, Ranse turned his head.

That quickly, Daniel took advantage of the distraction and ran his opponent through with the sword. He put so much force behind the stroke, he toppled Ransom Clary and pinned him to the crude pine floor.

Ranse groped at the sword quivering in his belly and cut his fingers trying to remove the blade. "Damn it all. Those women *are* cursed. I hate when Robbie is right. Look, cousin, you got to take care of Custis. He won't put up much of a fight unless he's told to, and I'm all he's got. Bury me next to my kin. Give your word 'cause I'm done for."

"You have my word."

"I'd watch out for poison and knives if you really plan on marrying this one." Ranse gave a grin that might well have been the grimace of death. What light there was passed out of his mean, brown eyes.

Daniel drew Pandora into his arms and kissed the top of her black hair. "I shall have to add Amazon warrior to my list of endearments."

"As you should."

The terrified screams of a man sounded outside the cabin. Daniel placed his foot on Ranse's corpse and pulled his sword free. Pandora gathered up the knives. Both ran to help their companions.

~ * ~

Bear-Who-Walks-Like-A-Man should have taken his quarry easily. A man distracted by watching sex is easy prey. But this bear-faced enemy proved to be a canny fighter, a worthy opponent. When Bear put the knife to his throat, his foe threw all his weight backwards, taking them both down and pinning Bear's arms in the process.

This man, who had helped to steal their food and frighten his mother, rolled aside and drew his own knife. Soon, both were in the knife-fighter's crouch, swiping at each other when they saw an opening. Their dangerous dance took them away from the cabin and closer to the woods.

The man called Robbie, taller and heavier, shot out a leg and caught Bear in the knee. He toppled. His opponent tried to drive his blade downward, but Bear held him off, arms straining. He prayed silently to the spirit of the bear clan to give him victory over his enemies.

A strange figure shot past their struggle. From what little Bear could see, it had the face and furry belly of a bear but the arms, legs and long, gray hair of a human. It bleated hoarsely as it ran. For a second, the man, Robbie, looked up. Bear set his feet in the man's stomach and pushed back, flinging him across the path taken by the weird creature.

A huge, dark form rose up behind the white man and appeared to hug his body to its chest. Huge claws sunk into Robbie's back. The sow bear set her teeth into his neck. Her prey screamed and screamed. The Seminole began to back away slowly. He noticed a small cub crying for its mother and made certain not to get between it and its dam. Beyond the spot where the she-bear savaged the women's kidnapper, a second cub watched from the safety of a tree.

Behind him, Bear heard a familiar voice. "Into the cabin, *amigo*!"

The Spaniard was not dead then, but Robbie soon would be. The sow bear dragged the man into the bushes. Her cub followed after, sniffing at the trail of blood. The cries of terror continued as Daniel pulled Bear inside, and Pandora shouted to Miranda to run to safety.

~ * ~

Longleigh raced in stocking feet across the sand to reach Miranda. The huge thug was standing now, a knife gripped in his hand. Jason raised his pistol as he came into range, tripped on the edge of the dock and lost his grip on the weapon. It skittered toward Custis, who simply stood there staring. Jason snatched up the gun and fired. Nothing. The ball had come out or the powder had spilled, and now the stupid thing became merely a club.

He grasped it by the barrel and swung at the knife hand of Miranda's captor. His weapon dropping to the boards, Custis flailed and swept the delicate Miranda off the edge of the pier and into the water. Jason repeated mentally over and over, "She can swim like a dolphin, she can swim like a dolphin," to keep himself from diving in after her. If he could not defeat her abductor, he would be no good to her at all.

Rather than try to reach his fallen knife, Custis grabbed Jason's wrist and squeezed until he dropped the gun. "Don't hit me," he said, releasing his grip.

Jason put up his fists. "Very well, let it be boxing. I've had training, you know. Prepare to defend yourself." He assumed the proper gymnasium stance.

"Don't hit me," Custis repeated, covering his face with his hands.

Jason peppered the larger man's belly with several quick punches, then went for the jaw, but Custis had already crumbled into a ball on the dock.

"Don't hit me. I ain't done nothing wrong. Don't hit me, Pa." Custis rocked back and forth on his heels, keeping his head covered with his arms.

Beyond him, dragging the rope Custis had tied to her ankle, Miranda straggled from the water in her dripping white wedding dress and climbed onto the sandy slope.

"Jason, please leave him alone. He surrenders," she called out.

Even though soaked through, Jason thought her a fetching sight with her damp curls framing her lovely, heart-shaped face, her wet garments outlining her slim, sylph-like body—a fit subject for an ode on a Grecian urn. Something jerked on the line still dangling in the brown water. Miranda tumbled to the ground. Frantically, she tried to untie the knot, but the rope drew her inexorably backwards toward the maw of a large alligator.

What had Bear said? Get on their backs, hold their mouths shut. Jason positioned himself above the gator and launched onto its tough, bumpy hide. Easier said than done. No one had mentioned the powerful thrashing tail, the great clawed feet. Still, he threw himself against the head and pressed down. The gator tried to throw him off by tossing its head side to side. With each toss, Miranda's white limb, exposed to the knee, came nearer to the reptile's jaws. Of course! He needed to force the alligator to open its mouth and let her go.

Jason made a fist and pounded hard on the armored snout. The mouth opened like a portcullis full of iron bars. Miranda drew up the rope and scrambled to safety. A man screamed over and over. Pandora shouted for Miri to get into the cabin. Custis continued to rock and mumble on the dock. No help there. Jason threw his weight on the gator's head again. The jaws snapped closed. And now what? How did one dismount?

He'd brought a knife, of course, but had put his trust in the pistol. Now he searched for his blade and finally gripped the handle. He pulled the gator's head up with one arm under the snout and stabbed at its softer, more vulnerable throat while he continued to ride the leathery back.

From the cabin doorway, Miranda cried out, "Oh, don't hurt it. Just let it go."

"I would love to oblige, my dear, but I believe I have no choice."

Gators do not die easily, he learned. He had no idea how many times he thrust his knife into the beast's throat before it went limp, becoming dead weight in his arms. Cautiously, Jason climbed over the reptile's head and went to Miranda. She cried in his arms—either mourning the gator or relieved at their deliverance. He decided never to ask which.

Twenty-nine

True to his word, Daniel set out to find the remains of Robbie with Don Diego to show the way. They took rifles ready to fire if the bear should charge. Miranda begged them to allow the mama and cubs to live, while at the same time urging Daniel to think of his own safety.

Bear, the Seminole, stripped the belly hide from the alligator and dressed out the tail and other useable meat. Pandora put water on to boil for a bracing cup of tea. Then, she tackled the job of preparing Ransom Clary's body for transport. Subtly, leadership had returned to her and Daniel.

Turning the tea making over to Miranda, she asked her brother to assist in lifting the corpse onto a blanket. Even in the dimness of the cabin, she could see his face turn pale as she folded Ranse's arms across his chest and closed the dead man's eyes. She raised the legs while Jason lifted the heavier torso.

As she drew the blanket over the body and prepared to bind it, Jason remarked, "You know, despite all of Papa's bloodthirsty teachings, I've never killed a man…wounded a few in duels that now seem ridiculous, but not killed. Daniel did this without remorse."

"You should not have to kill anyone in the civilized world."

"Panny, I believe we have traveled far beyond that realm." He stared out the open door of the hut to where Miranda stood dumping tea into the kettle of boiled water. Bear threaded chunks of alligator tail onto a stick and set the meat to roasting.

"Indeed we have, brother. Far beyond the pale."

"I am not sure I am fit to live in the American wilderness."

Pandora finished tying the blanket shut with a piece of rope she had cut with her bloodied stiletto. She pointed the knife at Jason. "Do not dare to suggest you will not marry Miri. No matter what these scoundrels said, she is as pure as the day you met her. We kept them off by using our wits. Besides, this swamp is hardly Ariel Island, where I believe a poet could live in total satisfaction."

"True, but I am loath to think I would live off a woman." He hung his head.

"Don't be ridiculous. You know Papa will double your allowance if you marry, just as he did for Joshua. Not to mention marrying an heiress is a long-standing tradition for younger sons. Do go and ask Mr. Bear to help you haul this carcass to one of the boats. And Jason, you have at the very least provided us with dinner." Pandora gestured to the roasting gator meat. "Oh, and be sure to bring Custis back with you. I suspect he will do no harm now that Ranse is dead, but we should tie him up, don't you think?"

With the body stowed in a dugout and Custis prodded to the cabin at knifepoint, they gathered around the fire to eat and drink. They'd hardly begun when another dugout appeared, being poled through the shallows by the Spaniard. Daniel sat in the middle behind a blood-soaked sack made from one of their blankets. They left their burden in the boat and came to sit with the others.

"Not much left of the man." Daniel accepted a tin cup of tea. "The she-bear tore his head off and gutted him. Her family had had its fill by the time we arrived. We found Don Diego's dugout unharmed and that made it easier to bring him back. As I promised, I will bury Ranse and him by his brother. I think there is no need to go all the way to the hills, which would be foolhardy, in fact."

Miranda pressed her hand to her lips as if to suppress her rising gorge, but she managed to murmur, "It is the way of animals to eat their prey. They do not kill for pleasure. You did not harm the sow or the cubs?"

"No, they scented us and crossed over to the next island on an old beaver dam. I had no desire to kill an ally."

Bear nodded. "Spirit of bear clan. I call her. No kill."

"Absolutely," Jason agreed.

Bear gestured toward Custis, who sat, feet bound, with his back against the hut. He picked at a few bits of gator meat Miranda had put on a leaf for him. "You make him slave?"

"A white man and our cousin, certainly not! But I am at a loss about what to do with him," Daniel said.

Custis raised his shaggy head. "Ranse is dead. I got nobody." Tears ran into his dark stubble.

Miranda took him a cup of tea. "Do not worry. You shall come live on Ariel Island and have your very own cabin. I have a childhood friend who will teach you all about the island, and you will help us save the turtles. I believe you and Ponce will get along very well together."

"Are you gonna marry me? Lady Pandora kinda frightens me. I don't want her no more."

"No, sorry. I am promised to Jason Longleigh." She shook a finger at Custis. "It was very bad of you to take us from our loved ones."

"Yes, ma'am."

"Dear God, another of Miranda's pet creatures!" Daniel exclaimed.

"Well then, that's settled. Shall we pack our provisions and attempt to get back to the settlement before dark?" Pandora stood and briskly brushed off the rose-colored gown, now far beyond repair.

Bear doused the fire and covered it with sand, while the others loaded the boats. Reluctant to ride with the dead men, he took the two women into his dugout along with some of the supplies. Daniel, more familiar with boats and the swamp, steered the second with Jason and the remainder of their gear. The Spaniard came last, bearing both bodies and the bound Custis back to the settlement.

They arrived at the cluster of cabins before sunset. Not wanting to draw wildlife, Daniel, Jason, and Don Diego immediately started on the graves. Bear got a fire going and filled a pot with gator meat and water to make a stew. He stretched and scraped the hide of the beast clean and saw to watering and feeding horses. The ladies made another attempt at corn cakes, this time placing them far enough from the fire to avoid burning the outside before the inside cooked. With a huge dose of molasses, their offering was passable.

The women took the privacy of the cabin, while the men slept on its raised porch. They locked Custis in the fur cache even though he had given them no trouble at all. He followed Miranda's orders as docilely as a bear with a ring in its nose.

Dawn came too soon, but it was best to get going before the heat set in. They prepared tea and ate the extra corn cakes before setting out. Custis sat, hands bound like those of his former captives had been, on his own horse. Daniel saddled the thoroughbreds. The horses of the two dead men remained. Don Diego took one. Bear began to saddle the other.

"No, my friend and brother in the bear clan. Please take this fine steed for all your efforts on our behalf." Jason offered the reins of the thoroughbred to Bear-Who-Walks-Like-A-Man.

"But that horse belongs to my..." Daniel began. Pandora stilled him with a hand on his arm.

Bear nodded gravely. Then he added a bit of something in his own tongue. "I name you Alligator Slayer, no more Jay's Son. Take hide."

He offered the skin, still on its stretcher. Jason accepted it with the same sort of serious nod. "*Vaya con Dios*, Diego, and my Seminole brother." The don and the Indian mounted and rode off toward Spanish Florida.

"You will have to carry that hide, Longleigh. It's bound to get gamey and it is *your* gift. You ride the nag since you gave away Roger's thoroughbred."

"This isn't such a bad mount. He's not pretty but very sturdy, I am sure. I will see your brother is repaid for his loss—somehow. After all, he did say not to spare the thoroughbreds during our pursuit."

With the women riding each behind their men and Custis' animal on a lead, they set out for Ariel Island. Having no need to hide their tracks or study the trail, they took a more direct route back to the coast, but night still fell long before they neared the islands. They stopped in a place with water and grass for the horses, made a simple meal for themselves and bedded down each in their own blanket around the fire.

Miranda, disturbed by all she had endured, dozed lightly while all three of the men snored lustily. She heard a "Psst" that at first she mistook for the rattle of a snake, but no, the sound came from Pandora, who slept between her and Daniel. She started to reply but held her tongue when Panny whispered, "Daniel, are you truly so very exhausted?"

"What? What?" Her brother answered, roused from his sleep.

"I asked if you are too tired."

"Too tired for what?"

"To go beyond those bushes for a short time and celebrate our reunion."

"I assume you do not mean fireworks and festivities."

"Oh, there might be some. I thought of little else during the long nights of our separation."

"Careful. Don't wake the others."

Miranda listened to their stealthy movements and even a giggle from Pandora, who never giggled, when they had to return for a blanket. More suppressed giggles, then panting and some very heavy breathing.

Miranda rolled closer to Jason. "Are you awake?"

"How could I not be? Why don't they simply break off limbs from a tree and hoot at each other like apes before copulating?"

She curled up very tightly against his turned back. "I don't know how she can do that after those men touched us."

"Let me assure you, being with the one you love is entirely different, Miranda." He spoke with some strain in his voice.

Rhythmic groans began to issue from Custis, bound hand and foot and rolled tight in his blanket. Miranda peeked over Jason's shoulder. "What is wrong with him? Should I see if I can help?"

"Dear God, no! Your cousin is simply—ah, stimulated by what he is hearing and is indulging in a bit of self-pleasure, I suspect. Stop your ears."

"Self-pleasure." Miranda considered the word as if it were a sweet and exotic treat. She rubbed herself lightly against his back.

He turned and took her in his arms. "Dearest, you do know I am going to marry you as soon as possible. Perhaps we could have our wedding night now," Jason suggested, his voice breaking a bit.

"I'd like that." Miranda tensed, sensing something he did not. A faint musky aroma reached their nostrils. "Don't move! Stay very still. Just let the snake glide over you. I am sure it will not bite if we remain calm. Pandora and Daniel must have disturbed it." She breathed ever so lightly.

Jason froze. Even Custis stopped humping his cover. The engaged couple stayed so close together, the serpent climbed over them as if they were nothing more than a log in its way. Its cool, dry underbelly slid along Jason's cheek and passed over his shoulder. Its sinuous body dipped as it passed along to the smaller mound of Miranda and slithered down her side. The thick, black reptile vanished into the night.

"Venomous?" asked Jason.

"A moccasin, I believe, but it has gone away. Now we can do as we wish."

"I am sorry, my love, but a snake crawling across one's face is very—deflating."

"Mammy Ida! I know she is up to her old tricks. I am a woman grown now and should be able to do as I please. Everyone gets to have pleasure but me. It is a pleasure?"

"The most exquisite pleasure in the world, but Miranda, if Ida sent a message, it was a very potent one. Panny told me you found copperhead snakes where they are rarely seen and used them to defend yourselves. We must be thankful for that. We shall wait for our wedding night."

A suppressed cry came from beyond the bushes, followed by a loud gasp, then silence.

"Not fair, not fair at all," Miranda pouted and rolled away from her husband-to-be.

Thirty

They rode into town during the supper hour, but the spring twilight lingered over the steeple of the white, clapboard Methodist church and its small parsonage. "Hold up," Jason said. "I do not believe I am willing to postpone our nuptials another moment, dearest. If you agree, we shall marry right here and now."

"Yes, Jason, yes!" From her position behind him on the horse, Miranda hugged his shoulders and laid her face against his back.

"The women might prefer fresh gowns and flowers, Longleigh," Daniel suggested.

"I've never had a desire for a large or fancy wedding. Here and now is fine with me, my Wooly Goat." Pandora took a moment to enjoy the expressions on the faces of the others at the nickname she had for Daniel, though perhaps, Wooly Ram might be more apt.

Jason was the quickest from the saddle and the first to knock on the parsonage door. With his dinner napkin still tucked in his shirt, the Reverend Abel Humbert answered the door.

"Glory be to God on high, Peggy! The lost lambs have been found."

Issuing orders to an assortment of children to stay seated at the table, his plain, plump wife joined the minister. "Do look at them, so raggedy and travel-stained. To think you came to us first to give thanks."

"That also, but we have another cause, madam." Jason presented the preacher's wife with a courtly bow. "We desire to be married before returning to the island."

"A double wedding, oh my! Please bring your ladies inside and allow them some time to refresh themselves. A bride should not go to the altar besmirched. I have water heating for tea and 'twill do for washing. Come, come inside. Reverend, do take the men to the mudroom to brush their clothes. I will bring the necessities for shaving."

The men trooped past the dinner table surrounded by wide-eyed children. Custis, who had managed to dismount with his hands tied in front of him, lumbered after Jason and Daniel like a forgotten hound. Like any stray dog, he eyed the family's grits, greens, gravy, and slivers of ham as he passed. "A real live bad man," the oldest boy whispered.

Peggy Humbert herded the women into the cramped bedroom she shared with her husband, presented them with a comb and brush, and pointed out a small mirror on a stand. She picked up the creamware pitcher from its bowl and hustled off to her kitchen for warm water. Pandora stared at her face in the mirror.

"We do look ghastly. I am browner than ever. Fortunately, Daniel does not care." She plucked out the few hairpins that had survived the journey and let her hair fall straight. Drawing the comb through her tangles, she said, "I rather look like I am about to marry the gypsy rover of the song."

"Yes," Miranda replied, a bit jealously. "How absolutely wonderful. Is it wonderful, the wedding night, since you and Daniel have had several already?"

"I wanted to reclaim him last night. After he threw off sleep, he wanted to reclaim me. Sorry if we kept you up. But I would say, better than wonderful."

Mrs. Humbert returned with a pitcher of warm water. Her guests stripped down to their undergarments and washed away what dirt they could. Without embarrassment, Panny reached into her crotch and withdrew the stained rags.

"Such a pity to have your monthlies on your wedding night," Peggy Humbert commiserated. "Just put them in the water to soak out the stains once you finish."

"No, we used these as a ruse to put off our captors."

"How very clever you are." The minister's wife regarded the grimy, tattered gowns laid out on her spotless bed quilt. "I am sure these were once very fine frocks, but they will not do. I haven't much to offer, but perhaps you would accept my Sunday best and my newest gingham."

She took the folded dresses from a standing closet and offered them. "We can pin them up the back and tie them with my girls' ribbons under the bodice to make a fit."

The Sunday best, a dark blue edged with the barest minimum of white lace on its sleeves and bodice, fit Panny fairly well. She took up in height what Mrs. Humbert used in girth. Cinched with a length of white ribbon, it would do. Miranda, in slightly faded, yellow-checked gingham, looked the country lass once they had lapped the back with pins and tied the gown with a strip of sunny yellow material. The preacher's wife stood back. "I know exactly what else you need."

She hurried from the room, pausing to prompt her children, "If you have cleaned your plates, you may take them to the kitchen." She passed out of her front door and into the yard, rimmed by pickets and a flower garden. A moment later, she returned with two withes of blooming mock orange. Crossing the two sides, she bound both into a chaplet with yet more ribbon and set one on each bride's head.

"Ah, yes. Such lovely hair, the both of you, and now the crowning touch to show it off. The reverend has prepared the chapel. If you will come with me."

Cries of "Mama, Mama, can we come to the wedding?" stopped them at the front door. "If you are very quiet and well-behaved and mind your manners. Mandy, hold the baby."

Trailed by the seven little Humberts, Pandora and Miranda entered the small church. Sunday's faded flowers still sat on the altar. Two fat candles capped in brass flickered in the dusk beneath a simple wooden cross. His hands still bound, Custis sat in the front row like the closest of kin. The Humbert family piled in behind him as the brides took their places next to their well-brushed and newly shaven grooms.

A small boy leaned over the pew and asked Custis, "Did you kill someone, mister?"

"No, I thought I was gonna get married is all."

"Oooh," said the child, as if that explained everything.

Pandora smiled at Daniel. Jason and Miranda, too deeply entranced by each other to notice anything else, had already joined hands.

The vows proceeded smoothly, well past the objections part. Custis did have enough sense to stay quiet. But, when asked for the rings, Jason simply shook his head, indicating he had nothing to offer. Daniel tapped his shoulder.

"My mother's wedding band for Miranda. This for you, my Indian Princess." He held out a simple circlet set with a ring of very small rubies. "I've had them in my pocket since our last ceremony. Regina has my mother's jewel chest, and she let me take my pick."

"Moving along then," the preacher prompted. "Place the ring on the bride's finger and repeat after me." They did and sealed their vows with a kiss.

Reverend Humbert produced two marriage certificates, beautifully embellished with garlands and cheerful cherubs, and filled in the pertinent information. The grooms exchanged the pen to witness for each other.

"Who shall sign as a second witness?" the pastor inquired.

"Me, me! I can write my name." Custis stood up, holding out his roped hands. "Ranse said a man should be able to sign his own name. I practiced and practiced. I miss Ranse."

"Allow him," Miranda said quietly.

Cautiously, Jason approached the hairy giant of a man and began to untie him. Daniel drew out a pistol and a knife. The preacher gasped at the sacrilege of carrying weapons into God's house, but did not object, considering the size of the man and the possible threat to his children. Custis grasped the pen in his large fist, dipped the nib into the inkwell and laboriously made an "X," following that sign with the letters, all capitals, C-U-S-T-I-S C-L-A-R-Y. He smiled through his bristly whiskers.

"There, I done it. It's harder with a pen and paper than on my slate with chalk."

"Yes, it is," Miranda agreed. "Do we really need to bind him again?"

"Sometimes your warm heart overcomes your good sense, sister. If we are to take him to the island, he must be tied. He may be more cunning than we know and seek to upset the boat." Daniel signaled to Jason to tie the rope around his cousin's wrists. He placed the certificates inside his jacket.

Custis held out his arms. "I don't mind, 'cause I'm going to a good place. Cousin Miri says so."

Unable to sit still any longer, a Humbert offspring shouted, "Can we ring the bell, Pa?"

"Hmmm, no. At this time of the evening, people will think a house is on fire. Allow the newly wedded to pass."

Evidently, the oldest daughter had sneaked into her mother's pantry. She tossed a handful of rice as the couples went down the aisle. Most of it landed on Pandora, who shook her head like a steed annoyed by flies. One very ugly bridesmaid, Custis crunched after them.

Accepting the pastor's good wishes, Daniel pressed a coin of generous value into the man's palm. He led the group to the stable where they'd left the horses. More money passed hands for a late-night rubdown and a bucket of oats for the animals that had done many days of double duty.

"What do you say we take rooms at the inn and travel to the island tomorrow?" Jason suggested eagerly. "I am sure we are all fatigued and need the rest." He yawned hugely to support his case.

"We have enough moonlight to row across the inlet to Caliban, I think. I'd prefer clean sheets and a full bath tonight. I know Roger and Regina will be waiting for our return."

"But should we be taking the ladies to the docks at this time of the evening?" Jason continued his debate with Daniel as Pandora watched with a knowing smile on her face.

"Look at us, man. We have a rifle each, pistols, and all the knives and weapons collected from the Clary boys. I doubt if anyone will challenge us."

At the wharf, they found a waterman asleep in his craft. Awakened, he appeared to be too deep in his cups to row. Daniel parted with the last of his funds to rent the shabby vessel, and the man staggered off to spend his fee at the nearest tavern. Jason seated the women and Daniel took up the oars. He followed the path laid by the moon across the water to the island. They tied up at the pier and rang the iron bell to notify the people in the mansion of their arrival.

A servant opened the door of the house on the hill. Light seeped out from the oil lamp hanging in the hallway. Roger appeared in silhouette, armed with a pistol to greet unexpected guests who came in the night. Never mind that the real threat had arrived in broad daylight not too many days earlier.

Daniel cupped his mouth and shouted, "Roger, we have returned with our brides."

The message unheard, the door shut tight. The newly wedded and Custis began the long walk up the drive. Halfway up the hill, the mansion opened again and sent a river of people, white and black, flowing out to meet them. They carried lanterns and candles against the night, a greeting of fairy lights. One form, dressed completely in white from ankle to turban except for a red apron about her middle, towered over the rest and matched Roger Clary for size.

Miranda dropped her husband's hand and raced up the hill. Avoiding her sister-in-law's outstretched arms, she embraced Ida around the waist. "Mammy, I am married at last to my one true love."

"Of course, you are, *bébé*. Mami Wata watched over you."

"God Almighty watched over them," Regina Clary corrected. She turned her welcoming arms on Pandora and clasped that lady to her bosom. "Does this mean I am now related to the Longleighs of Bellevue twice over?"

"Indeed, I suppose you are family now," Pandora answered, untangling herself from the embrace.

"With so much good fortune all in one day, I am nearly overcome." Regina fanned her face with a hand. "Come inside. We have the most wondrous surprise for you."

Roger Clary thumped the grooms vigorously on their backs and turned the tide of well-wishers back toward the house by leading the way. Custis, smiling with delight at this welcome, ambled along in the crowd of family and servants, none of whom remarked on his bonds.

Roger's wife darted past all of them and placed herself before the closed doors of the grand parlor where the nuptials had failed to take place. "Oh, wait until you see!"

Pandora leaned over and whispered to Miranda, "Do you think she has gone insane from her ordeal with the kidnappers? Are the wedding guests still trapped inside surrounded by dead bouquets, do you think?"

"No. Roger would have locked her away and freed them by now. She does feel the isolation of the island keenly. What is a paradise to me is a prison to her. Perhaps she is a little touched."

Without waiting for a servant to do the duty, Regina swept open the doors, turned and dropped into a deep curtsy. "May I present to you the renowned Duke and Duchess of Bellevue in the flesh and our dear pater, Eustace, returned safely from abroad!"

Thirty-one

"Papa!" Jason said.

"Mama!" Pandora echoed.

"Look, Daddy. I am now a newly married woman." Miranda held up her small hand to show the wedding band. She knocked her chaplet of orange blossoms askew in the process, but still managed to drop a small curtsy in the direction of the duke and duchess.

"Is she not charming?" Jason remarked, his eyes alight with love.

Daniel said nothing. He watched his father's piggy eyes and greedy face and waited. The explosion came immediately.

"Daniel, you were to prevent this travesty of a marriage to a penniless, untitled third son. Let me see the proof."

Reaching into his coat, Daniel presented the marriage certificates to his father, whose face gradually empurpled.

"So, these marriages have just taken place. Have they been consummated?"

"No, Daddy, not yet."

Miranda blushed in the prettiest way possible and looked at her shoe tips. Pandora's cheeks went dusky for another reason entirely, but she did not take her gaze off of her parents' faces.

"You see, we should have spent the night at the inn," Jason grumbled.

"You have married Lady Pandora, my son." Eustace Clary's chest expanded like a bullfrog's pouch. "Perhaps her twenty thousand pounds will make up for the other debacle. I see you have captured one of the kidnappers and disposed of the rest. Good work, boy."

"Which would have been unnecessary if you had returned Miranda's bride price to your cousin's kin in the first place." Daniel put the blame where it deserved to be.

The duke cleared his throat, making a loud rumble, and all turned his way. He sat enthroned by Regina in a massive armchair fit for a king. With his greatcoat, laces, and white silk stockings, lacking only a wig and a crown, he might have been a potentate from the previous century. With her skirts spread across a dainty ladies' chair, his duchess rested by his side. Before them on a low table, Regina had set out her finest coffee and tea services surrounded by the best small treats the plantation could provide at this late hour: tiny biscuits stuffed with shaved ham, honey cakes, sweet strawberries, pralines, crustless tongue sandwiches, slices of fruitcake, a cheese and nuts.

"I'm hungry," Custis whimpered from his place behind Miranda, as if he hoped this regal man would share his feast.

The duke held up his hand for silence. Quiet fell so absolutely, the ticking of the case clock in the hall, the mantel clock over the fireplace, and even the tock of Eustace Clary's gold watch could be heard in the room.

"As I have said before, my son is not a pauper. His allowance from the estate will be doubled. However, it is not the Longleigh way to live off an heiress. He must return to London with his bride and pass the bar if he expects my blessing and future support."

"But, Papa, I have seen Miranda's island and believe I could live there happily all my days."

The duke raised his brows when Miranda looked directly at him and began to speak in her child-like voice. "Before we came to Caliban to be married, I spoke with Ida."

"Of course, you did, dear heart, since you lacked your mother. I must have that same chat with Pandora tonight," the duchess interrupted. Pandora did not quite meet her mama's eyes.

"Not that kind of talk, Your Grace. We spoke of the Longleighs' abhorrence of slavery. We thought of ways the island might support all of us without the need to exploit the labor of others. Remembering our short sojourn in Brighton, I proposed we might make a resort of Ariel Island with seaside cottages and a lovely tropical garden for strolling. We would offer sea bathing and horseback riding and nightly lectures on the flora and fauna of the region."

"My son, an innkeeper!" the duke thundered.

Unintimidated, Miranda continued. "My, no. Ida and I would be the innkeepers. Jason will be our poet in residence, giving readings of his work and others'. During the day, he could engage the young men in the healthful exercise of fencing, not for pay. Everyone will dine on fresh vegetables and the fruits of the sea—with the exception of turtles. I would teach our visitors to leave the nests alone and invite them to layings and hatchings."

"All very well and good, but what of your slaves, young lady?"

"I will free all my people but allow them the use of their homes and provide a small salary for their upkeep of the gardens and their catches of fish. They might also expect gratuities for their services from the guests. Of course, they would be free to leave if this is not to their liking."

With Miranda's eyes on the duke, only Daniel, standing in support behind her, noticed that their father's complexion, which had faded back to his usual florid hue, now purpled up again. It did not bode well for his sister.

"Do not believe I will permit this folly. I have not signed over your dowry to this landless lord as yet, nor shall I ever! Turn one-thousand acres of the finest Sea Island cotton land into gardens. Free the darkies so we might all be murdered in our beds if they don't simply run off. Never, never, never! Unconsummated, this marriage does not stand. I will lock you away to whither as an old maid before I consent."

Eustace, seated on the other side of Lady Flora, pounded the low table with his fist. Coffee and tea sloshed from half-consumed cups. Strawberries rolled to the floor. A tiered cake plate toppled over—as did the master of the plantation, face down in the tongue sandwiches. Roger pulled his father up by the neckcloth before he could smother and spread his bulk out in the armchair matching the duke's in size and opulence. One side of Eustace Clary's face sagged as if it had been crushed in the fall. The arm and leg on the same side of his body hung lax. He choked on garbled words.

"I always thought my father would end this way, in a fit of apoplexy," Daniel said without a great deal of sorrow.

"He is not dead as yet."

Roger glared at him and called for a half dozen servants to haul their immense master to the first-floor guestroom. During the hubbub of harsh words and the removal of Eustace Clary's bloated body, Custis retreated behind one of the tall open doors and made himself as small as he possibly could, no easy trick.

"Oh, I had prepared that chamber for your wedding night, Miranda," Regina said as she wrung her hands.

"Jason and I will be happy wherever we are together."

"Then, an upstairs room. The men may bathe in the mudroom, if they wish. I will have water brought to your chambers. Now, I must go tend to Daddy Eustace and send a servant for the physician. Your Graces," she said, bowing away with another deep curtsy. "A place has been prepared for you also. Tell any servant your desire, and you shall have it." She backed through the doorway, murmuring, "So honored, so honored."

The duchess rose, went to Miranda, and enfolded the girl in her arms. "Welcome to our family, dear child. I said from the first, you and Jason were meant for each other. I do so want to take you back to England and introduce you to the rest of the family."

"Yes, as *I* said, you will fit right in with the Longleighs," the duke added.

"I am sorry to say your father is a most unpleasant man, Miranda. So, my advice at this moment is to go forth and consummate as quickly as possible before your papa recovers or your brother decides he must carry out Eustace's wishes. Go along, go along with our blessing. Isn't that right, dear?" Flora turned toward her husband.

"I suppose. But you, Jason, will return to London and finish what you started before you become—" the duke made a sour face— "a poet in residence. If that does not work out, you can always fall back upon the law."

"Thank you, Papa, Mama. You have ensured my happiness."

Jason took Miranda's hand in his and tugged her toward the stairs and the bedrooms above. Miranda dug in her heels and stopped in the open doorway to beseech the duchess.

"Please, do you know how the eggs of the Galapagos tortoises fare? Have they hatched?"

"I am sorry to say we do not know, having taken ship slightly over a week after you. But the creatures are in good hands. We have hired a turtle keeper, Mr. Amos Gantry, to herd the beasts on clement days as we believe they like to graze. It will keep them from my pineapples. He seems a most competent man and will see to the young as well."

"I have married into the most marvelous family," Miranda declared, as Jason gave her hand another gentle tug and lead her away.

That left Daniel and Pandora to face the formidable couple. The duke regarded them for a moment before speaking.

"I understood, young man, that you and my daughter sailed away to America to prevent a marriage. Instead, we arrive to find two have taken place. What do you have to say for yourself?"

"During the voyage, we learned our differences were not so great. When we were cast away on the island, as Regina might have told you, we conceived a great pas—, a very great liking for each other."

"Did you compromise my daughter?"

"Papa," Pandora cut in, "I would prefer to say simply that *our* marriage has been consummated. What's done is done. There is no help for it now."

"So, you have succumbed to wedlock and will give up your causes and curb your sharp tongue."

Her back very straight, her black eyes flashing, Pandora answered right back. "Not at all. Daniel has agreed to give up his birthright for me and turn over his slaves and land to Roger. We will return to England where he will practice law and fight by my side for emancipation and the equity of women."

"A substantial sacrifice. You do know she will be a great deal of trouble?" the duke said to his new son-in-law.

"Yes, but I also know she will be worth the effort."

"As are all Longleigh brides." The duke gazed fondly at his wife. "Run along then. We can discuss the details and your adventures in the morning. The duchess and I have had a very long day, landing here only hours ago. I look forward to a bed that rocks for other reasons than being at sea."

Flora rapped him with the fan hanging from her wrist. "Then go upstairs and await me if you are certain your back is healed. Daniel, prepare to greet your bride. Pandora, remain with me."

Both men grinning happily, they retreated from the field and left it to the women.

"Come sit beside me, Pandora." The duchess patted the chair her husband had vacated.

"Yes, Mama."

"While I realize you have passed beyond the usual pre-nuptial preparation, do you have any questions you wish to ask regarding congress between a man and a woman?"

"I don't believe so. We seem to go along very well on our own. Daniel taught me to swim—in more ways than one." Pandora avoided her mother's eyes.

"Marvelous, isn't it?"

"Truly."

"That's my girl. I knew beneath that harsh exterior you presented to the world, a true Longleigh lurked, waiting to come out. Now, you left with only the clothes on your back. I brought along a trunk for you, and being the matchmaker I am, thought to pack some very exquisite nightdresses. Of course, these garments never remain on for very long, but they do serve to intrigue the male of the species. Just one word of advice for marital bliss. It's best to allow a man to believe he is right at least half of the time."

The duchess rose and linked Pandora's arm with her own. "Let's go enjoy our husbands."

"You are an extraordinary woman, Mama."

"I like to think so."

~ * ~

As soon as the women passed the door where Custis crouched, he wormed his way up the wall to his full height and bumped it shut with his shoulder. He did the same to the other, then made his way to the spoiled feast on the low table.

"I'm hungry," he said to no one at all.

Taking a seat in the duke's chair, he grabbed several small biscuits with his bound hands and stuffed them in his mouth. A cascade of crumbs fell to the carpet. He scooped up cakes and berries and drank the remains of all the beverages. At last sated, he leaned back in the armchair and slept.

Thirty-two

Loathe to leave his bride lest something else go wrong, Jason Longleigh waited patiently as she bathed behind a screen and drew on a modest nightdress left out for her by Regina. She tiptoed quickly to the bed and drew up a light spread to her chin.

"I'm going to wash now. I do not mind if you watch."

He folded back the screen, shed his clothes and stepped into the shallow tub. Miranda retreated under the cover like one of her turtles into its shell. Standing, he paid special attention to the areas he had been unable to cleanse at the preacher's house. He meant Miranda to enjoy the spectacle. Once, he thought he caught her peeking out from under the cotton coverlet. He used the toweling to dry himself, but went to her naked, and parted the mosquito netting that veiled her like the Sleeping Beauty in the old fairy tale.

Drawing down the cover where she hid, he covered his most intimidating parts with the folded cloth and revealed his bride. She lay in her white gown with her hands crossed over her chest, her eyes closed tight, her curls spread on the pillow.

"Miranda, my love, what are you doing?"

"At the ladies' academy, the other girls said this is what a woman must do—fold her arms, close her eyes, and endure."

"Did Ida tell you that also?"

"No. But I thought colored women might be different."

"Last night, you were eager for me to take you."

"Last night we were in the dark and fully clothed. Tonight, we are so near to naked and illuminated by candles. And your parents are sleeping right next door, not to mention Daniel and Pandora on the other side."

"I doubt they are sleeping."

As if to prove his point, some merry shrieks came from the chamber housing the duke and duchess. These were followed by something large crashing onto the bed, which began to emit a rhythmic groaning of its ropes. From the room on their other side, both could just make out Pandora saying over and over, "Daniel, Oh, Daniel, my Wooly Goat," and the breathless response, "My Amazon, my goddess, my Indian Princess."

"Frankly, I wish we had it over and done with on the beach directly after our engagement. We had more privacy," Miranda whispered.

"You shock me, my darling. No, not really. I can assure you women of all races enjoy the same pleasures. Tell me what Ida said."

"Her advice did not have much to do with me. She vowed all would come naturally since we loved each other so, but I did not like when Ranse touched my bosom."

"You did not love him. When I touch you, you will feel differently, I promise." He unfolded her arms and ran his hands up under her gown, going gently and slowly until he reached her small breasts and rubbed them slowly with his palms.

"Nice?"

"Yes, very nice." Still, she kept her eyes closed.

"What else did Ida say?"

"She said men liked to have their snakes handled, and I should not be afraid to touch you, since I am unafraid of real serpents."

"Ida is a wise woman. Here, let me in next to you. Feel free to use your snake-handling abilities upon me, my beloved."

Her little fingers tiptoed down his torso and found the snake already stretched to its full length by the time her hand arrived. "Oh, warm and hard and velvety, not cool and scaly at all."

She stroked his shaft up and down, then surprised him by cupping his balls. He startled.

"Did I hurt you?"

"Not at all. Please, proceed."

"Ida said I was not to neglect them. Aren't they furry, just like small animals?"

"I suppose so, but you need to stop now."

"Am I doing it wrong?"

"No, you are doing it too well. Allow me to show you how pleasant this can be."

He found the silky curls between her legs and stroked her cleft. He tested and found her damp. But she was his first virgin, and he would take care. He drew off her gown and suckled those small, sweet, pink-tipped breasts while keeping up his attention below. When she arched and raised her hips, coming naturally as Ida said, he plunged into her warmth and made her his wife.

~ * ~

Daniel caged Pandora against the wall outside the dining room with his strong arms. "Tell me, Mrs. Clary, what did you enjoy the most about our wedding night?"

Pandora did not seek to escape. She clasped her arms around his neck. "When you removed the stiletto from my limb and kissed the cut I made to preserve myself for you. And then your kisses moved higher and higher to my most private parts."

"The *mons veneris* where I worshipped you with tongue and lips."

"Yes, this time I recall it very well. Do we really have to go into breakfast? No one knows we are up since you helped me dress. We could go back to our bed."

"It is ten already, and I believe I heard your parents arise earlier."

"Yes, they always have mighty appetites in the morning."

"A kiss then, before we go in and face them."

Daniel leaned in and entered her mouth with his tongue. Pandora returned the love play. She must have given them away with a groan because Regina burst from the dining room.

"There you are. Do come in and see. I've prepared an English wedding breakfast for you. The duke and duchess are waiting to begin. Please do not tarry." She all but pushed them forward.

"We have those dreadful smoked fishes, kippers, I got off Captain Fulton as well as the usual eggs, a cold ham, sausages, bacon, and a rabbit pie. Toast, biscuits *and* scones with butter and three kinds of jam. Coffee and tea plus a syllabub I had Cookie whip up, though it isn't keeping well in this heat. We are nearly into May, so that is no surprise. We might have to settle for the champagne." Regina's ears seemed to prick up like an eager pup's as she heard light steps on the stairs. "Here come our other bride and groom. Go in, go in. I must congratulate them on being truly wedded."

As Regina went to intercept the other couple, one of her housemaids fled screaming from the parlor. "Missus, I come to clean and that big, hairy man be standin' right there by the table making his water into yo' best teapot."

"Roger, Roger! Where are you?"

Her husband emerged from the guest bedroom, where he kept vigil by his father's side. "Cannot my father die in peace? Isn't it unseemly enough that carnal acts took place in nearly every bed chamber last night during the very time when the doctor needed all his concentration to bleed his patient?"

"Nothing went on in ours," Regina reminded him sharply. "I was up half the night tending to Daddy Eustace, then rose early to order the feast for the newly married. I cannot do everything. You neglected to lock up our kidnapper and now he has defiled my best teapot." She pointed at the doors to the parlor.

Custis stood there fumbling his trouser buttons with his bound hands. "Sorry. Didn't see nowheres else to go. Couldn't find a pisspot."

Roger glanced past him into the parlor. "Other than eating like a pig, he has done little harm. Boil the wretched pot. You, sir, come with me. We keep a lockup for recalcitrant slaves. You can bide there until we hang you."

"Cousin Miri said I'm not a slave. I'm blood kin. She's gonna give me a house on her island."

"We shall see about that. March." Roger, keeping well back, pointed toward the rear of the house.

Speaking from where she stood on the staircase, Miranda implored, "Please, brother, I did make Custis that promise. He is our cousin and only did as his brother told him. I will care for him. Perhaps he could be locked up just now for Regina's comfort and we will take him with us when we return to Ariel."

"In my opinion, he will slay you and escape, but I will do as you wish. Your death will not be on my hands because I have warned you."

"How is Daddy?"

"Not well. After the doctor took his blood, he descended into a coma and never said another word. I have set Ida to watching him so I might break my fast." Roger eyed Jason Longleigh standing at his sister's side. "I suppose you are now his legal wife."

"I am and so very happy."

"Mark my words, wedded bliss does not last. March, you filthy beggar," he decreed and seized a cane from a nearby hallstand to prod his captive in the right direction.

"Custis, I shall send you a tray of breakfast. Go along peacefully now," Miranda called after them.

Regina put her hands on her hips. "I cannot boil my best teapot. It is edged with gold that will flake in the process. Men never understand. That aside, do come see the feast I have prepared for you. I want to hear all about your great adventure and your escape from those ruffians while we eat."

She led the way to her dining room, where the other guests had begun to help themselves. The duke looked over his heaping plate and gave his son a knowing grin.

"Pardon us for starting, but I thought you might be abed until noon, and I do have the appetite of a bear this morning."

"I am ravenous myself, Papa."

"And I," Miranda asserted in her childish voice.

That set the duke to laughing and his wife to scolding his manners, but shortly they were all seated at the large, polished mahogany table to satisfy those appetites. Regina, eating lightly, opened a notebook very similar to the ones Miranda used to record her natural observations and took a pencil in hand.

"Now, begin your story right after I was left on the dock."

Pandora told the women's tale, since Miranda had no inclination to do anything more than gaze lovingly at Jason. "We did perpetrate several tricks on our captors, one of which I cannot mention in mixed company, but I will gladly tell you later in private for your notes. Miri, do tell them of your putting the copperhead snakes in Ray's bedding."

As Pandora expected, her new sister-in-law ended her part by saying, "I did not mean to kill him."

"I left all the signs I could for Jason to follow: startling wildlife, leaving footprints, breaking plants and scattering petals, even leaving behind a silk rose on a lily pad."

"Good girl, Panny. You did not forget my training," the duke boomed.

Daniel reached into a pocket and drew out the very rose to Regina's delight. "Oh, a sacred artifact of your terrible ordeal. May I touch it?'

She stroked the crushed and sullied silken petals. "I don't suppose you would part with this, Daniel."

"No, he would not. Nor would I part with the red rosebud Ida gave me for luck. I carried it in my bodice throughout our adventure." Pandora glanced beneath her lashes at her new husband.

"So I discovered. We have too many fond memories of both flowers to spare them. We should enshrine them in a jeweled box." Daniel kept his face perfectly straight.

"Of course. That is what I would do," Regina said a trifle breathlessly. "Go on, Lady Pandora. What next?"

"I believe we made the ordeal as terrible for our captors as it was for us. They set us to cooking, and we poisoned their meal with holly berries. Miranda assured me no one would die, but we made them very ill indeed, weakening them for Daniel and Jason—and our friend Bear-Who-Walks-Like-A-Man. Our Indian savior was half Shawnee, Papa, though he says he is Seminole now."

"Do I possibly know him?"

"Too young, I would think. He had a mother named Corn Tassel."

The duchess clapped her hands. "Could she be the same Corn Tassel I hoed maize with in Chillicothe?"

Looking at Flora's soft and well-kept hands, Regina exclaimed, "*You* hoed corn! Do you still have the hoe?"

"My, no. It was a wretched tool made from the shoulder blade of an elk. My dear husband presented me with an iron hoe as my very first gift from him." The duchess held up a hand before Regina could ask. "No, I do not still possess it. I had to leave it behind, though I do have some souvenirs of my days among the Shawnee at Bellevue Manor."

"Good memories, those," the duke said, almost misty-eyed.

"You were not the one hoeing the corn, my love."

"Bear and his mother did know the Longleigh legend," Jason added. "I rewarded him generously for his assistance in regaining our ladies. Roger, I did forget to mention that. An ordinary horse seemed too paltry for the safe return of your sister, so I gifted him with one of the racers—the gelding, not the stallion."

Roger, who had remained grim and silent throughout the meal, raised his head, his face turning nearly as red as his father's normal visage. "My best money-winner!"

"Really, I had no way of knowing that. I thought you would prefer to keep the other for breeding purposes."

"I will ship you a mare covered by my best sire to take care of the matter," the duke offered as if the expense were of no concern to him.

Regina gasped at the language being used at her table. Flora patted her hand. "The Longleigh men rarely watch their tongues. I must apologize for them."

"I do understand. They are men of action and derring-do and speak as such." Regina placed a hand over her heart. "Please, Lord Longleigh, let me hear of the rescue."

"If you will call me Jason, since I am your brother now." He related their adventure, leaving out only the killing of the cottonmouth along the creek, since that part would upset Miranda. Regina scribbled his words as fast as she could.

"May I ask why you are writing everything down?" Jason inquired.

"I have a small aspiration to become an author."

"More of her ridiculous fantasies. Why, she thought these islands would be some kind of tropical paradise when they are working plantations just like those in Virginia," her husband growled.

"I have done my duties according to my mother's training. I have borne your sons. If you cannot spare me this one dream..." Regina covered her face with her hands and wept.

"There, there, my dear. I will see your book is published—with illustrations," the duchess said, glaring at Roger Clary.

He rose from the table. "Daniel, do you suppose you could spare our father a few moments of your time and a prayer for his recovery at his bedside?"

"Of course. Pandora, perhaps you could tell Regina your cunning trick with the stiletto, if I take the rest of the men with me."

"Still wearing it, Panny? You see, one should never be without a weapon." The duke beamed at his troublesome daughter and beckoned Jason to follow him in order to pay their respects to the dying.

The women prepared themselves to listen with second cups of tea, scones, and biscuits. They clustered round the end of the dining table.

"I cut myself with my hidden weapon and made our captors believe we had our monthlies."

"What boldness!" Regina marveled.

"My clever girl," the duchess said. She hugged Pandora's shoulders. "My last daughter married in true Longleigh fashion, flying in the face of all convention. I am so proud of you."

Thirty-three

The men stood solemnly around the death bed of Eustace Clary. Roger led them in a prayer for his salvation.

"Amen."

The broken bellows of Eustace Clary's lungs still pushed the air through his open mouth. Though the man's piggy, brown eyes stayed open in their folds of fat, they showed no recognition of the people gathered by his bedside. Cloth in hand, Ida stood nearby to wipe the spittle from his lips.

"Ida, if you will excuse us." Roger Clary indicated the door. She left to linger in the hall.

"If I had my way, I would honor my father's last wishes, nullify Miranda's marriage, and squash her absurd scheme to turn Ariel Island into a resort full of freedmen."

"I assure you we consummated our marriage last evening." Jason preened a little. The other men watched while he puffed out his chest and slicked back his overly long, black hair.

"How could you do that while my father lies dying?" Roger thrust his face toward Jason from across the bed.

Leaning over, Jason poked him in the chest with a long, aristocratic finger. "Life goes on. Nor do I find Miranda's plan ridiculous."

"Ahem, I believe a seaside resort might make a good investment. After all, Brighton went from fishing village to valuable real estate practically overnight once the Prince Regent began frequenting the place," the duke said.

Roger bristled. "We have no royalty here. We are all equal."

"Except for your slaves and your women, naturally, a problem you will have to deal with someday. However, I suspect if you can lure a governor or one of your senators for a visit, the result will be the same. If an influx of funds would facilitate the building of the place, my purse is open." The duke spread his arms to show his proposed generosity.

"I refuse to allow any construction until this year's cotton crop is harvested at the end of summer. The plantation has its debts to pay, and now according to my father's will, it will be divided into three parts. None of us will be able to manage."

"Brother, I will gladly sell my island to you. I have pledged to Pandora to return to England and study British law. I am particularly interested in maritime legal matters. With Great Britain having such massive fleets, I should prosper." Deferring to the duke, Daniel added, "I will also use my legal training to forward Pandora's causes."

"Good man!" The duke pounded Daniel so heavily on the back he nearly landed on top of his father's mound of stomach. "I lose a son to America, but keep my little girl at home."

"Ah, Papa, do you think, since Daniel plans to be a barrister, I might skip..."

"No, Jason. You will return to England with us and finish your training as I said. Give the rest of the family time to know your bride. In all fairness, naught can be done before the cotton crop is in. Apply yourself, and you might be able to return next spring and begin building. Mark my words, Clary, the resort will be a fine investment. I suspect Miranda is a tolerant mistress and most of her hands will stay on for the wages. Shall we shake hands on our agreement?"

The four men crossed hands above Eustace Clary's heaving belly. They had no way to know if he heard the deals being made before the breath left his body, but suddenly he coughed and gasped as if to speak. His eyes bulged with the tremendous effort. He rose up from his pillow and fell back upon it, dead.

~ * ~

The women were summoned to clean the body and prepare it for burial, to cover the mirrors and stop the clocks. They talked as they worked.

"Dear me, I recently purchased three bolts of the most exquisite material from Captain Fulton and now I shall have to dye all of it black." Regina sighed as she draped the dresser mirror with an old sheet. "I confess I was not as fond of my father-in-law as I should have been. He lacked delicacy. Roger is much like him, but with education and manners that make him much more bearable."

"Would you allow me to purchase some of the fabric beforehand? I would like to send it as a gift to the Reverend Mrs. Humbert for her kindness in loaning her gowns for our weddings," Pandora asked.

"Certainly. At least someone will be able to enjoy their luscious colors. We will send her a length from each bolt, a gift from all of us at no charge to you, Lady Pandora."

Ida rolled the body in order to sponge the hairy backside of the corpse before they dressed it for a final appearance in an extra-large coffin being crafted as they worked. She finished that side and began to work on the other after laying a clean sheet beneath the bloated buttocks.

"Miranda, you are a married woman now and might stay if you wish, but perhaps it is not so good to see your daddy naked."

"I will stay and do my duty by my father. But could I ask a question first?" She stood on tiptoes to whisper in Ida's ear and the servant bent to meet her.

"No. Greed and temper killed the mastah. Nothing more. Fat, choleric men do not live long lives. Now *you* tell me. Did you sleep well last night?"

Each woman in the bedchamber knew Ida did not mean sleep precisely, but implied something else. "Do tell," said the duchess, who had been relegated to a chair with her feet up on a small footstool since Regina insisted she not lift a finger.

"I cannot tell." Miranda's blush suffused her face. "But I will say I could not be happier. Jason tells me more is to come. I should not have said that." She covered her entire face with her hands.

"Good, very good. Then, you had no need for my potion. I hoped to prepare some elixir for you, but this…" Ida gestured at the body. "Got in my way."

"Potion, did you say? I've heard of such things, but always regarded them as a bit of humbug. Never really needed any," the duchess said with great interest. "Are they truly effective?"

"Very," Pandora blurted. "I don't advise you try it. I mean, one likes to recall one's pleasures, not be driven out of one's mind."

"Really, Pandora? Did you experience this personally?"

"I stumbled upon its effect quite accidentally."

"I will prepare a new batch and see each of you gets a bottle. But use it sparingly, just a few drops in the wine, no more." Ida grinned in that knowing way of hers.

In a small voice, Regina said, "I would like to have some, too."

"There, another adventurous relative of the Longleighs." The duchess offered her praise.

~ * ~

Given the heat on the islands as the calendar moved toward May, the body of Eustace Clary did not stay long on display. Surrounded by scented candles and sweet-smelling bouquets, he lay in his huge coffin lined with some of the gold brocade Regina had purchased for curtains. Daniel brought his sloop over from Prospero Island to ferry the same guests recently invited for the weddings. They came bearing more flowers and foods for the funeral feast, making the occasion nearly as festive as the former event. For practical purposes of transportation, the Episcopal priest came to the island rather than hauling the bulky corpse to the church. He blessed the body and gave a eulogy lauding the dead man, "one of the most prominent planters in Georgia," for his business acumen and prosperity. The minister made no mention of charity or love of family or kindness toward those he owned.

No one actually wept tears for Eustace Clary, a blustering and greedy man, but they did try to appear bereaved for the sake of the family. Perhaps the knowledge that he would gain a second island softened the loss for Roger, who remained somber but not bereft. Regina dabbed at her eyes even though they were dry. Usually so soft-hearted, Miranda declined to weep. She remarked quietly to Jason beside the grave in the small family cemetery, "A pity my mother must endure him lying next to her for all eternity. He was not a good man."

Wearing their hastily dyed black gowns and deep veiled bonnets, Miranda and Pandora boarded the sloop the next day along with their husbands, the duke and duchess and Ida. They sailed for Ariel on a light breeze and a cooperative sea.

Impressed by Daniel's handling of the small ship, the duke remarked, "Pity none of my sons wished to join the Navy."

Jason, leaning on the rail beside his father, remarked, "On a calm day like this, even I can enjoy the experience, but believe me when I say I am not cut out for a life on the ocean. I was dog sick my first week out on the *Sea Nymph*. All that plunging up and down, rolling from side to side, day after day after day. Even thinking of the return trip...Papa, are you certain I must pass the bar?"

"A Longleigh finishes what he starts."

Looking slightly green, Jason said, "Excuse me, I believe I will go sit in the cabin for a bit."

The duchess took his place. With her husband, she watched the rich cotton fields of Prospero pass by, its dark workers laboring in the rows grubbing out weeds with their hoes.

"What a substantial sacrifice Daniel has made for our daughter."

"Hard to imagine anyone giving up land like this willingly, but I am sure that is how he won her. Good to see Panny showing some of the Longleigh warmth, too. They should get on well together. Daniel appears to have some interesting skills: sailor, barrister, and a man not afraid to kill in defense of his loved ones. He is a useful addition to the family like Leo McLaughlin, but neither one is good enough for my daughters. Why have so many of our children been involved in kidnappings prior to their marriages? Cannot any of them get to the altar in the usual way?"

The duchess threw up her hands. "Only three of the ten, not so high a number if we do not count my own capture and Danelagh's little sojourn with our Thalia or Kate's incarceration."

"I do count them!"

"But, noble or commoner, there never has been a man good enough for your daughters, dearest. Yet, all of them are wed now and happy with their choices. I feel rather old and useless."

"You—never old, never useless, heart of my heart. There are other matches to be made outside the family."

The duchess sent a coy little smile in her beloved husband's direction. "I have come to understand Miranda's island possesses several structures similar to the wigwams of the Shawnee, and I have obtained a bottle of magical elixir from the hand of Ida."

"Do tell, my love, do tell."

~ * ~

Arriving on Ariel Island, the duchess exclaimed over the towering palms, the charming, airy house. "I have specimens exactly like these in the conservatory but have never seen them growing in their natural environment. Your home is quite lovely, Miranda dearest, but you should consider adding a wing. The Longleighs tend to have large families."

"My love, our line nearly died out before you came along," the duke corrected gently.

"Simply be prepared. Jason is his father's son, even if more delicate in manners."

Miranda assigned the best bedchamber to her new in-laws. She deposited Custis, unbound, in the overseer's unused four-room house built of tabby. It sat halfway between the slave quarters and the big house.

"We use a headman style of organization here," Miranda said, "and they prefer to be among their people. The cottage was going to waste. However, Daniel and Pandora must have my quarters in the house. Jason and I shall stay with Custis for the time being."

"What?" Jason said, dismayed.

"Come, dearest, we will be embarking for England in a few weeks. I am happy wherever you are."

"Yes, certainly, and I with you, but he will be in the room next to us as we—sleep."

"Custis, you will be very polite and well-behaved and pretend to hear nothing at night."

"Yes, Cousin Miri. I like it here, but I'm hungry."

"Again? I believe I have taken on a giant to feed."

Once everyone was settled, they partook of a fine dinner.

The duke applied gravy to his mound of grits. "Do you remember boiled maize, my dear?"

"Yes, tasteless as ever. No offense meant, Miranda. I simply have never cared for it."

"When the duchess was enslaved among the Shawnee, her owner, an old hag called Snakeroot, slapped her hands for adding too much salt to the boiled maize. Perhaps that is why she does not savor it."

"You, a slave?" Miranda wondered.

"Obviously, Regina has not shared her book of Longleigh adventures with you. It is entirely fantastic, of course. Though Mama *was* enslaved by the Indians for a short period of time and rescued by Papa." Pandora took up another biscuit and added honey. "I believe I am becoming fond of these. I seem to remember something special about the honey."

"Not now, my Raven. We will speak about the uses of honey later." Daniel patted her hand.

"Honey can be quite marvelous," the duchess went on. "But any term of slavery is not short when one must endure it. You do see now why our family has abolitionist tendencies."

"All's well that ends well." The duke rubbed his hands together as if starting a tremendous task, planning with his usual energy. "We must summon a surveyor and have a good map of the island drawn. Then we can plan where to place the cottages and how to lay out the gardens. What do you think of building a large inn near the dock with an assembly room that could be rented out for special occasions and used for dancing and lectures otherwise?"

"A wonderful idea if we can raise the capital," Miranda said.

"No need to worry on that account, I assure you. Now about the primitive shelters you have dotted about the island. Some people might enjoy a more rustic experience. Before we leave, the duchess and I will test them for comfort." He eyed his wife in a most lascivious way.

~ * ~

The *Sea Nymph*, loaded with timber, furs and hides, and any cotton left over from last year's crop, dropped anchor off Ariel Island on the first of June. This time Captain Fulton came fully prepared for the transport of guests of quality, even to the point of relinquishing his roomy cabin to the duke and duchess.

Pandora had been given the task of seeing all the baggage got aboard and reached the proper chambers. Aware of this great responsibility, she carried a checklist and ticked off each item with great efficiency. Mama would see what a competent organizer she had reared—when the duchess made an appearance. Pandora's parents had gone off two days before to the wigwam. Shortly after, they had settled near the beach, taking with them a thick mattress of Spanish moss and a huge hamper of picnic food and wine among their supplies. A fog blanketed the area, sealing them off from the big house and their children. They had not been seen since.

Pandora frowned. Miranda had a similar list of delicacies the duchess desired for the trip. Although her new sister swore her island's preserves were as good as any other, her mother insisted she beg some of Regina. Preserved figs, lemons and oranges in great quantity, and soaps scented with specific oils simply had to be obtained for her comfort. Strange, her mother was rarely so finicky.

Daniel took Miranda first to Caliban, then to town to seek out these luxuries. Leaving his sister to shop, he and Jason set off to satisfy the duke's request for some fresh game to start the voyage: a deer or two, perhaps a dozen rabbits or some pigeons. In the end, the hunters returned with two young bucks and four turkeys. Regina supplied potted rabbit from her larder to make up the difference. Ida watched all these activities with that enigmatic smile she so often wore.

Aha! So Ida had sent the fog to give her parents privacy, and all these demands were simply a ruse to keep the children occupied. Normally, Ida and Horace, Daniel's newly freed body servant, would be checking lists and seeing to supplies. Instead, they merely stood by if needed and carried on a desultory conversation.

"Off to see the world now you are free man," Ida said. "The question is will we ever see you on these islands again."

"Wit' Old Mastah gone, you and Ponce free. You stayin', Ida?"

"This is my home, too."

"And mine if I got someone waitin' for me."

"I'll be here, Horace, long as the sun sets in the west."

Did the climate or all the oysters consumed make everyone want to mate like wild March hares, Pandora pondered. No time for that. They were to board the *Sea Nymph* in the evening and have a small celebratory gathering before leaving on the morning tide. She reached the end of her list and gave the crew leave to take the many trunks and boxes, each chalk marked for ownership, to the ship. Where were the duke and duchess? Time drew nigh to depart.

Shading her eyes, Pandora watched the progress of an open carriage coming down the palm-lined road from the house. Jason, Miranda and Daniel faced away from her. The duke sat across from them with a mighty smile on his face. Next to him rode a strangely dressed woman, who had to be the duchess if one could see behind the veil draped over her straw hat. Her arms were covered with white cotton sleeves, her hands with gloves and the entirety of her chest by a tucker coming up to her chin. Though her gown was made of light muslin, Mama had to be sweltering.

Upon arrival, the duke helped his wife down first. Miranda followed, carrying a small basket and the large feather pillow the duchess had been sitting upon. Daniel and Jason jumped down, and the group gathered on the pier to await the return of the ship's boat.

Pandora tried to penetrate her mother's veil with her gaze. "Were you stung by bees, Mama?"

"No, merely a bit burnt by the sun. It will pass."

"But you have always cautioned me to guard my complexion. How did this happen?"

The duke bellowed out a laugh that sent the seagulls scattering.

"Oh yes, your father with his bronzed skin that never burns finds this very amusing. Come over here. No! Do not take my arm. Don't touch any part of me."

When they had gotten away from the men, the duchess confided to her daughter and Miranda, who had followed. "I did just as Ida said, a few drops in the wine. But the duke being so much larger of frame insisted he needed more. Indeed, he seemed barely affected, but as the day went on, I developed a great thirst—caused by the fresh oysters plucked from the sea, I believe, and I drank from his cup. I felt as if I were on fire, threw off my clothes and plunged into the sea, where your dear Papa and I cavorted for some time. I know not how long. We stayed on the beach afterwards, reveling in the sunshine."

"Oh, I see where this is going," Pandora muttered.

"But clouds hung over that part of the island," Miranda said.

"I assure you the sky above us remained quite clear. I felt no pain until this morning when we awoke to greet the dawn in our usual way."

"Are you in a great deal of agony, Mama?"

"Oh yes, even my bottom."

"Mama!"

"Oh, come now, Panny. You are a married woman. Surely you know a woman may ride on top. There, I've shocked you again."

Pandora stuck out her lip as if she were a child once more. "You have shocked your children all of your life, why should now be any different? I do know that, thank you very much."

"Never fear, I have brought a goodly supply of Ida's salve for burns." Miranda held up her basket. "And a few other necessaries from her supply of herbs." Now she blushed.

"No more elixir, I hope. I do not believe I could survive it. The duke was insatiable. He is still grinning like an ape this morning."

"Not that. Ida said I am very young and need to learn to be a wife before other responsibilities come my way. She says Jason and I should enjoy our first year of marriage without other worries."

"Do you mean she knows a way to stop conception?" Pandora asked avidly.

"Hush! Do not let the men overhear. This is women's business only. I will explain when we have some privacy. Here comes the boat. Let me put your pillow down on the seat, Duchess."

"What a boon this could be for women's equity. Imagine how much women might accomplish if not burdened by childbirth and large families."

The duchess put a hand on Pandora's arm to stop her from following Miranda to pry out the information. "While I might have wished for longer intervals between births, I have never regretted bearing a single one of my ten. Keep that in mind before you do anything hasty."

Regardless, Pandora had no chance to pursue the topic. The men climbed into the boat first to assist the women. The duke lifted his wife and set her gently on her pillow. Pandora jumped into Daniel's arms. Miranda hesitated and turned back. She went to hug Ida, who had exerted her new freedom by proclaiming she would remain behind and see the gardens laid out in the fall and the tabby cottages built in the spring.

Embracing the young lady she had raised, Ida kissed Miranda's forehead. "Go on now. Learn to be a wife. It's best no one stands between a wedded couple. I will be here when you return. So will Ponce and Custis. I think they will be friends. Remember the offering

I gave you. Cleave to your husband. I know he will be gentle with you."

"I love you, Mammy, and will miss you so." Miranda kissed the black woman's cheek and then accepted Jason's hand into the boat.

The voyage began with supper and champagne. In the morning, the *Sea Nymph* got underway before their party assembled for breakfast.

Jason helped himself to a small portion of eggs and dry toast. Miranda poured his tea and fixed it with sugar and lemon as he liked. He gave her a grateful smile.

"Still a little queasy, but doing better than last time. Maybe it's the change of cabin mate," he said, smiling across at Daniel. "Where is my seaworthy sister today?"

"Unwell," Pandora's husband answered.

The duke looked at the duchess. "Panny is never unwell. Perhaps you should see to her, my darling."

At that moment, Pandora entered the room. She took a sniff of the rich aroma of coffee, eyed the yellow mounds of eggs, put a hand to her mouth and retreated to her cabin. Daniel rose to go after her.

"No," the duchess said. "Let her be. I know that look. She will feel better later in the day. Congratulations, dear boy, you are going to be a father."

Pandora did feel well enough to come up on deck toward noon. She approached Miranda and her mother as they stood near the rail examining an object Miri held, a mirror adorned about the rim with pretty seashells.

"I made this for Ida. She told me it was her most prized possession. I am to give it to Mami Wata to ensure a safe voyage and quick return."

"Mami who?" asked the duchess.

"A water goddess who is often full of mischief."

"I can attest to that," Pandora said. "I hope you will share Ida's secret with me nine months from now."

"Ida says the sea is ruled by a woman, not a man with a big, white beard."

The duchess, still swathed in clothes to keep the sun off, considered. "Yes, I could agree with that. The wide ocean is both bounteous and temperamental. The tides flow according to the phases of the moon. I see her point."

"Well then, here is our offering, Mami Wata. Watch over us."

The mirror sailed through the air. A wave broke over the bow and sent up fingers of foam that caught the offering in midair and carried it into the depths.

Epilogue

In late afternoon, the twenty-second of December, 1815, the servants lit the lamps early. Candles waited on the hall table for anyone who needed to make their way around Bellevue Hall. A moderate snowfall and the impending dusk discouraged the men from hunting. They holed up in the billiard room to smoke and while away the time until supper.

Each involved in whatever pastime they preferred, the Longleigh women sat by the fire in the drawing room along with two spotted dogs sleeping near the hearth. Despite the poor light, Miranda worked on her observations of the park's fallow deer and illustrated her notes beautifully, even the rutting scene. Kate, come up early with Joshua from London for the holidays, sewed yet another child's gown for her son, who seemed to outgrow them weekly. Still wearing her rich brown hair shorter than the other women, she bent over her needlework, glancing up now and then, the golden flecks in her eyes enhanced by the firelight.

The duchess preferred to read, as did Pandora. Pandora rested her book on top of her huge belly for the tenth time. She wore a loose gown, tied down the front with ribbons, and the softest of slippers.

She'd been allotted the most comfortable chair nearest the fire and given a footstool to prop up her swollen feet. Mostly, she wanted to arise and wander the room, but the effort to get out of her seat required too much energy. This book failed to engage. She snapped it shut.

"Honestly Mama, I do not know how you endured ten confinements. There is no possible way to remain comfortable. The child should have been born last week. I arrived here in November for my lying-in and feel as if I shall never return to my interests in London."

Miranda, eyes still on her notes, replied, "Calculating the arrival of a baby is not an exact science. They come when they come, sometimes early, sometimes late, not nearly as reliable as turtle eggs. Besides, we know there were several possible conception dates before..." Miranda stopped herself. "Before we returned to England. We knew the exact date the tortoises copulated and Mr. Gantry said the eggs hatched within two days of my guess, based on the size of the reptiles."

"You have my sympathy, Panny. But really, by the size of you and the fact that you have dropped, you should not be waiting too much longer. The midwife has grown fat living in luxury here since the first of the month. That miscalculation has cost the duke. I do hope the infant arrives before the rest of the Longleigh horde," ever-practical Kate replied.

"Tut-tut, Kate, how unkind to refer to my grandchildren as the Longleigh horde, though they are numerous to be sure. This year, I have embroidered a special stocking for each with their initials upon it for St. Nicholas to fill. No more quarrels about who received more nuts or candies. I have those cunning wooden toys I purchased in Georgia to stuff in each pair of shoes: Indians with tiny bows and arrows, wheeled-alligators, chickens that peck on paddles, dancing ladies and gentlemen. I believe I have a clogging mule as well. Each family will receive their own infant tortoise, of course. We shall have to keep the ones meant for James and Justin here at Bellevue until those boys settle down. As only ten hatched, my friends will have to wait for theirs and be satisfied with sacks of exotic manure." Her brow wrinkled, the duchess closed her book, too, and gazed out the window at the falling snow.

"The children will fight over their gifts as usual, and your friends are not much better. No amount of planning can prevent that," Kate answered.

"More tea, Pandora?"

"Heavens no! Within fifteen minutes I would have to find a way to get out of this chair in a hurry."

A light scratch on the drawing room door drew the attention of the ladies. Busby entered with a package addressed to the duchess. "All the way from America," he said. "I thought you would want it brought to your attention at once."

"Yes, indeed. Good man, Busby. If the post has come, the roads are not so very bad then. The rest of the family will be able to get here before Christmas and Boxing Day."

The duchess carefully removed the waterproof wrappings to find a sturdy box. Inside the box lay a dozen small books bound in blue leather and stamped with silver, the Longleigh colors.

"Look, we have Regina's book at last, right in time for Christmas. She says in her letter the regular copies are merely bound in paper. These are a special gift to her literary patroness. That would be me. It is entitled *The Further Chronicles of the Longleighs, as told to Mrs. Roger Clary, nee Regina Hopewell, now aligned with the noble family of the Duke of Bellevue twice over through marriage, and especially dedicated to Lady Flora, Duchess of Bellevue, and heroine of* The True and Exciting Adventures of Pearce Longleigh. Well, that takes up most of the first page. Regina has filled the rest of the space with her autograph."

"Something to lift the melancholy of this dreary day. No wonder the Druids burned bonfires all night long." Pandora reached out a hand for a copy and remarked, "Even my fingers are swollen. I could not take my wedding band off if I wanted."

"You don't want to. You are simply cranky with discomfort. Believe me, I cursed your father up and down during my first travail. The others came easier. Daniel has given up so much for you, Pandora, and we, all of us, are proud of how swiftly he passed the bar. He impressed those stodgy barristers with his knowledge of nautical matters from the start. I suspect they loved luring such a fine mind away from America to serve the British Empire." The duchess handed Pandora a volume along with her reprimand.

Miranda wandered over to get her own. "The snow is very beautiful. I've never experienced it before, but I believe I prefer the warmth of the islands." She flipped through the book idly. "I thought those old legal crows were very hard on Jason, making him wait and wait until nearly the end of the term for acceptance. Perhaps they knew his heart did not truly belong to the law. I am excited for his epic adventure poem, *Jason Longleigh's Journey,* to be finished. That will show everyone where his real talents lie. Oh!"

Miranda stopped chattering abruptly. She held up the book and showed one of the illustrations. A young woman, wild of hair and eye and dressed in diaphanous clothing, held two thick, writhing hourglass-marked snakes in her hands, preparatory to throwing them on a sleeping man. All of the women found the page in their copies. The caption read *The Abducted Virgin Bride Takes Revenge Upon her Captor.*

"Why, I would never hold a snake in such a manner. Serpents must be grasped firmly behind the head lest they bite. I handled the reptiles with sticks. Pandora will tell you so. Nor would I ever throw them on a sleeping man. I did not mean to kill Ray at all."

"I absolve thee of killing Ray Clary. The snakes did all the work," Pandora huffed as she made the sign of the cross. "You should be glad they portrayed you as strong, even if a little crazed. I appear to be a complete ninny in my portrayal. Just look at this."

She showed another illustration of a young woman with long black hair prostrate in a dugout canoe. This heroine strewed the water with lily petals from a bouquet clutched in her hands as her oblivious kidnapper paddled on. A single deep pink rose, hand-colored by some woman paid to embellish the illustrations, lay on a lily pad in the foreground.

"*Lady Pandora Leaves Signs for her Brother, Lord Jason Longleigh.* I did a great deal more than that." Panny turned the pages furiously to get to the end of the story.

"I rather like the frontispiece showing Jason on the back of the alligator, though judging by the size of the hide we brought home, the beast was not quite so large, nor was the knife he used to stab the creature in the throat. *Lord Longleigh slays the Behemoth of the Swamp*," the duchess read with satisfaction.

"More romantic twaddle," Kate remarked.

Pandora pushed herself upward. She shook the book in the air. "Not a single mention of the ruse about our monthlies or our poisoning of the food. And see here, I am shown cowering in the corner while Daniel fights Ransom Clary to the death. Regina has totally failed to mention that I fought, too, and in fact stabbed the man in his buttocks."

Kate laughed out loud. "Huzzah, sister!"

"Panny, remember your condition. Upset is not good for the baby. Here, Regina explains in her letter that her editor felt women attacking and poisoning men sets a poor example for female readers. Women are to be portrayed only as caretakers, the gentle goddesses of home and hearth. Violent deeds must belong to the men. The snakes were allowed for their exotic contribution to the tale. As for the monthlies, she could not bring herself to mention that in print," the duchess said.

"Oh, I could just—just tar and feather the woman, sister-in-law or not." Pandora threw down the book and stamped her feet on it. "This is even worse than the one written about you and Papa—which I have never seen in our library."

"I assure you, there is a copy way up high in a dusty corner. Mr. Meriwether made certain we received one and asked for our endorsement, which was not given. Still, it sold rather well in the former colonies. But please, Panny, do not stomp that way. Oh, now you've done it, broken your water all over the best carpet. Kate, summon the midwife. Miranda, fetch a maid to clean up the mess. Pandora, to your bedchamber."

As the duchess issued her orders, Lady Pandora Clary watched a puddle form around her hem and soak into the Aubusson rug. A sudden twinge crossed her belly.

"I suppose this means the baby is coming. I've never leaked so badly before."

~ * ~

Tomorrow the days would grow longer bit by bit, but tonight darkness reigned. The men in the library heard the infant's cry as the hall clock struck midnight. The two sounds competed in volume. Daniel Clary stopped pacing.

"My child is born."

"Yes, indeed. One of the proudest moments in a man's life, a first child," the duke said. He poured out some fine cognac and proposed a toast. "To a healthy child and a safe delivery."

Jason, Joshua, Daniel and the duke clinked their glasses together. As they drained their cups, the footsteps of the midwife sounded in the hallway. With the precious infant heavily swaddled against the drafty corridors of Bellevue Hall, the gray-haired woman in a fresh, clean apron presented her bundle.

"Your son, Mr. Clary. A fine, healthy boy. What will you call him?"

Daniel accepted her burden gingerly. "He has Pandora's straight dark hair. My wife, is she well?"

"Right as rain. Takes after the duchess when it comes to child bearing. A mere eight hours of travail for her first. That is very good," the woman added, since men were always in ignorance about such matters.

"Yes, Panny does have her mother's child-bearing hips. Let me see my newest grandson. Another excellent addition to the Longleigh line." The duke held out his big arms and cradled the baby like the experienced father he was. "What is your name, dear boy? Tell Grandpapa so he can write it down in the family Bible tonight."

"Given the day and time of his birth, I believe we should call him Christian for his own protection. Pandora did say we must give

Jason a nod as a middle name. He played a great part in bringing us together and aided in her rescue."

"Aided! I led that rescue expedition and Bear-Who-Walks-Like-A-Man took no small part either. He should be honored, too. Let me see my nephew, Papa."

Reluctantly, the duke handed over the babe. "It's about time someone in the family acknowledged their membership in the Bear Clan."

"You think Christian Jason Bear Clary would do? Won't the Anglican priest be upset by the oddity?"

"Nonsense, I pay his living. We have already conceded him the name 'Christian.' Besides, he has become inured to the vagaries of the Longleighs. I hope that gentleman outlives me. I'd hate to break in another vicar and have to explain once more that we shall have heathen names if we wish. We usually throw in a saint's name, too, as a sop to the church."

Jason gazed down on the infant. "Next year I might hold my own son in my arms, Papa. If Miranda runs out of herbs before we get back to the island, that is."

"Those potions never work. Miranda needs feeding up and more red meat. That is all. Assert yourself, son."

"I do, nearly every night, but she persists in saying we need time to ourselves before starting a family."

"Don't let her talk to Kate, or I will never have another," Joshua said. "My turn."

He weighed the boy in his arms. "I would say my son was bigger at birth."

"Joshua always claims everything of his is bigger. Ignore him, Daniel. His boasts only mean he regards you as part of the family now, another brother to be kept in his place. I think we need an additional toast." Jason raised his cup. "To Christian Jason Bear Clary, may he live long and prosper."

Pleased, his face flushed with pride and the drink he had imbibed while waiting, Daniel added, "And to my Lady Pandora: Amazon, Goddess, and Indian Princess."

~ * ~

The midwife returned the babe to his mother's arms. Pandora raised the flap of the blanket that covered her son's face.

"I do hope his eyes will remain light like Daniel's, green as sunlight on the sea."

"There is some hope. My first and last sons do have my gray eyes. Well done, Panny, well done. You bore the pangs like a true Shawnee without screams or complaint. Your papa will be so proud when I tell him." The duchess beamed at the last of her daughters to wed.

"Still, the ordeal is terrible, no matter how well borne. We should have sent Miranda from the room. Now, she will keep all her herbs to herself and never share them with us lest she run out," Kate said.

"When I am back on my island, I will send you some. However, I am unafraid. Jason and I will have a family—when I am completely ready and Ida stands nearby to attend me."

"Wait just a moment. We must have our own toast." Kate dashed from the room and returned shortly with four small stemmed glasses held between her fingers and a decanter of sherry. She poured and handed each a libation.

"To mother and child. To all women who are not gentle doves, but stronger than any man knows."

Meet Lynn Shurr

Lynn Shurr grew up in Pennsylvania Dutch country but left to wander the world shortly after getting a degree in English literature. After living in several states and Europe, she picked up a degree in librarianship. Her first reference job brought her to the Cajun Country of Louisiana. Eventually, she became director of a library system. For her the old saying, "Once you've tasted bayou water, you will always remain here," came true. She raised three children near the banks of the Bayou Teche and lives there still with her astronomer husband where she writes, paints, studies history, and roots for the LSU Tigers and the New Orleans Saints.

Other Works from the Pen of
Lynn Shurr

Lady Flora's Rescue: Book One of the Longleigh Chronicles. - Lady Flora follows the man she loves into the American wilderness not knowing he plans to remain there. Will he choose love over his own liberty?

The Perfect Daughter: Book Two of the Longleigh Chronicles. - When a fascinating gentleman rejects perfection, what must a young lady do to gain his love? Perhaps, seduction.

Daughter of the Rainbow: Book Three of the Longleigh Chronicles. – Shy but lovely Iris Longleigh is passionate about only two things— painting and Lord Valls, who will not marry her due to a secret he harbors.

The Double Dilemma: Book Four of the Longleigh Chronicles – The Longleigh twins wish to marry only twins and find them in an isolated castle on a forbidding coast. The adventure begins!

The Greatest Prize: Book Five of the Longleigh Chronicles – Jilted by the man she was supposed to marry, Kate sets out to prove she can win a greater prize.

Lion in the Heather: Book Six of the Longleigh Chronicles – Lady Euphemia adores all things Scottish—including the laird who steals her for his bride.

A Taste of Bayou Water - a prequel to Blessings and Curses. When Celine Landry refuses to leave Cajun Country to marry

billionaire Jonathan Hartz, what else can a brilliant techno-geek do but try to become Cajun?

Blessings and Curses - Adrienne and Pete—is their love real or are they the victims of an old traiteur's love potion?

The Courville Rose - Can four souls find love in two bodies?

A Place Apart - A wounded warrior and a society girl both seek seclusion on the same deserted island. Sparks fly!

Letter to Our Readers

Enjoy this book?

You can make a difference.

As an independent publisher, Wings ePress, Inc. does not have the financial clout of the large New York publishers. We can't afford large magazine spreads or subway posters to tell people about our quality books.

But we do have something much more effective and powerful than ads. We have a large base of loyal readers.

Honest reviews help bring the attention of new readers to our books.

If you enjoyed this book, we would appreciate it if you would spend a few minutes posting a review on the site where you purchased this book or on the Wings ePress, Inc. webpages at: https://wingsepress.com/

Thank You

Visit Our Website

For The Full Inventory
Of Quality Books:

Wings ePress.Inc
https://wingsepress.com/

Quality trade paperbacks and downloads
in multiple formats,
in genres ranging from light romantic comedy
to general fiction and horror.
Wings has something for every reader's taste.
Visit the website, then bookmark it.
We add new titles each month!

Wings ePress Inc.
3000 N. Rock Road
Newton, KS 67114

Made in the USA
Columbia, SC
15 November 2022